Jock Serong is the author of *Quota*, winner of the 2015 Ned Kelly Award for Best First Fiction; *The Rules of Backyard Cricket*, shortlisted for the 2017 Victorian Premier's Award for Fiction, finalist of the 2017 MWA Edgar Awards for Best Paperback Original, and finalist of the 2017 Indie Book Awards Adult Mystery Book of the Year; and *On the Java Ridge*, which won the Colin Roderick Award and, internationally, the inaugural Staunch Prize (UK) and was shortlisted for the 2018 Indie Awards. He has won praise for his trilogy of historical novels *Preservation*; *The Burning Island*, which earned him the ARA Historical Novel Prize and the Historia Award for Historical Crime Fiction (France); and *The Settlement*, which was shortlisted for the Voss Prize and the ARA Historical Novel Prize.

CHERRYWOOD
JOCK SERONG

FOURTH ESTATE

Fourth Estate
An imprint of HarperCollins*Publishers*

HarperCollins*Publishers*
Australia • Brazil • Canada • France • Germany • Holland • India
Italy • Japan • Mexico • New Zealand • Poland • Spain • Sweden
Switzerland • United Kingdom • United States of America

HarperCollins acknowledges the Traditional Custodians
of the lands upon which we live and work, and pays respect
to Elders past and present.

First published on Gadigal Country in Australia in 2024
by HarperCollins*Publishers* Australia Pty Limited
ABN 36 009 913 517
harpercollins.com.au

A catalogue record for this book is available from the National Library of Australia

ISBN 978 1 4607 6535 7 (paperback)
ISBN 978 1 4607 1715 8 (ebook)
ISBN 978 1 4607 3768 2 (audiobook)

Cover design by Darren Holt, HarperCollins Design Studio
Cover images: Paddle Steamer illustration by Shawshots / Alamy Stock Photo; wheel pattern
by hpgruesen on Pixnio; all other images by istockphoto.com and shutterstock.com
Author photograph by Fred Kroh
Typeset in Bembo Std by Kirby Jones
Printed and bound in Australia by McPherson's Printing Group

MIX
Paper | Supporting
responsible forestry
FSC
www.fsc.org   FSC® C001695

Cities, like dreams, are made of desires and fears, even if the thread of their discourse is secret, their rules are absurd, their perspectives deceitful, and everything conceals something else.

— Italo Calvino, *Invisible Cities*

ONE

Thomas Albert Wrenfether was a man unusually exposed to fortune.

Generous and charming, he won the affection of everyone he met. He grew up the only child of a wealthy Glasgow family, surrounded by love and comfort. He found schooling easy, was a graceful athlete and a friend to all. He was funny enough, and mischievous enough, that the tearaways saw him as theirs, but somehow studious enough never to cross a teacher. If he had an obvious fault, it was that he was too trusting. But his parents believed it was a good fault to have.

Thomas's father, Malthus, was an industrialist, though the coarseness of the word does no justice in explaining the lightness of his touch. He could persuade people like few others: bankers, employees, his family, so he could vault from scheme to scheme – some succeeding, some quietly foundering – with such agility that the family's wealth built steadily over the years and his reputation floated above reproach.

In his role as a financier of steam engines, Malthus came into possession of an American automobile, an outlandish piece of experimental technology promising romance and freedom, in its American way, to those bold enough to take the controls. Malthus, being such a man, took delivery of this vehicle in May 1890, and declined the salesman's recommendation to employ a driver. It would be he, a man of destiny, who would steer the complex carriage through the streets of Glasgow, while timid men eyed him with envy.

The contraption came from the dock on the back of a wagon drawn by two labouring horses. When Malthus pointed out the irony of this arrangement to the driver, the man only stared in silence, a horse himself in the moment. The automobile was brought down with great care, the tarpaulins swept off, and the exquisite thing revealed drew the breath from their mouths. The polished lanterns, the glittering of its glass and metal, the lustrous rubber tyres, the sheer athleticism of it, separated it from the other things it appeared to reconfigure: a kettledrum and a steam engine. It rested lightly on its springs, poised to leap away, laughing. The bystanders clapped with joy.

Three days after the delivery, one sunny spring Friday morning, Malthus loaded his wife, Emily, and their ten-year-old boy, Thomas, into the vehicle with the aim of driving from Bothwell, on the eastern fringe of the city, to the seaside resort of Largs, a trip he calculated would take them four hours. They wore their best clothes: he a morning suit, she a hat tied in place with a silk scarf, and young Thomas a miniature copy of his father's attire, an outfit he himself had chosen for his adoration of the man.

Thomas sat crushed into the passenger seat beside his mother. Beside them, Malthus clutched the steering wheel in his gloved paws. The seat was made from polished leather, studded like a Chesterfield couch, but it was narrow. Neither mother nor child wanted to sit in the passenger compartment behind the seat, which, being enclosed, might lessen the thrill of cutting through the air and smelling the engine's rich fumes.

The automobile was called a Great Arrow, Malthus told his boy, hollering over the wind. *The motor is as strong as twenty-five horses.* Thomas tried to visualise all of them hitched to the front. *Why, the President of the United States owns one just like it.* Thomas's father was prone to grand pronouncements like these, and, as remarkable as these facts were, another of his utterances, there behind the wheel, would lodge in Thomas's memory all the way into his own middle age. *The man who designed it was famous for making birdcages.* Thomas tried imagining himself as a delicate bird inside this ornamental cage. He raised a finger to the inside of the big glass square in front of them and tapped on it, as though his fingernail were the beak of a finch.

The trip accorded with Malthus's estimate, and the family arrived at Largs in time for the evening meal, grouse in a white wine reduction. They were surrounded by admirers at the private hotel, and Malthus walked them in groups around the automobile, pointing out the brass lanterns and squeezing the bulb of the horn. He explained internal combustion, and gasoline, and vulcanisation. He was offered and indeed accepted many drinks, and the toasts and the cigars and brandies occupied him until the small hours of the morning, while his wife and son slept upstairs.

In the morning, young Thomas noticed over breakfast that his father looked unwell. This was nothing new to him. He had seen it before when his parents had hosted their business friends in the family home and the staff had been left to deal with the mountains of debris afterwards. His mother encouraged her husband to take more water, and he retorted that he had never been better.

By the time the family began to make their farewells, there were concerns raised that another day of rest might be wise. Emily privately indicated to Malthus that staying longer would only cause more feasting. They could rest at home. And Malthus, brimming with enthusiasm, was already relishing the prospect of another long drive. He stepped onto the running board to wave to the crowd, the Great Arrow tipped obligingly on its springs, and, as he hauled himself into position behind the wheel, his wife and son braced themselves beside him on the seat. With a yelp of the horn and a cloud of blue smoke, they drew away into the landscape like some fantastic vision that had descended upon the people of Largs.

Not twenty minutes later, Malthus oversteered on a steep bend in the road and lost control of the gorgeous automobile. It lurched onto two wheels and careened into a culvert, striking the embankment nose first with sufficient force to kill Malthus and Emily Wrenfether instantly, slicing and impaling them upon shards of the windscreen, their necks broken by their forward momentum, their eyes still open to the world's possibilities.

Young Thomas, ten years old and now at the other end of fortune's random swing, was catapulted far from the wreckage and landed completely unharmed in a bed of heather beyond the culvert. He lay there stunned until a local farmer, who had heard the impact, came to fetch him, and he was carried away to the farmhouse, without having to witness the carnage on the other side of the embankment.

TWO

When the necessary administrative measures had been taken care of, Thomas Wrenfether became the richest child in all of Scotland.

He had only the vaguest awareness of this fact, which registered as a comforting sense that he would never experience material hardship. But what comfort it provided was dwarfed by the immensity of his grief. He missed the feel and the shape and the warmth of his mother, her soothing words and her smell. The objects that had been hers were a source of longing: if he saw any of her jewellery, he would burst into uncontrollable sobbing. Indeed, many household items were quietly removed, lest they set him howling with despair.

And his father was as heavy a loss, although in different ways. He had cast an enormous shadow over Thomas's childhood but, within the shadow, Thomas had admired his father, had mimicked, memorised and idolised him. The fact he was physically gone altered but did not diminish the man's ongoing presence in his son's life.

Now, as an orphan, Thomas was forced to call forth all the reserves of optimism conferred upon him. Fortunately, his moderate nature was an asset in those trying years. His tastes were not extravagant and his passions ran to ordinary things like football, duck shooting and falconry. He lived with his cousins in Edinburgh, amply funded by an executor's trust until he was old enough to take his leave of them.

When, finally, he moved on, his cousins grieved for the loss of him, because he was a good boy. But it was clear to all that there was a restlessness developing in him, unappeased by the enjoyment of accidental wealth.

He took on the family's business interests under the guidance of longstanding managers who were loyal to the deceased Malthus and his likeable son. Upon having access to his father's records, Thomas experienced the shift so common to children coming into adulthood: he understood his father was imperfect, and idolisation gave way to a more balanced form of affection. For he found Malthus had failed to patent several of the most valuable inventions of his businesses, allowing unscrupulous colleagues to purloin the concepts and set up elsewhere. For a time, under the advice of the managers, he tried litigating against the opportunists, succeeding only in making his lawyers richer.

But his good luck came in waves alongside his misfortunes, and he chanced to meet and to marry the daughter of one of the patent thieves, a woman six years his junior and as lovely and as forthright as her father was not. Lucinda Grace Deal was viewed in Edinburgh society as a good match for Thomas, a woman who carried her high breeding without arrogance.

She had studied architecture, an enterprise encouraged by her parents. Her scheming father had made his first fortune developing health spas and hotels on the shores of Lake Maggiore, and he shared with her his plans for ever grander resorts, imagining her talent would save him money on the first drafts of the hired architects.

Lucy was said to be an exceptionally skilled draftsman. But it was the suffix '-man' that ensured she never practised her craft in any formal way. Although her father's influence had helped secure her enrolment in Edinburgh University's undergraduate degree, where she had excelled in every subject, nothing could move the Royal Institute of British Architects to allow her registration among the profession. She drew in her spare time, she drew for pleasure. She studied the civic buildings of Europe and even the ships of the line. And as she and Thomas built themselves a home, she involved herself wherever she could in the design of things. But these were not rehearsals for a career. These acts of hers were forlorn, the twitching reflexes of a talent that could not be employed.

Soon, however, another event swept Lucy and Thomas off on a new course. In October 1911, they discovered she was pregnant.

* * *

The pregnancy was a joyful time for both of them, a time when Thomas felt that his wife had never been more beautiful, and Lucy knew she had never been more loved.

But the looming date of the birth, calculated by Lucy's doctor to be somewhere near the Easter of 1912, had a curiously opposite effect: it magnified worries Thomas had, before then, always harboured privately. Now they were to be more than husband and wife, now he was to be responsible for a child, he came to doubt his adequacy. Money had sheltered him, affection had cushioned him – what example could he be to a child? When he tried to express these fears to Lucy, she insisted he was everything she could wish for, and their child would adore him as she did. But the feeling nagged at him.

At first, when he was assailed by this fear, such reassurances were enough. But soon the fear drove him, became a reason to be up and ahead of the day, long before the dawn. No matter the challenge, Thomas would find a way, because his lovely wife was delivering them a child, theirs alone in the whole world, and they would raise it, boy or girl, with unwavering attention to every need. So ardent was this desire in Thomas that he fell into the delusion, so often seen in first-time parents, of believing they were the first couple in history ever to take on this awesome responsibility.

With a month to go before the predicted date, Thomas decided he and Lucy should take one last holiday together as a couple – the last time they would travel alone and not as parents. Not knowing whether love divided itself with the arrival of a child, he thought they should immerse themselves in it, undivided, one more time.

He arranged an overnight stay on a Saturday at a spa resort on the coast, a few hours from the city. It would take them most of Saturday to get there and most of Sunday to return, but the time would be spent in conversation, and the evening at the hotel would be theirs. Lucy understood Thomas's preference for a carriage, despite the slower pace. She did not protest, knowing the fear of motor cars still haunted him.

They were approximately an hour short of the hotel, according to their driver, when Lucy first shifted uncomfortably in her seat. Thomas didn't comment, assuming the long, bumpy journey must be hard on her body, given its state. Then, shortly afterwards, she shifted again, and this time uttered a small groan.

'Darling?' he inquired.

'I'm …' There was confusion on her face. 'Quite a rumble. Perhaps I'm hungry.'

Hunger, of course, was not the issue. Only moments later she grimaced, squeezing her eyes shut and gritting her teeth. They spoke over each other, he to begin saying, 'My dear!' and she to cry, 'The baby!'

* * *

They were somehow able to get Lucy to the hotel – Thomas was always hazy on the details afterwards. There was a motor car, they laid her out on its seat and it sped away, and Thomas followed in the carriage with its driver, pushing the horses without regard for their welfare or for either man's safety.

When Thomas arrived, a footman joined him at the door and hurried him through the spacious lobby, up a flight of stairs to a first-floor room. Lucy was in bed and a doctor was present, an elderly bald man with a long nose and bony hands that rested on the bedcovers like the claws of a bird.

Lucy writhed and cried out, unaware of Thomas's presence, and he realised how accustomed he had become to her acknowledgement of him. Here she was, buried deep in a crisis of her own, and he an irrelevance, as dumb as the bedpost.

The doctor saw him and raised his hands, directing Thomas away. He shuffled back out the doorway, the doctor following and introducing himself. Thomas immediately forgot his name and never recalled it afterwards. It was indeed the baby, the doctor confirmed. But it had got itself in a very awkward position and would have to be cut free for the sakes of both mother and child. The doctor did not directly ask for Thomas's consent, nor did he seem to have asked it of Lucy, who was past caring about such things. The volume of her cries from the bed was rising, adding to the urgency of the doctor's words.

People were rushing in, bearing towels and metal contraptions and bottles and rubber tubing and other items beyond Thomas's understanding. The world was racing away from him and he felt he had no idea what was occurring. He pushed past the doctor, back into the room, and cupped his hands under his wife's damp, hot chin. Her eyes sought comfort, and she recognised him. He kissed her forehead and apologised to her, though he did not know why.

He was entrusting his impossibly precious wife to a stranger, an affectless functionary who might be a genius and might equally be a charlatan, and there was simply no choice. The bird-like man was tugging at Thomas's sleeve, asking him to please leave, as a cot was wheeled in.

'Why is she not in a hospital?' Thomas asked feebly, though he knew the answer. There was no time. Lucy's body clenched as a powerful contraction gripped her.

'Now, please,' the doctor said.

Thomas pulled away from the bedside without breaking his gaze upon his wife, bumping into people as he went. Then he was out in the hallway and the door had been shut in his face. The carpet underfoot soaked up the sounds from the room, muffling them, but they remained audible. Footfalls, calm voices, sounds of metal and glass plinking in professional contact, but mostly the cries, rising to screams, weirdly distant, beseeching an end to the pain.

He was led by an aproned woman down the hall and back down the wide staircase, then taken around a corner in the hotel's lobby to a bar where couples, ignorant of the drama upstairs, were eating and drinking contentedly.

Arms guided him to a chair at a small table against the back wall of the room, away from other diners. A balloon glass, brandy. A silver bowl with nuts in it. He found himself mechanically feeding nuts into his mouth, crunching down on them and tasting nothing. He tried the brandy – it was chemically warm, and that was all he could say of it. The warmth spread through his insides, but he was barely conscious of it. His mind was racing. What were they doing up there? How long would it take? Had he seen the last of his beloved wife?

He pushed the nuts and the brandy away. The head waiter must have been watching him and taken this as a sign the starters were complete, because a flotilla of waiters now came and removed the bowl and the glass and laid down cutlery, draped a napkin over his lap and presented a pale soup that smelled strongly of vegetables and pepper. A pause: more staff, a plate of hot bread.

He stared at the meal. The staff had retreated. Time passed and the steam stopped rising from the soup. The fragility of his good fortune had been laid bare. So, this was how life went.

They came and took the soup and brought him beef. Then they came and took the beef, gone cold, and brought him cream and fruit. And with each re-setting they watched him with deep concern.

He shook himself from the stupor for long enough to ask one of them, a boy, whether there was any news. The boy scuttled off, perplexed, and returned with a newspaper. Thomas stared at it dumbly before he understood the confusion. He tried reading it, but the words on the page would not convert themselves into meanings. An older man returned with the answer to his original question. There was no news.

This could go on for hours, he thought. He had heard talk of confinements stretching through an entire night or even longer. But then, he realised, those were not caesarean sections.

He wanted liquor to dull the pain of waiting, but he also did not want it. It seemed wrong to anaesthetise himself against the ordeal his wife was having to endure.

He stood and looked around. The other diners had gone, and now he was an island, standing in a sea of tables and chairs. He looked to the head waiter, who swept a hand towards the door. There would be no need for sir to concern himself with the account. He nodded, set one foot after the other and headed for the staircase.

The nurses were coming down. They saw him and averted their eyes, each carrying a burden: implements on trays, bowls and bedding. The third of them, the heavy one after the young girl and the redhead, carried towels splashed with fresh blood.

He hurried upstream against the downflowing women to the door, where he banged with a fist and demanded entry. 'What is happening? What is happening?' It had been many hours, though time had taken on an eccentric quality. They had no right to withhold information from him, no matter how terrible it might be.

The avian doctor emerged, pulling the door closed around his body to allow Thomas no view into the room. 'She is fine, Mr Wrenfether,' he began, though his voice was terse. 'You have a baby daughter, very frail, but with luck both will survive.'

So, who was the 'she' who was fine? It had to be Lucy, it *had* to be – although the moment he had the thought, he felt the betrayal of the infant he had yet to meet and to love.

'Allow me a moment. I will see if they are ready for you.' The doctor disappeared and Thomas was left standing in the hallway. The tide of women leaving had ebbed now. He was alone with the carpet and the wallpaper. The smells of the hotel, food and pipe smoke, wafted up from below.

After an unreasonably long time – wasn't he simply asking a question in there? – the doctor reappeared and granted him entry. He followed the man through the door and felt the air change: it was thick with corporeal smells of muscle and fluid. There was no sound, only the silence of aftermath.

Lucy lay resting, propped up by a bank of pillows. She was drowsy, half aware of his entrance, and he realised they had drugged her. She wore a nightgown he did not recognise, and the curving rise of one breast showed in the soft light where the gown had been shifted aside. The bedcovers were drawn up to the breast and, for a moment, Thomas did not see the tiny bundle resting half under the covers between her arm and her chest.

Mother and child were afloat in the darkness, voyaging somewhere, utterly serene. As he saw the vision, and the emotion came down upon him, Lucy's eyes found focus and she responded to his joy, bestowing on him a faint smile.

He took up a chair, reached out and lifted back the swaddling of hotel tea towels. An angelic face, framed by a fuzz of dark hair, shifted in response to the movement.

So it was that Thomas Wrenfether met his daughter, his only child. He could no longer contain the tears, and he leaned into

the warmth of mother and child and allowed the sobbing to take
him over.

*　*　*

Lucy decided the girl would be called Annabelle. Both of them
fell in love with her instantly, their love made more urgent by
the fact Annabelle was so frail that the light appeared at times to
shine right through her.

The family spent three weeks at the hotel, waiting for the
baby to gain weight and the mother to heal before the doctor –
whose name was Varvinsky – would let them go home. During
those idle days, Annabelle grew to be a strong feeder, visible to
Thomas only as a ravenous pair of eyes wrapped within layers of
clothing against his wife's body. The hotel's female staff would
come to visit, would sit through their breaks with Lucy, asking
her questions and cooing over Annabelle.

Thomas had the benefit of endless income from the astute
investment of the family's capital. There was no urgency about
leaving the hotel, then, and what little correspondence needed
addressing, he resolved over coffee in a quiet hour each morning.
He filled his days with reading, beginning with newspapers over
breakfast, and progressing to periodicals and novels as the day
went on. He would move to a sunlit terrace if the day was fine, or
otherwise into the saloon. He made friends among the patrons,
starting anew with the couples who had seen him in extremity
on the night of the birth. He tried tennis, and found himself to
be quite competent at it. And when his wife was asleep and his
daughter wasn't feeding, he would sit in the semi-darkness of the
room, staring in wonder at the life force they had created, the
tiny heartbeat pounding away at the centre of the world. Her,
her, a mighty thing in miniature.

*　*　*

Annabelle Wrenfether recovered from her precarious start. Too social to crawl, she insisted on bumping along on her backside so her whole body was upright and alert to the world. She became so proficient at this that she could scoot along without using her hands, leaving them free for carrying food or waving to admirers.

As she grew, the Wrenfethers' many friends commented on the remarkable bond between father and daughter. Uncharacteristically, perhaps, for a man of his time and social standing, Thomas took an active role in raising the girl. He would get down on the floor and engage with her in nonsense games about made-up worlds. He would correct her sternly when necessary, interventions that hurt him more than they should have. He had thought it impossible to love anyone as much as he loved Lucy, but now he felt a new kind of love and was happier than ever.

Through the tumult of raising a baby, Lucy kept a shrewd eye on their fortunes. She began selling down the family's business interests and investing in stock options. Lucy's mother had died many years before, and when her father died of a stroke later that year – after a few happy months of being a grandfather – Lucy inherited, along with a villa in Lubriano and a Vermeer, the very patent he had stolen from the Wrenfethers. And though the managers of the Wrenfether firm sighed with satisfied bloodlust when the fruit of Malthus's genius finally came home, she promptly sold it off.

Lucy never took possession of the sizeable payment. Instead, she took in her lovely hands a bundle of share certificates for an ancient and august shipping firm known as the Maindample Line.

THREE

With less to worry them and with vast riches safely invested, the Wrenfethers began to look further afield.

Thomas, in candid moments, would confess to Lucy that he could not imagine emulating his father's successes. He resented the comparisons that longstanding employees made. They recognised his kindness to them. They even loved him for his uncanny physical resemblance to his father. But everyone knew he lacked the heedlessness, the contempt for consequence, which was a mark of his father's boldest business moves. Thomas, for his part, remembered the same impetuousness as the seed of the family's disaster. If his father's instinct lived in him, he would suppress it.

Late one night, as they lay together, the frustration in him boiled over. He had been outflanked by a more aggressive competitor, and a vital financier of the family firm had been seduced away. 'I will never understand why ordinary decency is not enough,' he complained. 'Perhaps I will never have the ruthlessness to be truly successful, and I am fairly sure I don't want it.'

'Be your own man,' Lucy answered. The faint light of the half-moon found its way into their room and fell on her hand where it stroked his hair. 'Strike out in some other direction, my darling.'

Such pronouncements, witnessing both her sage view of the world and her abiding confidence in him, made Thomas love

Lucy even more. But the shadows persisted, more frightening than he admitted to her — doubts that assailed him at the most unexpected times, coming upon him silently like rising water. If he did not kick out against them, he would drown, he feared, but the kicking seemed pointless. The doubts could be blamed on circumstances, but they were not external to him, not the product of people's unintended slights. They came from within.

And then the shadows would lift, as suddenly as they had arrived, and life would go on.

He and Lucy began to buy up more stock in the shipping line, until they had enough to win Thomas a seat on its board. The prestige of it was unassailable: to Lucy it was a vindication and a banishment of his self-doubt. These men were shipwrights, retired captains and navigators, men for whom maritime jargon and mystique were second nature. There was even a polar explorer among them, for goodness' sake. This was a step towards the kind of corporate seriousness his father would have esteemed. The press trumpeted the dynastic implications of the Wrenfether scion taking a major directorship.

Then came the board meetings. Through tedious debates they tolerated his presence and smoked with him by the massive boardroom fireplace afterwards for long enough to show good manners. But they never invited him into their confidences. They did not seek his views about their private investments. And he, for his part, made sure to vote with the majority and avoid any kind of disagreement. He wondered at times how he had found himself in this position, among these people. Had he catapulted himself into a world to which he was ill-suited? Had he been weak to abide by his wife's counsel? The thought alarmed him: their unity of purpose was the source of all stability.

At the time of the board's annual general meeting in 1915, Thomas found himself an ally, a Sardinian director named Jorge Ximenon, who said as little as Thomas did in board meetings, but not for reasons of unfamiliarity. No, he had a long family history in shipping, although the man himself was an enigma. It was rumoured his family history also took in sedition and fabulous, untraceable wealth, although Thomas was too fair a man to be swayed by rumour.

Thomas took to watching Ximenon across the table, fascinated by his dark eyes, his black moustache, and the watchful quality of his gaze. He inhabited his stout frame with supreme self-confidence. His life was his own secret business and no-one else's. How such a man came to be in the company of the obsequious, the arrogant and the vain was a mystery. Behind his back, they referred to him as the Moor of Musselburgh – they had no interest in discerning a man of dark features from any other such men.

Over time, the two of them, Thomas and Ximenon, began a conversational habit: polite inquiry, a sharing of thoughts. They were outsiders, but they had each other. Ximenon was the only one who would offer to discuss the board papers with Thomas over dinner before the meetings, or suggest a bottle of wine in some nearby club afterwards. It gratified Thomas that Ximenon, despite his apparent guile, was as satisfied of the line's good standing as the papers themselves suggested. 'We are very fortunate men,' he said to Thomas. 'Even war makes us wealthier. It is not every merchant who lives in such times.' In the past, Maindample's times had included a strategic position supplying marsala to Britain in lieu of the port and sherry that had become unavailable due to war with Spain. More recently, the times were a bustling trade in consumer goods with the new federation of Australia, a place on the other side of the globe, foreign to both men but enriching them daily with its need for everything from porcelain to nursery furniture. Maindample had not lost a single vessel to the U-boats, and for every market the war closed, another seemed to open in its place.

One winter's night in December 1916, they dined in a Russian restaurant in the Grassmarket. Ximenon had introduced his friend to the delights of garlic *grenki*, and, as Thomas tore at the salty bread, he was reminded of the time Ximenon came into a board meeting in a heavy fog of garlic fumes and the members winced theatrically and moved their chairs away from him. One of their many acts of mean-spiritedness towards him, yet the generosity of the man was undimmed. Here he was, sighing lustfully at the soup and the wine, delighting in the fact Thomas had taken a liking to the *grenki*.

Once the main course of sturgeon had been consumed, the Sardinian began thoughtfully stroking his moustache. 'My friend,' he said, 'there are few men I trust as I trust you. Yours is a rare brand of integrity.'

Thomas was momentarily flustered. It felt like a profession of love, and he was unsure how to respond. He opened his mouth to do so, but his friend stopped him with a raised finger.

'I have known you long enough now to disclose to you something important.' He swirled the wine in his glass; they had both drunk a considerable quantity of claret. 'Something I have kept to myself for many months.'

Thomas had divulged plenty of confidences about his life, his marriage and his ambitions to this man, although Ximenon himself remained opaque. He nodded his encouragement for Ximenon to keep speaking, but first the Sardinian looked over both shoulders to ensure the waiter wasn't hovering.

'I have, through my interests in other fields, come upon a singular opportunity.' He sat back, checking that Thomas was suitably attentive. Apparently satisfied, he continued. 'A tremendous quantity of high-quality timber. From the Caucasus, although its exact provenance need not concern you. This timber is too hard and fine grained to be used in building. Far too valuable to be burned as fuel. It can keep a straight cut for centuries without bowing, yet is also easily steamed into a bend.' His hands were miming these activities as he spoke, the short fingers climbing the air between them. 'Resistant to rot, naturally buoyant, meaning its ideal application is in shipbuilding.'

He had crept forward in the telling and now he leaned back, satisfied with his introduction.

'How much timber are you talking about?' Thomas asked, although he knew the answer would likely mean nothing to him.

'Approximately three hundred tons,' Ximenon replied.

'And what is your plan?' Thomas asked. Again, the Sardinian looked sideways. Heavy jowls swelled from the line of the man's jaw, so that an impression of a younger, thinner face could be found. The yellow candlelight caught the unblemished skin of his forehead, and Thomas wondered if he was younger than he'd assumed.

'We build a vessel, hmm?'

Thomas nodded agreeably. It was part of what the firm did.

'This vessel is a paddlesteamer. You know the type?'

'Of course.' *Rivers*, he thought. *Americans.*

'And here is why,' Ximenon continued. 'In Australia, in the southern province of Victoria, they enjoy a robust economy and abundant wealth. Gold money, agricultural money, land speculation ... enterprise, my friend. Englishmen, Scots, Irishmen, wishing to spend their money in ways that they understand to be *aristocratic*.' His tongue rolled over the word with relish. 'None of it is remotely aristocratic, of course. They are chancers, Philistines with grand aspirations, but they can be persuaded to part with their money precisely because they wish to emulate the gilded Europeans they hear of.

'Now the transition from sail to steam is more or less complete, as you know. And very soon, it will be steam to diesel. So let us say this is a *cause célèbre*, an opportunity to settle the debate about profitability for good, and say to the world that sail is a thing of the past.'

The world. Thomas felt a giddy rush. 'This is no small thing you're planning.'

Ximenon leapt onwards. 'The city of Melbourne, their capital, sits at the head of a shallow estuary known as Port Phillip Bay. Narrow at the top, where the major river enters, and much wider across the middle. There's been a steamship company operating there for some years, three paddlesteamers on a tourist route from Melbourne to the holiday resorts further south. But there exists a *need* ...'

He took a pen from inside his jacket and, throwing a hand in the air to summon a waiter, requested paper. When it arrived, he began drawing the estuary, a diamond shape, narrow at the top and bottom and spilling wide to the west. 'Port Phillip,' said Ximenon, concentrating on his drawing. 'Melbourne here.' He made a dot. 'The tourist routes run down here' – he curled a line down the east side of the bay – 'but no-one is providing a service across the mouth of the river here at the top, and there is increasing settlement and industry on the western side.'

He looked up at Thomas, inviting him to see the beauty of it.

'A paddlesteamer has no rigging. It doesn't heel over. Ample deck space for the patrons to promenade, even leftover space for freight. There's two towns, here and here' – he drew two more dots – 'St Kilda and Williamstown. Four miles across there. A good steamer will cover it in half an hour and come back with the boilers barely labouring. But the key is to invest the voyage with drama. Pomp. So, rather than rush through eight crossings a day, you provide, say, two or three, make a conspicuous loop up here in front of the city, so everyone sees the vessel ... make *theatre* of it. And at a commensurate price, of course.'

'Which of our yards do we commission for the build?' Thomas was already caught up in the thing. The noise around them had faded to a blur and the candlelight glowed with possibility. Here was a man he trusted, with a proposal that was instantly appealing. He felt a terrible urgency to make the project happen before someone else thought of it, or the window of opportunity closed for some other reason.

The Sardinian smiled. 'Ah,' he sighed. 'It is not quite so simple. You see, the ones already operating there are iron hulls – so you can sail them across open ocean to a destination. The hulls were probably plated in, I don't know, Plymouth, Hamburg. Sail them over to whomever has commissioned them for whatever purpose they are required. But this one will be lighter and more nimble in operation, weighing far less in timber. That's the advantage. The disadvantage' – he raised a cautionary finger and the candlelight fell gold on the hairs on the back of it – 'is you have to ship the raw timber over and build it in the local yards. In the first instance, you might say that we would lose a commercial edge by not building it ourselves, but the local employment can be parlayed into political favour. Carpenters, boilermakers, painters. And the construction period generates anticipation. They will have a local press, I assume.'

Thomas thought hard, reached for a reason to be cautious and could find none. 'What about the board?' he eventually asked. 'Nine besides us, yes? I can think of two who are sufficiently forward-thinking, another two who will look for problems – I think you know to whom I refer. So, a substantial number of them are in play.'

'Yes, I know the two.' Ximenon smiled. 'You are right. We need to convince two of the remaining five in order to have a majority. But what I am putting to you is more far-reaching. In the first instance, we offer it to them as a company enterprise. If they decline it, we seek a dispensation to do it ourselves. Then the naysayers will become our allies – they will want the risk assumed by someone other than Maindample. You have family money, I am aware, and so do I. If they forbid the dispensation, then we must look at resigning our positions. There is no legal danger in doing so. They will be snookered, as we will have them on the minutes scoffing at the viability of it. They cannot then sue for lost opportunity.'

The headlong rush was more than Thomas could bear. The perfect ripening of the idea in place and time, the strategy for getting it past the board … He struggled to find a sober response.

'Why did you come to me with this?'

'Simple. You yourself have identified the conservatives on the board. I could not go to them. My research indicates the remaining five are financially beholden to other interests. They do not have the available capital to support this venture if the board declines to endorse it. And besides, MacCamish is a doddering old fool.' Ximenon looked deep into Thomas's eyes, seeking trust there. 'I need agility and integrity.'

In that moment, Thomas Wrenfether's life spun like a coin on its edge, though he had no way of knowing it.

'Too few of the beautiful things are left to us, Thomas,' the Sardinian said. 'The world is crowded with ugliness, impatient to befoul itself. When offered grace and light, we should open ourselves to it. This timber' – his eyes roved in search of an exact form of words – 'it will make you *weep*.'

Thomas felt a wave of happiness pass through him. Here was a thing his wealth could not buy: the trust and esteem of a renowned commercial mind. These meditations on beauty he could take or leave, but the trust was a precious thing.

'Leave this with me,' he beamed. 'I will talk to Lucy. I feel sure she will see the sense in it.' He extended a hand and Ximenon shook it vigorously. 'And do not think of paying for dinner,' Thomas added. 'It is the least I can do, since you have brought this opportunity to me.'

FOUR

Thomas rushed home full of excitement, but the stellar trajectory of his night soon faltered.

His wife heard him out, clutching a cup of tea. Her face, so adorable to him in the evening light, had been creased with worry from the beginning of the story.

'Why has no-one else thought of such a thing, if it is so clever?' she asked.

Thomas felt a surge of annoyance. The question was a good one, which was why it annoyed him. 'No-one thought of the biplane until the Wright brothers did,' he retorted. 'It only looked obvious afterwards. That's what happens with the best ideas.' He was standing as he spoke, gesticulating, and he thought he saw a hint of fear in Lucy's eyes.

'There will be less control over the construction if it's done on the other side of the world,' she persisted.

'We'll live there,' Thomas countered. 'People say Melbourne is wealthy and grand. We have no parents to think of now, only our child to care for, and the climate would be better for her there.' It was manipulative of him to invoke their daughter, but it was true, and he did not need to add that they would be far from the terrifying charnel house of the European war.

She sighed, took a mouthful of tea. 'We are not mariners,' she said flatly. 'We have made a good living by relying on the expertise of these people' – by whom she meant the board of

Maindample. 'To venture out to the colonies without their expertise, without knowing anything of this estuary, or who the passengers would be, or ...' She fell silent for a moment. 'Especially with—'

'Him! It's Ximenon, isn't it! You have never accepted him!'

She bowed her head; it was true. Despite having met him only a few times, she did not trust the man and nothing would dislodge the instinct. Even to exchange pleasantries with him was, for her, to swim against a current.

'What do you really know about him, anyway?' she asked.

'I've told you what I know and it is enough for me. He comes from Sardinia. He has independent wealth. He is well mannered and knowledgeable.' Thomas gave in to a meaner instinct. 'And he values my opinion.'

He saw the comment hit its mark, but Lucy recovered. She took no pleasure in pressing him like this. 'What do you know of his professional history, my darling?'

'He told me he was an ambergris broker.'

For a long, almost comical moment, they both looked baffled, and Thomas began pacing. She wondered if every marriage, no matter how loving, must eventually come to such a point.

'It is a federation, not a colony, in any event,' he snapped. This was new territory, the first time that married life had not presented itself as a perfectly aligned partnership. 'There are times when it is necessary for a wife to bow to the deeper understanding of her husband,' he began. 'I am more generous than most in consulting you, in taking your counsel, but there are occasions on which I must stand firm.'

A look of despair crossed her face, and he realised how deeply he was already committed to this plan, how much it distressed her, and he knew he had approached the entire conversation in the wrong way. The claret hadn't helped, and he was unable now to correct any of it. Yet he was not done.

'It was you who counselled me to be my own man,' he said. 'You told me to strike out in my own direction, and I intend to do so.'

* * *

An extraordinary general meeting of the Maindample board was scheduled on receipt of Thomas's letter to the secretary. Thomas and Ximenon met several times beforehand, crafting their proposal and researching the city of Melbourne, its people and their estuary.

On the appointed day, Ximenon and Thomas presented their idea and Maindample's board listened. They stroked their whiskers. Allies leaned inward to mutter; foes averted their gaze. Thomas observed the reaction and put it down to nothing more than having tossed a stone into an undisturbed pond. There would be ripples, of course. When their talking was done, and with no questions having been asked of them, the chairman indicated the balance of the board should retire to consider what had been put. They left the boardroom and adjourned to an antechamber, leaving Thomas and Ximenon there in the enormous room, surrounded by statuary and maps.

'They won't do it.' Ximenon was examining a bust of Francis Drake, peering as an optometrist might at the marble eyes. The remark was unexpected, and when Thomas didn't reply, he added, 'They lack the vision.'

Another half-hour passed, during which neither of them spoke and Thomas's foreboding grew. When an attendant knocked on the door and the board filed back in, not one of them would look him in the eye. He, a man accustomed to the good favour of the world, felt the beginnings of an unfamiliar dread on seeing the animus in their faces. They had walked out colleagues and returned a jury.

The chairman, a Yorkshireman named Haddock, waited for the room to settle and for the attendant to close the huge door, which echoed as it slammed shut. He looked once around the table and began to read from his notes.

'The board, absent Messrs Wrenfether and Ximenon, has met to consider the proposal put this day by those absentees, concerning the construction and operation in Melbourne, Australia, of a paddlesteamer, such vessel to be built from timbers supplied by Mr Ximenon at what purports to be wholesale cost.'

Those words – 'what purports to be' – struck fear into Thomas, and now he could see how badly he and Ximenon had miscalculated. The voice behind the grey whiskers droned on.

'In the board's view, the proposal lacks merit, both due to the obscure provenance and pricing of the timber, and due to our collective lack of expertise in the intended market, which would be' – he squinted at his notes – 'excursioning.'

A minor shift in the air had forced ash out of the fireplace, and it hung in swirls and settled on the polished table. The morning sun found places to alight: the head of a bust, a carved correspondence box, the wisped white hair of the treasurer.

'It is further the view of the board that Messrs Wrenfether and Ximenon have devoted considerable time and research to this venture' – Thomas brightened momentarily, believing he was to be praised – 'and have done so in pursuit of private profit, and therefore in breach of their fiduciary duty to devote their best endeavours to the benefit of the Maindample Shipping Line. In truth, this initiative was never intended to meet with the board's favour, but to be declined and thus to clear the way for the proponents to exploit it themselves. Such divided loyalty is to be condemned in the strongest possible terms.'

Thomas surveyed them all. Not a single eye met his.

'It is, accordingly, the intention of the board, absenting Messrs Wrenfether and Ximenon, to conduct a ballot in order to ascertain the board's continuing confidence in the stewardship of the aforementioned gentlemen.'

Thomas was slow to understand what was being said. But this moment had been contrived to deny him the time to think. Haddock reached to his left and rang the brass bell to bring the factotum back into the room. He whispered to the man, who scurried out, returning with a small, polished box.

'Each of you is possessed of notepaper?' Haddock surveyed their blotters and saw this was so. 'I shall put the motions as chair, to ensure they cannot be said to have come from any member individually. There shall be two motions. One, "That Mr Wrenfether retains the confidence of the board," and two, "That Mr Ximenon retains the confidence of the board." Members are to indicate their vote by writing "Aye" or "Nay" beside the numerals one and two on a sheet of notepaper, then fold it into quarters and place it in the box as it is passed around.' He rubbed his hands, looked down the length of the table at them with the grim satisfaction of unbending judgement.

'Mr Ximenon, Mr Wrenfether, although you are, of course, entitled to witness the voting process, you are exempted from the vote, as it pertains to a matter in your interests.' No-one answered. The ash had all come to rest. Even the dust hung still in the air. 'Let us commence.'

The ensuing scene was a blur to Thomas, a procession of disjointed images of his colleagues, already his former colleagues, staring at their blotters or frowning at their pens as though the word 'Nay' was impossibly difficult to form. Anything – a troublesome cufflink, a chipped fingernail, the dull stares of the statues – anything but look at him. The blur played out in a timescale of its own as he spun within a vortex, but he would remember scenes from it for the rest of his life. The box's journey around the huge table, the collation of the votes and the droning of the factotum, deputised as hangman. The solemn pronouncement of the chairman, the packing up and the leaving, the empty room. Ximenon with his fingers laid gently on Thomas's chest: 'This was all preordained.' A strange smile of destiny on his face.

This was professional disgrace. Thomas could not tell what it meant for his wealth, but his name had been rendered worthless. He had placed his family's fortune in the hands of an unknowable man, and then in the hands of these brutal mercenaries, the grandsons of slavers and the cousins of dukes. These men had entire mountain ranges named after them. They wagered ships over cards. And they had disposed of him with ease. There was the potential to litigate the matter, but the courts were filled with exactly such men, and it would not have surprised Thomas to find the bench comprised of their brothers and fathers.

His last hope was Ximenon.

FIVE

One rainy Friday evening in the winter of 1993, a taxi swept through the streets of East Melbourne, on its way from the city to Richmond.

That year was one of the few remaining when a great deal was known of the world but not yet so much that the world had become over-known. Small gaps remained.

The taxi driver had greeted his passenger with a faint nod through a slit of open passenger-side window. His head was a river boulder, heavy, and so devoid of the ordinary distinctions between flesh and bone it seemed entirely hard. His skin was slightly dark, his hair trimmed short, his nose crooked like a boxer's, and, although he was clean-shaven, his stubble announced its imminent return in the form of a darker shadow.

His passenger, a young woman, noted these things in the seconds it took to open the rear door and lower herself in. The driver didn't turn to her, but she saw enough of his face in the mirror to find something softer in there. He watched her; she watched him.

Her name was Martha. She slid across the vinyl seat, tossed her work satchel onto it beside her hip. She was dressed in a business skirt, an unremarkable jacket and low heels. Her hair was straight and dark, tied back without thought, so that strands appeared on her forehead. It was a lifetime habit of hers to puff at these strands when they touched her face. She fidgeted with her glasses and watched the light explode in the beads forming between sweeps of the wipers on the windscreen.

Martha was on her way home from work. She worked at Caspian Lawyers, the powerful commercial firm that occupied ten floors of a glass tower in the central business district. Her job as a junior litigator was the sum of her aspirations, having driven her through long hours of study and long weeks of internships, when her friends were out having fun. When she had ended a short and ill-advised marriage the year she was admitted to practice, it was the notion of having a *profession* that bolstered her self-worth.

And yet that profession did not make her happy. She had chosen Caspians from among three offers on the basis they had a Human Rights group. But despite the smiling and nodding in the interview, they had seen her exceptional grades in Contracts and Property Law, and had put her in Dispute Resolution. At each of the three six-monthly reviews since then, she had carefully raised the assurances about a placement in Human Rights – assurances falling just short of a binding promise – and each time had been told that, although her interest was noted, it was a 'tightly held practice area'.

Having missed out on her preference, she began to see herself as a battery chicken, a productive unit entrapped in a box, selling her life in six-minute pieces to her employers, who on-sold her life to clients, who passed the cost of buying Martha's life, by then wholesaled and retailed, to their clients in the form of some minuscule mark-up.

At Friday afternoon drinks, seated around the Caspians boardroom table, Martha's colleagues would unwind and flirt while the catering staff kept up a supply of finger food. Some lawyers would arrive late, complaining about the final urgent thing they'd had to finish. This was mostly a performance for the prestige of being the last to stop work. Others would open a beer, chat a while, then claim there was something important they needed to deal with back in their office. Martha knew this was unlikely. Nobody ever called after about five on a Friday, and, if they did, it was rarely for something that couldn't wait until Monday. Appearances were everything.

This particular Friday night, however, Martha had skipped drinks. She was due at a dinner party. The hosts were three of the other junior litigators, people who not only shared a sixty-hour working week, but also a house in Northcote. She was dreading it. She felt obligated. It was probably a good thing to do. She wasn't getting out enough. No-one should live alone at twenty-five. These thoughts circled and went nowhere.

When the taxi pulled up at her block of flats in Richmond, she asked the driver to wait. He lit a smoke, wound his window down under the perspex shield that let the smoke out but kept the rain at bay. Again, he nodded. He had not uttered a sound over the entire journey.

She went inside, checked the answering machine – nothing – and changed. There was no surprise in the flat, as it was only ever she who came and went. Everything here was orderly, everything in its place.

When she came out, the driver had done a U-ey and started on a second smoke. He glanced at her and flicked it out the window. He faced directly ahead and she sat in the back again – she knew this to be a good practice – gave him the address and resumed staring out the window. The vinyl slid under her jeans and she smelled cheap deodoriser and smoke. She hoped neither would cling to her.

East Melbourne again, the frontages wide and deep, impossibly wide for this close to the city. Thirty, forty years of this and she could live in one of these. Well, live, in the sense of staggering home to sleep in one between the endless days of work. *No, my husband is in The Hague right now.* Uphill around the edges of the Mercy Hospital and the Gardens and briefly onto Victoria Parade. Any right turn would plunge them into the heart of Fitzroy, but the one the driver took was unfamiliar to her, between a florist on one corner and a small bar on the other.

Then they were in the quiet streets, a place that felt full of secrets as much as history. The Napier Hotel flashed by, lit up, cosy. A drink: she hadn't brought wine. She could wing it and apologise – these weren't friends of such standing that she needed to care – but she admonished herself. It was how she got things done, admonishing herself. *Is this good enough? No, it is not!*

'Would you stop at the next pub?' she asked the Human Rock. 'I need to grab a bottle.'

Another of his nods. As if he had willed it, a beer sign glowed through the rain, hung from a wrought-iron rail above a doorway. It was at the end of a short run of shop awnings, one of which had a large fibreglass hamburger slowly revolving above it: 'Nick's American'.

The front of the pub was tall, but it looked nothing like the usual Victorian-era pubs of the inner north. Above the door, there was a small lunette window with timber frames and coloured leadlight panels, something written in gilt on the glass. The driver jolted the cab into park, and she saw 'L-O-V-E' tattooed on the backs of his fingers as they curled over the transmission. A faded manifesto, evidence of some long-ago life. The fingers were huge, and she sensed the compressed power in him.

She stepped out into the rain. The beer sign was reflected in the puddles.

A small booth served as a bottle shop, with doors to the left and the right presumably leading to bars. There were glass-fronted fridges behind the counter, a few racks of wine on the walls, a cigarette machine, a display of chips and nuts. The till was large and covered in brass scrollwork, with a window at the top where number cards popped up: '$1.43' stood there now, and Martha wondered what in this room could be so cheap, so oddly priced. A bare bulb hung from a power cord in the centre of the room. It was swaying – the breeze from her coming through the door, perhaps.

Something about this room was strange, stranger than the oversize till. She had never been here – it was the sense of the familiar that disconcerted her. She was not good at this. Concentrating on some file in front of her, something complex, certainly. But not taking close note of the physical world. She could find herself on a tram, sitting next to someone she knew well, who might sit there smiling at her absent-mindedness, and she would not notice them. But she had studied the taxi driver with a new form of intensity, and now here she was, ticking away in the bottle shop like a Geiger counter.

She waited for someone to appear behind the counter, and the odd sensation persisted.

Then another observation came to her – under the cigarette smoke and spent beer, there was an intoxicating smell, something wonderful and mysterious. It maddened her. She felt she should know it well, but the word would not come. She breathed it in again, tasting it, and ran a hand along the edge of the counter to feel the wear of innumerable transactions. This room. Perhaps it was nothing more than having spent too much time in an office tower.

Behind the counter, the ceiling was much higher and a spiral staircase wound its way up into the gloom, out beyond the fridges. She peered into the void. Still no-one had appeared to serve her. She was busting to wee; how had she forgotten at home? She tapped the silver bell on the bar; the *ding* reached back into the building and she could hear footsteps approaching, unhurried.

A young man appeared, somewhere in his early twenties, wearing a black t-shirt. He was thin, not especially tall, his hair long and chaotic. His skin was pale, his eyes dark.

'You right?' he mumbled.

'I need a bottle of red. Cheap red, like a lambrusco or something.'

'Mm. Okay.' He nodded but didn't move.

She sighed, remembered the other thing. 'Do you have a bathroom here?'

His face opened a little, like this was an easier request than the wine had been. 'Yeah, through there and straight along. You'll see it.' He gestured at the door to his right, her left. On it was a map of the pubs of Fitzroy, sagging from its Blu Tack.

'I, er …' She hesitated, looked into his eyes. 'Won't be a sec.'

Through the door, out into a darkened room; much larger, but the low ceiling continued here. There was a long bar stretching parallel to her right, lamps finding tints among the bottles on the shelves. Music played faintly somewhere but, again, there were no customers. And even if there were, they could not have sat, because the barstools were crowded into the far corner of the room: some upright, some tumbled. They did not appear to have been placed there in any deliberate way – maybe a drunk person had done it. It looked more like a football crush than a form of storage.

When she came out of the bathroom, she found multiple doors leading off from the bar and couldn't remember which one she'd come through. She tried the first but, despite looking like a standard internal door, it opened onto the street, and a cold blast of airy rain doused her before she slammed it. She tried another: again, the darkness outside and the flying flecks of rain. The night smelled beautiful, damp and clean, and for a moment she thought about abandoning the bottle of wine and just walking out into it.

A third door finally led back to the bottle shop. She looked at it with a frown, like it, too, had tried to mislead her. The boy was still standing there. His arms were propped against the bar, pale and sleek, and a bottle stood on the counter between his spread hands. Something about the way he occupied those clothes. Not how they draped on him, but how he moved within them. Were they borrowed clothes, perhaps?

His face was turned away, looking over one shoulder, to where an ancient woman was opening and loudly shutting cupboard doors, muttering under her breath.

'It's okay, Nan,' the boy was saying. 'Don't worry about it. I can get it later.' He sounded tired, as though this was a long-standing exchange between them.

The woman kept searching. The cupboard-slamming was done with a flick of her wrinkled hands, well practised, and the violence of it seemed to satisfy her. Then she stood to her full height, which was no height, really. She was dressed in a brightly patterned satin robe that was something like a kimono. Her white hair was piled high on her head, long strands swinging free of the combs she had jammed in here and there. She focused on Martha, her face pinching into a scowl.

'We're closed,' she said.

'No, you're not,' said Martha.

The woman's eyes widened. 'Oh, *hello*, you know better than I do?' The voice was uninflected with any indication of class or ethnicity, and laced with a distinct edge of threat.

'I'm sorry,' the boy interrupted. 'Course we're open.'

From behind him came a *tsk* noise and a loud sigh. The woman clattered off along the service side of the counter, to the left of the bottle shop, out of sight.

'Seven-fifty, alright?'

She looked into his eyes. The price seemed optional. Shit, he was gorgeous.

'Fine. Thank you.'

Martha passed him ten dollars. He jabbed a few keys on the till and it sprang open. Then he produced a long, narrow paper bag from under the bar, wrapped the bottle and pushed it towards her.

'Fine,' he echoed, eyes still locked on hers. 'Have a good night.'

She pressed a smile, jammed the bottle in her handbag and went out into the night, giving the door a sharp look on the way through, as though it might be going to send her somewhere else.

The taxi waited on the opposite kerb, a flash of yellow in the monochrome street. She climbed into the back seat again and steeled herself for the night ahead.

SIX

Martha woke alone in the flooding winter sunlight of Saturday morning.

The night had been forgettable. Unthreatening conversations about the Meaningful Things: the firm, some politics, a bit of family. It was depressingly predictable. These were the type of people who would start on the dishes, and their real opinions, as soon as she was out the door.

They'd cooked Spanish. It was, of course, perfect, but the garlic was sour in her mouth now. She got up and boiled the kettle, made green tea, went downstairs for the newspaper. It was huge, a weighty clump of folds incapable of being rolled up, and so delivered flat. It had been her first indulgence when she moved out of home, to ring the local newsagent and order weekend papers. It had felt grown-up. She liked to be conversant with the Middle East, new wines, the books people were reading and the CDs they were listening to.

She should get a cat, she thought. It was good to demonstrate affection for someone, something. But she worked insane hours. She would not get a cat.

The bottle shop. It came back to her now. Not the discussion of the Planning and Construction division and how their juniors were widely believed to be on a fast track to partnership, but the pub and the boy and the taxi driver.

37

She made toast and flicked through the paper. The rustling reminded her of something. She went back to her bedroom, to her handbag, and fished out the crumpled ball of the paper bag that the bottle shop guy had twisted around the wine. She'd scrunched it and dropped it in her handbag when she couldn't find a bin. She smoothed it out with the palms of her hands.

Large print, stylised cursive in navy blue on the reddish-brown paper.

The Cherrywood.

No address, no phone number.

Later, she would ask herself why that moment had ignited the fixation. The guy, sure, but she had walked past a dozen, a hundred more attractive men in the past week without deciding to search for them. The building, then? She had no interest in architecture, only a vague idea the place did not belong in its context. If it was a hundred years old (she had no idea), why had it stood in defiance of everything around it? Later, when there was so much time to think about how it started, she came to believe the spark was already inside her, and everything else was mere fuel. She had always had the need to understand, to rationalise. To shrug off the events of the previous evening would have been to accept that some things are simply inexplicable, and Martha could never let go so easily.

So, she went to the phone books. Nothing under 'C' in the White Pages but, just in case, she took the L–Z volume and looked under 'The'. Then she went through 'Hotels' in the Yellow Pages. Again, nothing. Odd, but not the end of the world. She remembered the route the cab had taken.

Martha put on running shoes and intervarsity trackpants, a shapeless polar fleece. Outside, she'd be an oddity on a Fitzroy Saturday among the pea coats and Docs, but she'd never cared. She was only passing through their scene.

She got off the tram as Victoria Parade neared the northeastern edge of the city. The boulevard formed a watershed here, sloping

east and west away from St Vincent's Hospital. She thought
for a moment, then started walking north, following what she
recalled of the taxi's path. There was a leaden gleam to the winter
trees, and the houses huddled behind them: terraces, duplexes,
converted pubs and shops. Martha had been inside one or two
of these artful deceptions, humble from the street but restored
down to the last ceiling rose inside. Private courtyards in there,
Jasper Hill and Boyds.

The taxi had pushed north for several blocks, so she was in no
hurry to recognise anything. But the further she went, the less
sure she was of her direction. There were the rundown student
share houses with their Tibetan prayer flags. There was the squat
rectangle with the Italian business name on a plaque. The flaking
facade, 'LABEL DIECUTTING WORK'. The Commission
flats were on the right, she was sure of it. Or was it the left?

She found a takeaway place called Malt House with a brightly
painted souvlaki on its awning. Was it a souvlaki she was looking
for? It didn't matter. Next door was a vacant block with a builder's
temporary wire fence, a tin sign on it: 'Sandbank Demolitions'.

She walked until her feet hurt. In the afternoon, she found
herself on Nicholson Street, admiring the delicate timber
tracery of Osborne House, so intricate as to mimic the trees the
timber had come from. Across the tram tracks, the Exhibition
Building lay long and airy and filled by the daylight. She had
sat law exams in there, curled over a small table for three hours,
never looking up, never allowing her thoughts to waver from
promissory estoppel and constitutional conventions. On this
afternoon, she saw the building with eyes for the beauty she
hadn't allowed herself to enjoy back then. It was a vessel in both
senses of the word, both containing and displacing, afloat on its
gentle rise to the city's north.

Her minor search hadn't worked. She found a tram and
began the rumbling trip home. She'd stuffed it up, that was all.
She worried about herself sometimes.

During the following week, the memory of the Cherrywood kept returning.

Martha had a lot on her plate. There was a long-building, slow-running dispute with a developer, in which they were acting for the state government, and it was due for mediation on the Wednesday in a room full of QCs in mufti, who would be settled over their notes like pigeons on tossed bread. She loved to be in these rooms, to hear the wily advocates in bargaining mode, their clean hands resting on open ringbinders and their eyes creased with cunning. The outside world would be staggered to see the good humour they brought to these auctions of public assets. They were bloodless, even when their preludes had involved public warfare, media campaigns, the deaths of careers. Far from making her cynical about the process, it was reassuring to see clever people arguing companionably over the smell of coffee until these things found their natural level and were settled.

The week would also bring the professional reviews, in which she would have to front her supervising partner and the HR manager to justify half a year's work and her coming year's salary. She knew she could justify herself. The figures arrived monthly in hole-punched 'CONFIDENTIAL' envelopes and they were running her way. She had the hours. The projections were strong. None of it had anything to do with the quality of the time she'd sold, the precious hours of her breathing life. Quality was a subjective human judgement and she knew her work was good.

But a poor performance in the review could sow the seeds of doubt in the minds of her employers. If she couldn't present an ambit claim for her own interests, how was she going to promote the interests of Caspians' clients over the efforts of her bright young rivals down the street?

It would be fine, it would be fine.

It all had a way of subsuming the personal stuff. Things got buried, as if by blown sand, so only the chimney-tops of love and other edifices remained visible. She would rise from her chair at lunch, and occasionally in the morning and afternoon, to make cups of green tea in the kitchenette, and she would stare at the little tap mechanism on the urn, willing the moment to continue while she had a reason to be there. These were the moments when her mind returned to the Cherrywood, and the boy. The unmoored quality of those few moments delivered her a secret thrill.

So, she contrived a reason to be in the firm's library. The thirty-six minutes could be billed to a bank without it affecting anyone's share dividend. She worked her way through the Melways, following the coloured streets up and down the page with her forefinger. Next, she moved to the microfiche and loaded up a list of liquor licences, followed by a registry of crowd controllers. Nothing. The partners had their desk terminals connected to the Internet, and she wondered whether that might contain information about pubs. But the Internet was like other prestigious things: the partners bought themselves Porsches at an age when they looked silly in them, and having the Internet on their desks meant nothing when none of them knew how to use it.

After those thirty-six minutes, she felt reasonably confident there was no Cherrywood Hotel in Fitzroy, Victoria, Australia. In fact, there was no Cherrywood Hotel in the entire state, and the historical search confirmed there never had been. She felt a glow of relief at learning this, as it resolved one aspect of her disorientation. There was no evidence she'd somehow left Fitzroy and wound up somewhere else. Given liquor licensing was a state power, she couldn't speak for the rest of the nation, but that was immaterial.

She returned to the Melways and admired the neat grid of Fitzroy's streets, then placed the book facedown on the photocopier and selected the rarely used A3 paper drawer. When the long page slid out, she looked both ways, rolled it up and slipped it into a postal tube she'd brought for the purpose.

Back in her office, she took the copied map and placed it under some other documents, so she had cover if someone came in. After a diligent half-hour of work, she recorded the whole lot – the mapping and the real work – against a property developer who was currently before a Royal Commission for using standover men against protesters. They wouldn't have time to check her billings right now, and she felt no compunction about having them sponsor her little project.

As the office emptied out around six, she took up the map again and, with a ruler and a fine-line pen, drew evenly spaced horizontal and vertical lines to create a grid of squares over the whole sheet. Seventy-eight squares in total. Some she could rule out instantly, like the three squares falling inside the Fitzroy Pool – *Aqua Profonda* – so the eventual tally was seventy.

Rather than take the tram home that night, she stood outside the office tower and hailed a cab: a small test of an idea that was only half-formed. She got in the front and studied the driver carefully: average height, silver-haired, thin. Maybe around sixty, reading glasses hooked on his shirt pocket. Delicate fingers, clipped nails. No tattoos. She asked him to take her to the Cherrywood, and when he asked her where it was, she replied that she'd been there at night and wasn't sure, but she thought it was in the backstreets of Fitzroy.

'Ah,' he grumbled. 'Change their bloody names all the time.' He flipped through his Melways until he found map 44 and slid a fingertip up and down the streets. Then he frowned, tucked the book back under his seat and drove into Fitzroy, making aimless laps of the minor streets until he sighed and gave up. She smiled to herself and asked him to drive her home.

For the next four months, Martha walked every one of the squares she had drawn, checking up laneways, asking in pubs and using the Olympus she'd had since her year of backpacking in Europe to take pictures of street signs and facades. Some of the signs were mere ghosts, flaking paint revealing nothing more than an advertisement when she crossed the street and looked back at them. None yielded any clue to the pub's whereabouts, but she took photos of them anyway. Inside the Labour in Vain, she drank a lemon squash under an old mural depicting a washerwoman scrubbing the back of a dark child until a white patch appeared. She waited until the bartender was busy elsewhere and took a picture of it.

She kept detailed notes at home, never daring to take them to the office. She cross-hatched the ground she'd covered on her photocopied map until the entire sheet was darkened with the frustrated scratching of her pen.

She chastised herself. She prized her own determination, her ability to make time count, yet here was a pursuit that yielded no result for time invested, a minor fixation with no end point. The boy and the pub: the pull they exerted on her was surprising. She wondered if it was the first time she had been addicted to anything, or whether it was really that she hated to be beaten. But she came to think there were more productive uses of her days.

The pub refused to reappear, and she reluctantly let go of the project.

SEVEN

One Saturday evening, Martha walked the northern footpath of Gertrude Street.

Time hung still in the city, in the warm golden light of summer, suspended after another day of the endless cricket against the English – an obsession she could never understand. There was an empty quality to the inner suburbs during the week between Christmas and New Year. The office was running on a skeleton staff and the partners had retreated to the Peninsula to race their couta boats.

She was walking to feel part of the world, to observe others. The traffic was sparse, the sound reduced to the occasional rumble and ding of an 86 tram. It had been six months since the bottle of wine, and she had long ago given up searching for the pub. These walks happened to take her through Fitzroy. The shops were more interesting, the buildings more lovely than Richmond's. There were more people out and about, more surprises around corners. No, it had nothing to do with the pub and the boy.

She crossed Brunswick Street, past the strange timber balcony hanging from a terrace on the corner, the structure always threatening to fall into the intersection. On her left, the Atherton Gardens and their Housing Commission towers. Ahead, a phone booth – two people in agitated discussion. A girl in a flimsy top, clutching at her blue arms, pecking forward at a man in jeans and a polyester soccer jersey. The girl pointed at him, tried to corral him inside the phone booth as he tried to slip free of its door.

'You said credit, Anthony! Fucking *credit*!'

Martha was coming towards them, and a detour at this point would have drawn attention to her, so she pressed on past them, eyes averted at first but then unable to help herself. When she looked up, she caught his animal eyes as he scanned the street for signs of trouble. A wild kick from the girl caught him on the hip – its aim was more central – and he staggered into Martha's path, saying, 'Sorry, sorry,' as he regained balance. The sounds of the girl's accusations, dissolving to sobs, faded behind Martha as she ploughed on.

The shops were closed, and human activity was clustered around the pubs. The smell, the disinhibitant waft that leaks from a pub doorway onto the street, struck her unawares in the middle of other thoughts, and she recalled *her* pub. She felt certain the pub wasn't here on the busy streets – not that she was looking for it anymore. It was somewhere in the narrow streets to the north, and in the back of her mind. Not that it mattered.

But if she *was* searching, if it was on this busy strip, with its art supplies and furniture stores and its trams, then people would notice it. People loved to bring mysteries to heel. It was the worst of human smallness, she thought, the need to make sense of enigmas.

Under the leafy plane trees, past the Builders Arms, the air thick with booze and smoke and human need. It was roiling in there, spilling over with life's hungers. Men, mostly, arguing and laughing, but women too, hair cut or coloured in ensigns of rebellion or indifference, clothes denoting a Saturday night for one's own pleasures and no-one else's.

There at her feet, a man whose dark face was lost in a bird's nest of white hair, onto which was plonked a yellow beanie. She nearly tripped over him as she peered into the public bar. He sat cross-legged beside the corner door, his back against the tiles.

Over his lap, he cradled an electric guitar, plugged into a small box amplifier. The amp was covered in stickers: Lord Jagannath beamed out at Martha and exhorted her to 'SMILE'. The cap at his feet was full of coins.

'Look out,' he said. 'Lady's on a mission.'

The man was talking to her, she realised. 'Yes, well, actually,' she began, 'I'm trying to find a pub.' The words surprised her, having been sure she was not.

The Koori man stood with an effort. 'Looks like you found one.'

'No,' she replied. 'Not this one. Another one.'

He was packing up the guitar and the cap and the leads that snaked to the amp. He started to lug the gear inside. 'Don't see what's wrong with this one. Wanna come and tell me about it?'

She followed his back as he wound his way through the crowd inside, shoulders parting to accommodate him and the neck of his guitar, closing again in his wake so she had to hurry through behind him. He grunted something at a girl in a Mudhoney t-shirt who was pulling beers, and led them to a quieter rear bar, where he placed the gear at his feet. He removed his yellow beanie, sat it on the bar and rested his hands beside it.

She took up the stool next to him, and he cast her a glance as though he'd never seen her before. As he did so, a drink appeared between his hands, a dark pint that settled upwards, against gravity, and overspilled the glass. Martha suddenly wanted one, and when the Mudhoney girl stopped in front of her, she indicated the man's glass, which was now tipped into the cavern between his whiskers. The girl nodded and poured her one.

Martha hadn't intended to wind up drinking with a stranger in Fitzroy, and started to worry, but then told herself one wouldn't kill her. Music snaked through from another room: 'Animal Nitrate', sweet and buzzing like a sonic hive.

The busker took another sip. 'What kinda pub is it?'

'Oh.' Martha had to think about this. What kind of pub *was* it? 'It's a strange place.' She thought of the Cherrywood's seductive smell, and suddenly realised the source of it. 'It's made of timber, like *only* timber. Two-storey. Lots of windows, a corner door with one of those … semi-circle windows above it. It has a bottle shop and a public bar and a back bar. But no-one really seems to go there and I only know it's in Fitzroy and it's …'

'Got a name?'

'Yes.' Why hadn't she simply started with the name? 'It's called the Cherrywood.'

'Cherrywood,' he repeated slowly. Martha thought she detected familiarity, along with a half-formed intention to conceal it. 'What else about it?'

How far to take this conversation? There were things Martha had seen, but even those took on a dream-like quality in her memory – the curvature of the walls, of the bar, the beams. The scattered barstools piled higgledy-piggledy in the corner.

'It's … I went there once and I knew where I was, or I … It was beside a kebab joint—'

'Love kebabs. You sure it was kebabs?'

'Yeah, but I've walked all around and looked at maps and I can't even find the kebab joint, let alone the pub.'

The man picked up his half-finished pint and dabbed it several times along the bar towel like it was a stamp, watching as it left diminishing circles of foam. 'Heard this before,' he said. He was staring through the low opening in the back wall of the bar, under the rows of spirit bottles, into the chaos of the crowded front bar.

'What do you mean?'

'People looking for things, finding they're not where they thought they were. See through there?' – he pointed at the front bar crowd – 'See how many blackfullas out there?'

He looked directly at her now. 'What do you really know about Fitzroy, love? You live here?' The 'love' was so neutral, he may as well have addressed her as 'mate'.

'No. I live in Richmond. Just pass through sometimes.'

He sighed, took a drink. For a moment, she thought the conversation was over, so she took a deep mouthful from the pint that had appeared in front of her. It was velvety and sweet, and its aftertaste reminded her of slightly burnt toast, though in a good way.

'What is this?' she asked him.

'Portogaff,' he answered. 'So, you don't live here.'

'Nope.'

'Well, all these people, right?' He pointed again at the front bar. 'Koori mob. So many here they used to call this street the Black Mile. Dirty Gertie. Come in from Fram, from Lake Tyers, Condah ...'

Martha must have looked blankly at him.

'Missions. They were coming in from missions. Taken from their families when they were little, from their mums and brothers and sisters and aunties and uncles. Whole lotta lies about em being brought up wrong. Put in care, or they put em with other whitefulla families, and when they're grown-up they leave that family, leave the mission and they *drift*, see? Like if you got a bird in a cage and you take it outside and you open the door of the cage, the bird just hops on top and stands there, then after a bit it starts making little flights, cos there's a thing tellin it home's somewhere but it's got no idea where.'

He flew his fingers around in the air between them.

'It's not just a Koori thing.' He was becoming more vehement now. 'All kinds of people, damaged people. Trying to find your people. So, they come to these streets for years, like a collecting place. "Hey, you from up north?" "Your lot from the river country?" Whatever, making connections. So, this pub, right? And the legal service, health service, housing board' – he counted them off on his fingers – 'Fitzroy Stars, the boxing gym. All about getting back to your people. Strong place for that. Started with the old ones ...' He began to count his fingers again. 'Thomas James, Margaret Tucker, Martha Nevin. Uncle William Cooper, come to Fitzroy from Cummeragunja. Ol Pastor Doug's church ...

'So, people are milling around, asking questions, night after night, like they gonna put the pieces back together. Cops come, council workers come, see all these blackfullas blowin this way and that, gettin raucous in the pub, and they say, "Why don't you lot go home? Can't hang round like this." And this lot say, "What do you think I'm tryin to *do*." See? Trying to go home, but we all lost now.'

His voice lost its vehemence. 'Anyway, you were saying you'd lost a pub.'

Now Martha felt ashamed that the thing she sought seemed so trivial. 'I don't know your name,' she said lamely. Instead of providing it, the man answered, 'True.' They both drank in silence. Someone called out to the man in friendly mockery from among the revellers in the front bar. He responded with a grouchy bark that hid a glimmer of amusement.

'I'm sorry,' she said, and wasn't sure why. 'It's just, sometimes I feel a bit lost. Not like the people you talked about, but ... I can't describe it. That pub felt like it might be a fixed point, and now I can't find it.'

For the first time, his face betrayed a particular solicitude. Was his care an indication she had stumbled upon something important, or had he seen madness and worried for her? This was, she supposed, the first fork in the road: not realising *why* someone has looked at you with concern.

'Thing is, you're not gonna find it by chasin it around.'

'I've been very systematic,' she replied. 'I've divided up the Melways page, and I've tried every combination of liquor licence—'

'No,' he said firmly. 'You might call it a system, but all you're doing's chasin a different way. Maybe you got to sit back a little and see if it comes to you.'

She thought about this. 'Okay. Have you ever been there? To the Cherrywood, I mean …'

'Er … no.' He was thinking, searching his memory for something. 'Maybe? I don't know. Mostly drink here, do my busking here cos I know this lot. Got no need to go wandering around the backstreets lookin for mystery pubs.'

'I never mentioned it was in the backstreets.'

'Yeah, we – didn't you? Well, if it was in Smith Street or Brunswick Street, everyone be seeing it, so it's gotta be backstreets, doesn't it?'

Martha had had the same thought. She had definitely been in a quiet place the night she'd found the Cherrywood.

The man reached down, picked up the guitar with a grunt and placed it across his lap. He searched up and down the neck, carefully placed his thumb and forefinger over a particular point on a string and plucked it. It emitted a high, unplaceable sound.

'Know what that is?'

'Ah, no.' She wasn't sure how basic this question was, as she'd never had time for music.

'Harmonic. Not a note. A *fundamental frequency*, they call it. Contains all the tones. See, any note, right – this one, or this one, or this one – you hear it as one note, but it's full of tones. Partials, they call em, little vibrations in the air.' He rested the guitar on the ground again. 'Now, you take the city, right. You want to have one city on a map so you can say, "There it is, there's the city. I can walk from A to B." The harmonic. But every single person in the city lives in it in a different way. I could say, "I had a picnic in that park," and you could say, "I had a friend died of an overdose there." Same park, same place. Tones. The city vibrates in millions of different ways, every hour, for every person in it.'

'Oh.'

'And another thing, same thing. Yarra comes in from the east and the Maribyrnong comes in from the west and they meet at the docks and then the whole thing flows into the bay, right?'

'Right.'

'Wrong. That's what's happening on the surface. Land can be flat on top and tilted underneath. Under the roads, country drains down from the north, down Elizabeth Street, and it makes pools and, whatya call em, aquifers, under Flinders Street Station, under all them trains. They were there when the whitefullas came, and they bricked em up, but they can't stop em flowing under there, and then you go deeper and there's other ones flowing in other directions, and down and down, criss-crossing but never meeting. Down, down, down. City sits on the top, vibrating. And if you could feel all those different ways it's resonating … then your map starts to look a bit silly, hey.'

His eyes went wide. 'The whole place is humming, love. It's making a sound but the sound isn't one note, and it's a place but it doesn't go on one map. It's a lie that it's just one place.'

She saw it now and knew it to be true. She had felt so alone, assuming day to day that everybody else belonged to one place, a city called Melbourne, that it was only her who didn't belong. Now she saw that everyone lived in a different city made out of their experiences, cities blurred by their countless subjective versions, overlaid upon each other and occupying the same place. This led to two conclusions: everyone was as alone as she was, and in the gaps between all these versions of the city, there were places that could hide a hotel.

The drinker in the other bar called out again.

'I'm sorry,' she said. 'I've been keeping you from your friends.'

The man glanced through the gap to the front bar, waved the backs of his fingers at the source of the voice in a way that was both affectionate and dismissive. 'Ah, he'll be right. I'll go see him.'

He got up off his stool, straightened and pushed the empty pint glass towards the back edge of the bar. 'Good luck with your pub,' he said, and he placed a hand on her shoulder as he passed.

'Do you need to take your things?' She gestured towards the guitar and amp on the floor under the bar. He looked at them.

'Nah.' His eyes met hers as he said it. This man had been to the Cherrywood, it was clear, and he knew the place well.

Or perhaps he had lost his mind once, and he knew that place too.

EIGHT

Jorge Borgius Ximenon was, as Thomas rapidly learned, a mercurial partner.

Sometimes Thomas's letters would be returned to him unopened. Sometimes the man would respond with such brevity that Thomas would be left wondering if he had inadvertently caused offence. Sometimes Ximenon would initiate contact himself, pouring streams of thought into some arcane matter and having his letters delivered across town urgently by courier. Sometimes the correspondents were private secretaries, or an accountant or solicitor: Ximenon was abroad, or he was unavailable or swamped with other work. Then Thomas would hear reports of him out at his regular haunts, perched behind mountains of food and wine, listening to unfamiliar pipe music and surrounded by unexpected company.

Lucy had withdrawn from her husband's affairs after his expulsion from the board. Thomas knew she did not want to distress him further – she had no need to point out how right she'd been. Without her shrewd perspective, he found himself prone to wild thoughts about this enigmatic man. He was no common fraudster, clearly, for the board of Maindample would have subjected him to the same scrutiny before accepting him as they had applied to Thomas himself. Besides, an ordinary swindler would move on, and he had remained faithful to his clubs and his favourite restaurants since the banishment. Thomas had tried to do the same, and it pleased him to discover that most of their friends were sympathetic, uninterested in the gossip, and only concerned for his and Lucy's welfare. He could not say the same support had been extended to Ximenon, as he had no idea what Ximenon's circles were and who moved within them.

This led him to consider a stranger notion: that Ximenon was a spy. For whom he might be spying, or in what subject matter he traded, was beyond reckoning. Thomas was humble enough to assume that nothing in his life, other than the obvious fact of his wealth, was worth reporting to others. But how had Ximenon been so well informed about their fellow board members? How had he come upon his wealth, and why hadn't he explained the source of the timber?

Specific doubts became more general. Why had he drawn him in? When he revisited Ximenon's earlier answer to the question – that Thomas was the only natural fit among the board members for this enterprise – he felt unconvinced. The pitiless flash of obsidian in Ximenon's gaze, so fleeting it could be missed entirely, marked him as the conduit of darker forces.

Thomas's resolve had hardened. Whatever the man was up to, they were bound to each other by this misfortune and he would not let him become elusive. To do so was to admit defeat, and circumstances had developed beyond that point now. The shipment of the timber had been arranged, a deposit paid to the shipper – Maindample's chief rival. Thomas had insisted, and he felt sure his wife would be proud, that the balance of his money was placed in escrow awaiting safe delivery in Melbourne.

There was a compelling reason for caution. Thomas had never seen the timber. It disconcerted him to be hostage to Ximenon's word that it existed. He didn't know what type of timber it was, only that it had preternatural virtues. He could summon it in his mind: tall, square stacks of it lying on a barge, bathed in evening light so the tone of the wood glowed, sometimes pink or mauve, sometimes a butterscotch yellow. In these visions, ropes and tarpaulins secured it in place, and the light was softened by wreaths of tar smoke, kept burning day and night to ward off the borers.

On awakening from such a dream, six months after their expulsion from the board, Thomas rushed off a letter to Ximenon demanding a meeting at the Russian restaurant for lunch.

* * *

Seated across the table from him, it maddened Thomas to find Ximenon as relaxed as always.

He went through his usual routine of inspecting the menu, grunting with satisfaction at the presence of his favourite delicacies and gasping theatrically when the *maître d'* read him the specials. He prepared a cigar and laid it aside, poured wine for both of them and settled back with a sigh and one arm over the top of the banquette. Thomas watched this ursine sprawling with newfound suspicion.

'So.' Ximenon smiled. 'What business have we to cover?'

Thomas had planned to take issue with the absences, the torrents and droughts in correspondence, the alarming randomness of Ximenon's attention. But here and now, his resolve wavered. He needed to confine himself. To open this up into a broad-ranging attack on his partner would only make things worse.

'My wife,' he began. 'She is a very intelligent woman. Very cautious. She asks me how I can be sure this is a good idea. Now, I mean no scepticism, and certainly I have no doubt as to your bona fides. But I need to know more about the timber.'

'Ah, hmm.' Ximenon exhaled, rolled his bearish head on his short neck. 'You do not trust its provenance?'

'I can trust its provenance and still understand my wife's unease about your connection to it.'

A shift, a glint of alertness in the Sardinian's eyes. He called for Lillet Rouge on ice, sat forward and delicately shifted the cutlery on the table in front of him. Thomas hurried to apologise, as was his way.

'You'll forgive my tone. I am ... anxious to be sure.'

Ximenon was distracted, looking for the head waiter. 'Do you think we could manage the boar's head?'

'I'm sorry – what?'

'I'm starving. But it is a lot, and the ... *pah*' – he waved a dismissive hand – 'the theatrics. But I think we should.' He clicked his fingers over his shoulder and ordered it. Then he fixed Thomas with an admiring look. 'This is good! You are becoming assertive, my friend. Please don't ever feel it is an intrusion to ask for information you are fully entitled to. But where to start? Tell me, have you heard of the Expropriation of Tiflis?'

'No. Go on.'

'No, of course.' He laughed a little, paused and drew a finger down the condensation on his glass, as though measuring the level of the story Thomas would need.

'There are lives,' he said eventually, 'ones unlike yours, where necessity takes strange and disturbing forms. People whose moral responses to the world are shaped by the extremes confronting them, and not by matters philosophically fixed – honour, mercy and so on.'

Thomas feared he was going to be subjected to some obscure monologue, but Ximenon was closing in on his purpose.

'So, two years ago I was in contact with some ... political interests in the Caucasus.'

Aha! So, he is a spy ...

'You are, of course, aware the Russian Empire is in its death throes?' Ximenon continued.

'Yes.'

'Imagine the men at the centre of those events, contemplating the fate of an entire nation. You expect them to be in gilded palazzi, don't you? But often, they are in safe-houses and in bars ... establishments far less salubrious than this one. Bolsheviks and Mensheviks, united in their desire to overthrow a corrupt regime but divided over the role of violence. The Mensheviks were steadier, more inclined to negotiation. The Bolsheviks, not so even-tempered. Years ago – how many? Must be, ooh, ten – the Bolsheviks, whose cause I sympathise with, I must add, decided to take matters into their own hands. They formed a secret committee within the revolutionary movement, met in churches, passed messages in code through the street urchins. These men were the bravest of the brave, on the run not only from the tsar and his Okhrana, but also from their own sworn comrades, their Menshevik brothers. They formed a plan to rob a bank in Georgia, in the city of Tiflis, to send an emphatic message about the evils of entrenched wealth, and also to raise money for their insurgency. What do you think of the morality of all this?'

'I might be more of a Menshevik, I suspect.'

'Yes. Though none of us has been tested, have we?' Ximenon sipped – the ice made a little melody – and returned to his story. 'They carried out their Tiflis plan. You will not know the place – an ancient city in the Caucasus, strategically vital for centuries. Almost exactly halfway between the Black Sea and the Caspian Sea, the womb of ancient Europe. None of which matters here.'

The waiter arrived with a tray of cutlery, implements Thomas would have called pickaxes and saws if he wasn't so sure they had specialised names in this environment. Ximenon sat back while the tray was positioned before them. He resumed speaking after the waiter withdrew.

'One of the two principals in this scheme was a young man who styled himself "Koba" – a political veteran despite his tender years, who had organised robberies before. Intelligent, cunning, a man completely committed to his cause. The other was his childhood friend, Kamo, who was little more than an excitable sadist. A dangerous thug, the type who finds opportunity in a revolution but has no intellectual grasp of the struggle. *You give me a grenade and I will throw it to behold the dismemberments*, yes? A necessary evil of uprisings, these people.

'Through compromised insiders, Koba and Kamo discover the schedule of the bank's cash deliveries. They make bombs. They form a gang of twenty – hard men, ones who would prefer to die under torture than to speak – and, one summer morning, they take up positions on the street corners around the great square of Tiflis, dressed as peasants, coats stuffed with revolvers and grenades. Only the maniacal Kamo dresses differently. He poses as a grenadier and sweeps loudly into the square in a troika.' Ximenon shrugged. 'Some people can't help themselves.

'The police are present because the authorities have been tipped off about the plan. All these people, watching these other people, while the city, unaware, goes about its business. Children, my friend. Children and their mothers, walking the sunlit streets. What do you think of the morality now?'

'This makes me uneasy, but you know it does.' The waiters were assembling in a guard of honour as the kitchen doors swung open.

'Yes. This is why you are a good soul. Others could justify what comes next. The cash delivery arrives by carriage, heavily guarded by horses and more carriages. This much is expected. When the delivery enters the square, the gang pounces, throwing explosives and firing their weapons. The carnage ... terrible. The dead and the dying, the screams and detonations and the spinning shrapnel from destroyed statues and plinths and windows and so on. A boy selling papers is decapitated by the flying buckle of a bridle, and it is said that a horse, having lost two of its legs, slides away from the scene, disembowelled but with its carriage still attached, while a robber with his scalp torn off tries to heave the cash bags from the carriage.'

Amid these scenes of carnage, the severed head of the boar arrived on a timber board, borne high by the head waiter. Its mouth was agape and stuffed with an apple, the ears and snout crisped by roasting, the eyes replaced with chestnuts, the smell of it rich with herbs and fat. A sprig of rosemary crossed its jaw behind the apple like the bit of a bridle. Thomas felt his appetite deserting him, while Ximenon took up the brutal cutlery and began to saw.

'They get away, all twenty of them. Quite remarkable, given what a chaotic effort it has been. Forty dead, and about as many fine horses. Most of the dead are police, but there are dozens of injured civilians blinded, burned, dismembered.'

'And the money?'

Ximenon heaped slices of the head onto their plates and tossed a few garnishes at each. 'Ah, you make me think I do not really know you. I tell you about disfigured women, murdered children, and you ask me about the money. They got away with about half a million roubles, but most of it – and this is the key to the story – most of it was in serialised bank notes. Traceable. Governments keep lists of these things, you know.

'A long stalemate ensued. The revolutionaries could not spend their money while the authorities were waiting for the serial numbers to reappear. But the authorities could not ascertain who had done this terrible thing once the trail had gone cold, and they took out their frustration on whatever groups had earned their displeasure in other areas. The Armenians suffered terribly, and, of course, the robbery was no work of theirs.

'The robbers moved first. They had a plan to convert the money. Somewhere, and the details are vague, somewhere in the countryside east of Tiflis, out towards the Caspian Sea, a deal was brokered involving a trade of cash for goods. The goods could then be on-sold and redeemed as untraceable cash, and slowly, slowly, the original bank notes would be fed into foreign currency markets, where the Russians could not reach them.'

'Goods?' Thomas felt like a mist was slowly lifting.

Ximenon was chewing extravagantly, already reloading his plate. He waited, swallowed. 'The goods were trees.'

'*Ah* ...'

Now he put down his knife and held up a hand: he did not want his audience getting ahead of the story. 'Eat, my friend. It will be getting cold.' Ximenon began heaping more food onto Thomas's plate with a pair of silver tongs. When he was done, he picked up his knife and fork, but instead of eating, he dabbed at the air with the tip of the knife.

'Everything went wrong, of course. Someone knew someone who knew a family who had run an orchard for generations, and their trees had contracted an infection – a root parasite or a mite or something, I don't know – which meant they would never fruit again, but it left the timber completely unaffected. The family couldn't sell the timber into conventional markets due to the trade rules preventing the spread of the pathogen, whatever it was. People didn't understand the science behind it, and they thought releasing the timber would put entire communities of orchardists at risk. This was the Transcaucasus – people under immense persecution, then and now, and therefore highly protective of their few assets. Hillsides covered in trees, acres and acres of them, and these people were confronted by the prospect of the whole lot being burned. To make matters worse, the bank – another bank, of course – was closing in on the family, seeking to take possession of the farm.

'So, they were the ideal supplier to the revolutionaries. There were negotiations. Preparations were made to harvest the trees and mill the timber, and very quickly it was done, stored on the property among these barren hillsides. Both parties had much to gain – or lose – and sometimes in these situations people become desperate. Discussions broke down ...'

'Oh, no.'

'... and the orchardist, his whole family, murdered. You must understand, we are now several steps removed from the original perpetrators of the robbery, the Bolsheviks. These people are intermediaries, common gangsters. It is impossible to transact such business without these entanglements.'

Thomas was gripped by the fear, once again, that he had no idea who the man sitting opposite him really was. Exactly *who* conducted such business?

Ximenon heaved a long sigh. He reloaded his plate again and ate, taking his time now. Thomas had barely touched his.

'The timber has come into my possession through brokers who, be assured, had no role in those terrible events. I am at the end of a very long chain of consequence. But perhaps we can do some good here.'

A group of businessmen came crowding into their corner of the restaurant and began to arrange themselves around the long table immediately next to Thomas and Ximenon's. They were loud and the air carried the smell of the booze on their breath. Several of them bellowed their greetings and examined the flayed skull of the pig as they pushed their way into their seats. They seemed harmless enough, but it was clear the conversation between Thomas and Ximenon could not continue at the table.

'We should walk the riverbank,' suggested Ximenon. He took up his cigar, called for the bill and paid it, as was customary.

* * *

They took a cab to the river and, as they began walking, the topic of the imminent voyage came up.

'You have made preparations to sail?' Thomas asked.

He received an inscrutable smile in return. 'I am not the one with a young wife and a child to consider,' Ximenon replied. 'The voyage will be very trying for them, you know.'

'Yes, but are you coming with us?' He was tiring of this indirectness – he knew he sounded irritated and he thought the Sardinian should hear it.

Ximenon stopped, leaned on an iron rail and looked towards the shipyards. 'My friend, I am not as young as I once was,' he began.

'None of us are.'

'Yes, but I have matters, you understand, people to whom I must attend. I am fortunate that you are among the few of my associates I needn't watch over.'

Thomas hesitated. 'Do you mean we must go without you?'

'Only in the first instance. I will follow, once various transactions are completed. But while I am disappointing you, I should say this – I do not think you should sail with your wife and daughter.' He saw Thomas's look of distress. 'The Irish Sea is as dangerous as it has ever been. These terrible U-boats. You should have them come later when things are put right.'

'I understand,' Thomas replied. 'But ... no business partner? No family? Why am I taking the burden of this entire enterprise?'

'I think you underestimate yourself. This venture is well within the range of your talents. The voyage will be a pleasure for you, and there is room in the accounts for you to pay yourself a generous viaticum. Once you get through these ... tensions in local waters, you'll have eight weeks to think and work. Enjoy it – study the ways of the purser and the cabin staff so you will be armed with ideas.'

'But there is so much to be done at the other end!'

'Yes, but it will take time. We must land the timber, find a suitable shipyard, have the steamer built to the specifications we already possess, using funds we already hold in safekeeping' – he winked – 'thanks to your diligence. And by the time those matters are complete, I will be there to assist you with commissioning the vessel and launching the commercial enterprise.'

This moment left a deep mark on Thomas. Here they were by the river, silhouettes in coats. Even at this late hour, the air around them was filled with the steam of industry and the sounds of life in its relentless forward motion. Below them, couples walking past, oblivious to anything but their need for each other, and he standing in the chill air at the rail, absorbing the one thing Ximenon hadn't said: that he existed apart from these ordinary instances of life, a man who catalysed the fates of others and was never used up in the reaction.

* * *

Thomas began to work longer hours, entrusting less of the project to his business partner as Ximenon himself withdrew his attention. The nagging suspicion never left him that he was being deceived somehow, but every invoice was paid, every contribution punctually made to the business account.

Lucy managed to accommodate all of this, relegating it to a place in her mind where it could be controlled, while her heart remained open to Thomas and more particularly to their daughter. At five years of age, Annabelle could play the piano, recite poems and mimic her teachers. She could draw faces with a witty eye for caricature. She was funny and insightful, according to the adults who met her. But there was a side to her they did not see: her deep attachment to her father. His preoccupations meant that it was becoming rarer for others to see father and daughter together, and, in truth, it was Lucy who did the practical things, the scolding and comforting and worrying that were so substantial with such a precocious child.

It would irritate Lucy to see Thomas arrive home late in the day and receive the affection that should have been hers after her labours. But she never gave in to frustration. Her marriage was mature enough for her to see her husband as a good man, but not the heroic figure Annabelle imagined him to be. Though she loved him, he was well short of heroic.

None of this mattered to the little girl. She would sit in open-mouthed adoration while her father told her stories of the magical paddlesteamer they would one day own, and how people would come from far away to ride on it. She would draw pictures of it, sometimes with the paddlewheel at the back and sometimes amidships, sometimes with two backswept smokestacks and sometimes one, stout and blackened like a locomotive's. It must never have occurred to her that her mother knew more of the required architecture than her father did.

For Thomas and Lucy, the move to Australia loomed ever larger. It was the lump in the bed, the stone in the shoe. Thomas could not bring himself to raise the subject of Ximenon's advice to travel separately. Given a choice between separation from his wife and child and placing them at risk out of a selfish need for them, he knew the right decision but could not bring himself to make it.

But he needn't have tormented himself. Lucy came to the realisation, on her own terms, that it was necessary for them to travel separately. She explained her logic to Thomas: given the length of the journey and the likely delays, it was vital they kept an office open for important correspondence. Lucy would be the shopfront in Edinburgh, handling financiers and insurers and the other nabobs who had commercial interests in the project. She would deal with Ximenon – it was implied, though never discussed, that she intended to keep an eye on him – and she would attend to their daughter's education. Thomas would go, establish a base for them in the faraway land, and, when everything was in order, Lucy and Annabelle would join him.

The words she did not say, and which Thomas read in the air between them, were: *If your steamer is torpedoed, there will be a surviving parent for our child.*

Thomas resisted this logic – the visible part of it – at first, but there was no other way to do it. The date for his departure was fixed, and, as it neared, he brought a manic concentration to everything he did with his family. He did not have any separate conception of himself: he had been loved by his mother and father, and, but for a few years after their deaths – before he met Lucy – he had never measured his will against the world alone. The idea of operating in a foreign land without his wife and child was more than he could contemplate.

These were the thoughts assailing him as he took his usual Saturday morning walk to the market, this time having made excuses so he could go there without his wife and daughter. He found the old Jew, Herskope, at his flower stall, and asked for tea.

'Must be serious then. Sit down,' Herskope jibed.

'I am going to be apart from dear Lucy for a time,' Thomas began. Putting words to the thought stung him. Around them the blooms exploded in erotic disorder, a riot of colour and scent. He bent his head to make room for himself beneath them and their smell enveloped him. 'I want you to supply her with flowers while I am gone.'

Herskope smiled. 'A lovely thought. Do you have in mind weekly? Or more often?' He took up a notebook and a pencil, took the calendar from the wall beside his counter and began to examine the columnar weeks.

'No.' Thomas had thought about this. 'I want them to arrive at random intervals so they feel like a surprise every time.' He produced a wad of bills. 'This should cover the months I have calculated, and if there is any left over, you may consider it my gift to you for your assistance.'

The florist thumbed his way through the money. 'I shall write you a receipt.'

'No, don't. We trust each other. And besides' – he smiled – 'I wish to cover my tracks.' They shook hands, and Thomas remembered to give Herskope the dates of Lucy's and Annabelle's birthdays, the only specific days on which he wanted the flowers to arrive.

The nights drew down to single figures. He clung to Lucy and sometimes got up in the small hours to sit and watch Annabelle sleep, to engrave in his mind the sacred curl of her fingers on the pillow beside her cheek. He would sit there and think, or quietly weep. It vexed him to find the pursuit of success should be so inimical to the keeping of happiness.

NINE

In the late autumn of 1994, Martha found herself at the MCG for a football match.

To say she was watching the match would have been an exaggeration. The conglomerate who had the contract for the new northern freeway link were so grateful for her department's work that they had invited the legal team to a private function high in the grandstands behind insulating glass. The administrative workers who had filed and searched and stapled and delivered in support of the contract were somewhere below in the stands, huddled in their overcoats.

Martha had studied the two sides and their respective paths to the game, so as to have a solid conversational base if called upon. The lives of the main players reminded her of Russian novels in their arcs: the princes and the counts, those cursed by scandal and those sufficiently powerful to be immune from it. There were sagas unfolding in those lives, down on the luminous grass below.

The senior partners and the executives from the client company were hot-faced with beeriness. Despite the paralegals having been banished, a handful of the most attractive assistants had been invited in to be pawed and flattered. Martha had a rule about drinking in these environments. She did not feel she was the target of these attentions, but nor did she want to blur any lines. She kept a chardonnay in her hand and allowed it to warm in her grip.

One of the partners bailed her up, breathing beer on her in his enthusiasm. A good man, she figured, and probably not a letch, but he knew no life other than this world of backslapping and private calculus. He must have been about fifty and, although she understood men came in endless guises, there was an asymmetry about him. He was overloaded with analytical ability, but as a corporeal being he seemed underdone. Was he ever barefoot? Had he ever broken a bone, gone outside naked? There were no spots and no hairs on his hands. Aside from the modest sweep of grey hair over his forehead, she suspected he was dimpled and soft like a plucked bird. None of this felt sexual to her, but she experienced an insane urge to *examine* him, to know if he was really there at all.

Through the moment of weird distraction, he continued talking to her. What she had done on the contract had 'not passed unnoticed', he said, and her future was potentially a stunning one. 'None of these others have got what you have.' He pointed uncomfortably at her sternum. This was not mere flattery or blundering flirtation, she thought. He meant it. Had she heard such things from a drunken employer only months ago, she would have been thrilled, would have lain in her bed later on, replaying the words, weighing them. But something had shifted inside her, and she responded to his enthusiasm with steely smiles and nodding. Eventually – perhaps a little wounded – he wandered off. This had the effect of leaving Martha socially stranded and was the reason she slipped out to find a payphone and ring the number on the Caspian Lawyers Cabcharge card.

She heard three staccato demands and a vague promise: 'What name?' 'Pickup address?' 'Ready now?' 'First available. And you're at the MCG, Martha?'

'Um, yes. Yes, I am.'

'Good. Come out to the Brunton Avenue side and we'll have someone there for you.'

And the line clicked dead.

She waited under the concrete hull of the stadium, the firm's Cabcharge card ready in her fingers. It was lonely on the street, and the shadows in the loading bays of the stadium made Martha nervous. There were people around her, fans of the losing side getting away early, but she felt exposed, and was relieved when the taxi drew up with its roof lamp switched off. It pulled over in front of her, past other waving hands. Her mind was still on the evening as she recited her address to the driver, looking past him and out into the night. He headed for Punt Road, but as the cab rolled past the trees of the old park, she changed her mind. At the lights outside the Cricketers Arms, she asked him to head left, back towards the city's north.

'Do you know the Night Cat?' she asked. A carload of the graduates were heading there after the match.

'Yep,' he said, and she looked at him now. As he made the left turn, the driver's right hand rolled over the wheel and she saw a faded green 'H-A-T-E' spelled across his fingers. It sparked a memory, one she couldn't place. He was a big man, perhaps a Māori or a Samoan. His face was in shadow: nothing about him was familiar, except for the corresponding 'L-O-V-E' on his left hand where it rested on the transmission. A shock of recognition: she had been in this cab before. He saw her looking, cocked an eyebrow.

'You good?'

She took the question seriously. Was she good? Was he checking for her disapproval of the tattoos, or inviting her to ask for the story behind them? She glanced at the side of his face again, and again he returned her inquiring look.

'Could you take me through Fitzroy?'

The ghost of a smile. 'That's how you get there, isn't it?'

'I know, but ... through the streets?'

If this was an odd question to him, he showed no sign of it being so. And ten minutes later, she was on the footpath outside the Cherrywood, not knowing how it had happened.

She had abandoned the idea of the Night Cat at some stage and remembered the elusive pub. This time, she took care to note her surroundings as she waited for the taxi driver to run the Cabcharge through the knuckle-buster: the corner of Brewarrina and Cadell, two signs in the lamplight under the bare limbs of autumn.

There was no burger place, or indeed souvlaki place, next door. No plastic food above the awning. There was a coin laundry about five doors down, deserted and lit in hard blue-white fluorescents; on the wall at the back of the laundry was a tourist poster with a picture of the Pamukkale hot springs. A silken drift of music from the terrace houses along the street – the Killjoys – voices and laughter in the air.

The pub was exquisite, she now realised. Complicated lines of timber, just as she remembered, arranged ingeniously so the building, two storeys tall and with dormer windows in its roof, seemed to float above the ground. This impression was heightened by the appearance of the neighbouring buildings: brick and bluestone terraces soaking up the darkness, multiplying the cold. The pub spoke of something else, an optimism in the curved latticing. It didn't demand a speech and a stiff bow, the way the heavy decorations of the old Victorians did. She'd never read anything about architecture, and knew only the handful of terms one might encounter, tossed around in conversation. Was this Edwardian? It seemed too eccentric to be part of a *movement*.

The cabbie looked up at the facade. 'Good pub,' he said as he handed her the receipt.

Martha stood on the footpath, trying to understand. She could square the receipt with accounts on the Monday, and it felt like a win over whomever was trying to confuse her. She had a stake in the ground, a reference point. In fact, she had several.

She went in, this time choosing the angled corner door with the little window above it, rather than the one with the bottle shop light. How many doors in this suburb faced into corners like this? How many pubs had vanished and been forgotten, devoured by progress, hidden, leaving only an angled corner door to hint at their former lives? As she took the brass doorhandle in her hand, her right foot felt unconsciously for a bluestone step, but there was none. Instead, a pair of heavy, short lengths of timber formed steps, cupped by years of passing feet. She stepped up; the door swung back at her and would have struck her in the face had it not stopped at the toe of her shoe. She pushed again and was in the bar.

The lighting was as she remembered it, but the interior was behaving this time. Stools along the bar, a long brass rail and ashtray beneath; a scattering of plain tables. Empty but for three figures on the barstools and the boy she remembered – her heart leapt – leaning conversationally on the bar opposite them. Clustered around an ashtray, they looked up at the sound of the door, then returned to their conversation. They were like him, two of them thin and the third shorter and heavier. Each had scruffy hair and a growth, and each wore a t-shirt and beaten-up Converses. Their jackets were piled on the bar further down. Some bohemian thing united them, an attitude they had cultivated.

As Martha approached the bar, the boy broke off from the huddle and came towards her. His face was welcoming, and she felt there was recognition there. But then she began to doubt herself: why had she come? Having found the thing that had eluded her, what was she trying to achieve? He greeted her in a soft voice.

'Can I have a beer, please?' She sounded nervous. She told herself to shut up.

He rested a hand on the taps. 'Draught?'

'Mm. Um, a light maybe.' The hand shifted to a different tap and, without him looking there, his other hand found a glass in the refrigerated cabinets at his waist level. He began pouring. As she watched the beer fill the glass, she couldn't believe her good fortune. He was here, running the bar, and he was everything she remembered him to be.

'Been out?' he asked, and Martha looked down. Suddenly the foolishness of this idea crowded in on her. She was dressed like a lawyer. She had barely any cash with her and no friends to make it look as though she was casually passing by. She had planned the search with precision, but it was dumb luck, not the search, that had delivered the result. And she had no strategy for its conclusion.

'I, er, yeah. The footy.' She smiled and he smiled back.

'Close game, huh.' He glanced up at the TV above the bar. It was showing the post-match analysis, men in suits arguing. Her eyes followed his and she saw scarves and decorative bottles and steins up there too, a tuba dulled by green corrosion, a teddy bear and a shield with brass plaques on it – commemorating the grandees of a local team or the successful drinkers of a million pints or something – a Tretchikoff bathing nude, wading in the tropics, and a marine chart of Port Phillip Bay next to a faded sepia photograph of a long ship on a calm sea. Knowing nothing of ships, Martha took a moment to realise it had no masts, but instead had a wheel at its centre.

'I don't know,' she said. 'I had to be there for work.'

He snapped the tap shut and handed her the beer. She touched his fingertips in the passing of the glass. They did not lock eyes – he was looking back towards the other three. *His mates*, she thought. She pushed him a fiver and he dealt with the till, another one like the one she remembered from the previous winter. When he hit 'sale', the drawer crashed open and she watched it strike him lightly across the hips. His fingers scooped the drawer and placed a pile of wet coins on the bar towel in front of her.

She took the beer and paused: this was awkward. An empty room, music coming from somewhere. She went to the nearest table and sat, feeling foolish. If she'd been a smoker, this was the moment to set her hands to work, fumble a cigarette. Instead, she placed her small handbag on the table and began going through it. At best, this could buy her two minutes. But the boy was at her side now, like he knew.

'Do you want to come and ...?' He indicated the others, still engaged in their conversation. She thanked him and took up the beer, along with a cardboard coaster stuck to the bottom of it, and crossed the bar to where they sat.

'This is Will,' said the boy, indicating the smallest of the three, dark hair swinging over his face, which he drew aside with a pale finger.

'Mack.' He indicated the one beside Will, heavier and friendlier.

'And Van.' Tallish, thin and a face wreathed in dirty blond hair. 'And this is ...' He looked blankly at Martha, then broke into a smile.

Martha introduced herself and shook their hands.

'Martha works at the footy,' the boy said helpfully. She was about to contradict him, then decided she liked the new identity. The three of them were neither welcoming nor rude. They were accepting of her presence, she would tell herself later.

They had been arguing about politics, and they resumed as though she wasn't there and without any further reference to her. The boy was half in their conversation, half out of it, eyes darting to her. She waited until she was sure they were on her.

'You didn't tell me your name.'

He seemed confused. 'You don't know it?'

'Why would I know it?'

He smiled then, and she loved it. There wasn't a care in the smile, not even buried deep. 'You don't have the slightest idea who I am?'

'Why? Are you famous?'

He smiled again. 'No, definitely not. I'm Joey.' He poked his hand out over the bar self-consciously and she shook it. She was more intrigued than ever. The other three were again locked in an argument about something.

'I don't work at the footy, you know.'

'You told me you did.'

'I said I was at the footy for work.'

'Oh.'

'I'm a lawyer. I have to go to mind-numbing functions sometimes. Nights of the living dead. Are these guys your friends?'

'Yes, tonight.' He looked at them, then back at her. 'They're very shy. That's why they're not so friendly, sorry.'

'Oh, I see.' She drank again. *Tonight?* There were still no other customers in the bar. 'Nice place you got here, pardner.'

'Yes. Well …' He looked nervous, fiddled with something on the bench below the bar. When he looked up again, his expression had changed. 'How did you get here?' he asked, and she thought it an unusual question.

'Got a cab. I live over in—'

'What did the cabbie look like?'

'Older, baldish. Had—'

'Tattoos on his fingers?' He nodded gravely. 'Would you like another?'

'You're quite interrupty,' she said, and he looked mortified. 'Where is everyone?'

'Oh, ah …' He made a show of looking at the watch on his thin wrist. 'It's early. They tend to come in later.' He looked around her shoulder as though *they* would come storming through the door. A pub that made no geographical sense, an empty bar on a Saturday night. The *feel* of the place. So why was it him who was perplexed by her?

He poured a beer, set it down and hung uncomfortably between the conversation to his right and her before him.

'How long have you worked here?' she asked.

Again, the reluctance. 'It's been a while now. I sorta lost track.'

'Do you live nearby?'

He tipped his eyes upwards. 'Upstairs,' he said.

'Handy for work.'

'Mm.' His resolve seemed to stiffen. He was not going to allow himself to be questioned. 'Tell me something about you. How did you find us?'

'First time? First time, I was passing in a cab and I needed to wee,' she said. He laughed. 'And I needed a bottle of wine for a dinner party. You served me. In there.' She gestured to her left, towards the bottle shop. 'Would've been ...'

'August last year.'

'There you go again, interrupty-man.'

'Sorry. But how did you—' His brow furrowed, then he said, 'The cab,' to himself.

'Then I—' She feared the next bit might expose her as an obsessive. 'Okay. Don't think I'm weird, right? I did some research to work out where I'd been, because I thought I had it wrong. I did some walking. Quite a bit of walking. And I couldn't find the pub again, no matter what I did.'

He was listening intently.

'How come you remember me coming here in August?'

He looked distracted by the question. It had taken him off a course he was set upon. The friends had stopped talking. The room was silent, so they all heard her ask, 'What's going on here?'

The silence continued. Finally, Joey shrugged, looked around and laughed. 'Not much, as you can see.' The moment passed, but she felt she'd lost control of whatever she was trying to do. He was no less attractive than she'd remembered, something like Che without the beard and the beret. Thin Che, poster Che, before he got all fat and cigar-sooted.

'I think I'd better be going,' she said. She saw disappointment on his face and it secretly thrilled her.

The friends noticed her slinging her bag over her shoulder. 'Going already?' asked Mack, and, as she smiled in return, she

saw that his wrist, resting on the bar, had a band around it. Not
a decorative one, a clear plastic one with a strip of paper inside
it, on which she could see typed letters. There were small holes
along the band to set it at differing sizes.

She looked back into Joey's dark eyes. 'If I wanted to find
you again …?'

He disappeared under the bar and came back up with a
notepad. Taking a pen from his jeans pocket, he scribbled on the
back of his hand to get it running, then wrote on a page, tore it
off and handed it to her. It was slightly dampened by the tips of
his fingers.

'Easy. Ring me and I'll tell you the address.'

She looked at the phone number, her mind racing to keep
up. 'Why don't you just write down the address?'

'Well, silly, I won't know where you're coming from until
you tell me.'

It made no sense. None of this made any sense.

'The phone number's missing a digit,' she said.

'No it isn't.'

* * *

Later the same night, Martha unlocked the door to her flat and
let herself in.

Nothing had moved from where she'd left it. Why would
it have? The dishcloth had dried over the steel curve of the tap.
The microwave clock was still two minutes slow, the washing
machine display still blinking. Objects and their relationships
to each other, trapped in unending sameness, fully known and
disappointing.

She threw her coat and scarf onto the couch, turned on the
heating to a temperature that would have matched the outside
anyway, for the sake of feeling the air moving in a room with
no opening windows. She switched lights on and off again to

pass from the entryway into the kitchen and then her bedroom. Once there, she stood for a moment, enjoying the scent of it, a combination of fragrances she liked. Everything was neat and ordered, except the pinboard on the wall.

It was a tangle of map pages, pictures and notes, some empty spaces, some unused pins. She pinned the phone number into an empty space. Next, she took a pen from the jar and wrote neatly on an A4 sheet, then pinned it to the board too:

RULE ONE
The pub moves.

TEN

Thomas Wrenfether's long journey in the winter of 1917 began with a shorter one, from Edinburgh to Glasgow.

Annabelle clung to her father's hand as they pushed through the deafening crowds of Waverley Station, while Lucy walked beside them. It broke Lucy's heart, and it sorely tested her resolve, to allow Thomas this obsession. The entirety of the scheme was his – except for the painful idea of sending him alone, which was hers – and she had no desire to see the venture fail merely in vindication of her counselling against it. There was no such selfishness in her.

As they waited at the timber-panelled booking office, which was stranded like a beached vessel in the centre of the cavernous hall, Annabelle craned her neck to look up at the glass mandala of the dome, and her own sorrow was eased by its delicate symmetry.

Thomas saw her staring up and his gaze followed hers into the immensity of the ceiling. He crouched so his eyes were level with hers and together they watched the shards of coloured light landing among the commuters, reminders of pointless beauty amid the rush. Lucy was frowning over the tickets, trying to locate the correct platform. As father and daughter looked up, Annabelle asked, 'Are we the only ones who can see this?' He smiled happily back at her. She committed the patterns to memory, and long afterwards she would see them and recite their visual logic to herself whenever life grieved her, as others might use a mnemonic or a chant.

After a night in Glasgow, they took another train to the port of Liverpool, where their parting felt like the tearing of flesh itself. The intensity of the city, a place that drowned soft words, made intimacy impossible. Surging human undertows forced Thomas to keep a tight grip on Lucy and Annabelle. A mass of humanity – traders, dun-coloured soldiers, nurses in uniform with blood-red crosses over their hearts – was boxed in here by the grey slick of the Mersey and the pale stone of the Three Graces.

Thomas found them space by the wharf. He found it hard enough to kiss Lucy, knowing her smile, her wonderful eyes, would be consigned to his memory for long months. Then he felt Annabelle's small arm at his waist as though it represented every ounce of love in the world, and he was doubly stricken. He tried consoling himself by imagining the child would rebound as soon as his wife walked her away and she saw a juggler or a dear puppy on the street. Then the pain would be his alone, and he would be gone.

Here was the iron steamship, a dour vessel that scoffed at the grandiosity of this passenger's plans. Here was dull reliability, steadfast transport, unexceptionally getting things done. From the rail, in among the liners and the passenger vessels and the remnants of sail that comprised the fishing fleet, Thomas searched across the harbour. At the industrial wharf, he fancied he could see the glowing block of the timber consignment. It was due to leave more or less simultaneously, he knew. The shipwrights in Port Melbourne had been appointed, and they had built the slipway and the cradles. A massive brace had been engineered for the laying of the keel, which would be made from the trunk of a mountain ash, sourced many years before in the Gippsland region to the east of the city, they said. Kiln dried, they said, and free from intrusions, rot, hollows and knotting: things he'd taken on faith.

He stood and watched his wife and daughter waving among the crowd as the ship withdrew, hoping they might be able to make him out against the loveless steel of the hull, among the other faces and hands touching the breeze in farewell.

* * *

The perilous run out of the Irish Sea passed without incident, leaving Thomas wondering why he had worried so much. Through the long weeks of the voyage, he read and slept, paced on deck, tipping his hat to the women who promenaded with their luckier husbands. He dined alone and excused himself when offered company. Over time, the labouring vessel came to feel like a reprieve from the matters that had bothered him back home. The people around him did not know who he was. They knew nothing of his wealth, his successes and failures, of the tailwind of advantage afforded him in life. He could be anyone, he realised, a man of undisclosed potential. He could be as enigmatic as Ximenon himself.

The steamer reached Port Said, where it lay in the heat for a fortnight while a dockside dispute raged over its resupply. After nine days, it was met by a mail delivery that had caught it up. Two letters: one in his wife's hand, postmarked 20 December 1917. The other addressed in heavy ink, bespattered, the cursive running forward in a way suggesting not impatience but a desperate kind of flight. It was Ximenon's handwriting, which was normally unhurried, extravagant even. Thomas had not read a word before he knew the letter was written in extremity.

An instant of indecision: both letters could be nothing but small talk, but more likely both could be vitally important. He decided to start with his friend's.

My dear Thomas,
I write in apology, and in warning, these being the duties of a
friend and ones I have neglected, self-evidently.

We Sardinians are famed for our longevity, but the likelihood is I do not have long. I find myself settling accounts, financially in some cases, morally in others. You trusted me. I was drawn to you by the quality I saw in you, the quality of need or vulnerability that some might unkindly call naivete. I do not think it was that. I think you were among strangers. You were searching for friendship and for meaning in your life, and I was able to offer you both of those. We are outsiders, each in our own way.

You were stoic through the ordeal of our exile from Maindample, a valuable confidant and friend. And again, the vital matter of trust. You looked to me to ensure we would have our vindication. I know – and perhaps you, too, know by now – I have both delivered on that promise and also failed you. The failure is bitter medicine.

So, regarding the latter, I wish to apologise. Perhaps your life would be stabler, better served by modest habits, if you had never met me. I have already caused you harm, and I believe there is more coming to you. I can see the love, laid upon the landscape of your every word and deed, that you have for your wife and child. I ought to have better respected its preciousness.

The timber comes with trouble. They are killing their brothers, again, driving children into exile across the Caucasus, again, as I write these words. Again, as ever they have done. The timber comes bearing grudges drawn up into the grains. It comes with enemies. They are implacable, and they will not rest. Guard your treasure, guard wisely your loved ones, your mind, your very life.

To my great regret, I know now I will not be joining you. I retain my belief that you are capable of making a success of our venture, and therein rests my sole consolation.

I must hasten now. Be vigilant. Be less trusting but no less optimistic.

I remain—
Yours in solidarity and friendship,
J.X.

A second reading, a third, delivered only bafflement. Why did he not have long? Who were these enemies? And of whom should he, Thomas, be vigilant? His instinct was to write back, to demand clarity and an end to these riddles, but he knew in his heart such a letter would yield no response.

He folded Ximenon's missive, returned it to its envelope and tucked the envelope into an inside pocket. Deep in thought, unsettled, he took up Lucy's letter.

My dearest husband,

Though little time has passed, the days are wearing long on me. I console myself with knowing you are out in the world, endeavouring to do something worthwhile, and it is your spirit of adventure that stokes my admiration for you. But I miss you, I cannot put it any other way. Poor Annabelle was distraught in the first days, and her first question upon waking each morning was, 'Are we going to live with Papa today?'

In recent days, she has ceased to ask, though I am sure it means she has come to some acceptance of the need for this absence of yours, and not that she despairs of seeing you again. We both go on, in our different ways, she with schoolwork and friends, I with the tasks necessary to keeping home and tending to the business in your absence. There are the comforts of friends, of course, though I fear at times they pity me.

I am so wearied by the weight of this sad world we inhabit. The war, the widows and the orphans. We had one another, and so many others have lost that vital connection. We must be together again, and as soon as possible. This is not the way we should be, the three of us.

Another thing. I imagine the news has not reached you yet, but Mr Ximenon has died. Oh darling, it is awful. They found his body floating near the piers of the Forth Bridge, and they are saying his hands were bound. A police detective came to the house and asked me about him, and about your relationship to him. *He did not seem suspicious of us, or of you, in particular. It seemed his interest lay chiefly in sharing the rumours he had heard: it was suicide (which would be odd, given the bound hands), or he was engaged in 'Mediterranean business practices'. I must have scoffed aloud, as he was very affronted and he told me Mr Ximenon was known to frequent the stables of various thoroughbred breeders, and he had interests among the furriers of the Alaskan red fox trade! I am not sure he understood the distance between Alaska and the Mediterranean. Then he told me Ximenon was a provider of labour for shippers of disrepute, and his connections to various orphanages were, in this context, not coincidental. They are saying he had deposited vast sums of money in banks overseas, but there is no talk of successors, or even of family. Who was this man, darling, who came into our lives and upended everything, only to evaporate before our eyes?*

I feel glad to have made a pest of myself about the insurance. You will think me impertinent, I know. Whatever this means for your business venture, I console myself with knowing your money — or if I may be so bold, <u>ours</u> — is safe.

I will come to you with a heart full of anticipation. I have the greatest of faith in you, and the only thing I will not share with you is your self-doubt. As for little Annabelle, I went through a moment just now of considering whether I should throw out what I have written and begin again. Of course, she idolises you, as she always has done. That has not changed. She draws your face, and exaggerates the whiskers! We cope with the absence in our differing ways, that is the truth of it.

We are coming to you, as soon as it can be done.

With all of my love,

L.

Lucy had included one of Annabelle's portraits with the letter, along with some sketches she herself had done, skilful elevations of the superstructures of a paddlesteamer, and details of window casements, shutters and finials for the flagposts. There were plans for a home in Melbourne, on the block Thomas had purchased, through agents, in Elwood. There was even a design for a weathervane, a fat, exaggerated sailing ship heeling over, with long streamers trailing from the tips of its masts. 'Suggest in Bronze', she had noted beneath.

Thomas hurried through these sheets, then went back and read the letter again, more slowly, studying each line for hidden meaning. The news of Ximenon's murder he received with horror: the rumours around it he treated with cold disbelief. It was not Lucy's fault. It was not even the detective's fault such hearsay was circulating, and Thomas could only judge Ximenon by the conduct he himself had seen. Thomas had not been fleeced. To the contrary, he had possession of the entire project, and would continue to have it unless and until someone came forward to claim Ximenon's share. Had he lost a friend? He recalled the nights of eating and drinking, the hours of conversation that had filled him with fascination while revealing precisely nothing of the storyteller. He recalled Ximenon's steadfastness in the face of the Maindample directors' calumny; the confidence of a man who'd seen every kind of bastardry before. Ximenon had orbited alone in the darkness of space, until his brief flicker of light was extinguished. There was no telling what his life had amounted to, only that death's ultimate power was reconfirmed when such a man – so evasive, so untouchable – met such an emphatic end.

For an anxious few hours, Thomas wondered if someone would be waiting for him at the wharf in Melbourne, some functionary with a notepad wanting to discuss a motive for binding the Sardinian's hands. And then he reassured himself that sensible men would see his interests were best served by his partner living a long life.

Besides, he realised, there could be nobody in this faraway place with the jurisdiction to ask such a question.

ELEVEN

On the Monday after her visit to the Cherrywood, Martha received a memo from HR. She was to report to a meeting with her group head and the HR boss.

She felt a surge of fear. It was irrational, she knew. Her numbers were excellent, and the hours she'd spent snooping over the mysterious pub had gone undetected. She kept her head down, never indulged in gossip, never took her sick leave or even her annual leave. She was a good productive unit. She used these indices to calm herself: nothing was wrong. Nevertheless, she watched the clock until the appointed hour, and could concentrate on little else.

In the meeting room on the floor below, the head of litigation – a mild and mildly sinister man named Douglas – waited with the HR head, Winsome Cannon, whose only distinguishing characteristics in Martha's mind were her perfect blonde hair and the fact she signed her letters with a coloured marker instead of a pen.

There was coffee. There were no notes on the table, no file on her. Nothing. This was a chat – she was safe. Or *maybe* – the paranoia surged back – there were no notes so there would be no record of what was coming. She stood wondering if she was supposed to shake their hands in greeting, and opted for a feeble wave, which immediately felt stupid. Douglas indicated the chair facing them, arranging his face into a bloodless smile.

There was some small talk. She had never been any good at it but she did her best. Douglas had been at the football match, and he hoped she'd enjoyed the hospitality.

'Now, let's get down to it,' he said, changing gears from his approximation of Social to his preferred mode of Dry Business. 'I think we can say you've impressed everyone in Dispute Resolution. Can't we, Winsome?' He looked at the HR head and she nodded so vigorously that there was a jingle of jewellery from somewhere on her.

'And you might think I'm shitting in my own nest here.' He looked sideways at Winsome, who mocked a frown. 'We're not supposed to talk like that anymore, are we? But, Martha, I'm being asked to let you go.'

Her heart thudded. What did this mean? Was she being praised *and* fired? She sat there dumbfounded. Could she get another job in a firm as good as this one? She stared back at Douglas and saw his face was changing. Millimetre by millimetre, his brows rose and his mouth widened in an effort to suppress something muscular. Then the smile broke and he opened his mouth to reveal gold dental work, and he began to laugh. He slapped the table so hard that Winsome jumped visibly in her seat and the contents of the coffee plunger rippled.

Winsome swept a hand over her newsreader hair and cringed. 'What he means to tell you, dear, is they want you in the Insurance division. We want to shift you across.' She raised her blue eyes to Martha as though this was a request and not a directive.

Douglas settled after a couple of self-indulgent sighs. 'Your new boss is Brandon Manne,' he said. 'You might know him. Youngest team leader, youngest equity partner in the history of the firm.' She knew him, alright, a vastly self-assured rooster who strutted the corridors in tight suits and pencil ties. 'He wants to build a young team, and he wants the best. You should be very flattered.'

Flattered. Did he mean honoured? Would he say 'flattered' to a male lawyer?

'So, I had a message on the answering machine from him at eleven last night,' said Winsome, shaking a bangle down. 'On a Sunday night. I mean, you know how hard he works. Are you ready for that?'

Wasn't me asking for this, she thought to herself. *How am I supposed to be ready?*

'And he was saying, "Get me Martha." So here we are, darling,' – *darling?* – 'Getting you.'

Martha still hadn't said a word in response. The thing was, there was no word to say. This was not remotely a choice. And if Dispute Resolution was a long way from Human Rights, Insurance was the far edge of the next galaxy.

'Now, you can see this isn't an interview or anything.'

But it's absolutely fucking real, isn't it, lady?

Winsome touched the hair again. 'I've told Brandon if he wants you moved, then there's a premium for moving you, and it's in the order of fifteen percent.'

Martha must have blinked in incomprehension.

'Your salary, dear. Up fifteen percent.'

'Yes.' It was the first thing she'd said in an eternity. She could think of nothing else to say.

* * *

It was arranged between two unseen secretaries that Martha would attend Brandon Manne's office at three to formalise the arrangement. She knew he had been 'building a team', as he'd put it in the firm's Friday newsletter the previous week. As well as the internal appointments, of which she was one, there were young lawyers poached from competitors or plucked straight from the Articles program. They were a type: the males were boorish, loudly ambitious and still laughing at the jokes that

passed muster in their private schools. They were shaped like
rowers. The females were intelligent, icy and beautiful, silent
foils to the laddish dolts around them. Reaganites, Thatcherites,
Young Liberals.

Martha knew what these observations implied. Manne had
selected her too, and it worried her.

At the appointed hour, she found him behind a wide desk in
a corner office. His secretary peered around the doorway first,
then nodded her in. There were towers of paper on the desk,
more towers on the floor. Steel trolleys of ringbinders. She knew
from experience that the contents of these piles were both of no
consequence and of massive, society-bending importance. There
would be pages in there with the potential to bring down a state
government.

He had swung his chair backwards so his feet rested, legs
crossed, on a low table in front of the windows that looked
out over the MCG, East Melbourne and, somewhere beyond
it, Fitzroy. Her heart went there for a brief instant. The two
walls of the office that were not glass were covered in posters of
album covers and live shows: the Clash, the Smiths, Springsteen.
No real thread to it beyond the access to tickets, or at least a
way of buying the posters. They were encased in glass frames,
sterilising their intended roughness. A shelf of books, eight grey
filing cabinets. Awards, photographs of himself and a beautiful
woman baring her perfect teeth.

He was sitting with his chair angled away from her – a
small expression of dominance, no doubt – and she formed the
thought that he was not a demigod but one among thousands
like him, drones in glass boxes stacked into the sky, endlessly
swapping paper.

He swung the chair round to face her and beamed, as though
she had surprised him. Clean-shaven, closely cropped sandy hair.
A wedding ring. There was a document on his lap, folded over
a bulldog clip.

'Sorry.' He sighed. 'Got to get through this.' He tossed it on the desk among the leaf litter of similar documents. There was a computer terminal damming up the paper at one end and a phone at the other, big enough to have the same effect.

'Yes,' he said. 'Right.' He rubbed his face. 'Now. You.' She was still standing. He waved at the chair in front of her. She sat. 'It's Insurance, so … eighteen fee earners, twelve secretaries. You have to share one, that won't be new to you. You were in what – Dispute Resolution? Pfft. Start somewhere, I spose. Report to me direct, obviously. Toots'll show you your office.'

'*Toots?*' She couldn't hide her incredulity.

'Donna out there. Loves it.' He raised his voice. 'Right eh, Toots?' Outside the door there was no sound in reply other than the absence of sound: the woman stopped typing momentarily, then resumed.

He pointed to his own chest, then at Martha. 'I work fucking hard. You'll work fucking hard.' A sing-song arrogance to it. 'Rewards are self-evident. Taken out the Insurance Council award *twice*. Young team, young. And we play fucking hard, so I hope you're up for it.' Did it matter, in the execution of this set-piece, that she was even in the room? He appeared to be looking somewhere over her head as he spoke. 'Big clients are the Catholic Church and MRG. Know MRG? Tobacco Council's insurer. Same job for both – interlocutory hailstorm until they starve, then you win it, then you kick em in the balls on costs. You don't want em getting up and having another crack. Clear?'

'Um, no. I haven't … done this before.' Such was the sudden distress welling up in her that she wasn't sure if by *this* she meant insurance law or pulverising the weak.

'What?' He was already in the process of turning away, and his eyes creased in irritation. 'I'll give you the other scenario. If one of these losers manages to make it into court and get findings of fact against our clients – and I don't care if it's some old cunt with lung cancer or a poofter who's decided to blame it all on Brother Edward – if one of them manages to make the point juridically, then the whole happy system collapses, right? And you and me are posting our résumés to Legal Aid.'

Martha felt the floor collapsing under her. The air-conditioning hummed into the silence.

'So, let's be winners, huh? Much more fun. Okay, that's the lot. Move your stuff as soon as you're ready.'

He took up a dictaphone and began talking into it like she wasn't there. She retreated, away from the light of the world and back into the anteroom containing Donna/Toots. His raised voice came after her. 'What's your ... Martha?'

She returned to the doorway.

'Team retreat this weekend. Friday night to Sunday arvo. Werribee Mansion, fucking nice place. Everything's on the firm. Anyway, you have to come. Toots'll sort you out.'

TWELVE

Four days after Joey had handed her the phone number, Martha spent her first Wednesday night at the community centre.

She could have called Joey's number, but it was too soon – especially after the awkwardness of her arrival in the bar the previous weekend. So, she had walked in Fitzroy again, thinking she might simply bump into the pub, or see the taxi. Or find Joey.

She wandered in something of a dream, ruminating over the worrying prospect of life as a Manne acolyte, imagining ways in which the pub might move itself through space and time, and rehearsing conversations in which she chided Joey for his elusiveness and they wound up arguing and then making up. Then she would learn about his family and the pet dog he had when he was five, and she would brush the hair from his eyes and he would tell her to leave the life she was living and come and live with him.

The trees pushed their roots up under the footpath, causing her to stumble once or twice. It was dark, but nothing was hidden or startling. It was the nature of an urban grid, she'd come to realise – nothing ever approached around a bend. So she was surprised when a low brick wall running to her left turned into a cypress hedge. She peered through a thinning of the foliage to see a short front yard and, beyond it, a yellow brick veneer building, a leftover from the seventies, with a plain pine-board sign out the front, lit by a single garden light: 'The Charitable Sisters of St Ondine'.

It was early, despite the darkness. As Martha neared a gateway in the hedge, she heard the sound of voices arranged in a choir, singing tunelessly. There were lights on, other noises, repetitive pops and clatters. She stood still in the gateway, reading the sounds. Then, without knowing why, she was moving, through the gate and down the path, following herself over a line of pavers in the lawn until she approached the front door of the building. There was a doormat made from tyre strips and coloured plastic, and a flywire screen, swung back to reveal a doorbell button with an illuminated panel over it, into which the householder could place a slip of paper with their family name. In careful letters, this one had been labelled 'CSOSO'. She watched her own finger pressing the button.

She could smell something cooking as she waited. The singing went on, as well as the repetitive popping sound, starting and stopping in random syncopation, somewhere at the edge of familiarity. The light changed in the frosted glass panels beside the door, and a shadow resolved into an approaching human. When the door swung open, Martha was struck by a wave of warm air, loaded with tobacco and food. It called to mind the security of childhood, the years when her parents had smoked as they cooked, and drove, and talked.

A woman stood there. Short, plainly dressed in grey trousers and a scarlet jumper, with glasses on a chain around her neck, their arms framing a small silver crucifix on another chain. Her hair was short, her face alert and inquiring. She made no effort at a greeting. Martha could see people were moving about in a tight hallway behind her.

As there was no question to answer, Martha introduced herself.

'Oh yes,' said the woman. Martha knew from her tone that she had once taught children. 'And?'

'I was just interested in what you're doing here,' Martha replied.

'Doing here …' The woman weighed the expression as though it were a bag of groceries. 'Well, this is a community centre.' Her brow furrowed. 'Are you selling something?'

'No, I—'

'Oh okay, well, come in then.'

From that moment, Martha had the feeling she had joined something, that she was part of whatever it was this woman did. As she followed her narrow back down the hallway, she realised the woman hadn't said her name. 'I'm Martha,' she repeated, thinking this would break the impasse. But the only response was 'Righto.'

They came to an office, a cluttered room filled with folders and books and a picture of Jesus with His heart out. It smelled strongly of cigarette smoke. A bar heater burned at ankle level, the cord snaking away behind a bookcase. The overhead light from a bare bulb was comfortingly dim; a lamp focused a brighter beam on the desk.

They sat, and the woman took up a clipboard and a pen. 'So, you're a bit late for tonight, but I guess you can join in and see how you go,' she said. 'If you want.'

'I'm sorry?'

But the woman was looking down at her clipboard. 'So, speaking, ping pong or choir?' The pen hovered.

'I – I'm not here for any of—'

'You want a feed then? Or do you want to talk about something?'

Martha folded her hands on her lap. 'To be honest, I was passing and saw the place and I wondered what you do here.' She wasn't sure if this might seem brazen or strange to the nun. But it was the truth.

'Ah. Right.' The nun reached across the desk and found a packet of Winfield Blues and a lighter, tapped one out and lit it. As she did so, she offered the deck with a raised eyebrow and a grimace. Martha declined with a hand. The nun looked sideways at the door.

'We've got a few minutes. You see the sign on the way in? We're the Sisters of St Ondine, only I'm the last one left. Everyone's gone now' – she said it with a flat finality – 'and recruiting's a bit slow these days.' A long draw on the cigarette. 'We had a convent on Victoria Parade, big old place you might've seen. Once it was only me, the diocese sold it to the council and the trade-off was they gave us this community hall nobody wanted. So we do some things here …' She stopped herself. 'Is this the sort of stuff you were wondering about?'

As Martha nodded, the nun added, 'Not a journalist, are you?' Seeing she was not, she continued. 'Most nights we have this little gathering. Homeless people, addicts, sex workers. They get a choice – speaking, ping pong or choir – and they do two hours of the activity and then we feed em. All's we can't do is accommodate them. Got no beds.'

'Forgive my asking – if you're the only nun left, who's we?'

'Er, me. I cook something while they do their thing, and then we sit down and eat together.'

'And you, what – you talk about religion?'

The nun looked baffled, then laughed. 'We're not the Hare Krishnas, mate. It's a community service.' There was a distant *brring*, and the nun stubbed out the cigarette in the ashtray, which Martha noticed was emblazoned with the Hawthorn Football Club logo. 'Oven timer.'

She got up and walked out, and Martha understood it was intended she should follow, around a short corner and into a brightly lit commercial kitchen.

One side of the kitchen was lined with a steel service bench, and the bench was framed in a large opening that looked over what must have been the main hall of the community centre. Out there, about a dozen ping pong tables stood in rows, each attended by two players. They were young and old, rockers, goths, sickly-looking kids and middle-aged men heavy with lithium and sadness. The insane clattering of ping pong balls filled the hall, and Martha realised it was this she had heard from the street.

The nun was bent over an oven and, presently, she rose with a large baking tray, gripped in a cloth mitt. 'How many out there?' she asked.

Martha darted back to the window and did a count. 'Twenty-four.'

'Right. So, eleven speakers and nineteen in the choir. Need the other one.' She returned to the oven and came up holding another tray.

'What do the speakers do?' asked Martha.

The nun had produced a spatula and was dividing the first tray. It was meatloaf. 'Plates,' she commanded, and indicated a cupboard with her eyes. Martha went to it and started counting out fifty-six plates. 'They debate, mostly. Make speeches to each other. Read things aloud. Builds confidence, helps with finding jobs. Even literacy, for some of em.'

Once each plate had been loaded with a brick of meatloaf, the process was repeated with potato gratin. As Martha moved the plates from the island bench to the service counter in the window, people began to appear and set the ping pong tables for dinner: plastic tablecloths, cutlery sprouting like celery from milkshake containers.

The nun was watching her. 'What do you do, anyway?'

'I'm a lawyer.' It had always been a good thing to say. *I'm a lawyer.* The parenthetical things it carried: *I got good grades*; *I'm well paid*; *I'm diligent*. But it felt shameful in this building.

'Oh yes.' The nun's careful reply seemed to underline the shame. 'What kind of law?'

'I was doing dispute resolution, then they moved me into insurance, but I'm planning on doing human rights.' She brightened. There. That fixed it.

'Human rights, huh?' The pale eyes fixed on her, unimpressed. 'Good for you.'

An argument broke out in the dining room. The last game had entered a tiebreaker, or so it seemed from the shouting, and the combatants refused to be evicted from their table. A small girl, wiry and wan, put two plates down on the table and dropped the corresponding cutlery with a clatter. She waited until the ball crossed the table once more, caught it deftly and put it in her mouth. With a single crunch, she destroyed it and spat it out.

One player vanished into the crowd. The other was a large, heavy man of maybe thirty, with hair down over his shoulders and a chaotic beard. His face was buried beneath the hair and the beard and a grand set of eyebrows, so he was mostly nose and some cheeks. Martha worried that some sort of physical confrontation was going to take place, but to her surprise the man merely dropped his paddle on the table with a clunk and slumped his shoulders. As a plastic chair arrived behind him, he sat and scraped it into position for the meal.

Martha took a plate of food and sat down next to the man. Through the hatch, she could see the nun working. The chairs filled up: people around her had their heads down, eating. Some wore the signs of recent violence. Almost all had an air of weariness, like the struggle to withstand their various ills didn't amount to a tragedy but only to a tedious and repetitive cycle that left the sufferer exhausted. Martha knew enough to recognise that nothing here was sanctioned. None of it was branded by a charity or government. There was no evidence of a technique, a program. They were merely gathered.

She stole a look at the big man beside her, forking meatloaf into his beard. He was muttering between mouthfuls. His eyes darted with surprising alacrity to catch her looking.

'The tables are killing us,' he rumbled.

'Pardon?'

'Killing us.' He peeled up the plastic tablecloth in front of him and pinched the edge of the table between thumb and forefinger. With a little effort he broke a chip off the edge and held it up between them.

'Asbestos sheet, nailed to a frame.' She studied the fibres protruding from the chip and felt an urge to rear away from the raised hand. His eyes became wild as he surveyed the diners. 'Wait till they start coughing. That's the first sign.'

Martha rolled the tablecloth back over the exposed table.

'You can breathe through your serviette, if you're worried,' the man suggested.

When the meal was done, the patrons shuffled back out into the night, some in groups, some alone. A few stopped to talk to the nun, and Martha saw her handing over twenty-dollar bills to some of them. When the last patrons had gone, and as Martha was beginning to wonder why she was still there, the nun bustled back into the kitchen and hollered, 'Right! Plates on the bench, please.' There was no-one else left – she could only have meant that Martha do it. Martha looked out across the dozens of plates and glasses on the tables, the piles already brought across to the bench by the diners, and wondered how the nun was coping with this workload.

As she moved around the room, Martha felt more at home, and the clearing and the wiping down and straightening up began to feel like tasks with value. This time had no measure and therefore no price, which was why it had value. When she was done, she moved back into the kitchen and found the nun at a deep sink, scouring one of the huge baking dishes. Trays and utensils lay on a rack to her right, and Martha took up a tea towel and began drying. The smell of cigarette smoke was overpowering, and it took her a moment or two to realise the nun had a smoke burning in an ashtray on a shelf at eye height. As she loaded the baking tray onto the drying rack, the nun swept the rubber glove off her right hand and took a deep drag from the smoke, then rested it again in the ashtray. A bluish tinge was muting the fluorescent light of the kitchen. Martha would have to air her clothes to get the smell out.

'How'd you go with Rodney?'

'The man beside me at dinner?'

'Mm.' The nun pulled the plug and the soapy water began to gurgle away. The gurgling became a series of loud *glonks* as water hammer echoed through the walls.

Martha considered for a moment what to say. 'He didn't talk much. He told me the tables are made of asbestos. Is that true?'

'Yep.' The nun was back on the smoke again, squinting. 'He's schizophrenic, quite florid. I think they've changed his medication.' She ripped off the other glove and stashed them both in a cupboard under the sink. 'I'd prefer the tables weren't asbestos, but …'

'I mentioned I'm a litigator,' Martha said. 'I see the cases. Sometimes it takes decades, but it kills people, you know.'

A cloud of smoke. 'Aha.'

'Don't you think you ought to get rid of them?'

The nun took down the ashtray and stubbed the dart in the bottom of it. 'These people don't have decades. They've got ping pong.'

She started snapping off light switches, and section by section the big room disappeared into darkness, and, after it, the kitchen. The only illumination was the yellowy light from the nun's office. She headed there now.

'Thanks for helping out,' she said. 'You right getting home?'

Martha understood she was being dismissed. 'Can I come back next Wednesday?'

'See how you go,' the nun said. Martha wondered if she doubted she'd return. 'I can always use the help.'

THIRTEEN

The life Thomas found when he landed in Melbourne was surprising to him.

It was affluent, as Ximenon had foreshadowed, busy and forthright. But the people struck him as lacking regard for breeding or social position, a tendency which was amusing to him rather than alarming. Their adenoidal speech, their habit of lounging on anything near to hand, as though the world needed propping up, or they did. And perhaps they did: they drank an inordinate amount.

They had arranged themselves into suburbs echoing the mores of the Old Country – Kew for the ownership classes in the low hills over the river, Richmond for the workers on the flats closer in, where the flowing water powered the workshops that made the city's boots and hats and corsets, and swept the effluent of every process out to sea. There were Williamstown and Sandridge by the water, and the far-off resort town of Brighton to the south. But the divisions the suburbs might have represented were loosely observed. Exceptions were everywhere. At his age, and being the heir to a fortune, Thomas might have expected deference. But none of the people who knew him were impressed by such things.

It was late January, and although the pall of war hung over even this distant place, there was a welcoming brightness to the city. The sunlight was more intense than anything Thomas had experienced, and the mid-afternoon heat was sapping. He was told the heat was often broken by a storm from the southwest, a lumbering pile of thunder and heavy rain, the city's reward for sweating through the dry spells. But no such change had happened yet.

His instinct aboard the steamer had proved right – he could reinvent himself here. He would be able to go about his business in anonymity, trusted and trusting. The men he would meet were all engaged in some form of speculation, whether in property or gold or liquor, and the loose metric of reputation was the only force opening doors or slamming them shut. The city was seized with a feverish rush to exploit every resource before the next man off the boat took the chance.

He had secured a rented house in East Melbourne and taken Lucy's plans to a builder to begin work on the family home in Elwood. The builder complimented the work, noted the neat signature, 'L. Wrenfether', in the corner and asked if the architect was his brother.

In a scant few months, Thomas told himself, he would welcome his wife and daughter to the home, and have easy access to the shipwright and the paddlesteamer's future berth at St Kilda. He retained a fondness for horseback and an abiding suspicion of motor cars, and decided he would ride to his work each day when the house was ready and the stables done, and the two dearest women in the world were by his side. But for now, there was a vessel to build.

So came the day in February 1918 when Thomas Wrenfether stood at the sober iron gates of Rosstrevor & Son, Master Shipwrights & Surveyors of Port Melbourne, with rolls of plans under his arm and carrying a satchel stuffed with correspondence. He was greeted by a man coming out, a very short man in a boilersuit and cap, with a marvellously sprung face. He beamed in greeting, sending wrinkles in every direction under the cap, and led him into an open shed where another man stooped over a dismantled band saw.

Coramand Rosstrevor was older than the short man who'd greeted him. He was tall and lean, his face chiselled in stone as though barnacles might colonise the crevices. His blue eyes fixed upon Thomas as he shook his hand. The grip was crushing, and Thomas found himself involuntarily drawn to examine the hand inflicting such pressure. It was huge and weathered.

He did not begin by offering tea or commenting on the weather.

'You will want to see your timber,' was all he said. The accent was Highland Scots, a cut-basalt match for the demeanour. Rosstrevor's letters had been warm and expansive. Thomas surmised that someone had written them for him: this man measured his words.

Rosstrevor wiped his hands on a rag. They walked through the busy yard, past lighters, a sloop, dinghies and yawls on sleds. A stout ferry waited on a slipway while carpenters worked planes over its hull.

'Arrived a week ago,' the man was saying, as he led them through a maze of tin workers' huts and latrines. 'Must have powerful connections.'

'I did once, I think.' He had addressed Rosstrevor's back: the shipwright couldn't see the doubt on his face.

Under their feet, the land was gradually becoming the sea. Gravel and grass gave way to flat rock, sand and slicks of algae. Where the gravel ended, long planks were set upon stumps, and crabs scuttled under them, away from their approach. The smell changed to a metal-tang rise of weed and shellfish, ajar in the damp of the retreating tide.

Ahead, four pairs of curving steel ribs reached skyward from two trolleys on rails. Laid within them, the backbone joining the ribs was a mighty length of timber, a yard deep and sixty yards long. It curved up at each end, but ran straight and flat for most of its length. Thomas knew it to be the mountain ash trunk from Gippsland, the one they had dried and fashioned into his steamer's keel. Warm satisfaction welled inside him. His plans were becoming real, physical things, and men worked upon them with adzes and planes.

Rosstrevor was watching him as he studied the slipway. Evidently satisfied his client was pleased, he nodded to their left. 'Something else you'll want to see.' They rounded a corner between two piles of dark, encrusted beams, and suddenly it was there before them: the square tower of stacked timber from Thomas's dreams. In the afternoon sun it glowed golden-red, vascular and mortal and utterly unlike the vague pastel Thomas had imagined. It was strapped onto platforms of some lesser timber, a substance unrelated to that inferior material; unrelated to anything else in the yard. Its edges and corners were so finely grained and precisely cut that the lengths met at perfectly square ends. Only careful examination showed the giant block was in fact made up of individual planks and beams.

Thomas left the long plank he had been walking on and crossed the saltmarsh. The shipment towered above him, receiving the light of the afternoon, radiating it, exuding light of its own. He breathed out, puzzled by his reverence for this inanimate material, for this singular, monolithic *thing*, comprised of thousands of things: separate planks, trees, histories. He placed his hands on it, at eye height, and drew his fingertips down the surface. He did not feel an irregularity, not a bump in the grain, not a solitary splinter. Rosstrevor had silently joined him.

'What do you mean?' Thomas asked. 'What do you mean, I "must have powerful connections"?'

Rosstrevor ran a hand across his chin in thought. 'You do know what this timber is?'

Thomas panicked. This was a thing he should know. But then he remembered. 'Of course. It's New England mahogany. Export grade, free of impurities and inclusions.'

'Who told you that?' There was no cynicism in Rosstrevor's tone, only interest.

'No-one told me, as such, but my late business partner, Mr Ximenon, did all the bills of lading and so forth, and I distinctly remember he wrote it—'

'You've been misled, Mr Wrenfether. He might have had reasons to use such a common euphemism. This shipment is pure cherry.'

'Cherry?'

'Aye, sir. No mistaking it.'

Thomas fell silent, his mind racing over this further revelation.

'When you first wrote to me, I thought the idea quite unusual,' Rosstrevor said. 'Not impossible … simply never received a shipment like this. And never done a timber paddlesteamer. The ironsides these days go off to the sheet-metal boilers. This stuff' – he walked up to the stack and it glowed above him in the pale sky as he, too, rested a hand on it – 'more likely see a cubic yard of it, make a clock or a piano. Something fine, lasting. Never used for scrap or firewood. Or … no. Glass-blower makes his mould in a fire of cherry. The wood's like the fruit, full of sugars that respond to the heat. So, I spose that illustrates the point: if it must be burned, it's only burned in service of something else that's art. But to make a whole vessel from it … Well, wish you'd spoke to us first.'

'Was it inadvisable?' Thomas felt the anxiety rising in his throat.

The shipwright grimaced. 'No. Just not something you see often. Ever, in fact.' He had produced a small brass instrument from the pockets of his boilersuit and was rolling a thumbwheel as he spoke. 'An odd thing to do, to mislabel it. And not an accident, I don't think. Perhaps your people had concerns about … provenance.'

'I can assure you of our bona—'

'There's varieties to be had here,' Rosstrevor continued. 'Gippsland, Tasmania. Ash, Celery Top, King Billy, Huon pine … each got its own personality.'

Ximenon had never mentioned this, and now it seemed so obvious. Why had they not simply used local timber?

'Don't know whether to call it a strength or a flaw, but cherry is adamant. So, you use a hard timber like that, the vessel is rigid. Passenger never knows what it is they're feeling, but the hull responds to the water more … *brightly* than, say, oak.' He pressed the small instrument to the surface of the stack and operated the thumbwheel. When the device made a click, he removed it and examined it in his hand.

'Brightly?'

'Imagine the difference between a shod horse and an unshod one.'

Thomas's anxiety gave way to puzzlement. Rosstrevor hadn't refused the job, nor mocked the idea, but there was a reservation in him. 'What is worrying you about it?'

Again, a shadow of misgiving. 'Talk in the office, eh? Want you to meet my head carpenter.'

He walked them through more sheds, and past crates containing bolts and shackles and chains of various gauges. When the land reasserted itself over the reach of the tide, they came to a timber structure, an office inside. On the walls, large sheets of paper marked the progress of vessels and the movements of craftsmen, lists of figures and dates. A heavy steel clock. Tools rested on pegs, brought in from the sheds like farm dogs reprieved from their labours and invited into the house. Indistinct shapes in the gloom, steel fittings or lead weights or bells or joist-heads. A spacious worktable, cleared but for a few pencils and a paperweight.

There were two people inside the office: a thin boy of perhaps fourteen, who was tending the fireplace, and, seated at a plain wooden desk, off to the side of the dominant table, a heavy man with dark skin.

Rosstrevor spoke first to the big man, whose powerful legs were spread either side of the chair he was on. 'Oremu, this man is the client, Mr Wrenfether. The paddlesteamer.'

The man's face registered a look of realisation, as if Thomas's appearance solved a riddle for him. Thomas, for his part, stood confused, wondering if the head carpenter was going to appear at some stage.

'Oremu here worked at Keefer's boatshed in Beaumaris. Joined us but recently.'

'What were you working on there?' Thomas asked. *What are you working on here?* he wondered.

'They had me excavating the cliff behind the shed.' Apparently unsure how much more to divulge, Oremu fell silent.

'You make it sound like you were digging a drain, friend. Tell Mr Wrenfether about the work.' Thomas could see Rosstrevor held this man in high regard.

'Seeking out materials for the museum,' Oremu said. 'Natural history. Sharks' teeth, big as my hand' – here, he held up a massive palm – 'turned to black stone. Little fossils of sand dollars, evidence of dinosaurs.' He chipped the words out, enigmas from a lost past. Thomas conjured a cliff emerging from the fog and offering up eccentric treasure. 'Soft cliff, orange gravel, like mud when it's damp.'

'And this un here,' Rosstrevor went on, indicating the boy, 'is my son.' The boy stood to attention and proffered his hand without speaking. His eyes were solemn. Thomas wondered at their respective ages: the boy still awaiting adulthood, and Rosstrevor seemingly approaching old age. Rosstrevor asked the boy to make tea.

Thomas addressed himself to Oremu once again. 'You are a scientist, then?'

'Self-taught.' It wasn't an answer. 'All the collectors there are self-taught. It is science but it is a … trade.' He appeared to stop himself.

'Ah. A man of varied talents, then.' Thomas was unsure how to bring this conversation back around to business.

But Oremu did it for him. 'I was fascinated by your timber,' he said. 'I wrote letters—'

'With my blessing, of course,' Rosstrevor interjected.

'Trying to understand what we are to work with.' His voice was deep, with a slight accent, beyond the local one, that muffled the vowels. An intriguing smile played at the corners of his lips. Thomas understood that he was looking at the head carpenter.

'And what have you found out, sir?'

He gestured at a stack of paper off to one side at the return end of the desk. 'Your Mr Ximenon, who I understand is deceased' – he shot an inquiring look at Thomas, who nodded – 'had a stone-fruit orchard in Extremadura, many years ago. Trees died in a drought, a dispute over irrigation. Couldn't get water to them.'

'Oh.' Thomas forced a smile. This story was wrong. Or the other story, the one Ximenon had told him, maybe it was the false one. The boy appeared at his side, presented a cup and saucer and poured tea. Thomas looked up at him: the boy was thin, his hair unkempt. He thanked him and received a nod in return.

'The seed stock for the original trees came from Seville, from a bankruptcy sale. A merchant had gone broke trying to buy West African slave families, to give them their freedom, and had to sell everything off.'

'How on earth did you discover this?' Thomas wondered whether to challenge Oremu about this version of the history, then decided against it.

A heavy hammer plinked on a rivet outside. The carpenter picked up the sheaf of papers and hefted them. 'You write enough letters …' He smiled. 'It became very interesting to me, the repeated misfortunes. On and on, back into time.'

'Cycle of well-intentioned failures,' offered Rosstrevor, who had been listening closely. These two must have known each other down through many years for their sentences to appear as the products of one mind. It was an interesting choice of words, 'cycle of well-intentioned failures'. The Caucasian story Ximenon had told him, despite its violence, met the same description.

'When it arrived here we had it dried for a month in a kiln near Bacchus Marsh. It felt like it didn't want to go in …' Oremu looked confused by his own words. 'Then the kilnsman suffocated on fumes while it was there.'

A silence descended over them.

'A pattern,' the carpenter remarked. His voice had taken on the quality of recitation. 'Two families – your Mr Ximenon's, and this other lot, the Ardeleans. Always fighting. My correspondents took me back to the fourteen-hundreds, and they were fighting back then. Deeper than the sea, Mr Wrenfether.'

Thomas didn't know what to make of this gloomy digression, beyond the sense that the two stories of the timber's origin might not be contradictory, as he'd first thought, but braided somehow, and much older.

'What are you going to do with this paddlesteamer of yours?' Rosstrevor asked.

'Ah!' This was a well-practised routine for Thomas, one he could trot out for financiers, sceptics and gossips. 'The paddlesteamer, as you know from the plans, is quite grand in dimensions, so we imagine it performing a dual role carrying bulk freight across the mouth of the Yarra estuary, from St Kilda to Williamstown and back—'

'Thus, the keel,' interjected Rosstrevor.

'Thus, the keel,' Thomas agreed. 'And she will also carry passengers, in the open air during daylight crossings and, in the event of weather, having resort to the spacious cabin for their pleasure and comfort. At one hundred and fifty-five feet in length' – his voice was rising to a spruiker's pitch – 'she will be substantial enough to weather the gales on the bay in late winter and spring. And on her wide, generous deck, the cream of Melbourne society will promenade in the sun when conditions are fine.'

His hands were going, as they always did when he was enthused about something. He now imprisoned them behind his back. He had expected this short speech to have a salutary effect on the two of them, as it had on others, but their expressions were inscrutable.

The carpenter entwined his heavy fingers and stared at them. 'It worries me,' he said. 'I am quite traditional about such matters – a vessel is one thing or the other, bulk carrier or ferry, never both. How will it handle the top-heavy loading of cargo? Have you given enough thought to this keel? We have begun laying it, as you know. I am not the engineer, but when I calculate the top weight and lateral force, I do not see how your vessel will remain stable. It is one thing, sir, to have six or eight hundred people standing on the deck, and quite another to have cargo stacked ten feet high.'

'Or times,' added Rosstrevor, 'you might have hundreds of people on your decks and there is a sight – a whale, a grand vessel – and they rush to one side.'

Thomas was still absorbing this when Oremu added, 'And why have you opted to have the wheel at the stern and not amidships?'

'Simple,' Thomas snapped. Their combined assault was irritating him. 'By clearing the deck of the large obstacles of the wheel boxes at the sides, there's more space for the very things we've discussed. More cargo, and loaded lower, if that is your concern, and more paying customers.'

'I see' – the carpenter was pained again – 'I see how it fits with the commercial objectives, but a rear-wheeled paddlesteamer is a riverboat. It is designed to travel more or less in a straight line on flat water. It cannot pivot about its mid-point the way a mid-wheeled steamer can.'

'Fine,' Thomas replied, morosely now. 'We will only be travelling in a straight line, and we will only be sailing on flat days. The bay is essentially no different from a river.' But he could see how it was.

Rosstrevor had been deep in thought. He spoke up now. 'Are you *certain* you want her the way she is in your plans, Mr Wrenfether?'

Ximenon had organised the plans. Thomas couldn't remember for the life of him where they had come from. But the business was built around the vessel being this way, and it was too late to change things. He was being too accommodating, he decided. 'I wish to proceed exactly as we have agreed,' he said curtly. 'If you feel this is beyond you, I will take the project to your competitors. They may welcome a lucrative contract.'

On hearing these words, Rosstrevor's whole demeanour changed. 'Please, do not misunderstand. We are interested, to be sure. We can employ fifty, sixty men on this. The point is … Oremu and myself' – he pointed at his carpenter – 'we are worried for you, sir. Makes us more inclined to do the work, and to do it with care.'

Thomas looked from Rosstrevor to the carpenter, who sat at his desk nodding, with newfound vigour. 'It is so, Mr Wrenfether.'

These were good people, Thomas decided, and they did have his interests at heart. His outburst had been a miscalculation.

'I am willing to be guided on the matter of side wheels and stern wheels. Clearly, I am not the expert.'

'Gracious of you, sir.'

'What about propulsion?' Thomas asked. 'Are you satisfied with the coal burners? With the boiler?'

Oremu looked to his employer.

'Aye,' said Rosstrevor. 'Designs are good.'

Thomas felt his enthusiasm returning. 'De Carteret's. Birmingham, long history. We have used them' – he corrected himself – 'one of the major Scottish lines has used them for many decades.'

'And I see you have in mind a feathering blade design, for efficiency,' Rosstrevor continued.

Thomas nodded in recognition. He remembered the discussion with Ximenon and the engineer.

A frown crossed Rosstrevor's face. He was reading from a scrapbook of notes and drawings now. 'Course, we need to reconsider the gearing, if we move to a side-wheel design ...'

'Why?'

Rosstrevor grimaced, reluctant to embark on a technical explanation. 'Stern wheel applies force evenly across the stern of the vessel – the rudder controls the steering. But side wheels, it's the relationship between the two points of thrust. Both going forward at the same rate, same as a stern wheel. But one going forward, one astern, you're nimble. But then, too, we have to consider the fail-safe. If one wheel stops and the other's geared to it, they both stop. See?'

'As I say, I will defer to you on these matters, but I do not want the necessary engineering to hold us up any more than we can help.'

Rosstrevor made some cryptic jottings in his scrapbook. 'Anything you'd like to ask us, Mr Wrenfether?'

'You have worked on the paddlesteamers that service the bay, I hear.'

Rosstrevor rose. 'Yes, the *Ozone*, the *Weeroona*. *Hygeia*.'

'Those last two are Huddart Parker vessels.' Thomas tried not to show his concern, but Rosstrevor appeared to know what he was intimating.

'Your design is safe with us, sir. Never dream of giving Huddart Parker technologies to you, never reveal yours to them.'

'Good.'

Oremu watched the two of them with a frown. 'You know, I understand the utility of these vessels, and they have been a success in the southern half of the bay, but no-one has tried to run a ferry service in the northern half. Let alone directly across the mouth of the Yarra ...'

'Thus the opportunity,' Thomas replied. 'No-one's ever done a thing until someone does it.' He felt it sounded rude, but nothing about the impassive block of Oremu's head betrayed any offence.

The meeting ended there, and Thomas walked off into the warm evening of the city. These were good people, he told himself again. Good, steady people, of a kind he sorely needed after the loss of Ximenon. They could have their differences over the engineering and resolve them respectfully. He had been skating over the deeper technical issues, filling his time with thoughts of people and money. These men would not be so easily distracted.

Evenings such as this one struck him in the heart – perfect evenings carrying blossom and laughter and strange silver grass seeds floating like balloons on the northerly winds from the unknown interior of the continent, a place he hadn't seen and couldn't imagine. Nights when the air wrapped so close around a body, so gently, there was nothing to differentiate it from one's own pulsing blood.

Lovers passed and they murmured, walking with their heads inclined to whisper, to steal a kiss here and there. It would be him, when she came to him. It would be *them* doing the walking. Arm in arm, lovers once again, and his confidence would return with Lucy's counsel and her belief. When he missed her most, he knew it wasn't the paddlesteamer she believed in, but *him*. A woman who had had her choice of suitors had chosen him. What treasure he had gambled.

Without her, he couldn't locate the quality in himself, the one she must have seen. He wasn't brave, he wasn't piercingly intelligent or persuasive. He wasn't saintly. He was good, but only good.

They still talked about Houdini in Melbourne. They still marvelled at his insouciance, as much as they marvelled at him

looping a paddock at one hundred feet in his flying machine.
People are drawn to those who don't care, who don't feel
timidity, drawing reassurance from their own swagger. Maybe
it will work out, the spectator tells himself, seeing as it always
works out for the bold man.

It wasn't that Houdini escaped barrels, leapt from bridges
or slipped manacles. He escaped ordinariness, drudgery – *that*
was what people paid to see. He escaped the inevitability of
everyday life, and Thomas could do the same with his glorious
paddlesteamer. Lucy would have the man she deserved to have,
the man who defied expectation to make a truly wonderful thing.

FOURTEEN

Martha had wanted to hunt again for the Cherrywood that weekend.

The pub moves.

She remembered there was no bluestone step at the corner door. No grille in the footpath where the keg hatch should lead to the cellar. The pub sat light on the ground, so it could move. But why did the pub move?

By the Friday, at work, there was no talk other than about lifts to the team retreat. Martha didn't want any part of it, but she didn't own a car and she needed to get there somehow. She'd brought a bag of clothes, assuming things would work out. Also in the bag were a paperback, bathers and a notepad from the stationery cupboard embossed with the firm's ridiculous logo, two eagles lifting a breadmaker or something.

She ended up with two others – Heidi, a secretary, and a promising young stallion driving his own Honda Accord. He said it was the Limited package, something to do with the seat coverings or the suspension. Martha had volunteered to be in the front, navigating out of the city so she could have the Melways in her hands. The book fell open at maps 43 and 44, the alphanumerical grid in the blue margin around the edges. The suburb names spelled out in faint blue watermark over the detail of streets and railways, parks and rivers. Fitzroy.

She felt a little sorry for the girl in the back, who was young and seemed to be trying hard. She was friendly, determined to make conversation and apparently oblivious to the awkward dynamic. She'd brought her mum's pikelets in a cake container.

The stallion – Elliott or Evan or Eric, she mumbled it vaguely each time – wanted to talk about the Opportunity gifted to them by Manne in joining the Insurance group, possibly the greatest assemblage of talent in legal history. She wound the window down. The stallion cleared his throat.

'Bit cold, don't you think?' He had two jackets on hangers suspended from the coat hook over the back seat: a checked sportscoat and – she didn't have a term for it – possibly a golf top. A wolf in creep's clothing. Martha craned around to look at the girl in the back. She was reading a magazine and Martha's breeze was ruffling it, but she smiled anyway.

The stallion was still talking. Martha returned to the Melways, providing an update on directions before turning to maps 43 and 44 again. *The pub moves.* If so, it must move to an unoccupied space, otherwise it would require another rule – *the pub displaces other buildings* – and something about that felt wrong. So, the pub moved between vacant lots. There must be thousands of them in the city. Why had she focused on Fitzroy? Maybe the pub could even wander the rural back hills of the state. This was an interesting problem.

At the resort – a mansion in a paddock – Martha braced herself for the coming night. Dinner was in a small restaurant, Japanese, under lamplight. She was distracted throughout, trying to make conversation but plagued by questions: *Why does it move? Is it pursuing something? Or avoiding something?*

Manne sat at the top of the table, bristling with intent. He introduced the head of Litigation, a middle-aged man who then made a speech filled with wit and insight, and unmistakable fatigue. This was not his generation. How must it feel to be up there, she wondered, the company man spouting platitudes about their dazzling futures? There was a scatter of half-hearted applause, and the meal was served. Over dinner, Martha tried to summon the person she was a year ago, when this sort of gathering would have represented the pinnacle of her striving. These were people who would never have to endure the monotony of the outer suburbs and driving mediocre cars. Short of being prosecuted for something, their upward trajectory was assured.

The evening took a predictable course. The senior lawyers and most of the support staff slipped away early. The younger ones shouted for more wine and, later, trays of sticky-looking shots. Manne was the star at the orbital centre – never smiling – and they milled around him, obsequious and competitive.

Martha found herself at the edges, as she'd expected. She chatted to Heidi, found out she was playing rep-level netball. There was an atmosphere of compulsory hedonism now. The drinks kept coming, followed by shouts of 'Scull!' Plates of dessert lay unattended as people yelled over the music, danced and drank. Her father had told her a story once about the actor Oliver Reed, who'd been in a terribly important French restaurant and had got so pissed and overexcited that he'd climbed into the seafood tank and released the live lobsters onto the restaurant floor. While the *mesdames* and *messieurs* climbed onto the tables shrieking and bellowing, Reed splashed happily in the tank yelling, 'Be free, my little friends!' Martha had thought this was a tale about alcoholic extravagance, but now saw it in a different light. He was a drunk trapped in an awful room, a sentient being in a tank of his own, and it was either the lobsters or set the fucking place on fire with all of them in it.

She tried going to the bar to collect a round of drinks, to soak up some time without having to drink or talk. She was a little stumbly. The girl behind the bar, lipstick and a huge ponytail over a crisp white shirt, told her the tab had run out. Martha hesitated. She wasn't buying for anyone in particular and had no intention of paying for a large and non-specific shout. She returned the bartender's frosty smile with one equally insincere. *God, imagine having to serve us.*

The Honda stallion reappeared, as if summoned magically. He did a little gun thing with his index finger and an eyebrow and she realised he was offering her a drink. She said, 'White wine,' and showed him her teeth in appreciation. He raised his own drink to his mouth – something amber in a highball, a bit grown-up for him – then regarded her with interest.

'So, who lives in Fitzroy?'

'Pardon?'

'You kept flicking to the map of Fitzroy today. I was watching.'

'Oh.' She blushed. 'Nobody. Looking for a pub I heard about.'

'Which one? I did the whole inner north during uni.'

'I bet you did, cowboy.' She was hedging now, unsure whether this line of discussion should go any further. Whose secret was this, anyway?

'Nah, seriously. Which one?'

'It's called the Cherrywood.'

'Yep.' It was clear he wasn't sure. 'Timber place, two-storey?'

So, he did know it. This was interesting. 'Do you remember where it was?'

He scrunched his face. 'Napier Street?'

'That's the Napier.'

'Nah, nah, you go in off Victoria and it's on your left. Yeah' – he was pointing rudely over the top of his glass at her – 'across the road from a Spanish doughnut joint. Big fucken – what do you call em – churro, up above the door.'

He was spitting now. And he was wrong: Martha remembered looking across the road from the pub on the first night, at a row of darkened houses. No churros. Another one like him – taller and heavier – came crashing in and threw an arm around his suited shoulders. He flicked his fringe, cast an assessing glance at Martha.

'What's goin on?'

'You been to the Cherrywood, in Fitzroy?' the Honda stallion asked him.

'Cherry *Tree*? That's Richmond.'

'*Lemon* Tree. And it's Carlton, dickhead.'

The eyes of the interloper were resting, unfocused, on her chest.

'You got a boyfriend?' he asked, emptily.

'No. But I have an ex-husband.'

It had the desired effect, and as he moved away, she heard her name being called from across the room. Male, confident. Brandon Manne, leaning forward from his enthronement in a booth, hand raised as though to summon a waiter. He called her name again. Between the fingers of his raised hand was a credit card. He pointed the card at her now, and the message was clear. Others were looking, clapping, encouraging. One of them took the card from between Manne's fingers and ran it over to her. He had a wet patch on the crotch of his chinos. 'Whoo!' 'Do it! Do it!' 'Tequilas!'

Martha looked at the credit card, which bore the firm's name in raised silver lettering, and the word 'Corporate'. The music pounded and her head hurt. She was more than reasonably pissed. The girl behind the bar was watching with sour indifference. There were witnesses everywhere. The fucking partner had offered the card. There was no way this could be construed as misconduct, though the word made her hot with fear. Manne was ten metres away, assessing how she would handle this test of his. Somehow he had incited the mob while remaining clinically sober.

She handed the card over the bar. 'Yeah?' she heard over the music, and she yelled, 'Tequila.' She made a circular motion with a down-pointed finger. 'Do a tray, please.'

The bottle, the tray, a little army of shot glasses. Martha reached to pick up the tray and the girl put a cautionary finger on the other side of it, holding it in place. As she did so, she raised the card with her other hand. Unbelievably, she wanted to check that the corporate Amex of a major law firm wasn't maxed out.

The girl made a show of reading down the numerals on the credit card bulletin and, once satisfied, put the card in the slider and made an impression. She then put the card and the carbon copy on the tray in between the little glasses, and Martha took both and poked them into her clutch. As she carried the tray to the booth, she had to dodge two careening bodies, but she made it and a cheer went up. She smiled and everyone raised their glasses. One remained, and as Martha realised this, she also realised Brandon Manne was still watching her. He made a flicking motion with his thumb and forefinger towards his mouth. *Drink it.*

Eyes were on her now. The sycophants, following his gaze. She took the glass, shut her eyes and threw it back. It was fiery, then warm, then gone, and they were cheering. *Fuck them all.*

* * *

The restaurant kicked them out at midnight.

As the eight remaining lawyers milled around in the cold, one of the stallions put his suit jacket over Martha's shoulders. She was both repelled by the old-school chivalry of it and grateful for the warmth. 'We're going to BXM's room,' he said. To be referred to by the three initials of one's name was the highest badge of belonging, and all billing was processed under that code. The 'X' was a stand-in: it was reputed that Brandon had no middle name. But he billed a fortune, and BXM was his personal brand, his nickname and his numberplate.

Brandon unlocked his room and they filed in. Martha wondered what on earth she was doing. They were all determined to be the last to go to bed so it would be talked about on Monday. She didn't need to win their pissing contest, and she didn't need the endorsement, real or perceived, of BXM. She secured the armchair on the far side of the bed, her hand clutched stickily around the white wine she'd carried from the bar. People draped themselves on the bed, in the desk chair, cross-legged on the floor. Manne was going to hold court.

They hushed.

'So, this has been nice, huh? Good start to the weekend, everyone. We can load up on coffee in the morning and we'll get through the sessions. But don't any of you wimp it, okay?' He pointed a finger around the half-circle in mock accusation. Still no smile. You were expected to pick the jokes without signposting.

'What are we talking about tomorrow?' A stallion.

'You'll have to wait and see. But I want to explain the clients to you, do some stuff about expectations, performance. About our technique.'

'It's just fucken winning, isn't it?'

'Well, yeah, it's about winning, but there's more to it. You have to have a reputation for not giving a fuck. People need to expect when they come up against you, they're going to have a fucking hard time and you're going to be a complete prick. You got a dog? Pat your fucking dog at home. You come to work and you're kicking the cat. If they think it's going to be anything less than a total nightmare, right, they'll start taking advantage. So never give an inch.'

'Here's the method. I'm kinda pre-empting tomorrow, but I'll do it anyway.' He drew a deep breath. 'You take every point. Every point. This is what people expect of us. This is what makes us better than the second-tier firms. This is the thing, right? You take every fucking point and you concede nothing.'

He said 'right' a lot, she thought, convincing himself of every notion, even as he uttered it, by time-stamping it with 'right'.

He took a swig of beer, wiped his lips reflectively. 'I'll be auditing your files. You'll be running them, cause you get autonomy in my crew, but I'm going to be auditing randomly. And if I find any evidence of you giving ground, trying to compromise, I'm gonna haul you out and you can go back to fucking … whatever. Dispute Res. Banking. Fucking *Human Rights.*' He shook his head. 'Jesus, whose fucking idea was Human Rights?'

There was appreciative laughter. 'Land rights for gay whales,' someone said. They were welcoming an audit of their work, she thought, so they could show off their intransigence. This was the only life they could imagine, their singular *raison d'être*. To leave, to do anything else, would be to have failed.

'You can't keep doing it,' she said, before she considered whether to say it. Her voice soaked into the beige silk panels that clad the walls. Shocked faces looked around at her. Manne only tilted his head. 'There are going to be model litigant laws *requiring* compromise. You won't be able to stall people anymore. Costs penalties, strike-outs.'

The silence was suffocating. She was beyond caring.

Brandon Manne absorbed this for a few seconds, then began to applaud, slowly. 'Someone's doing their reading,' he said, and his appreciation seemed genuine. 'See? See? You gotta be *this* good' – he pointed at her – 'to stay ahead. And you gotta be fearless. Young whatsher … Martha here, fucking dead right. So, the challenge is staying ahead of the curve, right?'

He blathered on as though she'd never spoken. She felt sick. She felt trapped. She was stuck here with these people she now knew she hated, with no way home. She could go back to her room, but sleep would be only a brief respite from the torrential shitstorm of the weekend. Tomorrow the same odious worldview would be rehashed, in a PowerPoint and without the fuckings.

She took a sip from her wine: it was warm now, and cloying. Distractedly, she dipped a finger and ran it around the rim until the glass began to sing an eerie, high note. A thing she had done before, without thought, that now assumed a singular significance. She saw the face of the old Koori man in the pub, his callused fingers plucking the harmonic. Unseen waves resonating in unity.

A head swivelled at the sound. Martha stood. She would make her escape before Manne built up a new head of steam.

'Sorry, folks, I'm done.' There was a chorus of booing. She faked an idiotic smile, picked her way through the people on the floor and let herself out.

In her own room, she took two Panadol and a Berocca, and brushed her teeth. Flossed. The bed looked good. Her lips were dry. She wanted to find the lip gloss in her clutch. She delved in and, annoyed, shook the whole thing out on the bed. It took her a while to recognise the scrap of paper on which Joey had written the phone number. It was scrunched up, beside the corporate Amex. She returned every other object to the clutch except the phone number and the credit card. And, slowly, she picked up the bedside phone. She dialled zero and got an outside line. She hesitated a moment longer, then rang the same taxi number she had rung from the MCG the previous weekend. It was one-thirty in the morning.

The same woman answered. The same bright and interested voice, pleased to hear from her again. Would a cab at her room in twenty minutes be suitable? Martha thanked her and replaced the receiver, thought for a moment, then picked it up again and dialled the number on the scrap of paper. It rang five times before the call connected. Him, his voice sleepy.

'It's me,' she said, as though it should be enough, and of course it wasn't.

'Who?'

'Martha. I came visiting ...'

'Oh.' He sounded more attentive. 'Yeah. Hi.' There was a muffled sound like he was moving around in a bed. Stretching perhaps. She enjoyed the idea.

'I was wondering if I could …' He was waiting for her to finish the sentence. 'Could I, um? Hmm. This is awkward, hey?' There was a yawn down the line. She was losing him. 'I thought I might come over.'

'Oh. Yeah.'

'Would that be okay?'

'Sure. How far off are you?' He sounded sleepy again.

'Oh, I'm' – she looked out the window at the darkened eucalypts – 'I'm just round the corner, but I've got some stuff to do. How's an hour and a half?' She groaned inwardly.

'You've got some stuff to do? At one-thirty in the morning?'

'I'm a super-busy high achiever.'

He laughed softly. 'Sound like a pretty smashed high achiever. See you around three then.'

She was about to hang up. 'Wait … where's the pub?'

He gave her an address, and she wrote it down on the piece of paper with the phone number and stuffed it in the clutch. By the time the taxi came to a stop outside, she had repacked her belongings and, as she switched off the light and slipped out into the dark, she saw the light was still on in Manne's room. The cult of BXM, still in session.

The same cab. Behind the windscreen, the heavy features of the same driver. Love and hate. She heard their voices in the night, laughing too hard, braying like hyenas. This repudiation would not be forgotten.

FIFTEEN

The Cherrywood glowed out of the darkness like friendship itself.

The taxi idled, the driver staring straight ahead so only the left side of his face was visible to her. He'd taken the firm's credit card, and he appeared to understand the gravity of what she was doing. The near eyebrow moved slightly, an inquiry. She was too far gone now. She watched the card, trapped in its cradle as the slider passed over it, and felt a sense of something irreversible occurring.

She thanked him, he nodded silently, and she took her bags. There were birds beginning some kind of preliminary chorus as she crossed the footpath. The engine of the Falcon came to life and it drew away, and a light came on in the bar. The corner door swung open and there was Joey, mildly amused.

'Hi,' he said. 'Nice jacket.' The stallion's Henry Bucks number. She'd completely forgotten. He took her bag off her shoulder and deftly kicked the door open, as it had swung shut behind him. The steps were timber, as she'd remembered, and there was the same sense of the pub having little connection to the ground. This time, however, there was a giant liquidambar soaring from the footpath and touching the upstairs windows.

They bumped together as they passed through the door. Even as drunk and tired as she was, the touch carried electricity. She saw him put his hand on the doorjamb – more than put it there, he rubbed the timber lightly – and the gesture reminded her of superstitious people who feel the need to place a hand on the outside of a plane as they board.

He raked a bank of light switches and the rest of the bar lit up.

'You want something?' he asked.

'Could you make me a cup of tea?'

He smiled again. 'I'll have to duck out to the kitchen.' He took a beer glass with a practised sweep of the hand and poured himself a beer, then carried it with him through the rear door of the bar. She was alone with the pub, and its silence spoke to her.

The stools were lying down tonight. She went to the window and looked at the tree outside, which was entirely still. She looked back at the stools. These things were related.

Walking back to where she'd put down her bag, she ran a hand along the bar. A single length of wood, a polished beam, dark like caramel and differently knotted from the timber forming the walls, the floor and the furniture. Where those timbers seemed dry and weathered, the bar timber must have had a more privileged life: varnished, waxed, oiled – she didn't know. She bent and looked under it, wondering if the massive scale of it was a trick of veneering, but this only confirmed the beam was solid and immensely heavy. How had somebody put it here, and why had they used this particular length of timber for a bar?

She could hear Joey rummaging in the kitchen.

She took a packet of salt and vinegar chips from the rack on the bar and flipped it over – the use-by date was four years ago. Above the rack, there were two framed collections: cigarette papers from De Reszke, 'The Aristocrat of Cigarettes', and coasters. The paper roll was spooling over the top of the antique till and curling towards the surface of the bar on the customer side. She read the time of the close-off: three hours ago.

The light changed as she was reading, and she looked up to see the bare bulb, suspended on an electrical cord over the bar, was swinging slightly. She looked again at the stools, daring them to move. Now she felt unsteady, and placed both hands on the bar to regain her equilibrium. She was drunk: this was to be expected. The building shifted imperceptibly around her, faint squeaks and breaths of air passing between spaces, the taps and cracks of things cooling or heating. She became very still and imagined she could hear the water in the plumbing, the current in the wires, rodents in the walls. Taken in combination, they could add up to whispered words.

The building wasn't haunted, she decided. It was more like it was *living*. This place was no less an organism than she was, an unseeable matrix of circulating systems, parasites, things long dead and emerging anew. She imagined taking the entire structure and shaking it like a dollhouse onto a clean white sheet. She would see every spider and cockroach and millipede, and there would be untold millions of them, as well as the mice and the pigeons and crows and starlings and maybe even a skink or a blue-tongue under the floor. This might be a haven for invisible wilderness, here in the innermost suburb of the city.

The boy was still pottering in the kitchen. The plumbing. She'd been in the cab a long time, and she needed to wee. She remembered the way, a left out the door at the far end of the bar, past the crowd of relaxing barstools. Through the bottle shop, now in darkness. Out to the bistro, and left towards the two doors. Each bore a sign indicating a gender. The men's was a silhouette of a man in a top hat, and the ladies' a matching silhouette, her face daintier and with a ribboned bonnet on her head, under which her hair had been piled up to expose a thin, curving neck. Martha ran a finger over the sign and found it was enamelled, slightly chipped. Old. She was no closer to guessing the building's age. It didn't seem to want to discuss the matter.

She went in, and immediately felt a rush of love for the bathroom. The tiling was intricate, and high on the walls there were vents made of brass wire. The timberwork was delicate and more than functional: it was decorative. The sinks, even the toilets themselves, were of white china stamped with the word 'Cherrywood' in blue enamel, and the mirrors were edged in gilded timber so the viewer's face was framed, as in a picture, and the picture felt as though it had depth. She was an outlaw, a scarlet woman, a furious dame. She reached out to the mirror and her fingertips stopped at the glass, leaving smudges.

The door of the stall was locked by means of a brass latch – the type normally found on a sash window, but here they had been installed vertically. When Martha turned the latch to come back out into the bathroom, it spun uselessly on its spindle. She gave the door a slight tug to see if it would shake the latch loose, but it held. She puffed the hair from her face, bent down and examined it. Nothing appeared to be wrong. But when she tried turning it again, the curved lip of the latch would not disengage. She shook the door again, harder, without result. The door reached neither the floor nor the ceiling; there was no protruding object she could step on to climb over it, but the gap below it was high enough for her to squeeze under, so she did.

It took effort to arrange her body on the floor of the cubicle so she was pointed at the door and flattened enough to slide under it. The neck of the toilet bowl was between her knees, and only her belief that nobody had been in here for ages held back the horror of sliding face down on a hotel toilet floor.

There was a knock at the door.

His voice, politely inquiring. 'You okay in there? I heard banging.'

She sighed and stopped wriggling. 'You might as well come in.'

The door opened and Joey stood there taking in the scene. He had her tea in his hand. 'Getting to know the place,' he said finally. He came forward, reached down and drew her out from under the door.

She stood and dusted herself off. 'I know that looked weird, but I was … the latch broke. I was stuck.'

'Oh,' he said. He reached forward and pushed the door. It swung open.

'Oh, for fuck's sake.'

'It's like the thing with jars, you know?' He edged back around her in the doorway.

She was starting to smile now. 'No, I don't know.'

'Yeah, you do. Like when someone else takes it and the lid just comes off and it's like—'

She grabbed him by the front of the shirt and kissed him on the mouth. She hadn't given one second of thought to doing it. She hadn't asked herself, as she did with every other decision, what would happen if he resisted, if he was horrified. If he laughed at her. *God.* His body was passive for a moment, inert in her hands, then he began to react and he was kissing her back and holding her by the shoulders like she was something terribly precious or possibly dangerous, and the worst night she could remember had suddenly come good, and she told herself to shut up and enjoy it.

He took her by the hand, a delicious feeling she had forgotten, and led her back into the public bar. 'I've got to do a thing,' he said apologetically. 'Are you okay waiting here?'

He moved around behind the bar again, humming to himself. With a glance at his watch, he came around to the public side and shot the long bolts on the front door, pulled the blinds down and flicked the switches that operated the outside lights. Then he went to the saloon and the bottle shop to do the same. His movements were practised, almost unconscious, a dance Martha knew he had repeated over years.

When he returned to the public bar, he went to the antique till and peered at the display for a moment, then struck the key, which jangled the drawer open so it bumped to the familiar stop against his belt buckle. He flipped his way through the notes and coins, mouthing silent arithmetic, then removed the drawer and left it on the bar. Next, he went to the other tills

and Martha followed the sequence of noises as he carried out the
same routine.

Back in the bar, he piled the till drawers up in a stack
of three, then studied the shelves behind the bar. He chose
a packet of Benson & Hedges Extra Mild 25s, a red plastic
lighter and a packet of beer nuts, and deposited these on top
of the tills. He disappeared into the kitchen, gone for long
enough to boil the kettle again, and returned with an ornate
tea set on a tray.

'Would you excuse me a moment?' he said. Martha watched
him go, balancing the tray on the pile of till drawers, keeping
the little tower steady as he mounted the staircase. She listened
to the creaking of the treads as he ascended: although the pub
still seemed hostile to her, she had no doubt that his body and
the timbers were deeply connected.

He returned a couple of minutes later. 'You want to come up?'

There was a dizzy feeling of transgression in going behind
the bar. She was back of house, nearer the intensity of her
desire for him, and to the disconcerting touch of the building.
As they rounded the end of the low bench under the shelves
of spirits, Martha somehow cut the corner too close and the
point of it jabbed into her hip. Her small squeak of pain
caused Joey to look around. They came to the foot of the
spiral staircase and he began ascending ahead of her. The treads
were of heavy timber. The banister was smooth in her hand,
glossy with varnish and grooved by the incidents of history.
The walls came in closer, wallpaper peeling. There was a big
window halfway up, a curved pane of glass bulging outwards,
surrounded by small, coloured panes. Their feet were making
a hollow ringing now: these higher treads were made of ornate
wrought iron.

He had reached the top. It felt as though the ascent was more
than a two-storey building would require. The passageway
ahead of them was narrow and the ceiling low. To the left, a

heavy closed door with a brass plate said 'Committee Room'. Along the passageway, there were numbered doors on either side, such as one would expect upstairs in any pub. The carpet was scarlet with gold patterns threaded into it, more worn along the centre than at the edges. There were sepia portraits in frames at eye height, handsome people from an era when there was no requirement to smile into a photograph, so their faces seemed meditative, their expressions glazed. In a frame, a Millot compendium of brightly coloured feathers. More photographs: two adults and a child posing proudly beside a vintage car. A group of men in waistcoats and hats – one of them the subject of other portraits – standing on beams beneath the gigantic bow of a dry-docked ship.

The doors were identical, except for one on the left, which she assumed was a room facing over the street. Each door gave onto rooms she could picture – the iron-framed single bed, the plain wardrobe with six wire hangers, the bedside table with a lamp and the Conray bar heater that smelled of burning dust. A small table, a plastic chair. Salesmen, drifters, lovers, troubadours and tourists. Addicts. The lonely and the mad. Rooms to start and end lives. Except for that one door.

It had tall, narrow stands either side of it with pot plants on them. As she passed, Martha saw they were plastic, but even then they looked like they needed water. A geometric pattern on a small piece of paper was sticky-taped to the door. She paused briefly to look. It was a perfect circle divided into eighths, each eighth filled and coloured with painstaking lines in pencil. The corners of the paper were curled. The pattern was a marvel of draftsmanship, yet just imperfect enough to indicate the unassisted work of the artist's hand.

At her feet, the carpet was worn in a track that veered into the doorway and progressed no further up the hall. Joey had not given the door so much as a glance as they passed.

At the end of the hallway, Martha looked back and noticed the whole thing was curved. It was impossible to see back to the staircase they had ascended, though it had seemed longer than the external dimensions of the hotel could accommodate. Furthermore, the walls and ceiling seemed to narrow, so the gloomy end of the hall was imperceptibly tighter. *You're pissed*, she reminded herself.

At the far end, there was another spiral staircase, smaller and simpler. It curled through the ceiling, and she followed the boy up it. Looking at his calves and his worn shoes as they climbed the steps ahead of her, Martha didn't see that he was ducking to avoid the treads above. As she came around the first bend in the stairway, she smacked her head.

Joey stopped at the noise. 'You right?' He bent and peered down at her.

She rubbed her forehead. 'You must do that all the time, right?' He was a couple of inches taller than her.

He frowned. 'No. Actually, never.'

The coil of the stairway ended abruptly at a door. There was no landing – it was like reaching the top of a lighthouse. The door swung inward with a slight squeak, and Martha could see she was inside one of the attics. Across the room from her was one of the circular dormer windows she recognised from the street, through which the glow of the city lit the space. There was no light switch, and no light other than a small lamp beside a bed. He switched it on and the room lit up in warm yellow and the window now became the darkness. A pile of paperbacks on the floor beside the lamp, clothes on an open hanging rail inside the door, shoes in milk crates underneath the rail. It was neat, perfunctory in its sparseness.

They stood together in the small area of floor at the foot of the bed. 'Do all the girls complain about the climb?' she asked. He only smiled.

'How long have you had this room?'

'Well ....' He thought about the question. 'Few years up here. I was downstairs before. The corner room. Before that I had the little room facing over the kitchen roof ...'

'Is there anyone else here?'

He slapped the bed, raising dust in the lamplight. 'Are you ... um, do you want to ...?' He looked at the bed. And then he looked at her, standing in the teal dress she'd worn to the Werribee dinner hours before, streaked with grime from the toilet floor, and a realisation hit him. 'Your stuff!' He whacked his forehead comically with an open hand, and moved past her. 'Give me a minute ...'

'It's okay,' she replied. 'You don't have to.' But he was already out the door and clanging down the first staircase. Curiosity burned in her, a desire to understand him through the things he retained. The clothes were dark, not fashionable, and there was a hard-wearing practicality to them, suited to the life of a bartender. The shoes were strangely formal, like he'd raided his father's shoes. Brogues, plain business shoes, even a pair of tartan loafers.

The paperbacks were poetry, novels, nothing she'd heard of and nothing current. A mischievous thought occurred to her and she swept a hand under the bed. But she retrieved only chocolate wrappers and dust. Why would he have hiding places up here, anyway? The room itself was a hiding place. The whole pub was.

What's sustaining you? she pondered. *Where's the bit where you reveal yourself?*

There were some formal-looking oil paintings on the walls, small and bright and expressive. Bush scenes, women's portraits, a seascape. Something about the flat monotony of the seascape reminded her of Port Phillip Bay in winter.

Hung beside the seascape was an old promotional bill, a rowdy bunch of capitals and mixed fonts like the 'WANTED' poster that every kid got on a school excursion to Sovereign Hill, or an advertisement for a boxing match:

PADDLESTEAMER
EXCURSIONS

DEPARTING DAILY FROM ST KILDA PIER, AND VISITING WILLIAMSTOWN AND MELBOURNE'S FABULOUS YARRA RIVER.

THREE SAILINGS PER DAY
LUNCH CRUISE – DINNER CRUISE – EVENING CRUISE

VISIT ST. KILDA'S FABULOUS "LUNA PARK"
Your Captain: Edward Carville, formerly of the United States Navy

DEPARTURE TIMES
(weather and circumstances permitting)

St. Kilda Pier .... 12.00 midday, 5.30 p.m. & 9.00 p.m.
Williamstown Commercial Wharf ....2.00 p.m., 7.30 p.m. & 11.00 p.m.

Note: Arrivals are timed to allow connection to Williamstown and Port Melbourne train services, although no warranty of timely connection is provided.

FARES
Adults £2, Children Under Twelve, £1.
Infants Under Two Years of Age travel Free of Charge.
Concession available for A.I.F. Personnel and their Spouses.
Fares are exclusive of dinner service, incidental beverages and special events as advertised.
Fares are subject to review at the discretion of management and are correct at time of printing.

Latest dance and orchestral music provided on board.
Season tickets available upon request.

MENU
Luncheon Cold roast – Cold Corned Beef – Hot Potatoes
Dinner Salmon – Chicken and Ham
(Sweets – Custard and Apple Tart)
Supper Selected French Cheeses – Chocolates – Madeira

Agents **WRENFETHER & XIMENON Ltd.**   Enquiries by post/telegram via St Kilda GPO.

As she finished reading the poster, she heard his footsteps beneath the little staircase. She kicked off her shoes, whipped the dress over her head and climbed under the sheets. Surprisingly clean, for a boy. She sat up on the side nearer to the lamp, and positioned the edge of the sheet so it passed low over her breasts. She flicked her hair once, just before he came in.

He stood inside the door, a look of wonder on his face as he dropped the bag at his feet. 'Not how I saw my Friday night playing out.'

She looked at her watch. Four am. 'You mean your Saturday morning?' She felt clearer now, in the eye of a storm spinning drunk on one side and hungover on the other.

'Are you …?'

She poked the edge of the sheet down a little and arched an eyebrow in confirmation.

'Gosh.'

She giggled at the sheer goofiness of *gosh*. He looked briefly offended, then smiled. She snapped the lamp off and her eyes adjusted to the dark again. Him undressing, the silver-blue light from outside, the chromatics of frost. Then he was in the bed and they were together, and all of it became indistinguishable for her, the otherworldly room they were in, the fatigue and the sense of time slipping laterally across its own path. And him, so kind and unknowable. She whimpered softly while her searching fingers mapped his face and the bedclothes twisted around them and she felt the electricity of his skin on hers. What could any of it matter beyond this room – the streets and trams and offices and the city and its lights reduced to pinpoints from above, wars in distant lands, the idea of annihilation? None of it could reach them, two warm bodies in the dark. To be naked like this was to hold the whole world at bay.

At some stage she lay there awake, and him finally asleep, and she placed a palm on his ribs and felt them rise and fall. He had flung his arms out wide, one above her head on the pillow and the other suspended over the edge of the bed, pale and draped as Marat's corpse.

She ran her fingers down the fine dark hair over his sternum, then across the moving ribs and onto his arm. A vein bladed his bicep and forked at his elbow into tributaries that flowed over his inner forearm.

She took his hand and clutched it to her chest, held it like it would vanish at any moment.

Sixteen

The local winter came, a brand of weather more familiar to Thomas's bones. Far away, the war would be entering its fifth summer.

A new resolve crept into Lucy's letters to her husband. *I do not think it wise,* she wrote, *given the talk of sea mines and German raiders, to put our little girl to sea right now. Perhaps we might join you after the summer, when there is some hope things will settle.*

But how do you know when it will settle? he replied. *One might take the opposite view — matters may become entrenched and the possibility of sea travel will diminish to nothing. For as long as these people have resources of machinery and young men to expend, I fear they will continue. I am aware of my own selfishness in saying it, but I do not believe I could live through extended years of this loneliness.*

He hesitated, pen in hand in the darkness of the rented kitchen, a man in a pool of candlelight. The sound of laughter leaked down the street from a gathering. He added the words that captured his agony. *I long for your touch more than anything I can describe.*

She did not reply for a long time, as though his words had stung her, or indecision was tormenting her. *I cannot come,* she answered eventually. *We must wait, protect ourselves and most especially Annabelle. Remember always that I love you. This separation is as painful to me as it is to you.*

What if it were possible to write such a thing and not truly feel it? What if it could be committed to the page while the writer

felt the opposite? How would the faraway reader ever know? He
buried himself in the work, and although his new home was
ready and his belongings had been taken across town and installed
there, he lingered in the East Melbourne rental for another week,
absorbing the funereal atmosphere of the empty rooms. He ate less,
socialised less. He was surprised by his own capacity for sadness.

The American high-pressure boiler and the iron paddlewheels
arrived – Thomas had come around to the idea of a side-wheel
design. An ingenious clutch had been added to the gearing
mechanism so the wheels could spin in opposite directions,
making the vessel more agile. The Rosstrevor labourers filed and
painted the metal components while the steamer grew out of its
keel, sprouting ribs and stems and knees, then planks and decks
and fittings. Thomas drew hope from the sight of each day's
progress, like they were tending a sapling that would grow into
a mighty tree but for now required their constant care. In the
early days of the curving ribs, he worried they seemed flimsy.
But he was captivated by the beauty of the rich timber, spearing
into the sky with the grace of javelins. Only goodness could
come of such harmonies.

He saw Rosstrevor's boy, Joseph, at work on the precious
lengths of cherry, sometimes under the tutelage of the senior
craftsmen and sometimes alone, but always wreathed in
concentration, something approaching reverence, as his hands
moved over the timber. Thomas would make a point of
greeting him, but the boy was shy and would only offer slight
acknowledgement before returning to his work.

Oremu watched everything, perched like a flightless bird on
the scaffolds overlooking the work. He had a piercing whistle,
which he would deploy often, over a stray nail or a tool left
lying dangerously. He used gestures to convey his displeasure
once the whistle had done its work: flicked fingers, upward
nods. Somehow the men below him understood the nature of
the correction each and every time.

The vessel rose between the scaffolds, cradled in its slip cart. Thomas's favourite part of the operation was the milling, where the dusted craftsmen took lengths of the timber from the pile and ran them through powered saws and routers and steam presses to produce timbers that slipped perfectly into an absence somewhere on the vessel. The machines buzzed and howled and the timber answered back with a pop or a bang when the hot blade found gases in the grain. Fragrant clouds of sawdust settled in drifts around the men's feet, until at the end of the day the apprentices finished their shift by sweeping it up – eyes made ghostly in a mask of it – and bagging it for later use in lighting the furnaces. Some afternoons, Thomas liked to cup a handful of the fine sawdust, smelling it and marvelling at its silken texture.

For Thomas, this was not the assembly of components according to a plan, the building of a ship, but rather a reuniting of objects that had somehow lost and then found one another, laid beside each other on the bearers, slotted tongue-and-groove in perfect union. This was alchemical, he believed, something beyond mere physics.

The timbers were not only planks for the hull and the decks. They were cut and spliced into heavy beams that formed the cradle for the iron boiler and the gearing mechanisms, the base for the furnace and the framing of the superstructure. At each new stage of construction, as the timber was shaped to perform dozens of roles, Thomas found himself newly awed. This was fate in motion. This momentum, set in train by Ximenon, had outlived him. The history of calamities both Ximenon and Oremu had sketched for Thomas, the deaths and ruinations, would be extinguished by the hammers and saws of the Rosstrevor workmen as the timber sang in its perfumed dust. He had broken a sequence of misfortune, set the world to rights.

* * *

It was August, and Thomas was in Ballarat inspecting a foundry he had commissioned, when news of the accident reached him.

The timber, once again marking men for disaster. Oremu had been thicknessing lengths through a steam-powered bench saw when, as far as anybody could later establish, the blade struck a nail or a bolt and shattered, expelling shards of steel. Some of the shards passed clean through Oremu's right eye and lodged deep in the socket of his skull. Nobody could explain how a shipment of timber certified as clean and unused could have a spike buried within it, nor how the expert millers had failed to see it.

Thomas abandoned his meetings and rushed back to Port Melbourne. The carpenter had been released from the hospital but his plight was an awful one. Not only was the eye destroyed but the fragments were so deep that the doctors could not retrieve all of them without risking graver damage. His heavy body was propped on a cane, and when he tried to walk he tipped aside as though the ballast in him had shifted. He was stoic in company, but Rosstrevor said he had been weeping, and it unnerved him, as though an anvil had emitted the tears. There was a family to provide for, and Oremu's distress was compounded by his love of the vessel they were building.

'Thinks in curves, poor man,' said the shipwright. 'There's nary a straight line below the decking on this boat. Was his language, made him happy. But a man can't draw a curve unless he's got two eyes to compare off.'

Thomas notified his insurers, although he had no idea where legal responsibility lay. In doing so he experienced a moment of recognition. He was not his father, who would have insisted such things were the regular incidents of commerce and must not be taken as personal obligations. Stand distant from it, he would have said, for we are *owners*. A ghost should come with better advice, he thought.

At the bank, he made a large withdrawal to be given to Oremu's family, and with the money in his fist, he had another thought. At the post office, he sent off a wad of bills to Herskope in Scotland, with a brief letter noting how the months had raced by, and asking him to keep the flowers coming.

The darkness returned to him. He brooded under winter skies of sickly pewter. So far, he had buried his partner and lost his family, and now he had maimed a man, all of it in service of his grand vision.

* * *

One morning in September, Rosstrevor led a man across the yard to the perch in the scaffolds that had been Oremu's, and which Thomas had made his own.

Rosstrevor overshadowed the man beside him, who was of average height and proportioned to a robust athleticism. His hair was worn rakishly, breaking free of its pomade, thick and lustrous. Even at a distance, the amber locks glowed upon his head, tapering from narrow origins into a light-catching decorative feature about his ears. He was, Thomas thought, a pleasure to look upon. His face was split by a generous grin – the teeth evidently worthy of their tenancies in this fine head – and he darted from beside Rosstrevor to offer handshakes and bows to everyone he passed. In one hand, he carried a musical instrument, and, as he neared, Thomas saw it was a mandolin. They stopped at the foot of the scaffold, the man still rounding off a series of greetings, and Rosstrevor squinted into the sun.

'Young un here wants to ask you for a position,' he said. The man with him grinned eagerly upwards and Thomas climbed down. At closer quarters, Thomas saw he wasn't actually young. There was grog blossom, chipped and yellowed teeth, silvery wires of hair springing from his temples, mimicking the uncut strings curling from the neck of the mandolin.

'Ed Carville, formerly of the United States Navy and latterly of Little Lonsdale Street. Entirely charmed to meet you.' A bow that swung the mandolin high above him. An American. Of course. A southerner, by the lilt and the twang. The unsinkable grin hung suspended along with a hand, which Thomas took in a handshake.

Rosstrevor excused himself, polite to a fault. It appeared Carville was between postings, recently discharged from the Great White Fleet and looking to enter the ranks of passenger ferry professionals. He stretched the word 'ferry' in his drawl so it rose as an 'f' and dissolved into a fathom of disappearing vowels. Where others might have detected signs of disgrace in all this, Thomas saw enthusiasm. He did not baulk at Carville's lack of papers, nor at his suggestion that, given the hour, they should adjourn to the tavern to discuss the opportunity.

'Why would you work for me?' he asked the American on the way back to Rosstrevor's office. The man was still doling out waves and handshakes to men he had never met.

'Because what you are doing is brilliant!' he replied. 'People will come from far and wide. They will talk for a century about the magnificent paddlesteamer of Port Phillip Bay – have you thought of a name for her?'

'I wanted to name her after my wife, Lucinda. But there is another one by that name already registered.'

'It's a very sweet name. Nobody would mind, would they?'

'The federalists held a constitutional convention on the *Lucinda*. I think people would mind.'

Carville shrugged agreeably, then extended his arms wide. 'I should be asking you – why would you give me the honour of making me an officer?'

The true answer – that nobody else had yet applied – seemed a little unkind, so Thomas said instead, 'You have experience as a ship's master, I gather?'

'I will be honest with you, my friend.' Carville lowered his eyes in theatrical candour. 'I have never skippered a paddlewheel. But single screw, twin screw, sail, coal-steam and diesel, I have seen them all. I am awaiting my tickets and other papers from Boston, but I guarantee they will be available for your inspection very soon.'

'You've been at sea a good few years, then?' Their walk had taken them past the stink of the latrines, flies swarming noisily around the back of them.

Carville winked. 'More than you might pick from my sprightly looks, sir. Never lost a vessel, either, and that's including two years on the Newfoundland Banks.'

Thomas resisted an urge to clap his hands together in satisfaction. 'Excellent,' he said.

'But my particular skill, if I may say so, is with the passengers, sir. I am as much host as navigator, and do hope you will permit me the indulgence. Others' – he waved dismissively – 'can be deputised to give engine orders or plot courses. But to put the passengers at ease, to instil in them the romance of a voyage, is a grander thing by some measure.'

Thomas excused himself from Carville's second invitation to the tavern, and he told him he felt sure there would be a position for him. As he made this promise, he looked out the window of Rosstrevor's office and saw the hull planking had reached the gunwales, and the iron paddlewheels had been craned into position, with the framing of the sponsons closing around them. The superstructure, too, was there as a frame perched on the deck like the house on the Ark. Children were coming through the fence after school so they could sit on the lower levels of the scaffolds and watch the vessel's emergence. The estimate was three months: there was an irresistible sense of momentum now.

That night, he wrote to his wife and told her he had found a promising candidate to be master. He described to her a competent and naturally charming man, a 'gregarious optimist', whom he felt sure would set exactly the right tone among the passengers.

Her reply several weeks later was a surprise and an over-whelming joy to him. She had reconsidered her position and, given there had been no reports of attacks on civilian shipping in the Indian Ocean, she had been advised it was safe to make the voyage. She had booked passage for herself and Annabelle, departing on 30 January, and arranged to sell their home and to move their investments to Australia. *Should we come to any harm, I believe it preferable to going on without you like this.*

The agony of his loneliness would end, after all. They were coming to him, and he would have them in his arms by the end of the summer. His doubts had been mere phantoms.

SEVENTEEN

Martha caught a Swan Street tram before dawn on the Monday, wanting to be as early to work as she could.

When she climbed inside the old W-class, the lamps were still lit and the wood glowed like honey. She slumped against a window and looked up at the high rails running the length of the tram's interior, with their leather straps dangling. The gold lettering, 'Do Not Disturb Driver. Keep Feet Off Seats'. The joinery took her back to the pub and the way its timbers spoke to each other. Long-since milled and cut to function, sanded, varnished and well used, they nonetheless retained some secret inner life. Something was going on: the inanimate world was speaking to her and she was learning, for the first time, to listen.

At seven-fifteen she was back at her new desk in Insurance, the matter of the credit card weighing heavily on her conscience. She had eaten breakfast with Joey in the empty dining room of the Cherrywood late on the Saturday morning – toast with marmalade and butter in individual plastic servings. As she'd opened the side door onto the street – the pub obligingly letting her leave without misdirection – Joey had stopped her on the steps and drawn her close. She kissed him, smelled toast.

'That night I came in, after the football,' she began, 'why did you ask me if I knew who you were?'

He seemed puzzled for a moment, then he recalled it. 'Oh, you know. Bit of an event when we get a new regular.' She

frowned at him, and his face took on a new seriousness. 'I was …
Not everyone's as welcome as you are. I was trying to work out
what your angle was.'

And with that, he kissed her again and she stepped down
into the street. When he closed the door and his footfalls had
faded back into the building, she was left with the impression
that this was merely a pub she had walked past, a place that had
never offered such confidences.

On the Sunday, she had stayed in her flat, thinking and
reading. Was she in love? In the grip of a heavy crush, perhaps, a
bit in lust and definitely fascinated. Maybe those added up to love,
but she doubted it. How could she be in love with someone she
knew almost nothing about, and who she wasn't even sure she
could reliably contact? He had never evaded anything she'd asked
him, and certainly hadn't lied to her. It seemed she only had to ask
in order to resolve the things that puzzled her about him. But she
was carefully, deliberately not asking. Unknown, he was perfect.

But the building was not Joey, and Joey was not the building.
She catalogued its myriad insults and silent refusals, and decided
they were not coincidences. Late on Sunday afternoon, as the
light faded between the buildings outside, she wrote another
entry on the sheet marked 'RULES', which she'd pinned to the
noticeboard.

RULE TWO
The pub doesn't like me.

Now she waited, the credit card placed square on the front edge
of her desk, with the carbon copy from the taxi underneath it.

Brandon Manne swept in around eight-twenty, his customary
coffee in hand. Martha counted to fifty, allowing time for him
to settle at his desk, then she picked up the card and the slip and
walked into his office. He was jabbing at his keyboard, and the

fan in the back of the computer terminal was groaning into life as the screen lit up. He looked up.

'Yes?' There was no sign of condemnation, of forgiveness, of anything. It was unclear whether he even recognised who she was.

She held out the offending items, feeling foolish. 'I need to explain what happened on the weekend. I was … unwell.'

He looked at the credit card and she saw realisation dawning. Then it vanished under the cloud of his hostility. 'Take it to HR. Not my problem.'

She stood there a little too long, feeling a surge of anger. *Fuck you.* Yes, her escape might have come down to an inability to cope with the ugly grasping of his bonding weekend, but he was coping just as badly, a tactical wizard with the social skills of a fifth-grade bully.

'Fine,' she sighed, and started to leave. She had almost cleared the office when his voice came cold and clinical behind her. 'Don't take that tone with me, Martha. You did a runner. You clean up the mess.'

She didn't look back. She got in the lift that smelled of the morning's coffee trolley and angrily punched the button for the admin floor.

Winsome Cannon's nails were clacking on her keyboard as Martha walked in. She stopped, looked up and pushed her chair back, rushing to point to the conference table. In a fragrant cloud she swept around Martha to shut the door.

'Right,' she said as she settled. 'We've got a bit to talk about.' She studied Martha in a way that didn't look combative. 'Where do you want to start?'

Martha had rehearsed this moment. 'Well, you're going to want this back.' She pushed the credit card across the table. 'And you'll need this, I suppose.' She produced the carbon copy with the taxi driver's small handwritten receipt stapled to it by a corner. But Cannon was still waiting.

'I wasn't ... myself.'

Cannon studied the card and the receipt. 'You were feeling ill?'

'Yes.'

'Martha, you live in Richmond. This receipt is for a trip to Fitzroy.'

Martha couldn't believe she'd been so stupid. She should've thrown the receipt out and said she didn't get one. But Martha didn't operate that way, and knew it.

'I went to St Vincent's,' she stammered. 'Got ... got checked out.'

'Oh.' The silence stretched on for an embarrassing length. Finally, Cannon broke it.

'Martha, the door's closed, and what goes on in here is confidential. I hear things in this office that you wouldn't believe. Our lives inside this building are very controlled, but they're not necessarily the same when we leave it. Now, do you want to talk about what happened on the weekend?'

'I, er, stayed at a friend's place,' Martha managed to blurt. 'I live alone. I didn't want to be alone when I was unwell.'

Cannon took this in, thought for a moment. 'Martha, what kind of *unwell* was this? Were you physically sick, or were you ... sick inside?'

Martha was tempted to say every sickness happened inside, but this was no time for semantics. 'I'm fine, really. It was a long night and I needed to be ho— at my friend's home.'

Cannon smiled now, like an indulgent aunt at Christmas. 'A *male* friend? I think I'm beginning to understand the picture.'

'That's not—'

Cannon immediately put her hands up. 'I know, I know, it's your private business.'

'I can pay the money back.' Martha wanted to smother the prurient tone this was taking.

'You don't have to. That's not the issue. We understand your welfare is important. We're learning to take more care of this stuff. They're calling it "work–life balance".' A hair toss, indicative of a change of tack. 'But you may have some work to do to regain Brandon's trust. He's a hard taskmaster, Martha. He handpicked you because he thinks you're a talent. You know, you've done a little damage here.'

In the lift back up to her floor, Martha couldn't believe that what she'd thought was grand larceny ended up being nothing much. Then she tried thinking of it from Brandon's position: the cab fare was vanishingly small against the backdrop of what had been spent on the weekend. Her possession of the card was his fault – he'd surrendered it open-endedly. Cannon was right – the damage wasn't those things.

The damage was the revelation that she was not an adherent, and possibly not a *winner*. This was a credibility hit, a dent in the armour of commitment. It was in her nature to be worried about such things, but she was surprised to find the concern was only passing.

EIGHTEEN

In the following days, Martha's domestic life resumed its ordinary rhythm. She resisted the urge to ring Joey. She wanted to know more about the Cherrywood and to give away less about herself.

Since the Werribee Mansion episode, she had stopped taking meals from the evening trolley at Caspians. It was a protest, albeit a small one. She had begun to resent the firm reaching so far into her life that it actually fed her. The terms of the charity were unconcealed. By feeding workers, the business could keep them at their desks producing billable time, deep into the evening. It was this unsettling idea of the building secreting nutrients for its drones that put her off. There were lawyers in their middle age who stayed to eat, whether to set an example to the neophytes or because they hated their spouses or ground their teeth at the sound of their own children, and they saw the firm literally as their sustenance.

There was a void developing inside her where Human Rights had been. Within a week, Insurance had driven her away from her defining ambitions. And for every millimetre relinquished at work, a millimetre was taken up by the pub.

She made Wednesdays a firm commitment at the Sisters of St Ondine. The Smoking Nun never expressed surprise when she opened the door and found Martha there. She would greet her with weary ambivalence, then set her to work as though she had been desperately needed: scrubbing, sweeping, mopping, interceding in arguments out in the dining hall. She learned to officiate at the ping pong, to convene debates, but never quite to sing. As the regulars came to recognise her, they opened their lives to her, and she felt amazed at how much she didn't know. Deprivation, misfortune, the punishing business of negotiating the streets, day after day – the moments of extremity she had often seen but always turned away from, believing that anyone giving vent to their pain in public must be a drag on her time, or dangerous, or both.

On a lunchtime dash to the State Library, she found a hardcover history of Fitzroy and scoured it for clues among the weeds of Atherton Street, photographs of slums, of staircases and chimneys. The map in the frontispiece stared at her like a riddle, the schematic of an apparently simple labyrinth: a rectangle exactly one mile long and half a mile wide. Hoddle, the square thinker, had made one of his grids, bounded by grand boulevards to the north and south, and thoroughfares on both sides. The grid he had made was exactly the same size as the central business district of Melbourne. Had he imagined a future city springing up in the northeast to rival the original one?

She photocopied the map and studied it when she was alone. It came to represent a psychic prism, a refracting box. She wondered if the various spires and attics whispered to each other, if they suspended between themselves an unseen field of energy. She ran her finger across the page from west to east – Nicholson, Brunswick, Napier, George, Gore and Smith – then from south to north – Victoria, Gertrude, Moor, Johnston, Kerr, Westgarth, Alexandra. The half-mile width was itself divided into eight main blocks of one hundred yards each, then the smaller blocks were intersected by capillaries of laneways that must have traced back to the nightmen and their malodorous trade, anonymous passages between brick walls and tin fences she was sure held the secrets of the suburb's origins.

The names on the significant streets were relentlessly British, a roll call of kings and peers. The Woiworung had been there for an eternity, so the book said, but among the streets of Fitzroy she could not see a single word to reflect their presence, or even one foreign to the United Kingdom. The only concession to diversity in the nomenclature was the mixing of English and Scottish references.

She shifted the book in her hands one night and realised a significant feature had escaped her. The exquisitely perpendicular streets of Fitzroy – the framing of its grid – were not aligned north–south. The grid was skewed to the northeast. She went to the street directory and found all the grids of the inner east were tilted. The whole city of Melbourne bore the same inclination. What could this mean? She wanted to tell someone, to seize them and say, 'Look at this!' The sun could never set directly up Bourke Street from the river, as she had always assumed it did. Instead, it ran a slender hypotenuse of shadow uphill towards Spring Street.

She rummaged through the drawers of her bedroom desk and found the protractor she'd pointlessly kept since school. She laid it over the street directory and over the map in the history book: in both instances, the inclination was eight degrees east. Was this *magnetic* north? Why would that have been a concern for someone drawing suburbs on blank paper?

The book said the grid was old Fitzroy, or south Fitzroy, and its northern border was a thing called the Reilly Street Drain. It seemed like the drain had drained Hoddle's will: everything north of it was a miscellany, and thereafter, running north, the beautiful order of the grid broke down.

Night after night, the slip of paper with the pub's phone number looked down on her, pinned to the noticeboard. It would only be a matter of dialling it.

At work, she began to apply her time differently. Manne proved to be a poor overseer, preferring to watch the numbers and the files, rather than the people. So she was able to haunt the firm's library for long hours undetected. The librarians never interrupted her. She worked this way for two weeks, avoiding the Cherrywood over both weekends. She scoured the liquor licensing records again, trying different combinations of names, looking for names disappearing and reappearing at other addresses, for publicans who moved around. She watched, a spectator on the sidelines, as the temperance movement did its best to shut down the dozens of pubs that had sprung up in the early twentieth century, and as the women publicans fought back. John Wren was everywhere, securing graces.

The IT department was rolling out desktop terminals to more and more of the mid-level practitioners – by hierarchy, as every other privilege was disbursed – so there were fewer people working in the library now. Often she would be alone in there, stretched out at the communal tables recently installed to promote Collegiate Work Practices – a way to habituate clawed animals into playing nice.

There was only one other regular in the library: the firm's oldest partner, Mr Enmore. A man constructed from title and surname, too formal for lesser appellations. Martha had noticed the other partners ignoring him in corridors, like an oppositely charged magnet or, in this hyper-virile environment, a neutered dog. He never went to Friday drinks. He was dapper, often buttoned into a waistcoat. He wrote in longhand with a beautiful pen and he read the old calfskin-bound law reports. These had fallen so sharply out of use that many were displayed in reception as props to suggest the scholarly origins of the firm. He would wander out occasionally and return with one he had lifted from above the receptionist's head.

He had an uncommon ability to concentrate. On the days when he appeared, Martha would sneak glances at him over her own work. His head would always be down, brow furrowed, the pen making long sweeps. The cufflink at his right wrist would

make a solitary *clack* as he repositioned his fist at the left margin
to begin another line. Once, he looked up while Martha was
studying him, and he gave her a small and unreadable smile,
then returned to his work.

During the first few days of the library project, Martha
made a simple moral decision about how to justify her closely
monitored time. The insurers who looked after the Catholic
Church and the tobacco companies could sponsor her private
research, and in fact should be made to do so. If they were using
time and money to grind down deserving litigants, she could
redirect a little time and money. She began to record her hours
of research against them.

She figured the Cherrywood couldn't be more than a
century old, so she began with the drawings compiled by
Fitzroy City Council from 1890 onwards. Each drawing was
coloured in different shades to denote land tenures – lease,
crown, freehold, empty – revealing to her the places where the
pub might have been.

They had to be corner blocks, unless the pub somehow
reconfigured itself to adopt or discard a corner door as it moved.
She didn't think that was the case. In 1900 there were thirty-six
empty corner blocks in the grid. In 1925, there were twenty-
nine. The Cherrywood could have moved about as it pleased.
But by 1960, the number was down to nineteen, and she could
see every one of them. By now the council was reclaiming
slums to build high-rise Housing Commission towers, and
they'd taken up aerial photography to guide the project. In
1982, there were fourteen corners left, and in 1992, the number
was down to nine.

As of two years ago, there were nine places in Fitzroy the
Cherrywood could move between. This discovery led to another
idea: that the pub never left Fitzroy. The suburbs were boundless,
and there would be hundreds of vacant corners on the north side
of the Yarra. But the three times she had encountered the pub,

it had been within the Fitzroy grid. She felt sure this mattered in some way.

Shortly before 9 am on a Tuesday in June, she took the block of sticky notes from the table beside her and wrote on one:

RULE THREE
The pub cannot leave Fitzroy.

She looked up, still unconvinced by this one. It seemed even stranger than the idea that the pub moved around. There, not five metres from her, the silver-haired partner worked away at a pile of stapled photocopies.

She shoved the note in her pocket to add to the pinboard at home. Then she wrote down the addresses of the remaining blocks, knowing the Cherrywood could not elude her anymore.

NINETEEN

The ride each summer morning from the new house in Elwood to the yard took Thomas past the amusement park on the Esplanade. It was the work of Americans, copied from Coney Island, and it stood opposite the huge Palais de Danse, built by American brothers.

Hiring an American now looked like a strategy. If they had set their sights on colonising St Kilda, he would pinch an American of his own. When he had intimated to Lucy that he was considering Carville as master of his vessel, he was plagued with guilt, having already hired him. During a conversation at the shipyard, Thomas had seen Carville's eagerness as desperation to succeed – when in truth it was mere desperation – and had asked him if he would consider the position.

'*Master*,' he had breathed. 'Oh, my word.'

'You have the … the qualifications, the experience …' Thomas was unsure if he was asking or confirming.

'Of course!' A flashbulb grin.

'And you have the American flair to impress our clientele,' Thomas added; and Carville was not about to disavow him. 'I cannot precisely tell you a salary, but I will ensure it is commensurate with the responsibility.'

They clapped a handshake and Carville drew them into a violent hug. When they parted, Thomas repositioned his spectacles, which had wound up at a crazed angle. 'Now, will you need to confer with your wife?'

'Wife? Dear man, there is no wife! And *that*' – he pointed a salacious finger right between Thomas's lenses – 'is a drawcard. The society dames will buy tickets for their daughters! The whole world loves a captain!'

'Master.'

'Master.'

* * *

Thomas often walked along the foreshore early in the day, threading behind the backs of the two structures, theatre and amusement park, that fronted the Esplanade. It meant he didn't have to suffer the shocking cosmic joke of a giant mouth ingesting and disgorging tourists as the tramcar rattled past its row of shingle teeth.

The park was usually closed at this hour, so he saw these things in suspension, awaiting the crowds. At times, he felt the urge to linger there, imagining ... imagining couples seated in a delicate Ferris wheel, a Palais de Folies, straw boater hats craned back as the strongman hurtled down a tensioned wire suspended from the Turkish cupola. The cream-dollop white of billowing dresses in the sun, cumulus against the husbands' dark suits. Parasols and extravagant sun hats. Children in sailor suits and bonnets, posed rigidly for the man with his camera. A highwire in the holiday sky, the barometric drop of collectively held breath as a couple ant-picked their way across. A merry-go-round, brass poles and painted horses.

All of these possibilities were framed and enclosed by the eternal loop of the rollercoaster. It wasn't the rickety carts that captivated him so much as the timberwork, the slatted lightweight sleepers under the rails, the bearers holding them firm, then the latticing of beams to form the frame under the curving hills. It was a forest reconstituted as right angles, themselves in service of curves, the curves invoking the theatre of gravity as the carts slowed dramatically at the top of each hill, then plunged again. This was a magical contrivance, the engineering of a railway line into bridgework that left the view open through to the sea and the western side of the bay, giving a sense of open air under the squealing children in the carts, so they appeared to roll through the sky.

And further on, across the road and perched in the shallows, were the sea baths, another lattice of pretty timbers, another pair of Moorish turrets topped with flags. Nearer to what he foresaw for his paddlesteamer, the delicate architecture bathed in the reflective flats between high tide and low, a building unconcerned by the division between land and sea. The next triumph, after an amusement park in the dry sand and a bathhouse in the lapping water, would be a work of exquisite beauty that floated serenely away.

All the elements were there, easily obtainable in the imagination: the tesserae of a larger image. The people were hungry for pomp and thrills, and he could provide them. They were up there in the mansions, in the saloons of the Esplanade and the George. He needed to draw them down in the electric tramcar, get them past the amusement park and the theatre and out, out onto the bay. Somewhere in the interplay between painted timber and sunshine, this foreshore had the capacity to mesmerise. He would harness the magic, turn it into pleasure and profit.

* * *

As the hot, listless weeks of January passed, Thomas redoubled his efforts, aloft on frenzied energy. Somewhere under the drive, he sensed a void, but his momentum was such that he felt sure he wouldn't fall.

He interviewed and hired a crew, to be built around Carville, who sometimes came to the interviews and sometimes did not. He obtained a berth at St Kilda, had waiting rooms built with a bar and a kitchen, so his customers could come earlier and stay longer at either end of their voyage. The spectacle he was creating would ornament the shore when it berthed, an exotic seashell appearing and disappearing with the tide.

He sent workers out to foundries and iron sheds to find the best artisans, and they came back with brass fittings and glassware and ceramics and beautiful timber inlays. Chandeliers, shade cloths, a grand piano, huge pewter vases, carpets and rugs.

He fitted out the forward half of the saloon with chaises longues, the aft for social events, ensuring the entire space could be given over to extravagant galas. He had a stained-glass atrium built into the centre of the saloon's ceiling so as to refract coloured light over the room. The side windows of the atrium could be opened so the air would circulate when the gentlemen were smoking, and closed in the event of drizzle. A small side room was created in the saloon through the ingenious use of Japanese screens: a place for the ladies to gossip and adjust their hair, away from men's eyes. At the head of the room, he hung a clock, custom made for the paddlesteamer and featuring Roman numerals and the shipwright's name, 'Rosstrevor & Son', on its face.

He hired a composer to find him a brass band and a string quartet, and to write original music to be played in the excitement of those first minutes after departure. He signed supply agreements with fishmongers for oysters, breweries for beer and distillers for gin and brandy. He investigated installing a bakery in the steamer's restaurant so the passenger cabin would fill with the smell of hot bread. When he was reminded that the voyage would be so brief that the bread would barely be baked by the time the vessel reached the other side of the estuary, he found a bakery in Balaclava to deliver bread to the wharf on a schedule to match departures.

All of this he achieved in a mere two months, sleeping in snatches, eating as an afterthought.

He had uniforms made for the crew, modelled on what he remembered of the Maindample Line ones: royal blue with brass wire piping at the cuffs and collar, brass buttons and white gloves. Carville immediately took to wearing his around the Rosstrevor yard and, soon enough, to the tavern. His afternoons there started earlier and earlier, until they became the back end of his lunch, then he would not return to the yard for the rest of the day. He maintained there was nothing he was needed for – his real duties would begin when the vessel was launched. He would apologise, say he'd got caught up and wheel out that innocent smile of his. There was no malice in him, Thomas thought. Some people worked to a different clock.

In the dim interior of the main works shed, Thomas was surprised one summer day to see a familiar figure. Oremu seemed to have lost size somehow, and was still listing to starboard, still leaning on the cane. Thomas had long since acquired tea privileges in the Rosstrevor yard, and he boiled the kettle now, walked the two mugs out into the sunlight and helped the carpenter onto his familiar perch on the scaffold. Whatever skewing of ballast had taken place within the man was offset by his strength: he was still able to pull himself up from level to level, only requiring assistance when he staggered on the uppermost floor.

Once settled, he tipped his head upwards to take in the emerging paddlesteamer, or to warm his face in the sun. Thomas sat with him, their legs dangling in the free air beside the hull. The air carried creosote and bird shit and then the wind swelled from the other side of the yard, bringing with it the metallic tang of low tide. The hammers rang out over the snarl of the big saw – the very one responsible for maiming Oremu.

'I am so sorry for what has happened to you,' Thomas said. It sounded stiff, formal, which was not his intention.

Oremu inclined his head agreeably. 'Thank you for the money.'

Thomas plunged onwards. 'I don't – I don't understand *how* … I know nothing of these machines and how they work, but Mr Rosstrevor tells me there was nothing wrong with the blade, that there was metal in the timber. Which seems impossible to me.' He was rambling, wondering why he was explaining this, even as he explained it. 'The bill of lading said "fresh-milled new timber". There's no logical way …'

The carpenter was turning his head from side to side so he could watch the movements of the workers with his good eye. 'The doctor who tried to save the eye, he took out fragments.' Oremu made a vague gesture near his eye. 'Nickel, steel and lead.'

Thomas must have looked at him blankly.

'A bullet.'

'In a length of timber?'

'In a tree, once.'

'How does a bul— ' Thomas stopped himself.

'We have in mind the same image, I think.'

The hammers and the saws, the birds and the bright sunshine. Thomas saw for the first time that there were faded tattoos on his hands, arabesques of green and black, fading into his dark skin. He had lived other lives, this man.

'Your whole shipment is heartwood,' Oremu said softly. 'From deep in the trunk. It's the hardest timber the tree creates. I went through the stack once with the apprentices, trying to find softer lengths to bend for the banisters. There is not a limb in the entirety of it. All heart.'

A heart was a soft thing to Thomas, whether the organ or its figurative use. A heart yielded. He struggled to imagine it as a thing that was hard and dead.

'A craftsman thinks in radial terms. The tree grows from the centre outwards, and only appears to us to grow vertically. It is our biased perspective, nothing more. Centre outwards, adding rings as it goes. The vigour is in the layers just under the bark, passing water and nutrients back and forth, passing messages from the earth to the canopy. Busy streets in those layers, newness travelling up and down, pushed out from the centre by the tree's growth. Dying cells pass backwards into the heart, taking memory in there, to store it. Carried the bullet, I suppose. Young cells carry commerce, so they face the world.'

Oremu went on, his voice quiet. 'This *foreign body*, doctor calls it, that came out and blinded me – there is no reason it would be in there. But things of industry, things we use, they come here from Europe. People too, ships. Been there myself. Rotterdam, Groningen. Forgotten wars, famines, pestilence. Dead kings and broken stone. Nothing new can come from there. And things cannot be made new simply by crossing the ocean. What's in them remains there. There *is* no clean timber, no new coins.'

Thomas felt a kind of vertigo overtake him. The man was still hunting fossils, a mystic in the mud. These ideas – he barely understood them and yet they frightened him. The carpenter must have known it. He fixed Thomas with his one good eye as he sighed and took up his cane.

'Everything carries the old scars.'

* * *

The troopships had disgorged the city's men back into Port Melbourne and a new optimism filled the air. Europe was once again at peace, and this felt like a harbinger to Thomas, who believed great events connected themselves by invisible tendrils to smaller ones. No longer was the paddlesteamer a means to financial success: it had become an end in itself, a pinnacle of aesthetic beauty. His love of timber grew with each passing day, even as the world around him depended more on steel. Timber could retain sounds, or else every violin would sound the same. It could respond to motion: if it didn't, a pine boat would ride the water like a spruce one did. Its imperfection was comforting. It was, overall, closer in nature to the human condition than steel, which was lifeless, inflexible and prone to corrosion, to sudden, catastrophic fault. Steel was infernally born, and could tell no story. Deep down, there lay an origin for this preference of his, one that came to him lying awake and alone at night – his mistrust of steel could be traced back to the terrible demise of his parents in the Great Arrow.

His staff now numbered twenty. As well as the crew of seven, there were waiters, bar staff, passenger stewards, a bookkeeper and two cleaners. The stoker, Silas Whittle, had come down from the Murray River steamers and had with him his own personal shovel and bellows. He was slightly built and dark skinned, and although it was clear from his interview that he was not one for idle conversation, he declared he was a Yorta Yorta man, raised on a mission, and had renounced the demon drink some years back. His thirteen-year-old son would serve as his apprentice. Carville, who was putting in one of his rare appearances at this interview, seemed stunned by the hardness of the man: when Silas had left and Carville sat behind the letters of introduction describing him as 'tireless and beyond fatigue or distraction', he ran a hand through his hair. 'I suppose we are born to our occupations,' he sighed. 'This here man is no carnival spruiker.'

As Thomas watched Silas Whittle go, and Carville got up to excuse himself, he picked up an envelope that had come by courier from the mail ship. A letter, written in an unfamiliar hand. He sliced the envelope open and a pile of pounds sterling fell out. The letter was from an Amon Herskope, 'nephew and executor of the Estate of Abraham Herskope, late florist of the

Fruitmarkets, informing you Sir that our dear Uncle departed this life on the 22nd inst. and that our accounting for his Estate reveals the amount enclosed is owed to you under a standing agreement between you and our dear Uncle'. Thomas recalled the day he had sat behind the counter at Herskope's and made their arrangement, the scent of the flowers, the fecund humidity of the air. And he grieved for the sudden severance of that faraway friendship and for yet another connection to the life he had known.

* * *

Later in the afternoon, Thomas sat at the end of the outermost pier on Rosstrevor's stretch of the foreshore.

From here, he could look back at his vessel in its cradle, framed against the water. The timbers of the hull were the floors of ballrooms, swept by skirts. The white painted cabin was a summer house, a pavilion, a grandstand for cricketers. The louvres over the sponsons were the shuttered windows of a bathing box. The flags, the semaphores, bunting, suspended wires and ropes embodied the childish pleasures of a carnival, yet hinted at a place of repose. One might find a corner in the cabin where the sun leaned in from the northwest – for he had learned that inversion now – and open a book, sonnets perhaps, and allow the words their soporific effect until the eyelids drowsed.

The bottle-green paint below the waterline rhymed with the calm surface of the bay. The cast-iron hawse pipe at the bow had been painted black, and it looked out across the water like an eye daubed with kohl. The white of the superstructure reflected in the rippled surface among the dun-brown audience of lesser craft, their noses pointed in her direction. She was the woman in the room to whom every eye turns, tall and impossibly beautiful, stopping conversations, setting off currents of envy and lust, standing insouciant in the available space between unknowing and uncaring.

Her beauty was foreign. Although built within a square mile, every bolt and screw forged and lathed by local hands, she was yet another transposition. This estuary had never known paddlesteamers before the handful now plying the southern reaches of the bay, and before this one. His vessel was no different from the big terrace houses of Middle Park in the distance: local hands, local stone, but alien to the ground under them. Each was the summoning of a memory, an attempt at transplanting. In moments of pride, when he felt he was emerging from his father's shadow, Thomas was tempted to think his own contribution was the start of something uniquely local. But most of the time he doubted it. The plans were drawn by a foreign hand. The timbers were foreign, *created* foreign. When they had arrived in Liverpool for shipping, they were already redolent of some other place. Maybe the very soil they grew in wouldn't recognise them.

She was a curio. As much as he would like it to be the case, she did not belong any more than he did. She was a beautiful anomaly on this flat plate of water.

Somewhere far away, on a rougher sea and in a vessel of no great charm, Thomas's wife and daughter were on their way. The time that had elapsed had rendered their faces unfamiliar, but the remembered feeling of their warmth, their closeness, retained such a powerful hold on his imagination that he was able to re-make them, over and over, behind the lids of his closed eyes. And none of the material things around him, not even the exquisite steamer that rested there across the water, summoned a fraction of the desire he felt to be reunited with his family.

TWENTY

Late in the second week of her research, Martha discovered that Brandon had been called urgently to a Supreme Court trial in Sydney, and had taken two acolytes with him. No-one was keeping an eye on her, and her time recording was, she thought, impeccable. The six-minute units kept trickling in, shared between the insurers of tobacco and of myrrh, and categorised under vague descriptors like 'document searching' and 'file review'. Unwatched now, she began a methodical search of the newspapers on microfiche at the State Library.

Not knowing what dates she was looking for, she rifled through the long drawers of index cards under categories as they occurred to her. 'Hotels', 'Fitzroy', 'Publicans', 'Breweries', even 'Architecture'. Nothing came up. In desperation, she tried 'Melbourne History', and a re-direction card sent her to 'Port Phillip Bay'.

The Argus, 12 April 1919. A column, gossip really, by someone called Miles Wintergreen, writing under 'Saunterings'.

She sat under the grand ceiling with a photocopy of the page two article and she felt, if not the beginnings of understanding, at least a glimmer of some connection. She read it over and over, each time trying to eke a fraction more detail from it.

There was no other index card leading back to the Cherrywood that year, or ever after.

TWENTY-ONE

The taxi driver was the same man she remembered from before. He did not speak when she climbed in, betrayed no surprise when she said, 'Cherrywood, please.'

It had been three weeks. Joey hadn't made contact with her – she wasn't sure how he would find her, anyway – and at first she had resisted the urge to call. She wanted to create an impression of casual indifference, and to learn as much as possible about the mystery of the pub without simply fronting up and asking him about it. But the urge to see him gnawed at her until she relented and dialled the number.

Of course, he had said. *Anytime you like.*

So, it was Friday night, a reward for the week's restraint. The driver maintained a companionable silence, the radio murmuring beneath hearing. On the dashboard and the insides of the windows were stickers informing the passenger of many things: the fare rules, numbers for alcohol or drug counselling, the logos of credit card companies. But there was nothing to identify the driver. He wore a pale-blue polyester shirt with the word 'TAXI' in gold thread at the ends of epaulettes on his sprawling shoulders.

She watched the needle of the speedometer as it rose and fell in the traffic. Her eyes shifted to the odometer. For a moment, she could not believe she had looked at the very instant it clocked over to 800,000, but then she realised it was stopped at that figure. They drove long blocks of Victoria Parade, but the little tumblers did not move.

The Cherrywood appeared in another darkened side street, and she noticed with satisfaction that the address was among the six new ones she had found. The driver stopped at the door and she paid him. He tilted his head slightly as she climbed out. The dome light on the roof of the cab was switched off and the running lights were on, indicating the cab was not for hire. It slipped off into the night, leaving only the smell of oily exhaust.

The windows of the bar were dark in the middle of a Friday night, and she worried this was a symptom of terminal decline for a pub. Across the street, a fish and chip shop, lit up but also empty. Inside, stainless steel and posters – Gould League fish and a blonde girl on a motorbike. 'CHIKO: Hit the Hot Spot'. Outside, an illuminated plastic shark glowing on the awning.

The street was dark and quiet after the cab's departure. The light from the shop spilled into the street, filling the space under the awning. She crossed and stood at the glass. There was a tabletop arcade game in the window, two round plastic stools. She watched the screen roll by: it was Frogger. The cars and trucks came and went, right to left and left to right, and the plucky frog picked its way between them as though played by an unseen hand. When it had got to the riverbank, halfway up the screen, it waited, then jumped on a turtle, crossed to a log and another log. A turtle, a log, a misstep and a pixelated skull and crossbones. Instant death.

The purple glow of the screen lit the glass, lit her fingers and her face. The fryers were turned off, everything polished. The till drawer had been left open as a disincentive. The coloured screen blinked like a dying star in the void. It was the loneliest place she had ever seen.

She crossed the road back to the hotel, extra vigilant for cars and trucks. Rather than knock immediately, she walked the length of the pub on both sides of the street corner. Only sharp eyes, searching as hers were, would have noticed that between the timber at ground level and the asphalt of the footpath was a slight gap, the width of her little finger. She traced a hand over the lowest three boards, running parallel to the ground. They felt rough, serrated, and just as she had this thought, she felt a sharp pain and whipped back her hand. A bright drop of blood appeared on her fingertip: it had been sliced with razor precision. She dabbed it on the timber and peered closer at the wall, at first refusing to believe what she was looking at. But she was not mistaken. Barnacles. Long since dead, they had affixed themselves to the planks like they would not give up their prize. Between them were faint white swirls of encrustation, mostly rubbed off but still visible: marine worms, the type that appear on the pylons of a pier at low tide.

At the door, she thought Joey seemed happy to see her, and if her absence had concerned him, he didn't show it. She had bags with her, as she'd indicated on the phone, and he took them without comment. A delicious smell wafted through the empty bar.

'Cooking?'

'I had some prawns, so I got a fried rice and mixed them together. Kind of a paella.'

'Prawns?' Why was everything suddenly estuarine?

'Yeah. Want some?'

'Sure. Hey, can I stay a while?'

If the question had felt like a leap of faith, his reaction rendered it harmless. 'Of course,' he said. But he did look a little sheepish. 'Hey, I, um, did a thing. After I got off the phone. Come and have a look.'

He led them up the flights of stairs once again, with the bags hung from both his shoulders and bouncing on the banisters. The occupied room still had its pot plants and its geometric drawing: nothing had changed there with the pub's latest move.

'One sec,' he said, and he turned right, away from the bedrooms and through a door with a frosted window, embossed with the word 'Gentlemen'. He switched on a light, and through the frosting she could see the vague form of him moving around in there. He emerged seconds later with his hand out.

'Give me your hand,' he said, and he gently took hold of the finger she'd cut on the barnacle and stuck a band-aid over the cut. When he was done, he squeezed the hand so lightly that Martha thought she had imagined it, and then he led them into his room. Inside, it was unchanged from what she remembered. He went around the far end of the bed, where the attic window was, and threw open the sash so the night air came in, cold and fragrant.

'Now, be careful with this bit.' He stepped out of the window and stood on a narrow platform between two slopes of the slate roof. He reached back to her and helped her climb out so they were standing close on the platform, holding the window ledge. There were only a couple of metres of slope before the edge of the roof, the guttering and the dizzying fall to the street below. Up here, they were among the twigs at the height of the bare winter trees, and across the street, a large apartment block obscured the sky. There was a streetlight below them, which gave her an unwelcome sense of the height of their position. The shark grinned up from across the road.

'Now, follow me,' he was saying. He worked his way up the side of the little dormer over the window, wedging his feet in the flashing between the slate and the timber of the attic wall. When he reached the top of the attic, he lay flat on the roof and his fingers reached the peak of the pitch. Grabbing it, he hauled himself up until he was sitting astride it.

She told him he looked like a gargoyle, but he looked triumphant, silhouetted against the night sky. She took hold of a decorative timber piece and hauled herself onto the roof of the dormer, then followed him up to the ridge.

There, the most amazing view awaited her: the city, a phosphorescent hydra, sprawled and glowing. It occupied the ground and sky to the west of them as if it had drawn the electricity out of everywhere else, yet, lying downwind of them, it seemed to emit no sound. The light was yellow and white, encrusted with jewels of red, blue or green from neon advertising. There were moving points of light: the cars, of course, flowing in and out of the nested buildings, but also helicopters in close, a plane overhead, embers floating free.

She was so captivated by the view that it took her a moment to look down. Between the ridge they were on and a matching one parallel to it was a valley, a long, narrow section of roof sloping gently towards the street and the spectacular light of the city. And here, Joey had created something wonderful. He had taken a pile of thin bedrolls, dragged them out the window and laid them out so they formed a double bed. The bed was made, and at the head on both sides he had placed candles inside brass lamps that flickered warmly in the breeze.

She sat beside him on the downslope of the roof and let gravity take them down over the slate to the bed. There was a dark cloth bag slung over Joey's shoulder and he placed it down with a *plink*, rummaged in it and produced a bottle of wine and two glasses.

'What if I ... need to wee?'

'Always overthinking things.'

She took him in her arms and kissed him, her fingers ranging up his back to pull him closer. She shivered at the swell and fall of his breathing against her chest, the prickle of stubble, the angles of bone and muscle that shaped him uniquely. He smelled slightly of cigarette smoke, slightly of salt, or warmth, or something. He was new enough that every impression of him was intriguing, and she nuzzled at his neck for a moment, intoxicated by the unfamiliar comfort of him.

He took her hand and they lay back. From this position Martha could still see the city, but any trace of the neighbourhood, bar the very tops of the trees, was obscured by the roof's edge. It was a secret place: only the tops of a few church spires punctured the night sky between them and the distant nest of light. She concentrated on the air, smelled it deeply and found a note of the new blossom of spring.

'How do you know it isn't going to rain?'

'Overthinker.'

She laughed.

'Look at the sky,' he protested. There was a dusting of stars over them. 'Anyway, so what if it does? If the bedding gets wet, I can tip it over the edge.' He looked either side of himself. 'In fact, I might do it anyway.'

She shivered a little and shuffled herself so the bedcovers wrapped around the lower half of her body. He did the same, and she felt the warmth of his body in the space they occupied.

With a breath of breeze, she heard the passage of air through the bare branches of the street trees, and behind her a metallic squeak. A windvane, on the very peak of the roof's pitch, a fanciful rendering of a sailing ship in bronze that was nearly as tall as she was, its hull a fat belly and its oxidised sails cast in permanent swell.

'How's the finger?' He was looking out at the city.

She peered at the band-aid. The oddness of the injury reflected the strangeness around her. 'I suppose I should ask you how I cut myself on a barnacle at your hotel, sir.'

He smiled, looked down. 'We used to get oysters when I was a kid.'

'Can we talk about that now?'

'About your finger?'

'About everything.'

He sighed, waited a long time before he answered. 'I haven't told you any lies.'

'You haven't exactly been forthcoming, either.'

He took her hand under the covers. 'If something's difficult to understand, you don't just cough it up, do you? You kind of wait to build up trust.'

'So … I was hoping maybe we had some trust by now.'

'Maybe ask me what you want to know.'

She felt he'd cornered her into revealing what her hypotheses were. But they were good hypotheses, damn him. She was willing to risk it. 'I have this idea that there's a set of rules governing this building.' Her heart was in her mouth. It was madness, but she had been unable to find a more rational explanation. He hadn't reacted, so she plunged on. 'Like' – she watched him closely – 'the pub moves.'

Again, his guarded look. A lock to be picked. 'So, what's your question?'

'Is this one of those genie and lamp things? Is there a limited number of questions?'

'If it was, you just burned two. But no.'

'So, does the pub move?'

'I suppose so.'

'What's that mean – "I suppose so"?'

'It means nobody knows. Nobody's ever seen it happen.'

A gust of air swirled about them and the distant hum of the city became audible. She had clicked a barrel of the lock, or snipped the blue wire, and no alarms had sounded.

'How can you not know? It must be a hell of a thing, a whole pub getting up and moving …'

'I'm sure it is, but nobody's seen it. When you were a kid, did you ever read the Faraway Tree books?'

She nodded. 'There was Moon-Face and a lot of sandwiches. Lashings of something or other.'

'Well, you know how they'd have summer holidays and they'd go back to the tree and there'd be a different land at the top? The Land of … fucking Lamb Roasts, or Getting Around Upside Down or whatever. And if you were up there and wandering around the land, you could get stuck there when it rotated away from the top of the tree, remember? Well, when

I was a kid I understood the pub the same way. I never went too far away in case it moved and I couldn't find it again.'

'You were here as a little kid?'

'As a kid, yes. But not little.'

She thought for a moment. She needed to return to that idea. And *why*. Why the pub moved.

'I have this other rule I thought up.'

'Go on.'

'I've been here three times and all three have been in the backstreets of Fitzroy. So ...' She hesitated — she felt foolish again. 'The pub can't leave Fitzroy.'

'Spot on.'

Two rules right. 'What about North Fitzroy?'

'What, north of Alexandra Parade?'

'Yeah.'

'Nah. We've never been there. That's just Clifton Hill in drag.'

'So why can't it leave?'

He shuffled under the blanket and frowned. 'It's complicated. Has to do with land tenure. Leases or something.' He looked at her and a wry smile appeared. 'Your stuff. I don't really understand it.'

'But the building has to ... *move*?'

'You haven't heard of this arrangement?' He was teasing her. 'What kind of lawyer are you?'

'I'm serious. Moving's a human thing, a choice people make. But it sounds as if the people don't do anything. It's the *pub* doing the moving.'

He nodded. 'And you want me to explain it.' He lifted his palms helplessly. 'Sentient pub, I guess.'

It would only have sounded ridiculous to Martha if she hadn't heard the rest of it by now. But common sense had inverted itself and she had a chance to learn it again.

'So, something about the arrangement, the covenant or whatever it is, confines the pub to Fitzroy?'

'Yep. Imagine if it was stuck in Oakleigh, right?' He laughed at these things, impossible things, as though they were routine. He was exposed here, and hadn't yet chosen to confide in her. Her instinct was to disassemble this story, to study its constituent parts and understand it. But there was a danger, she felt. Too much pressure and he would clam up.

'When the pub lands …' she began. 'Is that the right term, *lands*?'

He shrugged and nodded. 'Good as any.'

'When it lands, how does it reconnect itself to the things you need, like water and power and sewerage and … how does it get alcohol?'

'Oh, there's people. They've got their own jobs, like a night-can man who does the sewage. Not the best job to be stuck with.'

'You mean … forever?'

He laughed, and it was just as well. The question felt ridiculous and the potential answer gave her vertigo. 'They're not ghosts, if that's what you mean. You can't stick a hand through them.'

'So, if the pub moves and nobody sees it move, how do they know where it is?'

'What an excellent question. They're … there's this little strong guy does the electricity, same guy ever since I can remember. As a kid, I called him Ash Man. He looked burnt, hair all sooty, clothes charred, like something had blown up in his hands.'

A story, a little character thing. He hadn't answered her question.

'What about the water?'

'It's not on mains. The building collects its own off the roof here.' He patted the slope of slate next to him. 'I've had to fix leaks and things a few times and I've been able to trace it back – it drains centrally to an old iron boiler behind the cool room on the ground floor, and it functions as the water tank. There's another one that works as a grease trap. They're pretty amazing. But we don't need as much water as you might think.'

He'd opened up on that one. So, there was nothing unearthly about the water system. If she did this for long enough, she could map his evasions. 'Of course,' she said. 'You can't have pipes when there's no guarantee there'll be anything to—'

'Connect them to at whatever point the building settles upon.'

She enjoyed that term, *settling*. The idea that a pub might come to rest on the earth, snuffle about and perhaps even wriggle a bit, an old dog in its bed.

Joey continued, 'So, the underneath is flat, and it sits on supporting beams that rest on the ground. I have to crawl under there sometimes. Worst claustrophobia ever. It's a gap of about two feet, depending on the ground under it. And the underside of the floor is matted with these pipes that don't go anywhere, like a rootbound pot plant.'

'These people, the service people ...'

'You're stuck on that bit, hey. You should ask Nan about it.'

She'd pressed too hard there. But now they'd got to Nan, another topic she'd have to return to. She needed to close off these supply questions before she came back to the Nan thing.

'How does the pub restock?'

'Blind luck, really. Sometimes, if we sit still for a while, a liquor rep comes by. Other times, I ring the companies and I ask for a rep from across town and say our regular guy has called in sick and could they do a delivery? So they don't understand the oddness of us not being on the list in the correct spot. They don't care – it's all commission.'

'Your chips are out of date.'

'Not much commission in chip-repping.'

'What about drinkers? Don't they wonder where the pub went, like I did? What if they want to come back?'

'Drinkers are heedless, mostly. And the ones who do want to come back – lost their jacket or whatever – they normally give up after a few days of looking. Not everyone has your level of persistence.'

'Just persistence?'

'What else?'

The light was only the two guttering lamps, a little upward spill from the streetlights below. He couldn't see her blush. Surely, he couldn't. 'Never mind. You're pretty secretive, you know.'

The enigmatic smile she loved and hated. 'I've answered your questions.'

'And I'm still none the wiser.'

He didn't reply, and she took the conversation to be closed. They watched the lights of the city, distant enough that she felt eerily in orbit above the familiar world.

'Hey, remember when I said I might need to pee?'

'Aha.'

'I need to pee.'

He laughed. 'Well, I've got to say goodnight to Nan anyway. Come on.'

He led her back through the window and through his room, down the corridor to the head of the staircase.

'Wait there a sec,' he said. 'I've got to get her things.'

He left Martha in the darkness of the passageway, her eyes wandering over the cornices and skirting boards, the timber filigrees marking little archways in the long ceiling. Timber everywhere, original and delicate. Not a single one of the skirts or cornices was straight. They had been bent, and placed, in pursuit of a very specific scheme.

The stairs squeaked. Joey returned, his arms laden with the till drawers, the tray with the tea set and smokes.

He led her to the door halfway along the corridor, the one with the drawing and the pot plants. Before he knocked, he glanced at her: a caution or an apology. 'Nan, you there?' Then he knocked lightly as he pushed the door open.

'Well, I'm not in fucking Acapulco, am I?' came the reply. Joey inclined his head back towards Martha, close behind him; she thrilled to the touch of his hip against hers. His look was one of weary amusement, like last night it had been Cancun or Waikiki.

He swung the door fully open, and over his shoulder Martha saw the woman she had last seen behind the bar now propped up in a single bed with a lamp burning on the table beside her. The lamp was draped with a filmy purple veil that made a tinted, scandalous light. Other veils hung over tables and a Japanese screen; beads ran and spilled into glittering piles. Colourful brooches and other jewellery lay scattered on a dark-red velvet cushion on the dresser. There were crossed tumbles of lace, of gleaming satin. The bed had an iron-framed head and foot, and where the enamelling had chipped away, the bare metal showed as rust. On another side table, a small and fierce-looking stuffed animal, chocolate-brown with mad tufts of white hair sprouting from the sides of its head, stood in perpetual snarl with its eye fixed upon Martha, the intruder.

Nan, star of her own show, was wrapped in a pink dressing gown, pulled tight around her chest so it presented only a shallow vee at the sag of her throat. The points of her toes made pinnacles at the bottom of the bed. There was so little of her, Martha thought, and yet so much.

'Bit late,' she cawed, with a glance at a small metal alarm clock under the lamp. Her eyes caught the tea set. 'Good,' she muttered, and the bed squeaked with her movement.

She took the teapot and poured. When she was done, she placed the mug on the bedside table and the tray on the floor, then indicated to Joey to bring the tills. For the first time, she acknowledged Martha.

'Who's this?'

'This is Martha, Nan. Nan, Martha.' Joey smiled benevolently as if introducing two children he needed to behave. But Nan's eyebrows took on a hawkish quality as she assessed Martha. To Martha, Joey added, 'Nan's my – what are you, Nan?'

'I'm your business partner,' she snapped. 'And who's *she*?'

'Martha's a friend, Nan.'

'*Friend*. Think it's smart having people around the till balancing?'

'I reckon this people is okay. She hasn't murdered me yet.'

'Hmph. Thanks for consulting me.' She made no attempt to address Martha, so Martha elected to say nothing herself.

Nan walked her fingers around the assortment of objects on her lap. 'Would it've killed you to bring a bowl for the nuts?'

Again, the indulgent smile from Joey. 'You had one from Monday.' He opened a drawer in the bedside table and produced a small bowl. While he did this, Nan took the packet between her molars and tore a strip of the foil away. The nuts plinked into the bowl, which went on the bedside table as well. Now, Nan focused on the smokes. She made a display of tearing carefully around the cellophane wrapper of the cigarette packet, then opened the top, peeled the metallic paper and delicately sniffed the inside. She pulled a cigarette half-out so it stood free of the deck, parked it between her crimsoned lips, and took the pack away. Next, she took up the lighter, but did not bring it to the cigarette. Instead, she extended her arm and waved it at Joey. It must have been a cue he understood, as he took the lighter and lit her cigarette. She drew hard enough to raise a faint crackle of combustion in the quiet of the bedroom, and Martha saw the hit of pleasure on Nan's features. She poured the smoke out in a billowing stream above the bed, between Joey and Martha, and turned her head slightly to fix Martha with a fierce stare.

'So, have you hurt yourself yet?'

'Pardon?'

The sharp eyes narrowed. 'You *know* what I mean. Has the building hurt you yet?'

Martha thought of her fingertip. The small and specific bruise on her hip. Her forehead. The toilet door, which now felt like a warning shot.

'No.'

A satisfied smile, hinting at disbelief. 'Better watch yourself. It will.'

'*Nan*.' Joey's tone was disapproving, and Nan's malicious grin abated to a look that said, *We'll be taking this up again, you and me.*

'Right,' she said, 'right.' She reached over the other side of the bed and produced a heavy ceramic ashtray with images of men in bowler hats and bright lettering. She sat the ashtray on the bottom sheet near her hip, then took the till drawers and placed them in the valley in the bedding formed by her lap. She took a cursory look at the contents of the drawers.

'Shit,' she said, looking at Joey. 'This the lot?'

'Nah, there's heaps more, but I've been systematically ripping you off.'

'Such a wit.' She glanced at a darkened corner of the room, and, following her gaze, Martha saw, behind a pile of unmatched shoes and a palm that was potted in a brass shell casing, a large, dark shape hulking in the gloom. A safe, with a brass handle over the lock, large enough that it was hard to imagine how the thing had been dragged up here.

Nan looked at Martha and saw her looking at the safe. She looked back down at the till drawers on her lap, unwilling to do any of the necessary business in Martha's presence.

'Righto then, that'll do.'

* * *

In the middle of the night, Martha's worry came to pass: it rained. She woke to the cold on her face, the sky darkened, and a shivering sound in the trees.

They bundled up as much of the bedding as they could and hurried back to the window, taking care not to slip on the wet slate. Once they were inside with the window shut, Joey remade the bed. They climbed under a huge blanket that itched Martha's skin, in sharp contrast to the softer feeling of the places where her body made contact with Joey's.

The rain became heavier, drumming on the slate and making trickling sounds around them.

'There's this dream I have when it rains,' Joey said. 'I hadn't had it for a long time, and then when the rain started tonight, it came back to me. It's like the building reacts to the water and comes alive a little bit, gets into your dreams.'

Martha understood. The pub felt the rain and responded to it.

'Anyway, you want me to tell you how it goes? It's pretty weird ...'

She said she did, and so he began.

'In the dream, the city has this network of channels. They run along the footpaths, next to the gutters, but they're deep and wide, like, a metre by a metre, and the profile of them is a half-cylinder, like the *levadas* of Madeira, but the difference is the surface is tiled with beautiful glazed tiles, deep ocean blue like the ones – do you know the ones on the Majorca building? And yellows, like perfect sandstone yellow, and bottle green and silver. And – you have to stay with me here, okay? – here's where it gets strange. The water in the channels is clear and clean, and there's a pumping station in the centre of town, probably under Myers, somewhere big and central, and the pumping station circulates the water around the network and it filters it and heats it to a perfect temperature for each day of the year. So in summer it's cold and refreshing and in winter it's body temperature and there's steam rising off the channels everywhere you look. And here's the weird bit. People commute in the channels. They'll get in at one point and there are little street signs in the tiling so, if you're wearing goggles, you can tell where to hop off one channel and into another one, and—'

'But what about their belongings?' Martha knew she was intruding with her logic, but she couldn't help herself. 'Their clothes and bags and shopping? What happens when they reach their destination and they get out dripping and cold? You can't go to a business meeting like that.'

'Well, it isn't in the dream, but I've thought about this bit. There's a network on the footpaths that matches the channels. There's little booths with warm air for drying off, and there's couriers. You'd hail one like a cab and say, okay I want to get from here to Exhibition Street, and they take your things on a bike or whatever and put them in one of the booths for you and you jump in the channel to make the journey. You see, the pumping station has little repeater stations around the network, and their job is to control the speed of the current in the channels. So if you're coming down the Collins Street hill from work towards the centre of town, then there's a gravity feed in that direction and you'd get up quite a thrilling pace. But if you need to go back up the hill, the water's pumped, and it's a bit more sedate.'

'It'd take a lot of power, pumping water uphill.'

'Takes a lot of power to run trams, too. But imagine it! People would travel in little groups and they'd be floating along at walking pace, chatting. Mums with kids. And you'd see ladies sitting at the cafés having coffee and their hair would be frizzed but nobody would mind. It'd become a point of pride having frizzy hair, like you were a true Melburnian. And people would come from around the world to see the city by ... by—'

'Yes! What do you call this thing? It can't be a *levada*.'

'I don't know. There might be a local Aboriginal word for water channels?'

'But wouldn't people damage the channels?' She was doing it again. 'Or have accidents? There'd be a rash of drownings.'

'A lot of people get hit by trams.' The energy had gone out of his retelling, and she wondered if she had spoiled the magical story. 'Maybe there'd be problems. But imagine how happy it would make people.'

* * *

The first traffic woke Martha before dawn, and she lay for a long time listening to the birds in the trees. The day's first light was appearing outside, spreading in the eastern sky, while the city remained under darkness. Joey was a fitful sleeper – she had noticed it before – but now at night's end he was at peace, curled towards her with a hand under his head and the wild hair spilling across his face. She searched his skin – over the visible side of his face, and down his neck and over the surfaces of his arms – looking for evidence of the life he had lived. Pale, lean but not muscled. No sign of exposure to the sun, but myriad clues about the things his body had seen. A bruise here and there, brown and fading. Old piercings that had closed over. Who had loved this person before she began to? Getting him to open up about the Cherrywood was hard enough, but understanding the corridors within him would be altogether more difficult.

A crow started up and curdled the reverie into something vulgar. Joey stirred. She kissed him, an offer of more certainty than she felt, and his dark eyes opened.

'I have to go in to work.'

'Oh, shit, mmh.' He thrashed about, dragged the hair out of his eyes, and stood. She laughed to see him collecting himself like this, standing bolt upright and naked from beneath the chaos of the bedclothes. She stood as well, shocked by the cold of it, and he held her close. He swayed a little and she realised this was a dance and she pressed him close and swayed in response and there was a moment when this was what they did and it was just the two of them there, in the crowded attic of the wandering pub at the beginning of the new day.

Joey had left her belongings in an empty bedroom on the floor below the attic, off the bending passageway. She went there and threw together an outfit, then dragged a brush through her hair. She wondered how Joey was going to deal with the rest of the bedding from the night before, and when she returned to his attic, she found him absent and the dormer window open again. She clambered back out to the valley between the roofs.

The answer was simpler than she'd thought. He had rolled the bedclothes into a bundle, then inched his way over to the edge of the roof. He was peering mischievously left and right when she found him, and when he was satisfied there were no passers-by on the footpath below, he tossed the bundle down.

'That's the thing about moving around,' he said, when he clocked Martha's look of horror. 'Neighbours might judge you, but they're not neighbours for long.'

They worked their way back inside through the bedroom window and headed downstairs to collect the bedding from the street. *Could this be a lasting thing?* she wondered as they embraced once more at the doorway. *Could it be as simple as this?*

The fascination followed her into work on the tram. The streets were offering her clues now. In the moments when the reverie lifted, she worried she was no different from those poor souls who get messages from their televisions, or lose themselves in madness trying to invent perpetual-motion machines.

The imaginings evaporated when she entered the tower, allowing the lift to suck her into the sky and the sterile world of the firm. She worked through the morning, head down, finishing the paper she would present to the research group over lunch: 'The Smoking Plaintiff – Contributory Negligence as Antidote to Asbestos Claims.' It was about redirecting the finger of blame away from the toxins knowingly placed in the path of workers, and onto their personal habits, like the small pleasure of a cigarette on a break. She knew it was an effective strategy. She also knew it was immoral. Only weeks earlier, she would have been able to compartmentalise it, remind herself she was sworn only to represent. But now it felt nauseating.

That night, the bedding restored to Joey's little attic, they argued in the bar, over the torn foil of kebabs she'd bought them.

It began when Joey made some slight and, she later thought, inoffensive comment about lawyers. About them being a breed apart, with their self-perpetuating cycles of privilege. None of it was wrong, or necessarily right. Martha had met many different people in her work, though she knew at some intuitive level they were more likely to talk of the housing market than the housing shortage. But it fed her misgivings, and whether it was tiredness, or being comfortable enough with him now to take issue, she reacted.

'I don't know who these people are, and I'm where you'd expect to find them.'

'You can't see them if you're surrounded by them. A fish has no concept of water because there's nothing else.'

Martha groaned and rolled her eyes at this.

'So, tell me then, who are you if you're not one of them?' he asked.

'This feels like an accusation,' she said.

'It's not. I'm really interested. I don't get out much.' He smiled, and the smile was unguarded. 'Tell me who you are.'

Now she had to think. She felt sure she was an outsider, but she'd never stopped to articulate why. 'I come from good suburban stock,' she began. 'The boring, devout part of it. I was taught to believe being judgemental was a virtue, and you were shrewd if you could spot the failings in others.'

Joey seemed interested in this. 'Is that right, do you think?'

She had never got to the bottom of this question. 'I think you should judge people, and you should act on the judgements.

I don't understand people who say, "Oh, I know he's an arsehole, but he's so entertaining."'

'Okay, but everyone's flawed. Everyone'd wind up alone if we took that too literally, wouldn't we?'

'Yeah, but the way my family applied it, it was more like envy. Those above our station didn't deserve their place, those below did. Which is remarkably neat, when you think about it. Too fat? No restraint. Can't speak English? No effort. We were the median standard of everything, which I guess is why they call it the middle class.'

'But I don't think that's how you'd choose to live. You don't seem like that.' Joey had got up, scrunched the foil and taken it to the bin behind the bar. He drew glasses from the top tray and poured them a beer each.

'Well, yeah, I'm interested in being kind as a result,' Martha answered. She sucked the froth off the top of the beer. 'You know, I'm not *naturally* kind, like some people are. I have to consciously choose kindness, and I suppose I want to. It matters to me.'

'I think class matters to you. You keep mentioning it.'

'Oh, shit. I do, don't I. It's the fact it's so inescapable. The sense that you're locked out of some things and locked into others, no matter what you do with your work or your friendships. The high can't fall, not in the fundamental sense. You can't even prosecute the privilege out of em. And the lowly can't rise, even if one day they can afford first-class seats.'

'So, which are you then, the high or the lowly?'

'I know I just said we were middle class, but really, it was muddier than that. Somehow my parents steered a course right between every indicator. Mum taught primary school, right? Definite working-class background, Maltese Catholic. First in her family to go through tertiary education, if you call teachers' college in the sixties tertiary education.'

'Was she ambitious? Like, materially ambitious?'

'She was ... hold the thought a minute. See Dad, he was a driver. He drove executives around in nice cars that the companies provided. But he was out of jobs as much as he was in them. Never his fault. The boss was a hypocrite or the clients were arseholes or he had no support. Impossible, as a kid, to know if they were sacking him or he was quitting, but it was one of those things that was Never to Be Discussed in the household, like money or sex. "Your father's left his job" was about as direct as it got. I was a smart kid, probably, but even smart kids can be incurious about such things, or—'

'Or they have an instinct for the things not to ask.'

'Or that, yes. So the weird thing was, you've got a teacher and a driver, and the driver's in and out of jobs, but they were ambitious. And to go back to your point, not professionally and not quite materially, but socially.'

'Aren't materially and socially the same thing?'

'No, not really. You might crave a nicer car or a bigger house, but those things are means to an end, which is that you want to mix with the people who have those things. The people with the BMWs make nicer vowel sounds, and you need a BMW to be in their company. So we lived in Millswood, in Adelaide. Really nice suburb. It's not like there's trust money behind this, you know? These two basic-wage earners, living in Millswood. I got sent to convent school and we had cars and once or twice we had holidays, but I had this unshakeable certainty we were faking it. There wasn't a cent left for the everyday stuff. Feeding the finance, constantly, and the minute the interest rates got the slightest bit of indigestion or Dad decided he couldn't stand the fleet manager, then it was crisis mode again and the company car would be gone. And none of it was ever discussed. It was like this, I don't know, pressure valve, this hissing panic. Like at any moment someone was going to explode.'

'Jesus.'

'And the whole cycle would repeat again once they were back on their feet.' She took a long gulp at the beer.

'But everything must have worked out alright. I mean, you're doing fine ...'

'Well, it worked out in the sense that they could keep doing it. But I knew. I absolutely knew that the people who could afford it, the girls at the school whose families were three generations deep in the place, they could see through us. They knew as well as I did what was going on. We were tourists in their world. Pretenders. They had exactly the right jeans, the right runners, before I even knew they were right. And every time I saved up and waited patiently to have the jeans or the fucking runners, I was five minutes too late and they'd be looking at me with pity. Big smile, forced smile. "They look cute on you." Meanwhile, they'd moved on to some other brand I'd never heard of.'

'You went to law school. You must have eventually ... caught up?'

'You never catch up. What's more, you can never go back. It's the weirdest fate to miss out on both the honesty of the working class and the networks of the wealthy. If you read my résumé, you'd see the suburbs and the school and the faculty and you'd say, "Ah, one of us," if you were a commercial lawyer. Or, "Get this princess away from me," if you were a real person. But neither thing would be truthful.'

'So how did it work out? The family stuff, I mean ...'

'You can't fight social physics forever. I probably saw it for what it was earlier than Mum and Dad did. They ran out of credit and broke up. And I got tipped out into the world. So here we are, hey.'

They were silent a moment. Martha felt she'd said too much, wondered if she was about to get teary. But having said such things, she wanted to make sure she'd got it right.

'The thing about living in the borderlands between two worlds is that you get hung up on authenticity. Even now. I feel like there's you, and here, and there's work and them. I want you to know I'm *me* and I mean well. I'm not … pretending to be something.'

'Don't you want them to know the same thing at work?'

He only asked questions, she noticed, so precisely directed that she felt like she was interrogating herself. He had revealed nothing, while she blathered on.

'Every day that goes by, I care less and less what they think.'

Joey cleared their glasses, came back and wiped the table with a cloth, enacting habit. 'Thanks.'

'For what?'

'For being *you* here. I'm glad it fell my way and not theirs.' He smiled the dreamy smile that had caught her and held her the first time she'd walked in, ten feet from where she sat now.

'Can we maybe talk about you sometime, Joey?'

He had crossed the room, was reaching for the light switches. 'Yeah, sometime.'

TWENTY-TWO

Rosstrevor inspected the paddlesteamer and pronounced her seaworthy. The yard needed to clear out its largest client. Thomas was adamant the maiden voyage must be an event, so it was agreed that, first, they would slip the vessel in the dead of night and, instead of having her pushed around to the berth at St Kilda that would be her home, they would take her out on the open water and test her.

On a hot and still February night, with the tide at its peak for the month, the paddlesteamer rested in its giant slipway cradle, high above the water. Having ascended by ladder, Thomas stood on the deck and looked down at the workers who had assembled in secret to witness the sea trial. Although he had instructed Carville to be there, Thomas felt no surprise when the appointed hour came and there was no sign of him. The crew had gathered on time, and in truth there was nothing they could not handle between them. But the absence rankled.

Rosstrevor's son was there, the boy Joseph, in a suit and hat. He moved around the pier, on and off the deck of the paddlesteamer, watching, learning even now, fixed with the possessiveness the young exhibit when they have taken to a thing – a thing mastered or cared for. He darted around under the cradle, removing sandbags and wooden chocks until the weight of the vessel was held only by the heavy chains securing it.

Thomas stood on the port side of the deck, beside the dining room windows under the raised cockpit. He braced his legs wide and told himself to take it all in. There was a muted three cheers and the chains were released from the sled. The early movement was slow and grinding, stern-first, before the wheels of the sled reached the thick tallow that had been used to grease the rails and the whole apparatus gathered speed. Then the men hauling on the ropes suddenly stopped and turned, and commotion ensued. Someone was running alongside the sled. A dark coat swirled as the figure jumped and took hold of the apparatus and began to climb the outside of the paddle box. Carville. Thomas recognised him when his hat flew free and his hair swirled in the breeze. He darted over, intending to reprimand him for his recklessness, but as he took Carville's outstretched hand and hauled him up on the deck, he saw the delight and excitement on his face, and also saw he was well drunk.

'I am ...' he gasped, 'so very, *very* proud of you, my friend!' And he wrapped Thomas up in a vaporous hug as the two of them fell to the deck with the growing momentum of the sled. When they stood again, it had gained pace, and Thomas felt his hair lift in the wind. They gripped the portside rail and each other as the angle of their descent steepened and the moonlit sea hurtled towards them. There were sounds of severing, of splitting, as the vessel came down the rails. It was a reversal of normal parturition, the newborn rushing from air to water, but the rending and tearing were unmistakably the trauma of delivery. With a roar of foaming water, they were afloat, bouncing gently to rest.

A tugboat closed in and began nudging the hull. Thomas watched the portside paddlewheel spinning freely, its blades dipping and leaving the water, a mesmerising clockwork that also suggested the power being held at bay. Carville paced the deck, calling orders from the practical – 'Give me the steam pressure!' – to the esoteric – '*Dolcissimo!*' Silas Whittle's furnace had been rumbling since mid-afternoon and now the head of steam took hold of the wheels, driving them through the sea – first port, then starboard, then both together. They ran the gearing in opposite directions, and Thomas marvelled at the perfect pivot this manoeuvre created, the sandy eruptions on the surface around them.

The vessel felt light under Thomas's feet, as hollow and buoyant as a paper lantern on the water's surface. He knew this would be the first and last time it would feel this way. Provisioning, fuelling and passengers, and all of the heavy furniture and fittings they had held back to keep the launch as light as possible – all of it would make her heavy, so he resolved to remember it.

They did a fire drill, extinguished the furnace and restarted it, purged the steam and ran it to red-line. They measured the vessel's stopping distance. And when it was done, they measured the remaining coal and water, the consumption and mileage, speed and distance. Rosstrevor made notes of every observation, jamming the pencil behind his ear to tap and prod as he moved about. There were small exchanges between him and his son, grunted almost, that were instructions or praise. The boy would go avidly wherever he was told to be.

An hour after midnight, the paddlesteamer was alongside its new berth at St Kilda. The tea rooms on the pier were dimly lit – enough for the small welcoming party to see what they were doing, but not enough to risk attracting a curious crowd. They were undetected.

Oremu was waiting on the wharf's edge, and at his feet was his carpenter's toolbox, unused for long months. The tug bumped the steamer into a right angle in the pier, so there was a walkway behind its stern.

Thomas and Carville stepped off, then lifted the long board lying at Oremu's feet, holding it against the stern of the vessel while the one-eyed carpenter screwed it in place. It was the final touch, a moment of solemnity that caused a tear to spill from his good eye.

The paddlesteamer had a name now, one Thomas felt sure would become a part of the city's history.

CHERRYWOOD.

TWENTY-THREE

When trouble came her way, Martha was blindsided.

She had been dividing her time between the hotel and her flat, coming and going in the night, relying on the taxi driver, who arrived without fail, spoke very little and never acknowledged the pact between them. The language inside her had changed: she decided she was in love.

While her male colleagues expected to be judged upon their unlimited potential, with their boorish demands to be admired, Joey seemed content to be judged on his present, quiet self – if he even bothered to think about judgement. And he was more tender, more thoughtful than anyone she had ever met. The exploration of a mystery was becoming the discovery of a new life.

Added to that, the weirdness around the corporate retreat had disappeared and she was back to her diligent best, a performer who met every benchmark, they would say. She was deep in the work, deep in the business of drowning a broken and addicted plaintiff in interlocutory documents, when one day, Winsome Cannon appeared in the doorway. She placed her palms flat on the doorjamb and rested her cheek on them, a move Martha thought looked like seduction in the silent film era. She was unable to say how long Winsome had been standing there, watching her with a serene smile.

'How are you doing?' she asked softly. The smile had a cultish quality to it, and the question was not neutral.

'Fine,' Martha responded. 'I'm good.' She placed the dicta-phone she'd been speaking into facedown on the desk. Then she remembered the video they'd watched during their induction, about how to get pesky conversationalists out of the room. She picked the dictaphone up again and ejected the tape, placed it in a cradle of completed tapes and wrote down its serial number. When she looked up from this confected busyness, she could see Winsome was not fooled.

'Can I ...?' She indicated the visitor's chair stacked with folders to make it an unwelcome stop: another tactic from the video.

'Sure.' Martha waited while Winsome lifted the detritus from the chair.

'How's work?' she asked when she had settled. A repetition of the first inquiry. She was stalling.

'It's good.' Martha gestured to the file open on her desk. 'Busy.'

'Good,' she smiled. 'We knew you'd be a good fit for this team.' An awkward silence. 'So, I thought we might have a little talk about things.'

Martha's mind raced over the possibilities. They'd stored up their wrath over the retreat and she was being sacked. They'd finally gone through her clearly expressed preferences and decided to transfer her to Human Rights. Or neither of these things – Winsome was just a gasbagger. Martha couldn't remember from the video how to get someone out of the office once they'd settled down for a chat. It mostly dealt with doorway lurkers.

A faint lift of her eyebrows was enough permission for Winsome to press ahead.

'Martha, it's no secret we think you're very gifted. You know, in the old days, the approach to recruiting graduates was to read the CV, have a listen to the candidate in interview, and if they didn't have two heads, you hired them. Nowadays, we're a bit more scientific about it and we do a bit of personality analysis.'

Martha had no idea where this was going.

'And the thing with you was, you aced the MBTI. Tightest correlation with desired attributes for a litigator we'd ever seen.'

You're assuming I answered honestly, she thought.

'We know you've got partnership potential ...'

There was a *but* coming.

'... but the retreat thing's got us worried.'

'The retreat thing?'

'Your sudden exit from the team retreat. The taxi back to Fitzroy.'

'I thought we discussed this.' Martha suddenly felt indignant. Her eyes darted either side of Winsome, like she might need to make a dash for the door. Winsome sighed loudly through her nose, and again Martha was struck by the idea that she was nervous, not angry. This was not the way power structures worked on these floors: there was anger, and there was work. There was no space for awkwardness.

'Brandon thinks you may have had an episode of some sort.'

'What?'

'We – we're not allowed to inquire into your private wellbeing, you see. Not beyond keeping an eye on men with exploding ventricles.'

Not usually the offending organ, Martha thought, but her mind was still on the notion of an *episode*.

'So I can't ask you if you're alright ... you know—'

'Mentally?'

'Yes!' Winsome heaved a sigh of relief. 'Mentally! So, you see, I'm in here on Brandon's behalf asking – *not* asking' – and she performed a dreadful, theatrical wink – 'if you're okay, you know' – she whirled a finger around her temple – 'upstairs.'

Martha was too shocked to reply, at first. They thought she was mad but they weren't allowed to ask about it. They'd been tiptoeing around her ever since the retreat weekend, and now she knew why. Some thread of compliance inside her snapped. 'This is off the record, right?'

'Of course.' Winsome's huge smile indicated she thought they were making progress.

'Then you can tell him, off the record, to get fucked.' She saw Joey inside her head, proud of her. She felt a wild thrill. 'On the record, I'm shipshape and loving work.'

Winsome did not move, but lowered her eyes. 'You understand that might not be the response I'm looking for?'

'Sorry. That's what I've got for you. Now if you don't mind—'

Winsome Cannon stood and straightened first her hair and then her skirt. She produced a business card, which she placed on the corner of Martha's desk. 'I'm not going to pass on any nastiness like that. We can get you an appointment with this guy any time. On us. He's called Bird. You'd really like him.'

* * *

The card lay in the top drawer of Martha's desk for weeks, buried under a jumble of pens and other stationery, until one day, without forethought, she took it out and dialled the number on it. Winsome Cannon had never followed up. Brandon Manne had never given any indication that Martha's insult had been conveyed to him. She had worried at first that any contact with the counsellor, or therapist, or whatever he was, would set alarms ringing in HR: she was flaky, she was unwell, she was not a *winner*. When the receptionist assured her that the very existence of an appointment was confidential, as well as anything discussed at that appointment, she went ahead.

It came down to curiosity: she wanted to understand the change that had come over her. The years of living alone, engaged in an endless conversation with herself, the monoculture of work: it had been enough, for a long time, and suddenly it wasn't. Talking to Joey about growing up had breached a dam inside her. Maybe it was time to take these thoughts to someone and ask, 'Is this all of us, or just me?'

The name on the therapist's framed certificates was Stephen, but as Winsome had intimated, he introduced himself as Bird. He was tall and thin. He wore elegant glasses, a close-fitting knit in mustard that few men could pull off. Everything about him was neat, his silvering hair, the slender watch on his left wrist, the draping of his limbs and the array of objects on his desk that said, *Yes, this is a staged display of personal effects designed to reassure you I'm a regular guy.*

It was clear from the beginning that he was serious. He spoke quietly, and rather than ask questions, he had a way of ending statements with an upward inflection, inviting a response. It was a technique, Martha had no doubt, but it was pleasant enough and did not seem insincere. He wrote on a notepad balanced on his knee, crossed over the other knee. The pen was an ordinary disposable blue biro. He frowned slightly as he wrote – concentration rather than displeasure.

'Those your kids?' Martha asked, nodding at a framed photo of him, a little darker-haired, his arms around two preschoolers in a rockpool in the sun.

'You like them?' he replied, and Martha secretly delighted in the misstep. He had, too obviously, sought her reaction to the image rather than simply saying yes, they were his kids and they were Amelia and Joel, the names she had picked up off the spiky stick-drawings of *Dad* she could see over the filing cabinet.

They went back and forth for some time, him seeking a rapport, working around trivialities and harmless interests, while she kept moving. There must be some sort of statutory limit to this jousting, she thought. Eventually, he closed in.

'Tell me why we're talking,' he said firmly.

'Why?' She smiled. 'Easy. My employers are worried about me.'

'Why are they worried about you?'

'Because I bailed on their weird corporate bonding session.'

His eyes shifted and she knew immediately that he'd been briefed about it.

'Is it ethically cool that you've got background on me?' she asked. She wasn't upset. It was a feint, a test of his resolve.

'My obligation is to you. I can gather information from elsewhere if it helps us. And nothing goes back the other way, beyond my plain conclusion about whether you need further help.' The default expression on his face, one of openness, hadn't changed. There was no trap here. So, she talked.

'I lived alone, until recently,' she began. 'And I suppose it's relevant that I've been married once before, briefly.' He wrote something, but did not interrupt. 'I know. Kinda unusual for someone my age ...'

He flipped over the pad and read the file under it. 'Twenty-six?' He shrugged. 'It's not uncommon.'

'What else?' she continued. 'Law school. I got ... high grades, a lot of high grades. But I'm not a freak, okay? I'm a normal person who happened to have a knack for exams.'

'Why? Why law?'

'I had options. Family wanted me to do finance, but I wanted to do something good for people. Sounds naff, hey. My heroes as a kid weren't athletes or musicians. They were humanitarians. Mary MacKillop, Mandela, Fred Hollows. So, if you've done your homework about what I do at Caspians, you'll see the irony.'

'What about your social circle at university?'

'There really wasn't one. I still envy those girls whose undergrad years were a prelude to their adult selves, you know, their politics, their intellectual tastes, their sexuality ... style, everything.'

'That didn't apply to you? None of it?'

'I think I more or less understood myself by the time I went to uni anyway. Did some careful exploring of things. But there weren't a lot of epiphanies to be had among the Young Lawyers or the Social Justice Collective. And I wasn't a big drinker, no interest in drugs. Led a very quiet life. I read a lot, but I don't think that's what you're after here.'

'You keep in touch with your folks?'

'Loose contact. They're long since divorced. I don't think they can imagine my life and I can't remotely picture theirs.'

'Do you ever grieve over the state of your relationship with your parents?'

'Oh no,' she said brightly. 'We drove each other mad. They did a reasonable job of raising me and I went my own way. They were addicted to drama. Judgemental. Absolute. It got to a point I couldn't abide it.'

'That's an odd way of putting it – "I couldn't abide it."'

'Well, that's how it was. I ran out of tolerance for intolerance.'

'Siblings?'

'None.'

'You said you married young.'

'Yes.'

'Do you think you might have been looking to rebuild something in your life? Companionship? An exchange of responsibilities with someone?'

Martha stopped, caught by the question. Why had she married Aaron: poor, uptight Aaron? A continuation of her mother's religiosity that she'd fought so hard to leave behind. 'I'm not saying you can reshape your life in the space of a year or two,' she said. 'The marriage was probably a mis— well, I mean it was obviously a mistake. But it was a throwback to the life I'd lived with my parents, yes.'

Martha hadn't discussed her parents with anyone, had barely even thought of them, until the conversation with Joey. And here she was, picking away at the sore again. It was easy to dismiss, to belittle. But she had loved them once, and she knew perfectly well that they'd loved her. Time tore it away, yet it was still there.

'Okay.' Bird pulled a face, almost a grimace. 'Look, I should dig into the rest of your life, outside of work. Between what

I'm told and what you're telling me, something's up. But I don't want to take you where you don't want to go.'

'I'm fine,' she responded.

'Hang on – your life's fine, or you're fine talking about your life?' He was smiling.

'The latter. And probably the former.'

'Off you go, then.'

'Okay … I'm in a relationship, and—'

'Sorry, let me test something on you. Are you in love?'

She puffed at her hair, and he appeared to notice. 'Yes. Yes, I am. Since autumn, so four months.'

'How many times would you say you've been in love?'

'Oh, I told myself I was when I got engaged, but it was wishful thinking, in hindsight. It didn't feel like this.'

'So, tell me about it.'

'He's a bartender. Don't know much about his background, to be honest. He works at a pub that keeps – you're going to have to bear with me here – it keeps shifting around Fitzroy.'

She watched his face for any sign of a reaction as she said it. There was none at all.

'Physically moving.'

'Yep. I'm not holding any of this back, okay? The pub moves – I can only find it if I'm in this one particular taxi – and I'm still working on understanding the hows and whys. A set of rules. So, you see, I quite like not knowing much about Joey, that's his name. Part of what I feel for him is bound up in him being … an enigma, I guess. The pub, on the other hand, I want to figure out.'

She was talking without inhibition, so she was surprised when Bird put a hand up and stopped her. He had been taking notes, but now something was bothering him.

'I want you to tell me more about this' – he flipped a page in his notepad – 'this Joey. You don't want to get to the bottom of him, like you do with the pub?'

This was interesting to her. His attention had been caught not by a pub that defied physics but by the nature of the boy. 'He's quiet. He's thin. His hair's long and dark.' She stroked an imaginary length of hair beside her own face. 'He looks like Simon from Ratcat.' Bird's face indicated the comparison meant nothing to him. 'There's this quality about him. I'd struggle to, you know, describe it, but it's to do with the silences. In my working life, I'm surrounded by people who feel the need to keep imposing themselves, reminding you they're there and they're impressive. He doesn't need any of it. You're drawn into this area of low pressure.'

'Conversational osmosis.'

She smiled. 'I suppose so. And it's more than that. He lives in this world of his own, inside the pub. You get the feeling he can deal with the rest of us okay, but he's performing when he does it, the way you might feel if you had to hold down a conversation in a second language. And there's this other thing about it, like he and the pub are intertwined and they're both in danger. Like I need to rescue him.'

More scribbling.

'Why ...?' he began to ask. Then he went on. 'No. Can I go back to this idea of rules? Maybe this is something to do with you saying Joey and the pub are linked. Why have you privately attempted to understand the rules that apply to the moving pub, when you could simply have asked the boy behind the bar, who you're in love with?'

'Two good reasons,' she replied. 'First, he's secretive about it. Like it's some territory that's his alone, and isn't open to conversation. Secondly – and this is strange, I know – but I like it to be this way. I want to explore it. I don't want someone to tell me how the movie ends. I want to go to him one day and say, "I figured this out."'

'Why?'

'I suppose deep down I feel it's what he wants from me.'

'So you'll be worthy of him if you do figure it out?'

She thought hard. *That* was a good question. 'No,' she said, eventually. 'More like it'll prove we're meant to be together.'

He scratched his head and repeated the almost-grimace. 'Let me test this a bit. If the pub moves around, why wouldn't it go to Ecuador or, I don't know, Mauritius or something? Why is it always within reach?'

'It's trapped. I don't know how it works yet, but it's bound to that very tight area, and at this stage I think it might just be Fitzroy. Do you know Fitzroy?'

'I've spent some time there, yes.'

'Joey said it's something to do with the terms of a lease, as he put it.' A sly smile at Bird to indicate this was not, in fact, how leases work.

'It's a square,' he said. 'You know – not a square but a set of right angles. A defined space.'

'Yes. Which might be something historical. A grid ...'

'Mm. Why doesn't anyone see it moving?'

'I'm not sure. Joey said it happens at night and there's never any sign that it's going to happen.'

'Okay.' He did some more writing in the notebook. 'Do you know *why* it moves?'

She liked the way his mind seemed to work like her own. 'I've got no evidence for this, okay, but I think it moves when it's under threat. And now you'll want to know who or what threatens it.'

Bird nodded agreeably.

'Again, this is only intuition. I think there are people who want to ... claim it. Recover it. I think it's about more than gaining, you know, commercial access to whatever ground it's standing on.'

'Hmm.' He wrote some more, stopped and pressed the other end of the pencil against his forehead. 'I want you to go back a step. Tell me about the taxi. I'm interested to know about the driver.'

'Um, he looks Samoan. Or maybe European. I don't know what kind of European – he hardly ever talks – but there's an accent, and his face or his, his whole *head*, is heavy. Like a Balkan general or something, but … he seems decent. Tatts on his fingers, *love* and *hate*.' She dotted fingertips along her own knuckles to demonstrate.

'So these people, the ah … the taxi driver and the bartender … they know about the … the pub's *other life*?'

'I think they're part of the other life. They don't seem to operate in *this* life. The first, no, the second time I went there, Joey had these mates drinking at the bar and they were like old friends and they were, you know, talking among themselves and … I haven't seen them since.'

'Which takes us to something obvious, doesn't it? Are there customers?'

'I've never seen one, but there are the usual things you'd expect customers to buy, like alcohol and chips and nuts, and there's even a commercial kitchen in there, and there are men's toilets and women's toilets, and—'

'So how does it make money without customers?'

'Why does it need money?'

'I don't know,' said Bird, and for a brief moment Martha thought he sounded exasperated. 'To pay Joey's wages?'

'He lives there. He eats there. He doesn't seem to need money.'

'Well, to pay the power bill …'

'There's a guy who hooks the pub into the grid and I'm pretty sure the whole thing's untraceable.'

Bird frowned again. 'One of these – what? – wraith-type figures.' He had been writing swiftly. Now he put the pen and pad down on the desk beside him.

'I didn't mention anything about wraiths.'

He uncrossed his legs and crossed them over the other way, rubbed his eyes, then folded his hands on his upper knee.

'Martha, you're a very likeable person. I mean – I like how direct you are. People come in here and they dissemble and they lie, and they try to convince themselves of things even while they're trying to convince me. But you're unusually open, and I appreciate that. So, I need to be open with you. This is – this is bizarre. You work in the most rational field I can think of. And you're excellent at it – everyone says so. But what you're telling me is irrational. It's not my place to judge it, so I am going to hand the problem back to you for a moment. What am I to do with it?'

She shrugged. 'I'm not unwell, am I? I'm not screwing up at work – I'm still doing the dirty stuff they want done, and in fact I'm doing it perfectly.'

He nodded: it was unarguable.

Now she was even more convinced he'd been briefed.

'See, I spent years hanging out with people who believed in God and the Trinity and the Old Testament. There's some pretty fucking – pardon my French – fucked-up ideas to be had around the place. So, let's say you're right and I'm delusional and none of this exists. How is the irrational alternative world I'm inhabiting any more batshit crazy than Christianity, or Thatcherism or betting on greyhounds? How is it any less benign than topiary or knitting?'

He was laughing to himself now.

'I'm serious. And the other thing is, it isn't irrational. In fact, it's the most rational thing I've experienced in my life. Here's a problem that challenges logic and engages all the critical thinking I can summon. That's got to be more rational than the lazy rubbish we *assume* every day of our lives. If rationality is about seeking objective verification, then I can assure you I'm at the peak of my game.'

He was silent for a long time, head bowed slightly and eyes directed, unfocused, somewhere near his shoes. Martha was

unsure whether she had vanquished a foe here, or gone too far
and found confirmation of her own fears.

'I need to think hard about this,' he said, eventually. 'Can we
talk again?'

TWENTY-FOUR

In September, Martha discovered a vacant room directly below Joey's attic. It was shaped more conventionally and had in it a single bed, a table and, most valuably, a wardrobe. Joey found her a key from a board behind a door in the kitchen. The board had on it a dozen large iron keys, each with a paper tag tied on by string, the tags bearing room numbers in faded cursive.

She hung up her work clothes and arranged everything else in the drawers. Her shoes she placed neatly, side by side, in the cavity below the hanging space, and she set out makeup, a perfume bottle, jewellery and other necessities in front of a small mirror on the table.

Winter had given way to spring again, magnolia flowers appearing like clumped snow in the grey mornings. Martha was still living between the pub and her flat, trying to maintain a little distance, despite the urge to be ever closer to Joey. He never came to her flat, and she never pushed the issue. She understood he belonged to the building, and this suited her fine.

She hung a backpack on the hook behind the bedroom door: it contained a pair of maroon Doc Martens she'd picked up from an op shop, already covered in grease and stains, a butcher's apron and a pair of safety goggles. Joey had suggested it was the kit of a serial killer, but its function was entirely innocent. Every Wednesday, she slung it over a shoulder and walked to the community centre. The Smoking Nun was teaching her to 'cater-bake', her term for the giant dinner trays she produced. The linear burns on Martha's hands and wrists, the soreness in her feet and calves, felt like the achievement of something real. One evening she sliced a long peel of skin and flesh off the side of an index finger grating carrot, and she watched the wound scab over, turn pink and fade through the weeks until it resolved in a flat scar that rewarded her with the short story of that Wednesday every time she looked at it.

She lay with Joey in his room at night, and read and talked, nestled in the crook of his arm by the light of the single lamp, dim enough to only blur the distinction between darkness and light. To get ready for work in the morning, she had to descend the spiral staircase to the passageway, then walk the length of it to the bathroom, boards springing and popping under the worn carpet beneath her bare feet in the dark. At the end of the passageway, after the bathroom and next to the top of the lower stairway, was the door marked 'Committee Room'. Not once had Joey mentioned this room. She tested the doorhandle one morning, and felt an illicit thrill in doing so, but it was locked.

In the early morning, the bathroom could be bitterly cold, even after she'd pulled the cord to operate the wall-mounted radiator and filled the space with the stink of smouldering cobwebs. When the radiator and the steam from the shower had done their work and the worst of the chill was dispelled, she would wrap herself in a towel and scuttle back along the passageway to the dressing room beneath Joey's attic. More than once on these pre-dawn dashes, Martha glimpsed shadowy movements along the skirting boards. They were always at the corners of her vision, always obscured by the gloom. Finally, one morning, a distinctive squeak gave shape to the movements: rats. She had known this already, she thought, but the idea still horrified her. She raised it with Joey. How, she asked him, did a pub with no customers and no stock of food have a problem with rats?

He shrugged. 'They've always been here.'

'But how?' she countered. 'The pub moves. The rats would have to be permanent residents.' The oddest things were increasingly assumed between them.

Joey only shrugged again. 'I guess they are, then. Besides, we haven't moved for a while.'

'I wanted to ask you about that. Why haven't we moved?'

Joey didn't answer for a long time. 'Are you happy?'

'Yes, of course, I—'

'Here? With me?'

'Yes, both of those things.'

'Then it shouldn't matter, should it?'

She agreed with him and let the matter drop, but it troubled her. She wondered if the pub was vulnerable when it settled.

She took to arming herself against the rats with a broom as she walked the passageway. And in this mode one morning, returning from a shower wrapped in a bath towel and thrusting the broom at a rat she'd cornered against the skirting board, she ended up outside Nan's room. The unfortunate animal backed itself up against the timber and, for a second, Martha felt sorry for it. Then she jammed the broom down hard, expecting to feel the squished bulk of the rat beneath it. Instead, she struck the empty skirting board with a loud bang. She cursed under her breath and jabbed the broom down again at where the rat had stopped. There was another miss, another loud bang, and the bedroom door swung open.

The movement gave Martha such a fright that she gasped and pressed a hand against the towel at her chest. Nan emerged in a heavily quilted dressing gown decorated with a pattern of palm trees and lotuses. Her hair was wild. On her feet were slippers that looked like parrots or macaws. Nothing about the woman's demeanour suggested the banging had given her a fright; rather, she looked irritated. Martha stared into her eyes, her once-beautiful face. The creases aligned themselves towards the expression of happiness, yet here they were, pressed into service as a fearsome snarl.

'For Pete's sake,' she snapped, her voice both polished and ordinary, like a cricket commentator's. 'Can you do that somewhere else, woman?'

Martha could only stare, open-mouthed. The first light of morning slashed its way into the heart of the building, streaming through the colourful room behind Nan. 'But there was a rat.'

'Of course there are rats, idiot.' Nan had her fists on her hips now, her feet planted indelicately wide. The parrots looked east and west. 'They're perfectly fine. You, on the other hand ...'

'Me what?' Martha felt her voice quaking, and she knew the sulphurous old bird could sense her fear.

'You're not wanted here. Plank-faced whore. Take your broom and buzz off.'

Martha looked dumbly at the broom.

'Nobody wants you around.'

Martha took a breath, felt bolder. 'Joey wants me around.'

'What the boy wants isn't the end of the matter.' She glared once more at Martha and slammed the door.

* * *

Martha hadn't needed to call the taxi again, because the pub hadn't moved for weeks. It maintained a steady presence overlooking a small park on the corner of Moor and Brewarrina streets. Gradually, its clientele built up as people were able to find it and return to it. Groups were forming, referring to themselves as regulars. There were demands: for food, for advance bookings, and even for rooms, and Joey was suddenly run off his feet. Nan disappeared from the bar during these weeks, although Martha was dimly aware of her presence from her coughs and shuffles behind the decorated door upstairs. Each night at the end of trading, Joey would patiently usher out the last of the stayers, collect the till drawers, the smokes and the tea set, and take them upstairs to Nan, though he didn't invite Martha to join the ritual again.

The rats increased their numbers by the day. Weeds grew along the gap between the foot of the pub and the footpath. One afternoon, a photographer set up a tripod in the park opposite and began taking photographs. As she walked home from the city tram, Martha found the man there and asked him what he was doing. He was a historian, he said, and he was puzzled about this building, so out of its era. It didn't appear in any of the main books.

Martha's alarm began to grow.

* * *

Although she had never deliberately made a secret of her life at the Cherrywood, it was equally true that Martha had told nobody else about it. Nobody except Bird.

Alone in her flat one night, she pondered the problem. She believed he wouldn't report any of their conversations to her employers, and she needed to test her theories on him. So she found his card and dialled his number. She waited until late in the evening to ring, expecting an answering machine, but evidently he had a diversion to his home line, as he picked up the phone.

'Can we talk again?' she asked him.

'Of course.' His voice was reassuring, as if he had been expecting the call. 'Do you mean now?'

'No, that's nice of you, but I'll come in.'

When she put the phone down, Martha examined the pinboard she had started making over a year ago. If maps were the scriptures of settled thought, about landscapes and history, then she had found a glitch in the iron will of cartography. The lists of names and dates. And in the centre of the board, the three rules. She took the piece of paper off the board and wrote down a fourth:

RULE FOUR
People don't control the pub.

And then, holding her breath with trepidation, she added another.

RULE FIVE
The pub stops moving if anyone falls in love.

TWENTY-FIVE

In the end, the timing was so tight that Thomas feared his wife
and child would miss the *Cherrywood*'s maiden voyage.

He pored over the calendar with Rosstrevor to determine
the perfect date for the maiden voyage, allowing an extra month
for Lucy and Annabelle to arrive, given any delays, and the need
to settle in. They opted for Saturday, 5 April, when the weather
might still be mild and the bay would likely be flat. The football
season was still a month away, and Melbourne's well-heeled
would be looking for a day out.

He notified the newspapers and sat down for interviews,
swallowing his dread. When he could, he offered them Carville –
'available only in the mornings due to his heavy commitments of
an afternoon'. Carville would wink and grin and promise tickets
for wives and mistresses, and make outrageous claims Thomas
would sometimes have to step in and correct. He was, however,
a wonderful salesman, and, more than once, Thomas wondered
if the man was better suited as a promoter than a mariner. The
journalists loved to know they were talking to 'the master', and
Carville peppered his commentary with obscure nautical terms,
which they would ask him to spell as they studiously took them
down. It gave the enterprise a ring of authenticity, even if he was
something of a song-and-dance man.

The articles began to appear, building to a crescendo as April
approached. Thomas was delighted to find the commissioning

of the *Cherrywood* was exactly on schedule. The days were filled with more trials: testing water systems, lights, instruments and particularly the steam engine. The work was done at the wharf, alongside the shore systems that needed just as much scrutiny: ticketing, boarding and disembarking, entertainment.

Silas and his son loaded tremendous amounts of coal into the hold and burned it day after day, checking temperatures and tolerances and soot deposits. They were both, father and son, limbs attached to the same unyielding core. Strong, dour, uninterested in conversation, they were what Thomas's mother had called 'born workers', a trait she admired in domestic staff.

A new moon appeared. His wife was coming. His dear child was coming. He ploughed on, buoyed by hope and beset at times by the familiar darkness, by the loneliness that blanketed everything. Carville bounced around him like a heedless pup.

On the Tuesday before the launch, the tickets sold out. Still Thomas's family had not arrived, and he fretted hourly. The austral stars exploded over him in a profusion he had never experienced before, as he walked the streets to and from the berth at St Kilda at the oddest hours. On the Wednesday, the couta fisherman at the pier greeted him in his customary way.

'Vrenfevver. How's the boat?'

'Wonderful, thank you, Septimus. How's the fishing?'

'Bah. No fucking fish.'

Thomas looked into the disappointed eyes, framed by wiry hairs that sprung from his brows and the bulb of his nose. 'There seem to be fish in your bucket.' He pointed to the catch, trying for an encouraging smile.

'Hmph. Shit fish.'

'What do you think of the weather?'

'For your big launch?' The fisherman assumed the air of a man who had seen every imaginable folly and could only laugh. 'Couldna picked a worse time, if you arks me.'

'Really? I've heard no word of trouble. Why do you say that?'

'Straight southerly. Never get em this time o year, but yer gettin one.'

'On Saturday? Are you sure?'

'Never been surer. Southerly. Pig of a wind. I won't even fish. Might go see the dogs.'

Thomas had no idea which dogs these were. The sea was glassy, the horizon made vague by an autumnal haze.

'An with them big tides,' the fisherman went on. 'Big tides. Arks me, Vrenfevver, I wouldn't be out in that thing o yours. Not then.'

Thomas thanked the man, not knowing what to make of the advice. The barometer by the door had shown no sign of change. Autumn had made the gauge so steady he'd begun to wonder if the needle had corroded in place at 'FAIR'. Septimus was drinking too much, he decided.

As time passed, and Thomas began to prepare himself for the disappointment of launching the *Cherrywood* in the absence of his family. Then, on the Thursday before the launch, a telephone call came through from the pilot station at the heads. The MS *Cordner* was steaming up the bay. The *Cordner*, embossed on the stationery of Lucy's letters. He dropped everything and raced to Port Melbourne, waiting until a smudge on the horizon became the plume from a smokestack, and a ship came into view. It was a slate-grey morning, the air clean and cool, and the edges of the vessel were sharp against the dull mirror of the sea. He could make out the *Cordner*'s portholes, then flags and railings and, finally, people. They had been apart for more than a year, and the little girl he saw in his imagination would no longer be that way. The ship was bringing him two different people. He choked down the panic.

The steamer neared. The engines surged in reverse and the water around the iron hull boiled. The linesmen hollered to the ship's crew and the hawsers were secured. Thomas's impatience mounted. He pressed forward in the crowd, apologising, and when he still could not see his family, he tried waving his hat. They were taking an eternity to position the gangplank, damn them. Other families had found their loved ones and were waving manically. Pocketbooks flew through the air, tossed by optimists with messages too urgent to await the gangplank. There were flowers, there were crying children. And there was Thomas, beyond anxious now, buffeted by elbows and hips.

When, finally, he found Lucy's smile, the instant was so remarkably clear and intimate that he couldn't remember not seeing it. The curve of her mouth, her teeth, the affection in her eyes. She was no different for the absence, her hair pinned back under a felt hat and her gloved right hand waving at him. The pewter brooch he recognised from their honeymoon gleamed on the dark material of her coat – *her coat* – and his eyes scanned onwards, and there, oh there was his daughter, so much taller and dressed in a paler coat, her face made bright by the sun on her tears.

Lucy leaned down and instructed her to blow a kiss by miming one with her own hand, and Annabelle blew one down to her father, and Thomas felt the months fall away and his agonies recede. They were together again and nothing would separate them now.

* * *

The three of them were crushed together on the back seat of a cab, Thomas, in his joy, even forgetting his lifelong antipathy towards motor cars. Lucy described a dull life in Edinburgh, a shapeless mass of time that merely passed, bringing with it nothing memorable or good. Annabelle seemed overcome at first, then found her voice and swung promptly to the other extreme, unable to stop talking about even the most trivial things. Thomas was filled with delight, drinking in the life in her, the character he didn't recall being so apparent a year and a half earlier. Here she was, even more enchanting than he remembered.

He had the driver pass by the pier so he could point out the freshly painted *Cherrywood* to them both. From the distance of the pier's length, they could see the private guard who had been posted – both to stoke intrigue and to keep the curious at bay. He was asleep in his chair.

Thomas had thought about this moment. He didn't want them to stop and inspect the vessel yet: the anticipation could be stretched out. He had booked dinner for them at a restaurant in the city, and he saved his descriptions of the paddlesteamer for then. 'In only two days, you will see her sail,' he told Annabelle over their meal. He saw, or thought he saw, admiration in her eyes that he had caused this miracle to happen. The girl's barrage of questions gradually faltered, and soon enough Thomas caught her eyelids drooping at the table.

Later, at home, he felt nervous about being alone with Lucy after so long, about how he could possibly be entitled to take her in his arms. What she might want from him, or not want. Time had robbed him of sureness. Somehow, she knew this, and she threw her arms around his neck and began kissing him before they had reached the bed. Over the grinding months of separation, he had simply existed, nothing more, his days measured by sleep and waking. Life was mere chronology, until now.

Now he was alive, and his fingertips traced across her cool skin and he could hear her breathing, feel her heart. To be alive was to be conscious of someone else's aliveness, he thought, the tiny sensations of her hair falling on his face and his shoulder, the softness of her and the mystery of her movements, both surrender and volition. They rolled over each other and every murmur and gasp was so perfect he wondered how on earth he had survived, how he had pushed this desire down so it wouldn't torment him. The world's beauty was here in its entirety, in the intimacies revealed to him, and titanic fears were helpless before the brush of her eyelash on his cheek.

The Friday was among the happiest days Thomas could remember. They walked together, taking in the still morning air that he had come to consider chilly, until he realised his wife and daughter, with their more recent memories of Edinburgh, thought it mild. They looked at the beach and he pointed out the grey line on the northwest horizon that was Williamstown. When they had eaten, he prepared the horse and led it with Annabelle riding side-saddle, the bridle in one of his hands, his wife's hand in the other. People recognised him, bid them 'g'morning' and doffed their hats to Lucy. He was recognisable not as the son of the legendary Malthus Wrenfether, not for being wealthy, but for bringing something to the city, a whiff of faraway Europe. Beside him, Lucy smiled to see him acknowledged in this way. She was amused by his evident pride, yet also uncritically happy for him.

The paddlesteamer shone brilliantly at rest in the sunlight, and Annabelle gasped when at last she had a clear view of her.

'There she is! The sum of all our efforts!' Thomas exclaimed.

The vessel rested so lightly on the water, it seemed possible she would float away on the air, that she was the progeny of zeppelins or greenhouses or the Crystal Palace of Hyde Park. There were staff everywhere, cleaning and provisioning and checking, and there on the high bridge behind the smokestacks was the unmistakable profile of Carville, arms raised above his head and hips swivelling in a libidinous dance.

'Ah,' said Thomas, biting down on his alarm at the spectacle. 'You will meet our master. I will be very interested to see what you make of him.' He thought Lucy would know how to read the man, his charm and his nonsense.

The men around the gangway welcomed the family aboard with a guard of honour. As Thomas crossed above the strip of seawater between vessel and wharf, he checked the four mooring lines: at the bow and stern and the two amidships, passing either side of the louvred sponson that housed the paddlewheel. He had been thrilled to find on the sea trial that the delicate louvres kept the water from splashing up onto the passengers, yet allowed for a pleasing sound of rushing water as each paddle blade emerged and feathered, spilling its burden of water into the centre of the wheel.

Inside the cabin, an old man sat practising on a double bass, while the provisioners bustled about them with crates and boxes. Annabelle ran the length of the room, breathless with amazement at the piano and the artworks, the sunlight through the coloured glass illuminating the timbers. Outside, a gull glared in the window, and she laughed and made a face at it.

Thomas took his daughter onto the deck and squatted beside her. He pointed up at the space between the tin funnels. There was the silhouette of the bronze weathervane he had commissioned: a fat, exaggerated hull and three masts in full sail, a stylised pennant streaming behind the stern. It had cost more than the rudder blade assembly, and was already greening in the sea air, but it was money well invested.

'It spins to show us which way the wind is going,' he said to her. 'Your clever mother designed it. Isn't it beautiful?' Annabelle did not answer: she was awestruck. 'Come along, little friend,' he said, and led her by the hand back into the cabin.

Inside, Lucy stayed close to Thomas, an arm tucked under his. When they passed through doorways, she relaxed her grip, then took up his arm again. It filled him with happiness, as did the brushing of her skirts against his leg, and her contented smile as she watched their daughter darting about the cabin.

There was a sound of singing, something Vaudeville growing louder, and the athletic legs of Carville appeared in the spiral stairway that led up to the bridge. He swept into the room, hair still wild from the breeze, and lit up at the sight of Lucy.

'*Ma chérie!*' he cried. 'Finally, we have our duchess of the silver seas!'

Thomas studied Lucy closely, and saw she was amused, maybe even flattered. You had to know her eyes to see it.

'You must be Captain Carville,' she said, her tone formal and faintly sceptical as she extended a hand. Carville took the hand and kissed it – Thomas knew this would be his way – then swept his free arm wide.

'Look at what your brilliant husband has done, madam! Behold the luxury! We are on the brink of something magnificent!' The crew laughed and Carville looped his arm in Lucy's other one, and with a look of mock-scandal on his face asked Thomas if it would be improper for him to show the duchess the wheelhouse. Thomas smiled in resignation and Lucy favoured him with a furtive roll of her eyes.

He wished those brief couple of hours would never end. That night, he told Annabelle stories about the magical steamboat and the characters who would sail on her, and when her eyes began to close, he placed a kiss on her forehead and shut the door silently as he left.

Thomas and Lucy lay together in the half-dark, fingers entwined, and he knew from her breathing that she was not asleep. He waited, his head on Lucy's naked chest, listening to her heart beating. When her voice came out of the darkness, it registered through her chest as well as in the night air.

'Where did you find Mr Carville?'

How had the man charmed his way into the room? 'He appeared one day in the yard, looking for work.'

'Where had he been before then?'

'Oh, navy, he said.'

There was a silence. Then: 'Did you check his history?'

'It's not something one would lie about, serving in the navy.' He could hear the defensiveness in his voice. 'You either did or you didn't.'

'Yes.' Three beats of her heart. 'Did he have any letters of recommendation? And what was the reason for his discharge?'

Thomas grunted in frustration, a helpless noise that was meant to suggest he was too close to sleep for this discussion.

'Mr Ximenon was the same, wasn't he?' she suggested. 'Just appeared one day ...'

He grunted again, then said, 'It was me that appeared. Ximenon was already on the board.'

'I do wish ... I know you have worked so hard, but I do wish you would take more care when you put your faith in these people.'

He resented this change of tone, this inquisition after the months of hard work. 'Don't you see?' he replied. 'The world is arranged thus. I can't say how it is among women, but men – there are some for whom life is a performance. There might be nothing under the surface – no-one knows. It's all magnetism, *charisma*. And then there are the rest, men who will only ever be the audience for it, wishing to be brought into such a man's light.'

'Dear God, Thomas. You are neither of those men.'

'Carville cannot help being what he is – my eyes are open to it. And I cannot help being drawn to him.'

'He is even here between us, then.'

'Please don't be foolish. He will bring us good fortune, and that is what matters.'

They spoke no further of the man, and, in time, the depths of the night took them both.

TWENTY-SIX

Bird wore a loose linen shirt that made him look relaxed, bohemian. Martha could see the thinness of his chest where the shirt draped towards its buttons, the chest of a sullen guitarist. Which was fine with her. She was distracting herself. He was watching her.

'You made the appointment,' he said. 'Which is good. I'd like you to tell me why you did.'

'I haven't been entirely honest with you,' she began.

'I know.'

Martha considered how he could have known. Perhaps her body language had betrayed her. Or the firm had had her followed and had reported the observations to Bird. This was idiotic, paranoid.

'I've been living in the pub. With Joey.'

'Is it making you happy?'

'Yes. Yes, it is.'

'Is this a sustainable way of life? I mean, can you live there and keep working as you are?'

'Does the firm need you to find that out?' She regretted asking this: it was unnecessarily aggressive. But it didn't seem to bother him.

'If we're looking at your overall wellbeing, it's a fundamental question, isn't it?'

It was, she knew it. 'I don't know. I'm still feeling my

way into it. But you asked me why I made the appointment.'
She hesitated, then plunged on. 'There's this other thing.
All this time I've been in love with Joey, the pub's stopped
moving. Hasn't moved in weeks and weeks. You remember
how I've been trying to figure out the rules about how the pub
behaves?'

Again, incredibly, he nodded as though it was the most
pedestrian thing.

'I think there's another one. If Joey's in love, or someone's in
love in the pub, it stops.'

Bird was still for a moment. Then he raised a thoughtful
finger. 'Let's park that for now, and we'll start with – suppose
you're right. Suppose love stops the pub. Does it matter?'

'Yes, I'm pretty sure it does. I think the pub's vulnerable.
People are starting to wander in, and it's just Joey in there, apart
from the old lady who lives in one of the rooms upstairs, and
other than counting the tills at night, she doesn't do any of the
work, and Joey's not going to cope, and if the pub needs to move
around, the longer it stays in one place, the fewer options it has
to be elsewhere when the available corner blocks are getting
taken up.'

'Mm. Yes.' Bird reached behind himself and took up the
notepad he had used in their previous session. He thumbed
through until he had the page he wanted. 'You might remember,
when we ended off last time, I said to you I wanted to think
more about the mythology – no, not the right term – the *psychic*
elements of a moving pub.' He thumbed a couple of pages. 'I did
some reading, you see. Some thinking. When you were little,
did someone read you the Faraway Tree books?'

'Ha! Joey asked me the same thing once. And yes, I read
them to myself.'

'That's interesting in its own right. Anyway, do you recall
how the land at the top of the tree would change without
warning?'

Martha stared at him, thinking he was mocking her. 'You think I'm living out children's books?' But he appeared completely sincere.

'No. I think the classics among children's books are signposts to the psyche. But let's bring it back to the pub. What's your understanding of the mechanics of the movements?'

'There are other people involved,' she said. 'People who come and do things like connect the utilities and deliver things, and the taxi driver who seems to know where the pub is every time.'

Bird was tapping his fingers on his knees, thinking hard. 'To some extent, in Blyton's world, physical elements can cross over from one realm to another. The children can visit the lands at the top, as you can visit the pub. Dame Washalot can tip her water out onto the ground – that is, beyond the tree – so it enters the understood world. There's a means of transition – Moon-Face's slide. And the Enchanted Wood works like a liminal zone between the two entities. You follow?'

She nodded.

'And what's the rule? What's the really big rule?' He seemed lit by some disturbing energy.

'I … It's been so long. I don't remember.'

'*The children must leave before the land at the top moves on.* To do otherwise, no matter the temptation, invites disaster. Tell me, have you ever been inside the pub through a move?'

'No.'

'Well, I have a feeling you mustn't. Forget Blyton for a minute. Think of this as an analogy for our own orientation in the world. There is a point at which you may be tempted into surrendering to this other state of being, and if you do …'

'None of this sounds very scientific.'

'I'm not a scientist.'

Martha decided to take a risk. 'Aren't you interested in whether I'm making all of this up? Whether it's *real*?'

'Ah. Whether it's real or not is of surprisingly little importance. If it's real to you, nothing else needs to concern us. You're experiencing it subjectively, just as I'm experiencing my reality over here. Are you comfortable with that?'

'For now.'

'Good, because I want to take this further. A cardinal tree rising through worlds is a potent symbol. Blyton didn't invent it. Think of "Jack and the Beanstalk". Norse myth. The ordinary mortal – you – leaves the roots at the foot of the tree and, as you ascend, you approach clouds. Roots to clouds. Strength, dependability, to vapour. The Babylonians, in their vanity, built a tower to heaven, and they left the known world by climbing it, and God struck it down.'

'It's a pub, not a tree.'

It was her habit to cut through verbal thickets like this.

He laughed. 'You know as well as I do, the elements are there. The grounded life that doesn't satisfy. The portal, the other world. *Ascent*. Whether those elements are exclusively inside you, or whether I could go to Fitzroy and find the same pub and the same bartender, is beside the point.'

'So, this is about me being unhappy at work?'

'I mean no disrespect, but it's not that simple. The things we hate and avoid are the raw materials from which we make the things we desire. It's the whole gist of the freedom thing. You need your career. It's the only track on which you can race that souped-up intellect of yours. But you hate the firm, you hate the economic notion of selling your life in little pieces. You hate the lifestyle, most of the people. So, you build out of it a world where time can't be bought and sold, where it's ephemeral.'

'So, it *is* a figment of my imagination.'

'There's simply no telling. I'm sorry.'

They sat in defeated silence for a moment. It was Bird who broke it.

'Martha, I wonder if I might share something of my experience with you.'

She nodded.

'I was involved in an activist group when I was your age. About unionism, not that it matters particularly. Hang on … No. I was a bit younger, actually. Still at uni. Anyway, they sent me to Canberra, to this big summit at the old Parliament House. And I don't know how it happened, but I wound up in a motel room by myself for about ten days and – someone had paid for it – and I had an … episode. Hard to define. I read feverishly, by myself on the couch in the motel room. Raymond Carver, for whatever reason. And then I spent days in the lobby of Parliament House waiting for MPs to come out, and I'd accost them about our cause. Literally march up and harangue them. Side note – it's remarkable we can do such a thing in this country. Maybe not such a good thing. Mostly, they indulged me, but looking back at it, I can see that a couple of them, especially the female ones, were edging away nervously. "I'll make sure my electorate office gives you a call," sort of thing. I think I thought I was a major element in the national conversation, and that's ridiculous – I was a kid, a volunteer – but it was important to me to buttonhole these politicians and tell them our demands.

'I did a lot of walking, a lot of sitting in the sun, letting my mind spin. And then I'd write – reams and reams of stuff about the cause – and late at night I'd screw it up and throw it in the bin, then I'd get up and unscrew it and read it over and add more to it, and then the same cycle, start to finish, again. And I remember I went to a menswear shop and I bought a silk tie that cost a hundred and sixty dollars. I still remember the price – an absolute fortune. I was totally convinced I needed that tie and I wore it for my haranguing work in the Parliament House lobby. And when the stint was over, I got on a plane home and went back to normal life like it had never happened.'

She listened intently, sensing this had been an unusual confidence.

'The point is,' he continued, 'I was very much like you when I was your age. I was a perfectionist. I was awkwardly intelligent, and by that I mean I could think through big concepts without ever delivering the cheeky quip that would endear me to others. I suspect you would feel similarly. You and I, we dwell on things. The volume is up, sensors twitching. There are times in our lives when the ordinary boundaries of our thinking, of our behaviour, can evaporate and we are left feeling our way into new modes of being. It's not something diagnosable, I don't think. What I experienced might go close to being framed as a manic episode, except there's nothing else in my personal history to support such a diagnosis. So, life goes on. And with you, I have no concern about you experiencing this thing. It's your life and your business entirely. But I don't want to see you damage your future prospects. I don't want to see others exploit you, or see you lose your way.'

He was looking at her with concern now.

'I don't want to tell you to do anything. I'm not going to recommend you get medicated or refer you on to anybody. I suspect your employers would like me to, to be blunt. You know lawyers. "Is there an answer? Why don't you just fix it?" There are things about us that aren't amenable to being "fixed". I want you to stay in touch, maybe come back sometime and tell me how everything's unfolding. I'd be very interested. I'm sure you could send my bill to your lovely employers again. Does that sound okay?'

It did, and she thanked him. She left the room believing she had discovered a like-minded soul, someone who, in his own words, was familiar with new modes of being.

TWENTY-SEVEN

There were people on the streets who seemed strange to her. People of whom she would have thought nothing in the past – slightly odd, out of place maybe. But cities harboured difference, and difference was no reason to stare. It was the context of an altered world, her new eyes, that lent these strangers added significance.

A woman with irises of caramel, a face that was old and wild and worn, passing in a cloud of smoky incense.

A man wiping his wet hands on a spattered apron as he approached, muttering fiercely and peering at her with intent.

It was the city, nothing more.

Darkness was falling when Martha reached the Cherrywood. The shark eyeballed her from across the road. Nothing had moved, and this came as no surprise to her. She was about to enter through the pub's corner door when she saw that, down the side street, a panel of timber latticework had been removed at ground level and was leaning against the wall.

She stooped to the opening, an arm-span wide and, when her eyes adjusted to the half-light, she saw Joey under the pub, about ten metres in, lying on his front and facing away from her.

She called out to him, and he grunted a reply, rolled over, but didn't otherwise move. So, she dropped to her hands and knees and placed her satchel just inside the cavity, then crawled in after him. The ground was cool under her knees. Spiderwebs had formed between the underside of the building and the ground, and when she reached Joey, he was propped on one side, resting on his elbow and studying a particularly dense web that stretched from a long beam under the pub onto some scraps of timber.

'Hi,' she said.

'Hi.' Joey showed no indication this was an unusual place to meet. Spikes of daylight crossed the gloomy space from the vents around the perimeter. As she looked up, Martha saw how the whole structure rested on the ground, on long heavy beams. The plumbing that came through from above ran along the underside of the floor but did not penetrate the ground. There were heating ducts, electrical cabling, and here and there what appeared to be hatches into the ground-floor rooms.

She suddenly felt foolish, lying there in the narrow space, facing him. Her work clothes were covered in muck already, and she could tell there was detritus in her hair from the webs and grimy crevices above. He was watching her closely, and the acuity of his gaze made him beautiful in the half-light.

'Can I ask you a thing?' he said, and when she didn't object, he continued. 'How do you – how do you feel about me?'

He couldn't have seen her blushing. She was panicking, trying to guess what the right answer to this question might be. She tested several responses in her head and each seemed fraught with danger. So she stalled. 'You aren't going to ask me how my day was?'

He only continued to watch her, a hopeful half-smile on his lips.

Here goes nothing. 'I feel all sorts of things, Joey. I'm … Okay, I'm very attracted to you.' Blushing again. '*Very.* I feel like I don't know you, and maybe the not knowing is my fault, that I don't want to …' She stammered to a halt. The sensation of being stranded like this was unfamiliar. *Fuck. Idiot!* 'I almost don't want to know the other stuff … just bliss out on never knowing.'

His head was resting on one hand and he reached out with the other to take her hand. 'Do you think you might love me?'

'I think it's very possible that I do.'

'Yes.' He said it calmly.

'*Yes*? What's that mean? Yes, you love me too, or yes, that was what you were expecting to hear? Yes, people often love me? What am I supposed to do with "yes"? Jesus …'

He was still peering at her. She had had this exchange once before, with poor Aaron, but she'd never otherwise reached a point in a relationship where declarations of love were tested. Then the understanding came to her, filling her body from the centre outwards like nausea. 'You're worried about the hotel, aren't you.'

'What do you mean?' His eyes gave the game away.

'It's another rule. We haven't discussed it, but I've worked it out. Love stops the pub moving.'

Joey's sorrow was now unconcealed. 'Everything down here's binding together.' He rubbed thoughtfully with his thumb at a beam beside his face. 'Everything's settling. The pub hasn't moved in ages—'

'So, is it just my love that's doing this? Do we have to love each other for it to happen? You could step in at any moment—'

'There's Nan. There's me. This is our *home*.'

'You could come and live with me in Richmond.' Why was she having to offer it? Why hadn't he answered and set it to rest? She was angry now. 'Why does it matter if the pub stops moving? You could build up some customers. Ha! Imagine running this business like it's a business.'

'If we stop moving, people start to ask questions. The stolen electricity. The lack of a licence. Rates, heritage overlays. We wouldn't pass anything, not the simplest inspection. Health department would be all over us. And once we shut, what then? Then we board the place up. Then someone buys it, demolishes it. Then it's over. The only protection we have is to keep moving.'

As she listened, she noticed the quality of the timber where Joey was still rubbing away with his thumb. Smooth, straight-grained, perfect.

'I'm part of this place, Martha. I belong here. And that's how you like it.'

'How I *like it*? Who do you think you are?' A strangled sob caught her by surprise. 'So, what are you saying, huh? You need to stay here and stop loving me so the building survives and you and Nan can go on doing your empty pub stuff? Sounds like what *she's* wanted the whole time.' Martha started to back away from him, with her head stooped to avoid the beams overhead, and the manoeuvre felt ridiculous, the world's most awkward way of storming off. She had shuffled halfway to the opening in the lattice when, inevitably, she smacked her head. As she cursed and rubbed it, he called to her.

'There's Nan to think about.'

Martha stopped rubbing. 'Who the hell's Nan, anyway?'

'She's kind of my grandmother. Or – no. It's a nickname.'

'*Not exactly* your grandmother. I should be expecting these things by now.' The exasperation overcame her. 'So what's the rule for Nan, then?'

He was looking down mournfully. 'If the pub dies, she dies with it. The Cherrywood's keeping her alive.'

Martha saw the pinboard back in Richmond, saw the list, and mentally added to it. *Rule Six. The pub is keeping Nan alive.* She waited until he had to look up at her. Then she spoke, carefully and deliberately.

'I wish I'd never said I love you.'

* * *

Night fell, and Martha avoided Joey.

She took the handful of things she had left in his room and placed them in the spare room below, then kept her Wednesday date with the Smoking Nun. The woman did not invite confidences, though she had revealed a quiet warmth over the months. Martha wanted to talk about the things that were troubling her, but the problem had become so large, the story so unlikely, that she couldn't imagine explaining it all again.

So, she waited until the ping pong combatants had finished their matches and the speakers had come in from the small room and the singers from the larger room, and their scruffy footwear had made its homely rumble on the floor, then she took the milkshake containers full of cutlery and set the tables, having first laid down the plastic tablecloths that hid the lethal surfaces from the diners.

Fish fingers, Marathon dim sims and a tri-coloured combination of corn kernels, peas and cauliflower from huge frozen bags. The visitors shook their salt over it, pecked away with the soy sauce bottles. They slopped green cordial from plastic jugs and guzzled it to slake the thirst caused by the salt.

Martha stood at the double sinks in her butcher's apron, scouring an oven tray with a ball of steel wool, while the nun made a shopping list. Neither of them spoke. Martha was always careful, in such proximity to the nun, not to inadvertently make bodily contact with her. To do so would have been disrespectful, she thought. The woman seemed to guard the space around her with crisp authority. Martha longed for such confidence, the unambiguous self-knowledge of it.

'Got the health department coming this week,' the nun said out of nowhere.

'The kitchen's fine,' Martha replied. 'What do they want?'

'It's about the tables. Bloody Rodney.' She said it without anger. 'He's rung their hotline to report the asbestos. And now they have to go through a *protocol*.' A caustic sneer appeared on her tired face, not for Rodney, Martha thought, but for the torments of bureaucracy. 'How did we ever get along before protocols, hey?'

'Do you want to move the tables somewhere? I've got a place I could store them for a while.'

The nun considered this through a long drag at her smoke, as though every option, even the devious ones, was up for grabs. She laid the pen down.

'Nup,' she said, eventually. 'Rodney's told them how the whole place works, evidently.'

'You must be furious,' Martha ventured.

'No,' she said. 'Rodney is the way he is. It's not malice, he just sees threats everywhere. We'll be right.' She took up the pen, doodled on a corner of her list. 'Sixty people out there tonight. It'd be a big call for them to shut us down over it.'

Martha went on scrubbing, watched the grey water under the suds, the shipwrecked pots in the depths. One department did not care about other ones, she thought. The Smoking Nun was wrong. This was just like her own work at Caspians. The wheels would turn implacably, and nothing was ever personal. The consequences, visited on real people at the far end of the system, were never visible.

* * *

At the end of the night, Martha bundled up the tea towels and lugged them in a huge cloth sack across several blocks to the laundromat.

An ordinary Victorian shopfront, graffitied and modified over the decades, at least until the seventies. The sign hanging down from under the awning said 'LAUNDRETTE' in red block capitals, but the signwriting on the front window said 'COIN LAUNDROMAT'. Inside, it was painted a cold grey-white, made starker by the intense fluorescent lighting. A colourful mural high on one wall above the machines, the marks of generations of students who would have frequented the place. On the other wall, a sign that read 'NO DRYING ONLY –

DRYERS ARE FOR WASHING CUSTOMERS ONLY' and
a tourism poster of Pamukkale. It looked familiar, but, try as she
might, she couldn't identify where she'd seen it.

Martha thought about the sign for some time. It didn't
initially make sense. Why would you wash a customer here,
and why would you do it in the dryer? She tried punctuating it
various ways in her head – no 'drying only' – and rearranging it –
no only-drying – but eventually she decided it was perfect.

The emptiness of the place, the waiting machines. Lids up on
the washers, hatches open on the dryers. *Choose me.* She looked
around nervously. Darkness on the street outside. There was a
locked door in the back wall – was there a family out there,
counting coins? The machine was a Speed Queen, its cream-
painted surface scratched with names and dates, presumably
done with the very coins that fed it.

She thought she heard someone come in, and she looked
around again as the tea towels tumbled in the washing machine
she'd chosen. No-one, nothing, just a large, dried leaf dragging
its way past on the footpath outside. She was calm. An empty
shop was not a cause for worry.

She fed her coins into the machine, then plunged the lever on
the slide. The machine rumbled into life, and, amid the noise,
she didn't hear a person entering the shop, though her peripheral
vision registered the movement.

She looked towards the door and a man was there. He was
short, dark-haired, with heavy eyebrows and a thick moustache.
He wore torn and dirtied clothes, a heavy serge jacket over suit
pants and boots. It wasn't the grime on the clothes that caught
Martha's attention but the fact that they – and the boots –
were burnt. There were charred edges at the sleeves and cuffs,
blackened holes here and there where it appeared a spark had
landed and then been patted out as it smouldered.

There was something in his hand that was long and pointed
at the floor. At first she thought it was a gun, and her heart

leapt in fright. She forced herself to look again and saw it was a jemmy bar, which was no less frightening in a deserted coin laundry.

The man was muttering to himself, looking around. He glanced at Martha, giving her no more attention than if she were a washing machine. Then he found the fuse box on the wall opposite and opened it, eyes darting over the rows of switches and fuses. He selected one and applied the jemmy bar, wrenching the fuse violently from the panel. There was a spark and a crackling noise. As the man jumped back from the fuse box, dropping the bar and shaking his hand in pain, Martha saw the washing machine had stopped.

'Hey!' she said.

The man looked at her, still shaking his hand. He returned to the fuse box and pressed the fuse back into its position. They both looked at the washing machine as it restarted. He chose another fuse and yanked it out. Nothing happened this time, and the man pocketed it and left.

Martha was alone again, the only sound a clanking from the washing machine. She looked at the floor and saw the man had left a trail of fine ash. It formed a penumbra around the shape of his boots, where he had been shocked by the fuse box. She leaned down and ran a finger along the lino, through the ash.

She brought her finger up to her face and licked the ash. It tasted exactly as she thought it would. She dusted the finger on the leg of her jeans and returned to her vigil at the Speed Queen.

* * *

When she arrived back at the Cherrywood, the lights were off. The bar door was locked, but she had a key. She let herself in and wandered through the darkness, familiar with the dimensions of the spaces and no longer bumping her body on corners or kicking unexpected nail heads that poked up from the floor.

She and the Cherrywood might finally be coming to terms, she thought; the irony was, it was too late.

She went to the spare room, lay down and stared at the ceiling. It had a plaster rose where the light was suspended by electrical flex, cobwebs around the cornices and enough dust to give the plasterwork a three-dimensional quality.

She needed to leave. She needed to return to who she had been, to find the old determination. Joey had never given of himself, had only passively accepted her into his world – a gesture that required nothing of him. And put to a choice, he had chosen the old hag, his sort-of grandma, over her. Her body twitched as drowsiness began to take her away. One day soon, she promised herself, she would get up an hour earlier, take her things to Richmond on the way to work and never come back here.

She slept fitfully, too cold and then too warm. She writhed about until the blanket had twisted itself around her and her head rested on a mean corner of pillow. The Cherrywood was restless, full of noises and tremors. She could hear the rats, the birds outside, the squeaking of timbers. A possum somewhere, hissing and snarling its tree-punk serenade. She smelled earth and ashes and damp and sawdust. Voices, having their own conversations and also whispering to her things she already knew, or had long forgotten then suddenly remembered. Laughter, sometimes deep and strong and pleasant, and other times cruel, like a joke was being told among the rodents.

Somewhere on the long journey of her sleep that night, the room filled with water, and it sloshed as though it was contained within a glass bowl that was tipping from side to side. The water wasn't drowning her, nor was it cold, and she wondered why anyone had ever drowned, anywhere, when it was so easy to breathe. But she was under something huge and heavy, something labouring on the surface of the water that had filled her room.

The shadows resolved themselves. She was lying under the keel of a boat, looking upwards at the planking of the hull, surrounded by a bright halo of sunlight. The image vanished as soon as it had formed and, in her semi-conscious state, Martha's orientation in the room came askew and she could not work out if she was back at home or still at the pub, if she was in her childhood home or asleep on calm seas in some gorgeous vessel, serenaded by strings.

* * *

When she woke, the light was wrong.

It took her some time to understand the problem. The blind was most of the way down. She stood and raised it, and immediately understood. The shark was nowhere to be seen. The liquidambar tree outside her window was no longer there, and in its place was the brick wall of the back of a cinema.

She felt dizzy, and her balance slewed left. The room smelled new and clean. She knew what it was, and she knew the reasons why.

The pub had moved, and this time she was a party to it.

TWENTY-EIGHT

The day after the Cherrywood's move, Martha's mood was turbulent.

At work, her thoughts returned over and over to Joey and the hotel. There was a curious elation percolating inside her. She was complicit in something secret and impossible. She thought back to the library, to the days when researching the Cherrywood was an uncomplicated pleasure, a game of cat and mouse she was steadily winning.

But she had not yet won. When she reviewed her methods, and the things she had discovered, she knew she was missing a vital piece. The taxi driver had known to come to Caspians. His reappearances weren't coincidence. He had singled out the firm, and her, for a reason. It followed that something about the firm was known to the custodians of the hotel. It maddened her. She knew she could ask the taxi driver, drop the question one day from the back seat, but there was the risk that he might spook, and never collect her again. He might not be the ally he appeared to be. If it could be done, it was better if she found the answer herself.

So, how were the firm and the hotel linked? It wasn't physical, architectural. One was rooted in the Yarra's sediments by a network of carparks and basements, soaring into the sky and made from Chinese granite, Pilbara steel, glass and cement and plastics. The other was timber and lay so lightly on the ground it resembled furniture. The two things could not be more different.

The people bore no obvious connection. Though both the firm and the hotel stretched back over Melbourne's decades, Martha's research had never tipped out a surname to link the two. In their brochures, Caspians talked about 'eighty years of Melbourne history', meaning the firm was roughly as old as the hotel. But beyond that boast, the firm showed little interest in its own beginnings. They were a young partnership.

Except, of course, for Enmore.

He had been there every day in the library, apparently absorbed in his own business. No-one knew what he did. No-one *bothered* to know what he did.

She was spinning with a kind of vertigo that had stayed with her since the previous night, a kind of vertigo that the Cherrywood's unseen movement had imparted to her. The building had irradiated her somehow, shaken her deeply, and she was left light-headed. She loaded up the billing software on her computer and entered Enmore's name. A handful of details came up. She chose 'client list', not knowing quite what she would be able to glean from the dozens of names that would appear. So, her first surprise was the list: there was only one name – Ardelean.

She selected 'files', and was surprised again. One file – 'General Advice'.

She pressed 'enter', but it wouldn't open. A small annotation told her it was restricted. She thought hard, scanned the screen for a workaround. There – 'Deed Lodgements'. This time it clicked open, and she gasped.

'Re: Cherrywood Hotel'.

One deed, last checked out of the strongroom two years ago. Before that, it had been six years. Enmore had one client. One file, in fact, and one solitary deed, barely ever looked at. How was this man justifying his presence? She thought of him facing her across the library desks and she understood he'd been watching her.

She wrote the reference number on the back of her hand and closed the terminal.

* * *

She requested the strongroom key from the deeds clerk, and when he asked what time she would be returning the document, she explained she was working late. The clerk, an elderly man, sighed.

'I'm not waiting around for you.'

'Well ...' She planted her feet.

He scowled, pointing to a small safe under his desk. 'Write this down,' he said, and gave her a code, which she also wrote on the back of her hand. 'Put the key back in there when you're done or they'll have me guts for garters.'

She waited until almost everyone was gone, especially Enmore.

As the heavy door swung open, she felt the shiver of entering a holy space. On the day she'd started at the firm, there'd been a tour, and they'd proudly told her the walls of the strongroom were four-hour fire rated. She had tried to imagine the intensity of a fire lasting more than four hours, twenty floors up in an office building. Deeds would be the least of their problems.

The shelves and drawers formed rows from floor to ceiling, filled not with the gemstones and currency of a banker's vault, but with paper, covered in incantations: secrets and promises and Damoclean threats. Voices from beyond the grave, whispering directions to the present world – *You may have this, if you do this* – the courting of absolutes like 'perpetuity' and 'never'. Some of it was on nondescript A4, some on scrolls of parchment with blobs of wax and swirls of cursive.

She used the strongroom every few weeks, and it never failed to unnerve her. What if someone shut the door? But no-one would shut the door without checking – this room, unlike any other room, could never be idly left open. If the door was ajar, someone was in here.

As she pushed deeper in, stepping between the stacks, her claustrophobia increased. It was a crypt. There being no possibility of entry for worms or rodents or for any moisture or warmth, it offered only mummification. She followed the little labels on the shelves that indicated number ranges and, shuffling sideways, she passed down to three digits, two, one … there.

She took the deed, locked the strongroom behind her and rushed to the copier to make a copy. When she was done, she reversed the process, replacing the deed, locking the strongroom again and locking the key in the safe.

Back at her desk, she read the copy she'd made, and ten minutes later, she had clarity.

* * *

The following days proceeded for Martha as storms of fizzing, sparking animus.

She wanted to *work*, to tear into something. She answered questions with a newfound impatience, wrote with open aggression, bordering on contempt. She raced across files, through meetings and in and out of conversations, as though the world was too slow and ponderous for her. In one instant, she felt liberated, secure and afloat; in the next, she was grinding her molars to fight back tears.

The group was gearing up for a trial. An action brought by a desperate and broke single mother who had blown her savings, her credit and eventually her family's money at an interstate pokie venue. Unable to stop, she'd begun siphoning money from her employer. Even then, she'd begged the casino to ban her, and they'd responded by offering her meal vouchers. By the time she was prosecuted over the till-skimming, she'd lost her job, her children and every vestige of her dignity. An enterprising plaintiff lawyer had issued a writ against the casino. And now came the wearing down: a sixty-page 'Request for Further and Better Particulars'.

> *If yes to any of the sub-paragraphs (a)–(f) above, give the usual particulars of any and all such instances, in each case specifying –*
> (i) *How many alcoholic beverages (hereinafter referred to as 'the beverages') the plaintiff consumed;*
> (ii) *Whether the plaintiff, and if not the plaintiff, which other parties, paid for the beverages, in each case specifying the terms upon which the beverages were purchased by those other parties; and …*

Shortly after her redeployment in the Insurance group, she had been appointed to the firm's Plain English committee. Within the same week or even the same day, she might be working on the manual that would be provided to every lawyer in the place, urging them to write and speak like a clear-minded civilian, while simultaneously crafting documents intended to exhaust and confuse with their tortured syntax.

She knew what had happened to the woman in Penrith. The woman's lawyer knew. The court knew, already, through the flurry of documents both sides had filed. And yet, this charade, this pretence at interrogation of the issues, designed to do nothing more than pile up the fees. They'd settle with the woman from Penrith, Martha had no doubt. It'd be enough money to put her back in a rental after the short stint in prison, but not enough to restore her worth in her own eyes or anyone else's. It'd be done on confidential terms to keep the media out of it and minimise the incentive for another plaintiff lawyer to try the same thing. Running the case was a risk to everyone's interests. As Manne liked to observe, the court might decide to make a point and, once made, such points were almost impossible to un-make. So, a settlement suited the system and its participants. First, though, everyone had to have their gobble at the trough.

As the afternoon of the Wednesday wore on into the evening, Martha grew weary. The woman from Penrith played on her mind. She was a person Martha had never seen in the flesh, yet she had furnished her with the look of the Smoking Nun and the voice of Nan, the harridan in the passageway. In her imagination, Martha armed herself once again with the broom and, this time, she swung it powerfully at the snarling head.

The clinical smell of the office was sharper now, a non-smell that was more noticeable after the Cherrywood's tones of timber and dust. The seams of these rooms were nearly as tight as the strongroom. The walls met the floor and the ceiling with such hermetic precision that sound could not pass between. The carpet, so perfectly firm underfoot, was a conspirator in this, grabbing words from the air and stifling them. The clicking of a word processor fell dead as the sound was being made, along with laughter.

She considered the idea that she had come to hate Caspians, her boss, everything they did and stood for. She'd felt it before, duller and less defined, but now the hatred was like a shrieking nerve in a molar. She could think of nothing else, and she wanted to wound the thing that was hurting her. And then she was moving, moving fast and methodically, before she could evaluate what she was doing.

She went to the filing cabinet drawers of the Penrith case, flung the top one open and stared in. She started to flip through the documents, looking for a place to strike. She thumbed her way to the divider that housed the senior counsel's advices and came to 'LIABILITY': twelve pages of careful argument in Arial 12-point, double-spaced, setting out the strengths and weaknesses of their case, assessing the worth of each of their witnesses and identifying the precise point at which they should settle and for how much. She released the binding clips and let the document weigh in her hand.

The Penrith woman hadn't chosen her fate. She hadn't gone looking for humiliation. The crazy woman in the Cherrywood's hallway wasn't born mean. She was in some particular state of pain. The pain came from life; what they had left was its enactment.

She took the advice document to the photocopying room. The two copiers sat like plastic pachyderms under hard lights. She went to the nearer one, ran off a copy. At the mailing station against the wall, she selected a large, plain envelope and tore off a square of stamps from the sheet. No-one saw her. The people she saw at this time of night were invariably deep in their own worlds, tired and indifferent to the activities of others. She knew to avoid the DX system: if the advice travelled by private mail, it narrowed the odds on who had sent it. So, she handwrote the name and postal address of the plaintiff's solicitor on the envelope, pressed the stamps into the top right corner and dropped the thing into the satchel she always carried to work. No record on the system, not even a use of the direct mail machine that could be traced. It was done, and it had set the consequences ticking, within five minutes.

She'd noted the Cherrywood's address when she left that morning, but she wasn't prepared to take a chance on it not having moved again. So, she rang the number, then found the same cab at the kerb outside the building. The driver, carved from stone.

'Good to see you again,' he said.

'It's good to see *you*,' she replied.

On the way to the Cherrywood, she asked him to find her a post box. From her position in the back seat, she saw nothing, at least on the side of his face that was visible, to indicate he sensed anything amiss. The knuckles with their tattoos rested at ten and two on the steering wheel. The night flashed by outside. She dropped the envelope in the post box and briefly wondered if life could continue like this.

* * *

Two mornings later, as she settled at her desk, Brandon Manne appeared in the doorway, coffee in one hand, papers in the other. Feline, somehow, in his suit. He grinned, teeth that could disembowel a herbivore. Even as she said the words 'good morning', she hated him for the ease with which he navigated the world.

'How's it going?' He perched one buttock on the arm of the visitor chair.

'Good. Going great.'

'Unreal. Casino thing good?'

'Yep. We're ready to file the request for further and betters.'

'That'll fuck em.' A wink. She wanted to retch. 'Best idea you had on this thing. Oh' – he waved the papers above his head – 'I found the senior counsel's advice on the copier. Some idiot, hey.'

He proffered the pages and she reached out to take them, watching him for some trace of knowledge. He held on to them for a second longer, as she pulled on the opposite corner.

'I figured you've got the physical file in here, so …'

She was sure her heartbeat had become audible, but she shrugged like it was one of life's mysteries. 'Thanks. I'll chuck it back in.'

The smile faded. 'Make sure you keep an eye on advices. They're as confidential as it gets.'

'Yep. Of course.' She moved a few items on her desk in the hope he would see she was busy, take the cue and leave. He didn't move, and the smile had gone.

'Can you think why anybody would be copying the advice?'

His tone was chillingly mild. She willed every muscle in her body to lie slack. She needed to let him reveal himself, to find out what he knew.

'I mean, I've racked my brains and I can't think of a reason you'd do it. Might check with the team this morning.' He made a clicking sound with the inside of his cheek, as if calming a fractious horse. The limber thighs in the too-tight pants unfolded and he loped out of the room.

When he was gone, she berated herself. What had she been thinking? And what kind of idiot leaves the evidence on the glass of the copier?

She examined the backs of her hands, as though they might break out in hives. But her body had reacted with nothing more than a slight tremor in her fingers. Why was she not more terrified? The hours, the years of patient study and self-sacrifice – everything hung balanced on the fulcrum of that document. She felt certain that her fate was sealed, and with that certainty came a surge of defiance, steadying her fingertips.

* * *

The following afternoon, Manne called an impromptu meeting in one of the conference rooms. As she made the short walk from her office to Conference 2, past the secretaries' corrals and the stationery shelves, Martha resigned herself to her professional suicide. She didn't fear it, perhaps even welcomed it, but she didn't want it to be protracted. She would leap on the grenade when it was thrown, blow herself to smithereens. She hoped at least their defence of the casino litigation had been dealt a mortal blow.

By the time she entered the room, the entire team was there, Manne at their head, again seated side-saddle on the edge of a table. In front of him, there on the table, was the very same envelope Martha had used to post the advice. Manne waited for the room to settle.

'Right,' he said, then, indicating a secretary: 'Shut the door, will you?' The stare he laid across them silenced every voice. 'This' – he picked up the envelope, dropped it again – 'is about the most fucked-up thing I've seen in legal practice.'

There was a collective intake of breath. No-one had heard Brandon Manne speak with anything other than titanium confidence. Now he sounded livid. 'For those of you who aren't aware, somebody' – he scanned the room – 'posted our senior counsel's liability advice to our opponents. It just happens, and I'm speaking to the person concerned here and not to the rest of you, that your stunt was unsuccessful, you treacherous cunt.'

The room was perfectly silent. It smelled of shock and fear.

'By random good luck, I'm on very collegiate terms with our opponent, and he's done the right thing. He's opened this envelope, realised what was in it, and he's resealed it and sent it back to me. And I have his word that he didn't read it.'

Manne's eyes were swivelling from one side of the room to the other. Every time they passed her, Martha felt sure they were pausing, letting her know he knew her to be the cunt. She searched her memory and there it was, the precedent that flew in the face of ordinary human decency and intuition: you owe a duty to your client and it overrides the niceties of fair play. Somehow the moron at McKetchelly and Spore had forgotten fourth-year ethics.

Manne had the envelope in his hand again. 'I'll find out who did this, and they'll be out the fucking door. They'll be reported to the institute, and they'll probably never work in the industry again. We've talked enough about loyalty, about the team, about the expectations of this firm. None of you are paid to moralise. And, in fact, beyond the boundaries of the files in front of you, you're not even paid to think. Now, get the fuck out, all of you.'

They started filing out, barely waiting to pass through the doorway before the whispered conversations began. As Martha headed towards the bottleneck, wanting only to be gone from the room, she heard his voice again.

'Martha, can you hang around?'

So casual, again. People were looking over their shoulders at her. She waited, wondering what her face was showing. The last stragglers wandered out and he regarded her coolly. 'Did I go too far?'

'No, of course not.'

'I needed them to know how dangerous this is. It's like a kid darting out into the traffic. You've got to rip them a new one so it imprints the lesson.'

Charming.

'Look, I want you to know I'm on top of this. Those copiers cover your work area and the two cubicles outside – so, you and the four secretaries. I've looked at their HR records, and it, aah ...' – he ran a hand through his hair and sighed – 'it should've been obvious. We've had trouble with Heidi Miles before. The thing over her sick leave, poor attendance record. She's – I mean, I don't need to tell you this, you're a woman – she's a malcontent. It's exactly her MO. You don't get your way, so you lash out. Anyway, she'll be gone by the end of the week.'

He clapped her on the back like this was a fucking football game or something, guided her out of the room and closed the door behind them.

TWENTY-NINE

Thomas took the horse to the pier before dawn on the Saturday. The bay was ruffled by the southerly, as the fisherman had predicted, but the sky was light and the wind was not worryingly strong.

It was just after seven when he arrived, and there was already a crowd. Something he had doggedly pursued was now the talk of society. He smiled, bid the press good morning and gave genial answers to their many questions. 'It will be a historic day,' he offered, 'and I hope you will each take the time to enjoy it.'

At the pier, there were children selling papers and cigarettes. Silas Whittle and his son were stretched against the near side of the *Cherrywood*, exhausted and covered in coal dust. The bins would be full, and a smudge of smoke from the forward funnel indicated that the furnace below was already warm.

The morning wore on. There were hands to shake, ladies to whom he needed to bow. These hours! They would end, however. They *must* end at noon, when everything would be set in motion. The mate was engaged on the lower bridge with the charts and the instruments. He had assured Thomas that the real skill lay in the engineer's role, keeping the furnace and the boiler and the gearing of the paddlewheels in optimal balance at all times. The mate's demeanour conveyed the gravity of his work: he was no understudy to Carville. He was preoccupied, frowning through his whiskers.

247

And where was Carville? It was normal for him to vanish in the afternoons, but he was a reliable presence in the mornings. The breeze was picking up strength. The windows rattled slightly on the windward side. The musicians were assembling on the bandstand while, outside, a brass band, apparently unconnected to them, started up a marching tune, and the crowd cheered. *Goodness me*, he thought, *it really is happening.*

The day gathered pace, and he ran to keep up with it. Lucy and Annabelle arrived at eleven, in plenty of time for the midday departure. They were beautiful, and the admiring crowd pressed around them. He tried to get to them, but could not. He waved, and Lucy mouthed a helpless 'I love you' across the sea of bonnets and hats. Annabelle waved madly, her joy uncontainable.

Midday, midday. Despite the promises in his promotional flyer, Thomas hadn't yet settled upon the timetable for the daily crossings, and his advice was that they should be adjusted seasonally – for the westerlies of winter and the easterlies of summer. Midday just seemed an auspicious time for a maiden voyage. People were pouring over the gangway now. The purser had been through his list and come to a tally of 803, of whom nearly fifty were press. There were municipal councillors, parliamentarians, a delegation from Government House, the Chief Justice's wife and her sister. There were harbourmasters, the owners of supply companies, an entire ladies' auxiliary, a hospital board, a novelist, six clergy, a librettist and a famous actress. Rosstrevor was there, patiently queueing to board, his face etched in a struggle between shyness and pride. He nodded when congratulated, and otherwise kept his own counsel. Not far from him, the bulk of Oremu occupied a space in the crowd. He, too, was taciturn.

Down the length of the pier and along the shore were the assembled ranks of those without titles, who had brought their children to witness the event, and the wind tugged at their parasols and swirled their skirts, and the children squinted at the flying sand. Nothing so momentous had happened since the Armistice, and here was a thing that was not grim and complicated, a thing that could be enjoyed in the moment: the maiden voyage of a beautiful vessel under the soft autumn sun.

* * *

The engines rumbled and the steam valves piped. The coal smoke leaving the funnels was graphite-black before the wind snatched it and hurled it away. And now, pressing through the crowd, came Carville, macabre somehow, a head full of grinning teeth like a carnival prop bobbing among the crowd – *Where has he been?* – and his hair in addled waves that made no secret of his dissolution. He was dancing again, lustfully. As the people pulled aside to give him access, recognising the importance of his uniform, he thanked them individually. Under his arms, pressed into each side, were a pair of ample women swathed in rouge and cheap satins. Thomas groaned inwardly at the sight. The crowd was roused by the master, his unbuttoned coat and his louche grin. This was not how it was supposed to be.

Carville careered through the dining room and the wheelhouse towards the spiral staircase, under the scandalised eyes of women, the amused eyes of men already a few brandies in, the condemning eyes of Rosstrevor and, beside him, the unreadable eyes of Oremu. But it was his wife's gaze that Thomas would remember. Her disappointment.

Carville could have noticed none of this as he stopped at the foot of the timber stairs and bent into a long kiss with each of the two women, blindly waving a hand as the crowd roared. Then he was off, spiralling up the stairs like a whirlwind had taken him away. Thomas rushed after him, excusing himself as he went, peeling away from the hands of well-wishers. When he emerged, blinking in the bright light of the upper deck, he found his master at the binnacle, frowning over the glass dial. He looked up at Thomas's approach.

'I have steam pressure at one-fifty psi, revolutions at fifteen hundred. I think' – he stuck a finger in his mouth like a child choosing sweets – 'about right.' Below them, the crowd on the promenade deck heaved with excitement as the sound and the billowing smoke presaged an imminent departure. Carville called orders into the brass horn mounted by the binnacle, and the wheels began to revolve. One rotated clockwise, while the other was in counter-revolution, so the bow of the steamer began to edge away from the wharf and its mooring lines tensed.

'Lines away, thank you!' Carville called theatrically to the men posted at the bollards on the wharf. Thomas had his hands on the rail, trying to follow a procedure he realised they had never practised. He had imagined this moment so many times, and in his mind it was always tranquil and grand, unfolding at a magically unhurried pace. The reality, he was now discovering, was more rushed. The men on the wharf lifted the big, spliced loops off the bollard heads and tossed them into the space between vessel and wharf. Each struck the surface of the water with a heavy splash.

* * *

In the lounge, Annabelle had waited patiently. She had smiled sweetly up at the adults she was introduced to, and thanked them solemnly for their compliments on her ribbons, on her shoes. 'Yes, I am very proud of my papa.'

At times, she felt overwhelmed by the weight of the conversation rolling overhead like a crashing wave. At the height of waists and hips, she was buffeted into a claustrophobic foreground of skirts and coattails. Halfway up an adult is less fragrant than their head is, she thought. She was under instruction to hold her mother's hand so they would not be separated. 'But I will always be on the boat,' she had protested when her mother had told her this. 'I cannot go anywhere else.'

This was the justification she allowed herself when her mother reached for her handkerchief. Annabelle glanced briefly at her now unoccupied hand and withdrew it. Bodies pressed, and the swell of the crowd took her from her mother's hip. She was away.

She burrowed through to the rear of the lounge where the crowd was not so dense and patches of the scarlet carpet could be seen. A solid turned post came into view and she laid her hand on it. The timber was warm, not tacky with varnish, as she had expected. She traced a finger around its curves and felt herself drawn to it.

The voices were less oppressive here. A slender brass chain had been slung from the post across to another one and, beyond the gate they formed, a compact stairway led below. The half-light of the stairwell felt like a retreat from the clamour, so she slipped under the brass chain and, keeping her left hand on the carved handrail, she made her way down.

There were brass fittings along the way, dim lights, as the stairway curled right and became a passageway along the backbone of the vessel. She was walking towards the front now, she thought. The sounds of adult feet came to her as knocks and thuds through the floor overhead. There were doors on either side, each with a brass number or a small plaque: 'Pump Access'. 'Starboard Gearing Compartment'. 'Strictly Crew Only'.

The passageway ended at a door – 'Forward Hold' – and she placed her hand on the latch that held it. A look over her shoulder: no-one there. Her head was spinning with the dizzy rush of doing something forbidden.

Inside, a large space was lit by four lightwells in the ceiling. Crates of vegetables and wine were piled on both sides, along with coiled ropes and canvases, mysterious tangles of metal and brass, glass floats and corked bottles.

She stepped forward into the hypnotising light. The long strands of hair that had escaped her ribbons were swaying on invisible currents of air, catching the sun. All sound was muted, and as she looked up towards the source of the light, she saw the heavy beams that carried the deck and the complex joins between them, pegged and interlocking like a wooden puzzle.

Drowsiness washed over her, and with it a vision that she was in a burrow under the roots of a tree, a place where she was warm and safe among secret hollows, encircled by the mass of the tree's heavy foot. She wanted to stay here in this place called Forward Hold. The light made pools on the floor and the shelves. Her mother would understand if she was gone a while. And her father was busy. He had more important things to worry about.

She hummed a little, traced her finger over the lettering on a crate. She could just … stay here.

From above came faint creaking, the thumps and scours of landed ropes, while deep below her the engines rumbled. The world came slightly adrift and Annabelle sensed motion. The *Cherrywood* was moving. The bottles in their crates began to plink against each other, and somewhere the vibration set a metal object ringing.

A sound nearby, no more than a dry shuffling. Behind her stood a boy, taller than her, a few years older. Dark and thin, watching her. How had he appeared like that?

'You're not allowed in here,' she said haughtily. 'This is my father's ship.'

He smiled, and the smile irritated her with its parental quality. 'It's a boat, not a ship. And what makes it his, hmm?'

What makes anything anyone's? she thought. 'He owns it.' Yes, surely that was the right answer.

'Ah, but my father built it. So perhaps I should be telling you off.'

She should have been outraged, but there was a mischievous smile in his eyes. 'It's lovely down here, isn't it,' he said. 'It feels like it holds you.' He was right: that was exactly how it felt. Forward hold. Although he was much taller, the boy was not looking down at her the way the adults upstairs did, was not about to ask her if she was proud of her father. She quite liked him.

'We should go up,' he said. 'It feels like we might be leaving.'

She followed him along the passageway and onto the stairs, observing how his tall, thin frame seemed to fit the confines below decks. His boots and clothes were well made, plainer than the other boys', and they lent him an air of seriousness.

He swept aside the brass chain for her. 'Come,' he said over the noise of the crowd. 'We can go high up and see everything.' Adults stepped aside for them. Outside in the sea air, he took her hand and led her forward. She looked down at her hand, clasped in his much larger one. She had resented her mother leading her about, but this felt different, like an adventure.

They climbed up another small stairway, concealed by the wooden box housing the paddlewheel, and, as they passed it, Annabelle could hear only the roar of the water from the wheel's revolutions. They emerged onto the flat roof above the lounge, an open space framed by a suspended wire. Sunlight shone down on them and the breeze whipped Annabelle's hair again. The crowd was thinner here, mostly men intent on watching the launch: seeking clues in the writing of the wake, the crew moving about among the passengers.

'I helped to build it, you know,' the boy was saying. They looked out over the milling figures below. 'So, I think we should call it *ours*, don't you? I am going to learn ev—'

He stopped mid-sentence, distracted by a commotion below.

* * *

When it happened, it happened so suddenly that no-one had the wit or reflex to intervene.

The *Cherrywood* was swinging rapidly away from the wharf.
The crowd was cheering. Churned water and sand arose in
the sea in response to Carville's improvised engine orders.
The swing of the vessel was more pronounced now there was
room for the stern to come around. The wind blew hard and
the semaphores snapped loudly in response. The cheering was
deafening.

Thomas saw none of this. Instead, what he saw were the four
mooring lines trailing in the water, the angles between them and
the *Cherrywood*'s hull narrowing dangerously. Carville hadn't
sent anyone to retrieve the lines. He was looking out to sea,
at where the bow needed to be in the coming minutes so they
could make their way west. He was whistling, one foot tapping
the boards at their feet. The stern line, three inches thick, was
creeping nearer to the portside wheel, and as the boat swung, it
was inevitable that it would be sucked in.

When Thomas looked down, he could see the smart blue
uniforms of the crew dotted through the crowd. They were
attentive, waiting to be told to do something. But there had
been no order. The engines were roaring louder and disaster
seemed only seconds away. He rushed to the portside rail and
saw the shock of white hair above the sea of hats.

'Mr Rosstrevor!' he shouted, but the shout was lost in the
crowd's happy din. 'ROSSTREVOR!'

Carville shot him a sharp look. The crowd hushed, at first
thinking the festivities were taking a new direction. Rosstrevor,
closest to the port beam, looked up at the bridge and found
Thomas.

'The mooring lines!' Thomas shouted to Rosstrevor.
'Someone must ...' He'd never learned the terminology he
needed. 'Quickly! Someone get them in!'

Why was Rosstrevor not on the bridge? he wondered, though
he knew the answer. This event had been arranged socially,
not practically. The master was a raised deity, and, as owner

of the vessel, so was he. Rosstrevor was a shipwright, a mere tradesman. Short of a structural problem emerging, he had no role here. But Thomas and Carville had been put, literally, on a pedestal, and no-one had remembered the true reason for having a raised bridge: the view all around.

Below him, Rosstrevor had seen the problem. He rushed forward at a speed that belied his age, shoving people aside as he went. He reached the gunwale aft of the paddle box, and there, in the corner that the sponson formed against the line of the hull, both he and Thomas above him could see the mooring line snaking its way towards the spinning paddlewheel.

The sound of the crowd vanished somewhere. Thomas could not hear the rushing wheel, nor the roar of unseen engines. He could not see Carville beside him, nor his own wife and daughter in the crowd, nor the sea, nor the bunting or the gulls. He could see only Rosstrevor, reaching with a pole he'd found, trying to flick the mooring line away from the wheel. But the stick was too flimsy beside the powerful wheel and its waterfall, and the waterlogged hemp of the mooring line was too heavy to shift from its inexorable course.

Rosstrevor's big left hand gripped the rail, while his right arm swung the pole, far below deck level. He braced a leg up high now, allowing him further reach, and Thomas could see the muscles in his back through his neat, sober shirt as he strained with the effort of smacking the pole on the churning water. The pier had receded far enough that no-one there could assist. The crowd on the *Cherrywood*'s deck had drawn back from him, allowing him room.

Suddenly, the balance in Rosstrevor's body changed, and he was too far over. The crowd gasped, but he never looked back, and there was only the clump of white hair above his jacket and no visible face to convey surprise or fear. His back foot left the deck, and he grappled frantically with the rail; he had abandoned the pole and was trying to regain his grip with his right hand.

There was awful panic in the movements, a wild desperation
from a man of conservative ways.

Men lurched forward, grabbing to save him. It was futile.
They could only swing at the space where he had been, for in
that instant he disappeared completely. The women screamed
and a hush followed, leaving only the roar of the churning
water and then ... and then a series of deep thumps and bangs.
Thomas looked back at the master at his binnacle, standing
motionless, open-mouthed with shock.

'Reverse!' Carville screamed, stung into action. He slammed
the telegraph back and corrected the order into the brass horn as
'All astern!' and by the time he had done these things, Thomas
had leapt the rail of the bridge and jumped across the roof of the
cabin then swung down into the crowd. They parted instantly,
so that he reached the rail where Rosstrevor had been at exactly
the moment of his horrifying end.

The paddlewheel was still threshing forward, although the
clutch and the gearchange could be heard deep in the hull.
The rope had pulled taut, and it led directly into the wheel ...
and now the paddles of the wheel came up with Rosstrevor's
body wedged in them, entwined with the rope. This bundle
had smashed its way through the louvres so his broken limbs
protruded among splintered timbers. The machine had
swallowed him, hopelessly entangled him, and as the blood
appeared in the open fractures of the crushed limbs, the water
from above splashed down and rinsed it clear. The blood
reappeared when the wheel finally stopped, and the shipwright's
corpse drained red against the white-painted timber as it hung
unmoving in the spokes.

* * *

The panic on board took many forms. Mothers shielded their
children from the appalling scene, as men crowded near the

sponson to offer help, or to gawk at Rosstrevor, broken open. The crew tried to restore order: someone directed the quartet to strike up a tune in the hope that people might come back inside the cabin.

The paddlesteamer hung paralysed in the water, and the wind held her broadside and began pushing her north. Thomas initially thought this was caused by the physical blockage of the body in the portside wheel, but the news was even grimmer – the engineer's boy relayed behind a cupped hand that the braking force on the wheel had stripped a gear. They could run one paddlewheel against the rudder to return the vessel to St Kilda, but they were underpowered. Thomas watched the smokestack and saw the effort had increased. He felt the rumbling under his feet, imagined Whittle and his son feverishly working the furnace. None of it was enough – the vessel was still creeping north, cold shadows on the gruesome tableau of the port side.

He took hold of a waiter who stood mute with horror by the cabin door, and ordered him to find a large tablecloth to drape over the shattered louvres and the body. Before the cloth arrived, he pushed through the crowd to examine the scene more closely. There was no prospect of extricating Rosstrevor. A part of his face was visible between the blades. It registered only disappointment, as though at the very last he had seen his fate and would have preferred it to be less public.

'Blow the horn,' Thomas directed a boy from the crew. 'Single long note. Then semaphores for distress. What are the …' He squeezed his eyes shut. 'I'm the owner. I'm just the *owner*, for God's sake! What are the semaphores for distress?'

The boy appeared flummoxed, as though presented with a snap test. Then he recovered. 'Black square and a ball, sir.'

'Good lad. Go and do those.' He looked shoreward, to the coloured dusting of spectators on the beach. They were too far away to understand what had gone wrong, but they would already be wondering why the *Cherrywood* was adrift, beam-on to the wind.

The crew attempted to shepherd the passengers into the cabin, but it wasn't clear they would fit. They roped off the rearward half of the promenade deck so the bloodied cloth over the louvres was no longer visible. Most of the men remained out on the bow, smoking and arguing about what had happened and what would happen next. The women and children were almost all indoors. Children pressed their faces to the glass, looking out fearfully at the sea and the sky. Only Rosstrevor's son, the apprentice, stood vigil at the body, bending to hold the cloth in place.

Thomas made his way towards the bridge before he'd formed any real sense of what he was going to do. Near the spiral staircase, something began to build within him, urgent and unfamiliar. Then he took the stairs two at a time, lifting his body by his hands on the banister.

The daylight, the breeze, Carville standing there, as broken as the man in the wheel. Thomas took two steps across the open space of the bridge, bystanders scattering, and swung a fist at Carville's head. He connected somewhere in front of his ear, felt the prick of stubble under his knuckles and the rocking of the man's head as the blow took him undefended. Carville dropped to his knees and Thomas took a bunch of shirt in his free hand, coiling to hit him again.

A crowd formed around him and Carville, shouting that he should hit him again, hit him harder, throw him overboard. Thomas looked in confusion at the hungering faces, unrecognisable as mere tourists, contorted with malice. Only one face was familiar to him, lower and partly obscured by the pressing bodies: his daughter's. Her haunted look, her eyes pooled with tears. In an instant, she was swept up by the crowd and was gone.

Carville looked up at him hopelessly, and Thomas couldn't bring himself to do what they wanted him to do, to club at the man's stupid head until he was senseless. He threw Carville into the corner of the bridge against the bright blue canvas dodgers that blocked the wind, and he slumped there in shame, unwilling to look up, or perhaps terrified of the second blow that Thomas couldn't deliver.

The wind was stiffening and, from where he stood, Thomas could see both the lee side, where the *Cherrywood*'s hull dragged the water smooth, and the starboard side, where the hull was pushing water. Between the *Cherrywood* and the land was a ruffle of breaking waves and a low, pale line in the water.

The engineer appeared from the stairwell, looking as though this catastrophe were just another frustration in a long and busy day. His eyes took in Carville, cowering against the dodgers, and Thomas, standing over him. He appeared to make a decision about command. 'Sir,' he said to Thomas, 'I've isolated the starboard wheel. We can run her against the rudder and try to make way upwind back to the – the pier, sir.'

'Yes, well, we're slipping north at quite a rate,' Thomas replied. 'Very well.' The engineer took off, with Carville scampering behind him, not a backward glance. For long moments, Thomas stood there in the wind, trying to understand what he could do. He heard the starboard engine straining as the *Cherrywood* swung upwind, so he wound the wheel until the rudder straightened the vessel again. But its inexorable drift to the north could not be stopped: the single engine was powerless against the gathering gale.

Thomas summoned the nearest crew member, a frightened boy with his shirt untucked. 'Get me the mate,' he said, and when the mate appeared, he asked, 'Why haven't we put down an anchor?'

The man appeared perplexed. 'Cap'n didn't give the order, sir.'

'We're blowing downwind without power and you're sitting around waiting for an *order*?'

'Well, yessir. How it works. Sir.'

'Right. The master appears incapable of doing anything. I want you to stop the engines for now and drop the anchor. It might … stop us, mightn't it?' *For God's sake*, he thought. *Why am I having to figure this out?*

The mate disappeared and, soon enough, Thomas heard the engines fall silent. In place of their rumble, he heard the winch at the bow, the rattling of chain and the splash as the anchor struck the surface. He positioned himself at a corner of the bridge so he could see the boil of aerated water where the anchor had plunged and the blur of racing chain, and for a moment he felt a flicker of optimism: perhaps this disaster could be contained. The chain was flying now, the vessel already well past the point where the anchor had entered, and the passengers were watching the manoeuvre with the same hope that Thomas felt.

Abruptly, the rattling of the chain ceased and there was silence. Thomas stared, unable to process what had happened. The *Cherrywood* resumed its downwind rush, unimpeded. The words formed in his mind as though whispered to him. *They didn't connect the other end.* It was too stupid, too farcical to believe, and yet it seemed perfectly of a type with everything else that had gone wrong. He fell against the railing and screamed into his sleeve.

When he looked up, they were hundreds of yards further north. Now the crew had taken the sheet away and were trying to roll the portside paddlewheel forward and astern to see if they could dislodge the body. The spectacle had the women weeping and the children shrieking in terror. Thomas took up the binoculars: no sign of assistance from shore. He swallowed down his shame and asked for the flares. As he stood there looking up, one arm aloft and the wick fizzing towards his wrist, he felt like an absurd statue, a roost for shitting pigeons. The flare ignited and the crimson light curved into the sky. The whoosh of its departure attracted the attention of those who had been staring at the body in the wheel, and the voyeurs were united with the hopeful and the horrified in following the parabola of defeat. *We are done. We have failed. Come and get us.*

The parts of Rosstrevor were coming away from the main and it was more than people could bear. His son wrestled in vain with the splintered timbers and his father's entangled body. Gulls swooped at the gore, scrapping and fighting. Inside, the vomiting started. The *Cherrywood* drifted on.

Looking north now, Thomas could see what the pale stripe was. A sandbank, lightly grassed at its highest point. Beyond it was another strip of deeper water, then the beach, the swamps, the mussel-cutters' beds and a long post-and-rail fence. He felt the strength of the wind and he knew there was too little space between the boat and the shore for anything to change, even if the wheel began to gain. There was too much pushing against them, and they were heading for the bank.

The boats were coming; that was something. He wondered why these matters were his alone to ponder, why he seemed trapped in a glass cage. His family must be nearby, among those crowding the rails. Lucy would know what to do, even here amid this madness. And Annabelle, nowhere to be seen, was so very much her daughter, resourceful and calm. It was he who stood rooted to the spot.

Four boats. Eight hundred people. He leaned over the rail and called to the crewmen among the crowd: 'Women and children first.' The call was acknowledged and it sparked a wave of pushing and shoving among the men, fists showing pale in their cuffs above the dark coats.

There were fishing skiffs, lighters and dinghies following further back, rowers straining. No care was taken to moderate their impact with the hull, and the fresh white paint ground off the *Cherrywood* and onto the gunwales of the rescuers. And while their crews shouted orders and the crew of the steamer shouted back, people took matters into their own hands and began to cross into the boats, which were slamming into each other, end to end, and into the *Cherrywood*'s hull. They tipped high onto their near beams as the weight of passengers threatened to capsize them. Somehow they filled without incident and the human pressure on the promenade deck was lessened. The sandbank was nearing now, and the boats hurried away from the *Cherrywood* to avoid being caught up in the coming stoppage. A handful of men, over-eager to help or perhaps angling to drop late into the rescue boats, wound up in the water and grabbed at the mooring lines still trailing on the surface.

They had covered perhaps three hundred yards from the pier now, and the birds that were massed on the sandbank took to the air in fright as the stricken paddlesteamer closed in on them. A crewman appeared at Thomas's side and pointed out that if the *Cherrywood* struck the bank beam-on, the wind and swell could tip her onto her side against the immovable object. Thomas gave the order to swing the rudder, and for a brief moment the steamer pointed downwind again. It felt like surrender, an acknowledgement of fate. With a lurch that caused people in the crowd to topple over, the *Cherrywood* struck the sandbank.

It was not the singular impact it might have been if they had struck a rock, or another vessel. Rather, it was a bump, then a long, slowing slide as the keel came up onto the sand and drove itself further and further forward. When Thomas looked over the edge, he could see the deep turquoise of the bay's natural depth, then the yellow-green of shallow water, and individual strands of weed on the bottom. It was perhaps only waist-deep amidships, and at the bow the sand was dry. They had timed the voyage to coincide with the highest tide of autumn, so they could venture deep into the Yarra River and show off to the townspeople. That decision would be their downfall, for there might never be a tide high enough to float them off.

The boats came in and circled again, flies on a carcass. More boats, different boats, their operators gazing up in wonder at this monument to folly. As they swung alongside, the crew organised groups of people to board each one, still battling the men who felt the importance of their salvation outranked that of women and children.

Thomas felt a presence at his side and recognised the society columnist from *The Argus*, a wet-lipped sycophant in a cheap hat who went by the name, or the pseudonym, of Myles Wintergreen. He placed a hand on Thomas's back and leaned in close.

'Oh my,' he breathed. 'Oh dear.'

Thomas looked at him helplessly. He had courted such people, and they would crucify him.

'You've not been here long, have you?' the columnist asked, and for a moment Thomas wondered if he was offering sympathy. Then the sneer took over. 'You'll never see scorn like the grasping classes of a new society.'

* * *

As the passengers made circles in their ant-panic, Lucy materialised near the main doors to the lounge and clutched her daughter.

'Where were you?' she demanded. 'Never do that again!'

Annabelle had no answer. She buried her face in her mother's skirts and concentrated on the sensation of her fingers in her hair. There were enough boats pulled alongside by now. They would be rescued, and soon this horrible day would end. For Annabelle, though, this did not mean relief: only a dull recognition.

Lucy knew there was no chance of finding Thomas, and she felt the worst of the danger had passed. They would be reunited later on shore. She gripped Annabelle, trying to control what she could. They were led to the gap in the starboard rail where a rope ladder had been lowered and people were descending to

the waiting boats. This was the lee side, facing the shore at Port
Melbourne, and the surface of the water was calm enough for
the boats to wait at the foot of the ladder.

Crew members in twos and fours brought out the crates
Annabelle had seen in the forward hold, to throw them
overboard. The talk was that, if they could jettison enough
weight, the *Cherrywood* might float free. The boatmen below
yelled obscenities in protest as tables and chairs, tureens and a
heavy Russian samovar rained down upon them.

When their turn came, Lucy lowered Annabelle through the
gap and held the back of her dress until she was sure the girl
had a firm grip on the ladder. The reaching hands from below
had her almost as soon as Lucy released her. Lucy removed her
shoes and went next. In a moment, they were seated in a fishing
skiff with a dozen others, scruffy-looking fishermen at the bow
and stern and a snowdrift of glittering scales at their feet. The
fishermen were still swearing at the pot-throwers, as more
splashes detonated around them.

'Wait!' Annabelle had seen the boy looking down, and the
cry escaped her. He appeared vacant, stunned, and was making
no attempt to move. 'Come now!' Annabelle called, and she
waved her arm at him. Her mother made a soothing sound and
tried to wrap Annabelle in a hug, but the girl wriggled free and
grabbed her mother's arm.

'We must take the boy,' she pleaded.

Lucy looked at her uncomprehendingly, and Annabelle
pointed to where the bloodied cloth still hung over the smashed
louvres of the sponson. 'His father.' Lucy understood at once,
and stood in the well of the boat.

'Send the young man down to us,' she called to the crew
who were looking down. 'That one.' She indicated Rosstrevor's
son, who still hadn't moved. His eyes were glassy. Men either
side of him guided him to the opening in the rail, where he
slowly came to life. Once he had been guided into the boat, he

looked at Annabelle and then at Lucy, a look that might have been gratitude or just confusion.

'My name is Joseph,' he said absently.

Voices shouted on the deck over a discordant music. The grand piano appeared at the edge and teetered momentarily on its pedal stem before overbalancing and falling. It hit the surface keys-first, sounding a brief water-chord before the hammers went under.

The fishing boat rocked in the wake of the piano's impact, eliciting a gasp from those on board, then it drew away from the *Cherrywood*'s side. Mercifully, its course took it along the hull and away from the sponson. But Joseph was looking over his shoulder, and he gazed in fathomless sorrow until they had rounded the bow and the tragic scene was no longer visible.

***

Many hours passed before it was all over. Thomas stayed with the *Cherrywood*, feeling he had inherited a captain's ancient obligation to remain after Carville fled on one of the boats. It was only him left, him and his dreams. Him and Rosstrevor.

To the northwest, Princes Pier was crammed with industry, sloops and ironsides waiting there, crates stacked high. The trains came and went from Port Melbourne in clouds of steam, and eventually the seabirds forgot the fuss and returned to roost on the sandbank, and, insultingly, on the *Cherrywood*. Smoke rose from the chimneys of Middle Park now, as the residents lit their fires for the coming night. Small craft came and went, tacking in curious circles around the wreck. Some of the mariners called out in sincere concern. Others jeered.

By dusk, the tide had fallen far enough that the aft section of the *Cherrywood* – its entire length behind the paddlewheels – was hanging off the plunging edge of the shoal, so the keel was exposed and unsupported. Thomas moved forward and stood alone on the promenade deck, then climbed down an abandoned rope ladder and walked over the dry sand to where the sandbank ended at the paddlewheel. He saw fish darting in the clear shallows, silver flashes against the dark varnish of the submerged piano. There was free air under the stern now, and creaking and yawning noises were coming from the timbers. There wasn't a trace of marine growth on the wood below the waterline – there hadn't been time for it to accumulate. Crucial timbers, deep within the hull and unseen, had started splintering along their grain, the copper nail heads, every one of them inspected by the rub of Oremu's fingertips, poking free like quills or stubble.

He returned to the bow, and shortly after sundown there came a groan from deep inside the ship as the splintering and popping of timbers accelerated. The sound gained in volume as the weight of broken things took down other structures, pipes and plates, and furniture and windows and planks. The deck under Thomas's feet leapt upwards and fell again, and then the entire stern half of the *Cherrywood* fell away from a fracture that had appeared underneath the cabin. The dining room windows shattered in concert as the sundering of the hull tore them from their frames, and the smokestack tipped drunkenly backwards. When it was over, the deck sloped away at a precarious angle towards the sea, and Thomas could see into the chasm thus created, where everything had tumbled and come to rest. The fracture exposed the workmanship and human activity and self-delusion in there, the carpets and drapes and teacups and glittering scatters of broken glass that would soon enough be sand again. The *Cherrywood*'s back was broken.

Deep in the night, long after Lucy and Annabelle had been taken away, and along with them Rosstrevor's poor son, he recalled the look his daughter had cast back over her shoulder, the grief and horror and … Was it shame he saw? A police boat came with short sledgehammers and saws to release Rosstrevor from his entrapment. The harbourmaster attached kerosene lights to buoys and anchored them around the wreck as Thomas wandered through the galley and tore at a cold roast chicken. Eventually, a boat was sent out to retrieve him, and he walked home to Elwood through the darkened streets, his hat pulled down and his coat collar up.

The house was plunged in darkness, but Lucy sat up in a chair, soft lamplight on her shoulders and the look about her of troubled sleep. She stirred when he came in but didn't speak. She only studied him with sorrowful eyes.

'It is done,' he said simply. 'The wreck has been secured.'

'Oh, darling.' She rushed forward from the armchair and tried to embrace him, but he held her awkwardly at arm's-length.

'I'm finished, aren't I?'

'No-one else was hurt. They can refloat it, surely.'

'Her back's broken,' he snapped, and his voice was unfamiliar to both of them. 'It's over.'

Her face was full of pity for him, but she stammered to find words of consolation. 'It's – it's … This is a setback. You have the insurance.' He let go her wrists, and she threw her arms around him, yet he stood wooden, unable to respond. 'You have the insurance and you can get the money and start again.'

They remained like that for a long time, a wife clinging to a husband who could not reciprocate the embrace, a sculpture in the dim room, under lamplight that spilled out the window onto the garden in the quiet street by the canal that led to the bay, whose waters lapped all night against the trapped and broken paddlesteamer.

THIRTY

SAUNTERINGS

by MYLES WINTERGREEN

The fair paddlesteamer *Cherrywood* was launched and trialled in secret, months ago, away from the prying eyes of the Melbourne public and indeed from the journalistic scrutiny of your humble correspondent.

Astute readers will recognise the context if I say that, 'thus undemonstratively was born this the most marvellous creature yet conceived by the art of naval architecture and the science of marine engineering'.

But secrecy oft conceals deeper malaises, fair reader, and all has come to farcical naught. Yesterday, before a crowd numbering in the thousands, the brief career of the PS *Cherrywood* ended in blue ruin, with the loss of one life, on a sandbank off Port Melbourne.

The particulars of the disaster have been ably reported elsewhere, but 'Saunterings' had the advantage of being present on board when events went awry. The *crème de la crème* of Melbourne society. A drunken captain. A loose hawser. A failed attempt at retrieval and a man overboard: a giant, in fact. Mr Rosstrevor, owner of the celebrated shipyard at Port Melbourne, became ensnared in the viciously spinning

---

paddlewheel and was there mangled and exsanguinated before the horrified onlookers.

The scene, it saddens me to relate, was one of unmitigated panic and sorrow. There was heroism and pluck at hand, as sundry fishermen and leisure sailors attended the stricken vessel, the bright skirts of Melbourne's mondaines fluttering down to the waiting boats like the petals of spring blossom.

The vessel remained stuck fast on the shoal thereafter, with Mr Rosstrevor's remains in situ. Every passenger was rescued, and the vessel's owner, a Mr Thomas Wrenfether, late of Edinburgh, remained with her until well after the beaching, which caused the keel to fall victim to the vessel's own weight, fracturing with the falling tide.

When 'Saunterings' took an evening stroll along the Princes Pier and looked out to the east, the poor *Cherrywood* could still be seen, dry-docked and misshapen, her unfortunate owner pacing the promenade deck with his bunting on the sag. One would surmise that difficult questions will follow, as the city awakes from this troubling dream.

THIRTY-ONE

Heidi Miles loved her job.

And this distressed Martha. Heidi wasn't there filling time. She had decorated her sterile office cubicle with photos and inspirational quotes. She smiled eagerly at the older secretaries and joined their conversations, even though they often concerned their children. She had no conversational authority among them, yet she laughed along when she was sure something was safely funny.

She arrived in the mornings in her runners, kicked them off under the desk and switched to a pair of expensive heels. The runners marked her as a kid, and in the early evening when she put them back on and draped the earphones of a Discman round her neck, she looked to Martha like a happy teenager and not a drone. She'd asked once if it was okay if she left, and Martha had pointed out that it was nearly seven and she should get a life. She'd been shocked, then saw the intended joke and smiled. The idea that this kid was a malcontent was a million miles from the truth. She was eager to learn, friendly and inventive.

These were the thoughts tormenting Martha as she stood on the wide footpath of Collins Street, commuters veering around her, lost in their own worlds. Her impetuous act of protest had cost someone else their job. Her own performance numbers were unimpeachable. She would be paid her bonus after the Christmas party, and the discussion about her advancement to senior associate would be renewed. And she would make her argument about a transfer to Human Rights and either it would succeed or their desire to keep her in Insurance would lead to a better contract next year. Playing by their rules brought the cast-iron promise of success.

Just not for Heidi. If the sanction of the institute didn't finish her off professionally, the lack of a reference from Caspians would work its poison. You don't just leave and reappear somewhere else in the glass towers if you don't carry an endorsement with you. She was gone.

Where was the cab? It was never late.

Heidi. It should have been clear to anyone with half a brain that Heidi wasn't the source of the leak. Manne was about as smart as they come. He was one of those people – one of those men – who had such an assured grip on the levers that his own ability and effort were immaterial to the collective force he could exert through subordinates. Martha didn't think she could ever be such a person. She depended on what was within her, and she had no mind for delegating and motivating.

Here it was, swinging out of the metal stream and along the empty kerb, the driver's hand half-raised above the steering wheel in what might have been apology. 'Traffic,' he grunted when she climbed in. They swept out from among the tall buildings and from under the tram wires into the side streets of Fitzroy, and at these times she felt, more strongly each time, she was coming home.

'I got you some Turkish delight.' She took out the carefully wrapped bundle of serviettes containing the treat from the working lunch on amendments to the *Insurance Contracts Act*. A faint puff of icing sugar rose from within the bundle as he took it in the wide tips of his fingers and placed it on the centre console. 'Good,' he said, and she took that as effusive thanks.

Heidi.

What had she done?

She looked at the side of the driver's head and, as the car idled at the lights, for the first time, he looked straight back at her. There was something asymmetrical about his gaze.

'You alright?' he asked.

Tears blurred her eyes. Her throat was tight. He looked back at the road as the lights changed, and she noticed one eye moved before the other. The right one was glass.

'I suppose so.'

The pub was where she expected it to be, next door to the block of yellow brick-veneer flats with the low seventies ceilings and the white iron railings. A bookmark in her head, those flats with their Howard Arkley planes. She wondered if the Cherrywood might settle again, if she might find a way back to Joey.

But Heidi.

Inside, she went past the bar, up the stairs and along the high passageway with its tattered carpet. The door with the pattern-drawing, sounds of movement behind it and a slit of light at its foot. Onto the small spiral staircase, and there she felt like this could be the habit of a lifetime, the curl of it and the banister in her hand and the sense of anticipation, the smell of the delaminating wallpaper, pleasant in its unpleasantness.

A beautiful perfume filled the air as she walked through the doorway of Joey's room: a thick clump of gardenias, glossy foliage and creamy flowers, stuffed into a huge tin canister. Where had he found such a thing?

It had been days. As though she had conjured him, willed him to be exactly here on the bed, an arm behind his head, its bony elbow poking high. He was reading a paperback, and, as always, he looked mildly surprised to see her, as though she could be anyone else in the world who came to this secret pub and knew their way through the building and up to this hidden redoubt. And then his surprise would give way to interest, as it did now, and he leaned forward and she bent down to him and he kissed her.

She touched the skin of his throat, studying it closely under her fingertips to be sure it was real. 'I'm sorry I said what I did.'

'I'm sorry I hadn't said the thing you wanted me to say. I do love you. I do.'

There it was. Had anyone ever said it to her? 'I love you too. I've never felt anything so clearly.' She curled on the edge of the bed, gave herself over to sweetness, and the voices of self-reproach fell silent. He pressed gently at her furrowed brow and she felt the knots unravelling. For a moment, it was enough.

'What does that mean for the pub? And Nan?'

He sighed. 'No-one knows.'

She told him about how she had leaked the advice, and about the meeting, and about Heidi. As the words formed and she spoke them, she felt increasingly ashamed of what she'd done. But the look of keen sympathy never left his face, and he heard her out.

'He's clever, isn't he?'

'No doubt about it. Youngest partner in the history of the firm.'

'He knows as well as you do that it wasn't Heidi.'

'Yep.'

There was a long silence.

'So, he lets you know he's onto you, and the pain and the guilt's yours to keep, hey.'

'Oh *shit*.'

'What are you going to do?'

She sighed. 'Nothing. I'm perfectly snookered, aren't I?'

He didn't answer. She pressed more closely into the crook of him and he dropped the paperback and draped his free arm over her. She had a vague thought about eating, or about how it could be that they were surrendering to the night at a quarter to eight.

None of it seemed to matter. She arranged all the cares in her mind: the firm, Heidi, the pub, him, Nan.

Into the darkness, she asked, 'Why is she called Nan?'

'Who?'

'Don't play dumb. The lady who lives on the passageway below us.'

'She's called Nan because her full name's Annabelle.'

'Not because she's your grandmother?'

'No.'

Joey's habit of literalism had run the query into the ground. Did he mean she wasn't his grandmother, or that she was, but it wasn't the reason she was called Nan? He didn't appear to do this to be obtuse. Rather, she thought it emanated from a way of seeing the world, unmediated by social conditioning.

'Does she frighten you?' he asked.

'No, but she's not very friendly.'

'She's … Old people get fixated on things.'

'What about the cab driver?'

'What about him?'

'What's his name?'

He laughed. 'You mean you've never asked him? It's Oremu.'

'There's something about his right eye.'

'He lost it in an accident.'

'Really? When?'

'Long time ago. I was a kid.'

'He's connected to here, isn't he?'

'Intimately.'

Again, the sense of him drip-feeding answers, accurate but minimal.

'I'm going to resign tomorrow,' she said. The words rested on the sheets between their bodies.

'It won't save this Heidi of yours.'

He was right. Manne was driven by malice and geared only to ratchet forward. Even an apology, a full explanation and her resignation would not be enough to move him. Litigators became great litigators by framing every difference as a battle of wills, and winning every one of those battles. He'd said as much himself at Werribee.

'You can't just let go of everything,' Joey was saying. 'It's the way you are, I think. Caspians gives you something to gnaw on. You might hate them, but without them you're pacing around the Big Cat enclosure yawning at the tourists—'

'With my big fucking teeth.' She mimed a roar of endless boredom and it caused him to yawn.

'You meant that,' he said. 'But seriously, you couldn't have anticipated it would go like this.'

He was right, of course. She already had a grasp of the practical things – how much money she had saved and how it would be relevant to their lives, and what the Cherrywood meant to him, whether he could leave it and how he would exist out in the world, where she felt he did not belong. He was a creature of the beams and the joists and the planks. Like Oremu, he belonged to a shadow world. The leaking of the advice and its consequences fitted a pattern. Here, too, she had interfered, and the exposure of a delicate creature to the world's brutality would be Martha's responsibility if it went wrong.

Things were closing in. The darkness had deepened. She couldn't tell from his breathing whether he was still awake. How long had they been silent?

'Joey?'

'Mm.'

'This needs to end.'

He didn't answer, at first. His fingers found her hair and traced their way through it. She concentrated on the sensation. The sorrow compressed in his body, escaping through his delicate hands.

'Yes.' His voice, right next to her in the bed, far away.

'Oh *fuck*, Joey.' She sat up. 'Stop saying *yes*! Why do you have to be so fucking *cryptic*? Would it kill you to disagree with me? Do you even understand why I'm saying it? I might as well have these conversations with myself!'

He sat up too, now. 'Well, I can disagree with you, if you wan—'

'Shut *up*!' She spread her fingers over her face and suppressed a scream of frustration. 'None of this is real. Neither of us is taking the slightest notice of the real world. You're some sort of captive in here and I'm making career decisions based on an imaginary future with you and there's a mad old lady downstairs and the fucking pub flies around the place doing God knows what. I mean, what a perfect metaphor for dodging responsibility!'

'You done?'

She watched him for a long time. 'No. There's something else.'

'Hard to think what else there could be after—'

'I'm pregnant.'

She needed to find the clues in his face that would betray what he felt, before he could find his poise. These words, this situation, were new in her life, and the charting of a course through it would start in this very moment.

She saw the shock register first. Then a wave of deep concentration, a stillness. A glimmer of understanding.

'Why do you think you are?' he asked, and she thought it a very strange question.

'I missed my period.'

'How long ago?' There was no force in this interrogation, only a mild curiosity. But this was far from what she wanted to hear. What was he *doing*?

'It's not just *late*, if that's what you mean. It's two weeks or something. Miles out.'

'Ah. Have you done a test?'

'No. No, stop asking me this stuff. I'm as regular as clockwork. Never been late in my life. You don't – you can't *know* like I do.' The irritation surged through her. 'Bloody hell, got a uterus now, have we?'

He reached to take down the clock from the desk by the bed, wound it with the little key that lived in a drawer under the clock face, and replaced it. When he turned back, he wore a look of utter seriousness.

'Do a test,' he said. 'You're not pregnant.'

She groaned in frustration. 'How do you know?'

'Look around you, Martha. Look at this place. Things stop. You're the one writing down the rules. Haven't you latched on to the deepest rule of the lot? Time stopped in here. Ages ago.'

The sinking feeling was upon her again. This sounded preposterous, but so did everything. There was no reason why this particular instance of weirdness shouldn't be true.

'How old do you think Nan is?'

She hesitated. 'Eighty?'

'Well, yeah, she's eighty-two.' He shifted where he lay, rearranged his hands. 'She looks roughly what her age is from spending enough time outside the building. Used to do stuff in the community, like helping homeless people. Thing is, she's been old a long time.'

'What?'

'You can't age in here.'

She thought about Nan, about her otherworldly quality, the restlessness in her. Nan.

Nan.

Him. She couldn't begin to process it.

'What's my period got to do with it?'

'Think about it. There's a mechanism within your body that responds to passing time. Between some age in your' – he indicated vaguely with his hand – 'I don't know, teens, and sometime in your middle age, there's a clock unwinding. Men can only measure the biological time in their bodies by things breaking, things wearing out. Or malignant things growing. And that stuff's irregular. But your cycle measures time, and the clock's stopped, Martha. You're in suspension now.'

Her instincts raged against the possibility. 'But even if you're right' – she found the evasion she had been seeking – 'I might still be pregnant.'

'If you were,' he said sadly, 'how would the pregnancy …?'

It stopped her cold.

'And besides,' he said, and she knew it was coming, 'I've seen this before.'

The room was quiet, the world was quiet. There was only the close smell of the space around them. The high dark corners of the walls were waiting for her to ask the question.

'How old are you?'

'I told you the first time we met,' he said carefully. 'I'm twenty-six.'

'It was the second time. And how long have you been twenty-six?'

'I thought this was about Nan.'

'I thought it was about my cycle.'

She could smell tobacco on him, could smell his clothes and hair that weren't quite dirty but smelled scruffy and endearing.

'I can still need,' he said, 'and you're something I need.'

They lay in bed under the shingles and listened to the night's distant traffic outside. There were still gaps in her understanding of the Cherrywood that felt dizzying, like stepping over a crevasse while the abyssal air breathed upwards.

His voice was soft now. 'Maybe it's been like this for a very long time. Maybe there's a cycle and I'm trapped in it, like Nan's trapped in it, like you're falling into it too. And if you go, the pub will be released and Nan will go on being Nan and I'll keep running the place and things will go on forever. But the building will get up and move, and it's likely you'll never find it again. Is that what you want?'

Later on, she would remember this conversation, and in the remembered version the building voiced itself in a distinct *creak*.

'I've found it this many times.'

'For one reason – Oremu wants you to find it. He's not talking to us about it. Whatever he's up to mightn't go on indefinitely.'

'You say you'll keep running the place.'

'Yes.'

'Joey?'

He smoothed the hair from her forehead, whispered, *'Don't.'*

'How old are you?'

'You can never come back if you make that decision.'

'How old are you?'

'Don't spoil everything.'

But with all her heart she needed to hear the answer. Things were becoming clear. Things that – he was right – she should never have contemplated. She held on to his hands in the darkness and it felt as though they were alone together in the universe and that there was no-one else to be found in its furthest clouds of dust to remedy this – not him and not Nan, no colleague or friend or wise counsel. The stark mechanics of it were hers alone to unpick.

'I need to know.'

His fingertips found her closed eyelids and traced down her cheeks, to rest with impossible delicacy on her lips.

'I was here at the very start.'

THIRTY-TWO

For Thomas Wrenfether, the days after the *Cherrywood* disaster were racked with shame.

The cheerers, the hat–tippers, the sycophants would not meet his gaze now, the worst of them carefully crossing the street to avoid him altogether. Children called out and scurried away, their friends squealing with laughter. He found Lucy in tears one afternoon, having been refused service at a bakery that used to offer her fawning welcome. He raged at that insult, wanted to go and kick their door in. The snubs directed at him were justified in his eyes, were all that he deserved, but to target his wife, who had counselled him against all this idiocy, was appalling.

Lucy tried to reach him, but he had retreated to some place deep inside himself. He existed in a strange state of functional despair, able to carry out the tasks required of him, but unable to see any prospect of redemption.

The morning after the beaching, as the police raided a flat above a liquor store in Little Lonsdale Street and took away the impostor Edward Carville, Thomas wrote to the insurers to seek an assessment of the wreck. He placed the words one after another without concern as to their impact. They could cause no consequence that might affect him. They were just words.

More distressingly, he had lost the ability to show any affection to Annabelle. At first, she tried distracting him, then bringing him cocoa, or toast, or even, with special dispensation from her mother, brandy. He, who had been so affectionate with her, who delighted in holding her hand while she spoke, had lost the power to move a muscle out of love for her.

But the girl's love knew no bounds, and rather than feel repudiation, she changed her approach. She tried writing notes to him and leaving them on his desk, or in the pockets of his jacket. She played the piano, delicately and with restraint, knowing he loved the sound of her playing more than anything. With perfect precision and entirely from memory, she drew the iron steamship that had taken him away. When she gave it to him, he thanked her politely and then looked down to continue his work.

He was there and yet he was nowhere to be found. He was an emptied husk, no longer the father she'd known, and his eyes appeared to focus on some point beyond her.

He wrote letters obsessively: letters to notaries, to salvage contractors. Letters back to Scotland, seeking to relocate his family away from this calamity of his making. Letters to relatives, arranging matters but never explaining himself or begging assistance. Nothing he did revealed him as a man who could see a future.

Lucy, for her part, made clear she had no intention of returning to Scotland. A humiliated retreat to their homeland was out of the question. She passed through stages in her response to her stricken husband. Like Annabelle, her default was kindness, and she tried everything, clutching at the cliff of his back in the bed, only to roll away in despair. Some form of pragmatism had to take over, otherwise all would be lost. She kept them fed, she hired and directed staff to run the house. She declined visitors, both the well-meaning and those hungering for scandal. She set up a new room for the orphaned Joseph, and the boy occupied it with silent, bewildered gratitude. She maintained the domestic correspondence, kept tabs on

Annabelle's schooling, walked the streets with her head held high. If the battle was lost within their walls, she would damn well win it on the streets.

And among the varied losses was one she never saw coming. She loved to be consulted about their business together and she knew she had insights to offer. But Thomas no longer asked. It was not that he doubted her judgement. He simply no longer cared for her ideas, and so, as the business withered and died, it became entirely his.

A month passed this way. Household things became sites of mourning. A drawing Annabelle had done, a round and wildly grinning head that was her papa, hung askew. Flowers wilted and dried in their vases, dropping speckles of seed. Things they had planted, things they had made.

Two months on, the press kept up their barrage as the short, cold days of winter arrived. Carville's first court appearance, rumours of a criminal negligence investigation into Thomas. Unfounded whispers about resistance from the insurer. Outright lies about Thomas making preparations to flee the jurisdiction. The wreck of the *Cherrywood* lay paralysed, gradually coming apart, and people saw what they wanted to see in its dereliction: a tragedy, a farce, evidence of hubris or criminality. Mostly, it was a subject to talk about, something to look at from the beach. The town talked incessantly.

Thomas ground on. He talked to no-one.

He spent a spiteful July afternoon with the insurers as they calculated the linear quantity of the timber. The actuaries made lists of figures, expressed them as width and length and diameter and degree of curvature and aggregate weight and thickness and countless other indices. No matter which way they formulated it, it seemed unbelievable there could be so much. They would tear off another leaf of their plan-sheets and try the entire exercise again in some other format. Thomas stood by, his legs going numb and his eyes blurring.

These had only been the trunks, Oremu had said, which meant, for every timber they had, a vast amount of other timber – the burl, major limbs, sub-branches, sticks and down to the finest twigs – had either been wasted or shipped off to other fates, collateral to the collection of this heartwood. How many trees, then, and what of the roots? Had the blossom of a village been taken so that spring was heralded ever after by some other signal – birds, perhaps, or shooting bulbs? Wild thoughts, unhelpful thoughts.

When he had extracted adequate concessions from the insurer, he organised the salvage and went straight back to Rosstrevor's yard to have them handle the demolition. The business was being run by the company accountant, William Cox, who shared the founder's reserved manner. He plainly saw Thomas as the architect of the disaster threatening his firm, and had made concerted efforts to erase the *Cherrywood* debacle from the company's history. Young Joseph was expelled from the firm by means of an official-looking letter and a wad of money. Still, Cox agreed to recover the timber, which meant having the same carpenters prise out the nails they had driven in only months before. Thomas had presided over the blinding of their head carpenter, the death of their managing director and the trashing of their reputation, but they would take his money to disassemble this embarrassment, this public reminder of everyone's folly.

Two long pontoons were manufactured out of barrels and planks, towed out to the wreck and fixed in position. For a day or two, the gulls occupied them and shat them as white as they had done the decks and structures of the *Cherrywood*. Then the workers came out in their punts and began the long undoing. They started with the things that were merely removals: the mouldering food and the bottles and the cookware and the crockery and the table linen. The bronze weathervane on the roof of the saloon. Then they moved to the heavier things: the coal in the hold, the remaining glass and the doors, bathroom fittings and furniture.

Within a fortnight, they had reduced both floors of the cabin to a skeleton that no longer interrupted the view from east to west.

At first, they stacked all the timber in a clear space in the Rosstrevor yard, for which Thomas paid a reasonable rent. This was no lasting solution, so he hired agents to find him more permanent storage and they came up with a vacant commercial block in the slums of Fitzroy, which he could lease for ten years and do with as he pleased.

'Sell it for firewood and you can sublet the space,' offered one of the agents, and Thomas only stared at him coldly. He'd paid a year of rent in advance.

New workers joined the daily voyages out on the punts: specialist carpenters, joiners and metalworkers taking down the superstructure piece by piece, preserving the long timbers whenever they could, carefully de-nailing and filling buckets with screws and bolts and washers. None of them questioned what they were doing, or why so much importance had been placed on caring for the timbers. Each could see with his own eyes that this remarkable grain, shaped to one use and deracinated to await another, continued to radiate a rare beauty.

When the superstructure was gone, the men began on the decking. The planks had been sanded to a silken finish, each precisely caulked against its neighbour, so any haste in lifting one could cause a splinter to shear away. The planks made weighty piles on the punts, laid neatly and strapped down to ensure their safety.

The workers hitched rides with the bullock drays that laboured the seven miles up Bay Street to St Kilda Road, over the river at Princes Bridge in the shadow of the busy city, and around its southeast corner for the long, straight run northward up Nicholson Street, with their wheels in the tramlines. The traffic would collapse to a standstill while the long teams made an elaborate hook turn at the Tankerville Arms and started eastward on Johnston, until they were deep in the side streets of

Fitzroy and, in the intestinal tangle of its course, nearly met the river again.

At the bayside end of the journey, they were stripping back the hull planking to get at the frame. One by one, the massive curved ribs were worked free from their beds and craned out, and the Ark was unmade. The ribs made the journey up Nicholson in a slow crawl between the trams, like a whale had been flensed in a railway yard.

* * *

In her room, upstairs in the Wrenfethers' silent house, Annabelle worked on a drawing of the Waverley skylight mandala in all its radial intricacy. She began by tracing around a saucer, then divided and subdivided the circle with ruled lines, using the sharpest of her pencils. Her tongue was pressed between her lips as she worked, her hand dusting away pencil shavings and graphite. The block of art gum lay waiting on the desk, but her line never once faltered.

She would win him over, win him back, and he would shine in the sky again, like he used to.

* * *

When the tide was low, the workers had access to almost the entirety of the hull's underside. No tide would match the one that had deposited the *Cherrywood* there, and some days they found themselves digging away dry sand at the bow. Within a month, the Rosstrevor crews had removed every last timber. The broken keel was cut into sections, but the other timber was taken away unmolested, and the Fitzroy yard was fenced off to protect its precious contents.

All was done. The only task left was to remove the two pontoons from beside the bank where it dropped away into deeper water. And on the Sunday before that task was due to be completed, Thomas woke early and put on his best suit. He took a heavy overcoat, placed a kiss on his wife's forehead; had she been awake, this would have surprised her, as he had not done so since the day of the calamity. He went into his daughter's room and was about to do the same to her when the girl woke with a start.

'Where are you going, Papa?' she asked him.

'Work,' he said.

'Wait,' Annabelle pleaded. 'You can't go yet.'

He stood above her, overcoat draped over his arm and hat in hand.

She wriggled out from beneath the blanket and padded across the room to the desk. The mandala was finished, glittering with colours that the original, in its faraway railway station, never possessed, but which her cherished memory had added. She held it against her chest, thumbs and forefingers like pegs.

'It's our sky-window. From the train station.'

She held the page out to him, but his body was already in the doorway.

'Papa,' she said. 'Papa, I made it for you.'

His eyes took in the beautiful, patient work, the act of love it represented. Still her arm was extended to him and still it was possible for him to accept the gift.

But then hope died in her eyes, never to return.

'I have no time for this,' he said.

* * *

Thomas left the house and walked purposefully through the rainswept streets until he reached the Rosstrevor yard.

There, he took the small dinghy he knew would be tied up at the working dock. In the well of the dinghy was a carpenter's box, which he had filled with railway rocks days earlier. He rowed with gentle strokes out to the pontoons, over the metallic winter surface of the bay. There was no wind, and so there were no yachts out, and no fishermen, either, due to the rain and the cold. There was nobody to be seen anywhere on the water or indeed the foreshore.

He whistled a low, slow tune to himself as he dipped the oars in the rain-poppled surface. When he reached the nearer pontoon, he tied off the dinghy and, with some effort, passed the heavy toolbox up onto the deck. He climbed up, his movements restricted by the thick suit and the coat. His good shoes were untrustworthy on the damp timber, but eventually he stood upright on the pontoon and looked out over the mournful water.

With the last notes of his whistled tune, he took the rocks from the toolbox and one by one placed them in his coat pockets, ensuring there was equal weight on each side. When he was done, he stepped off the pontoon.

The cold water shocked him, but not enough for him to resist. He kept his eyes open, and the descent was a blur of heavenly green. There was nothing to see, nothing that passed him by. It took no time for him to reach the sandy bottom. The long sides of his overcoat had spread into downswept wings during the slow dive, and now they settled out wide of him on the seabed, pinned neatly in place by the rocks, so that if anyone had been able to see him there, face down in the gloom, he would have resembled a great ray, laid out on the sand in wait of repose.

THIRTY-THREE

The morning after her reckoning with Joey was the last day before the long weekend, the last opportunity Martha would have to front up to Manne, to make an attempt to exculpate poor Heidi, and to end it.

She woke early, grateful to find her hands on Joey's warm body. He stirred when she did, and he kissed her neck. She left the attic, walked down the spiral stairs and took her towel from the brass peg behind the door of the spare room. Down the hall, past Nan's door – silence behind it – to the bathroom.

She stood in the warm mist of the shower, listening to the trickle and slap of water on the tiled floor. The taps were chrome, large and cumbersome, and the washers had reached the stage where they had become oversensitive to adjustment, so the faintest twist took the water from slightly above warm to scalding. This was the shower's only deficiency. The showerhead was old and generous – illegal now, she thought, before reprimanding herself that there must be a regulation or a standard, some minor something somewhere that governed these things. It wasn't as if parliament had debated and passed a law banning generous showerheads. This was the way everyone thought – in a stream of unexamined assumptions. Even lawyers. The showerhead was generous, that was the point, offering the water in a monsoonal rush that blanketed and soothed.

She had her head down, letting the water drum on the nape of her neck, and between the blurring curtains of her hair, she saw a spider, a daddy-long-legs, making its way up the wall below the taps. It had got to the level of her knees, and it proceeded by extending a long and delicate foreleg ahead of itself and tapping it repeatedly on the tiled surface, feeling for the droplets of water that clung there. Thousands of droplets waited to impede the animal's progress, each as large as it could become before its mass would cause it to lose purchase and run down the wall. The spaces between the droplets were too narrow for the spider to navigate. The front legs probed softly, *tap tap tap*, breaking the surface tension of the hanging droplets so they fell and cleared a little space. And sensing the clear space, the spider drew up its bracing back legs to advance its body a little, then began to probe again.

Martha thought about helping the spider escape the sudden change of weather in the shower recess. Another, contrary instinct told her this was the way of things, and to interfere here was to get in the way of heedless fate. Any moment, a random deflection of the downpour off her back or the top of her head might hit the spider squarely, knock it from its perilous ascent and send it spinning down the plughole between her feet. All of us, she thought. Any of us.

Maybe the spider was more calculating than it appeared. Maybe it was laying a web as it went, and each choice of foothold was underwritten by an invisible belay to a corner of tile. Maybe this was not a risk, but the ordinary business of being a spider: seeing the world from an altered perspective through compound eyes. Such a creature would speak differently of this building and its secrets.

She would walk into Manne's office, close the door behind her. She would call him a cunt. No, she would reprimand him for using female anatomy as a slur. She would remind him what a pathetic little man he was. She would tell him Heidi was innocent. She would confess.

Heidi. He would have already sacked her. He would not give her a chance to put it right.

Martha felt weak. A terrifying dizziness overwhelmed her, along with a sensation of the floor falling away, leaving her suspended high above the plughole. The power was leaving her legs, and they were filling with some viscous fluid that could not support her. Her vision crowded into sparkles and blurs.

She reached out a hand to steady herself by grabbing the tap, but the hand missed its target, and she was swaying, falling.

Falling.

The water was so perfectly warm, so reassuring, that she knew she would give in to it, fall with it, and she let it happen. Somewhere there was a deadened thud, a stopping of motion, yet the falling inside her head still went on, so that she was descending through the distance that separated her from the shower's floor, crystal fragments like silver sparks falling around her.

The floor appeared unannounced, so close that she could see the crazing of the old plastic, scattered with the broken glass of the shower screen. Rich, bright-red beginnings, flowing around her and spiralling, spiralling into the plughole. The shock coursed through her and she scrabbled like a shot animal, trying to find her feet against the broken shower door. It only cut her more, a small, piercing, faraway sensation she was aware of but unable to name. She hauled in a breath and screamed his name. Where was Nan? Would she come if she heard? What had happened?

She screamed again, though she felt sure no-one was coming. She was grounded; the spinning had stopped and each individual fleck of glass was inflicting its bright fire on her skin. Her eyes darted from the broken screen to the bathroom door, assessing options, and finally she stood and took hold of a soap dish set in the wall of the shower recess.

Blood in little creeks on her legs. Her hair hanging limp. Her balance returning slowly.

The pub had done this to her.

No, it hadn't. She had merely become overwhelmed. But she'd never fainted before, under any amount of pressure. The pub had done this to her, stepping up its campaign of harassment now that she had lived through a move.

She would never know. She looked around the silent walls, as though a confession was imminent. It wasn't, and the crime was deniable. What a mess. She ran the water over the cuts to wash away the glass, then wrapped a towel around herself, put a foot up on the vanity and began picking fragments from her thigh. There were footsteps outside and a knock, and she could see the vague shape of his head in the frosted glass panel in the door as she reached across and spun the doorhandle open. He entered, dressed only in shorts, and when he gasped, she realised how bad it looked.

'How ...?' He left the question hanging, rushed to the sink and ran water to wash her down again, dabbing with a cloth at the punctures and scratches as the bleeding slowed. When he was done, he wrapped the cloth over his hand and punched out the rest of the glass from the door.

He held her until she was calm, then left to find a broom, and she was alone again with the grim terrain of the bathroom, the bath with its old, slimy curtain, the washstand and mirror, the toilet. She examined her legs and found other bright lines of laceration where she'd slid onto one knee. The shards made a sparkling mosaic over the dull floor. She hung the towel on the peg on the back of the door, over the little sign that recited the rules of the *Innkeepers Act*, and left the bathroom.

She was walking the length of the passageway, headed for Joey's staircase, when the decorated door swung open. The noise of it, the violence of the latch and the creak of the door, startled her. There stood Nan, in a gown of burgundy velvet, her hair piled in combs, and blue thongs on her feet. She stared at Martha with open scorn, and Martha remembered that she was naked. It wouldn't have mattered; it had never mattered the countless times she'd done it, furtively, in the early mornings. The challenge in Nan's stare hung in the space between them, the crinkled pouches around her eyes contracting as she surveyed the cuts on Martha's legs. *Assessing what you've summoned*, Martha thought. She believed she could see the tiniest glint of satisfaction in those eyes.

You will not drive me out. I'm part of this now.

She tipped her head back and cruised slowly past, meeting the cold stare with a triumphant smile. As she passed the doorway, she felt the stare slide over the backs of her legs, the angry red cuts, and she slowed even more. *Lap it up, you old bag. You are not going to win.*

She would not be going to Caspians today. There would be no confrontation with Brandon Manne, no rescuing of Heidi and no restoring her credibility. No Human Rights, no partnership, no prospect of stability and optimism and progress and family. The eerie stasis of the Cherrywood's walls was the world now.

Up in the attic, she slid back into the bed, and when Joey had finished with the glass, he came back in and joined her, took her head and cradled it to him.

He'd found a miniature brown bottle and a cotton bud. When she asked him what it was, he said, 'Mercurochrome,' a word she hadn't heard since her childhood. Her memory of the stuff was that it was pomegranate-red and toxic. She declined as gently as she could, but she was adrift in his arms, having trouble separating the things she'd say from the things floating in her head as unspoken thoughts. *I feel like you're a figment.* She interlaced her fingers with his, seeking evidence that he wasn't.

Drowsiness overcame her, and he was stroking her hair, kissing her forehead. *I am a figment too*, she decided. *We all are, so it doesn't matter.* The cuts burned and they stuck to the sheets as she shifted and breathed, but none of it mattered like his presence did, carrying her, unweighted, across time and memory.

* * *

When, finally, she woke, it was nearly midday. She went back to the bathroom and washed the smears of blood from the floor and from the china of the sink and bath. She pondered the broken shower screen: how would a glazier ever come to fix it? Did the Cherrywood have nocturnal glaziers? She stuck band-aids on herself everywhere that wasn't visible beyond her clothes. None of the cuts were deep enough for stitching, but plenty of them were still oozing.

Joey had tipped the glass into a plastic bag. She took it and went downstairs, planning to go out and dump it in a street bin. But when she threw open the corner door of the Cherrywood and the light of the day assaulted her, she found something she hadn't expected: there was cyclone wire across the doorway.

At first, she dumbly shook it, wondering if it would simply fall over, before she realised it had been attached on both sides of the door. She stood on a barstool and looked down from the lunette window above the door. The entire frontage of the pub had been fenced in.

She searched the cupboards under the public bar and found three cardboard boxes full of broken-off, sealed bottlenecks, marked in Joey's hand with the word 'Ullage'. Next to them, a little wooden box with a dowel handle that was the pub's toolbox. Its tools were made of dark metal and timbers worn shiny, and among them she found a pair of tinsnips. She was about to shove the toolbox back into its space when the block letters caught her eye, carved into its end: 'OREMU'.

The taxi driver. This needed more thought, another time.

She started cutting at the foot of the doorway, then up one side, as a woman walking her dog watched with interest from

the street. By the time Martha had cut across the top and bottom
of the doorway and made an exit, the snips had worn a blister
into the side of her thumb.

She stepped down from the timber-slab threshold and looked
back at the Cherrywood, bound in an ungainly cage of wire.
The muzzled building looked back at her in sorrow, entrapped.
Nothing moved and no sound emanated, but she could feel its
outrage, and, knowing it well enough now, Martha heard its
grievance.

The wire was supported by poles every few metres, and in
the middle of each segment created by the poles, there was a
sign: 'Sandbank Demolitions'.

She looked up to see a sash window thrown open, a shock of
white hair blowing free in the wind. Nan gripped the windowsill
with eight blood-red nails below a furious scowl.

'What the *fuck*?'

The window slammed. Martha heard a door bang inside, then
footsteps pounding along the passageway, down the staircase and
across the public bar towards her. Nan came crashing through
the front door, flinging the cut wire aside, and stood with her
legs apart and hands on hips.

'BASTARDS!'

She lifted her nightdress and kicked at the wire, the impact
ringing through the links in both directions. She kicked again
and a blue Dunlop double-plugger spun through the air. She
watched it fly, then rounded on Martha, pointing one of the red
nails right between her eyes.

'Ever since *you* turned up!'

Martha edged back, unsure if she was next for a kicking.
Nan jabbed the finger at the cuts on Martha's legs. 'It knows
you're the problem, and that's why it's going after you,' she spat.
'Pity the boy's too thick to figure it out.'

She followed Martha's eyes, which were directed over her
shoulder, and spun around. Joey stood there, leaning against the

fence, his fingers interlocked in its links, his eyes filled with reproach.

'Not very nice, Nan.'

Martha was thinking fast, trying to grasp what was happening. Caspians would be behind this. She'd targeted the firm; the firm had targeted the pub. Coincidence or not, she needed to start putting things right.

'They'll be coming back,' she said. 'This is only the beginning. Nan, you can keep crapping on or you can tell Oremu to bring Heidi here.'

'Who?' she snapped.

'Heidi Miles. He'll know who I mean.'

* * *

The taxi pulled up at the Cherrywood at six that evening. The pub was open, a handful of customers peering at the wire either side of the door.

Heidi Miles was carrying large paper bags that, Martha surmised, must have contained the personal effects from her cubicle. Her face was set in grief, stony. She set the bags down, took up a stool next to Martha.

'I've never been here,' she said. 'Strange, isn't it ...'

'It grows on you,' Martha replied. 'I hope it wasn't a pain coming out here, but I really didn't want to meet at work.'

'Is everything alright?'

Martha looked at her, at the genuine concern on her face, and thought how little Caspians deserved such an employee. 'Yeah, fine. Just had a migraine. Everyone assumes you're piking when you pull a sickie on a long weekend.'

'Not with you, though,' Heidi replied. 'You're like a machine.' She was looking at the two fine cuts on Martha's left elbow and the one on her right hand, considering the implications. 'Is everything good?'

'Yeah, yeah, it is, Heidi.' Martha hesitated, then steeled herself. 'But I really need to talk to you.'

'Okay, well, plenty of time for talking. Now.'

'They fired you, didn't they.'

'Gross misconduct.' And with those words, she burst into tears. Martha waited while she collected herself. Joey was serving, chatting with two suited punters, his eyes darting to Martha and Heidi.

'Heidi, there's something I need to tell you about that.'

She sniffed, collected a tear with the tip of a finger.

'It was me.'

Heidi blinked uncomprehendingly.

'I was angry with them. I've been angry for some time.'

'*What?*'

Joey had edged closer, making a poor show of drying a glass. Martha pressed on. 'I wanted to do something to hurt them, and I figured sending the advice to Spores might jam a spanner in the works.' Martha watched her closely. Not a trace of the rage she was entitled to.

'But why would you do that? You've got the best job in the world. They love you!' She was wide-eyed with astonishment.

'Not much point going into the reasons. What matters is, it wasn't supposed to end up like … this,' Martha said. Joey put down the glass, picked up another. 'I didn't mean for you to get the blame, Heidi. That was Manne's doing.'

Heidi looked around the bar, looked at Joey, at the other customers and out the window. When she spoke, she was looking down at her lap. 'I fought so hard to get that job. Pretty much had to beg them. Takes me an hour and twenty minutes to get in there every day, and sometimes when you guys work late, I don't get home until ten.' She appeared to be on the brink of tears again, but she gathered herself. 'I didn't especially like them in Insurance …'

'Who didn't you like?'

'Come on. Surely you noticed?' She'd unexpectedly taken on the tone of an unwritten alliance. Outside the building, they were women and equals. 'Brandon.'

'What happened?'

'Oh, stuff. Comments at first, dumb stuff. Then it was questions – you know – about boyfriends, about my experiences. Jokes, meant to embarrass me. For a man who could easily reach the top shelf of the file storage, it's amazing how often he got me to reach things for him. I mean, I could put up with it, you know? Knowing I'd never have to deal with him outside work. But it made every day a constant battle. What's he angling at? Is there another way I can do this particular thing to avoid him? It makes life so tiring.'

'Would you go back if things were different?'

'Yeah, I would. There's other teams. But things aren't different.'

'They can be.' Martha took a folded piece of paper from her jacket pocket. 'On here is the time and date I logged out the file to access the advice. If someone did the work, they'd find it corresponds with the time and date I logged into the photocopier, which is also written on this. Oh, and I took your stapler to staple the copies and I kept it – it's still in my top drawer.'

She handed over the piece of paper and Heidi took it.

'Ask for a meeting with Cannon and one of the partners you trust. If they get nasty, tell them you're lawyering up. Don't get Manne involved. Tell them you figured it out and it was me. Ask them to ring me and confront me with it.'

'Why don't you fess up directly?'

'This way, you're not only off the hook – you can take the credit.'

Heidi Miles looked down at the sheet of paper, at the confession that amounted to a string of numbers. 'It'll end your career.'

'I don't want it to end yours.'

Suddenly, Heidi left her stool and fell on Martha, wrapping her in a sobbing hug. They remained that way for some time, while Joey slung the tea towel over his shoulder and the drinkers studied them in amiable confusion.

THIRTY-FOUR

The lifts of the Collins Street skyscraper, banked in vertical channels like the xylem of a mountain ash, were filled with professionals: legal, financial, strategic. The fashions, the facial expressions differed only by small personal increments. Men outnumbered women, and those women who did use the lifts were often young, junior in their reluctantly opening professions, or there in support of senior men.

So, when the lifts opened onto the reception level of Caspian Lawyers one November Friday morning, there was no missing the spectacle of the woman emerging.

Nan knew how she looked to them: short, unruly, formidable. She had done her lawless hair in the usual combs, but topped it with an olive beret, which jarred extravagantly with her alarming shade of lipstick. She'd escalated their clash with a geometric-print kaftan in browns, greens and mustards. Her mint-green pumps squeaked as she marched from the lift doors to the vast reception desk.

The receptionists faced the lifts and were separated from each other by the length of an average-sized kitchen. They were good at what they did, creating a sense of calm, of silence and distance, so the activity of those within the offices was rendered valuable and private. Their eyes were fixed upon the bustling woman, and their faces did not move. The judgements being made were invisible. She stopped at the front edge of their desk and glared at each of them as she fixed a pair of glasses to her face.

'I wish to see Donald Enmore.'

The receptionist on the left, whose name was Doris, stretched her lips into a smile, and rattled an inquiry into her computer terminal. An eyebrow over the beige box of its monitor. 'Do you have an appointment, Mrs ...'

'No, I don't have an appointment, Miss. My name is Annabelle Casamento. *Née* Wrenfether. Mr Enmore will see me immediately.' Her voice was flat and hard and unpleasant. She folded her arms over her bosom and planted her feet.

'Well, Mr Enmore *is* very busy, madam.' A large and significant work from the Heidelberg School behind Doris gave the illusion that she was standing in a smoky version of the Dandenongs. Her soft voice was pitched in deliberate contrast to Nan's.

'You and I both know, darling, that Donald has nothing better to do. So how about you quit the shilly-shallying and get him out here. I'd hate to have to—'

'One moment, please.' Her eyes lowered and shifted to her colleague, who hinted a shrug. 'Would you mind perhaps taking a seat?'

Nan scowled. Sitting might constitute a backdown. But she relented and took herself over to the long leather couch under the window that framed the eastern suburbs. She did not pick up *Harper's Bazaar*, or *Vanity Fair*. She did not feel the floral arrangement to test whether it was plastic. She did not look at the view or the receptionists, or fumble in her small handbag. She sat rigidly upright and glared at the opposite wall until a large glass door slid back and revealed the suited form of Donald James Enmore, standing there as though he had been suspended in that position, awaiting animation by some electronic pulse.

* * *

Until they both had teacups in front of them, Nan did not say a
word. When the tea arrived, her mouth puckered into a ferocious
painted moue.

The elderly lawyer blanched at the sight. 'It's lovely that
you've made the trip in to see—'

'*Why*, Donald?'

He arched an eyebrow. 'Why what?'

'Why did these Sandbank people fence off my hotel?'

Enmore had been standing. He placed his cup and saucer
on a corner of the table near to Nan and sat. She watched him
wince as he did so.

'You know why. It's out of my hands. My clients have certain
rights, which they are entitled to enforce. Your business has been
given ample opportunity to make good on its various deficits,
yet it remains in default.'

'It's not a *business*,' Nan scoffed. 'It hasn't been for decades
and you know it.'

'Annabelle … Nan,' he replied. 'You have my sympathies.
You've always had my sympathies. But I cannot place my clients'
interests after those sympathies. Do you think it pleases me to
have to do these things?' His blue eyes had lost none of their
power to captivate over the years, but she had always thought
there was something weak about the man.

'You know it didn't have to be like this,' he continued.
Something affectionate behind the eyes. 'Until young Martha
went across to your side, we could have played out a stalemate
for another generation – I send a letter, the pub shifts, I have to
find it again … I quite enjoyed that game.'

'She doesn't change anything, Donald.'

'Actually, she does. Let's recall it was you who called me and
told me she was living in the Cherrywood.'

'I was trying to have her quietly removed.'

'Yes, and we put her on to Bird, and all it did was entrench
her with you lot.'

Nan rolled her eyes to the ceiling. 'I was perfectly happy with the rats.'

'And that's not all. She's made a powerful enemy in here – one Brandon Manne. Equal parts arsehole and intellect, which can be a damaging combination. Martha did something very naughty with a confidential document and young Brandon is set on revenge. And he was able to trace her to the pub, thanks to your call. He pulled the Cherrywood file, did some hunting around and had the fence put up. As you can probably guess, that's only the first volley.'

Fuck, thought Nan. *The damn girl.*

Enmore's face darkened. 'It's not like it was, Nan. Ancient grudges, the nonsense about massacres and curses … all gone. Nobody can concentrate on last week, let alone last century. Everything's hurtling forward, don't you see? The average age of this partnership is thirty-nine, and they're nine-tenths men, which you'll be surprised to hear isn't a good thing. They don't do civilised disagreement, and they certainly don't do Marquis of Queensberry. They are interested in one thing. Money.'

'Get me the deed,' she said coldly.

He sighed. 'You know what it says.'

'Let's pretend my memory isn't so sharp, Donald. Go and get it.'

He leaned over the table, laid a bony middle finger on the phone. A female voice answered, and Enmore said, 'Felicity, would you be a darling and dive into the vault and bring me the Ardelean deed, please?'

A moment of silence. 'The one with the Latin?'

He smiled indulgently at Nan and looked down at the phone. 'Yes, dear, the one with the Latin. Thank you.' He took his finger off the call button. 'There you go. The Cherrywood file holds the distinction of being "the one with the Latin". I do miss the days when they were all ones with Latin.'

Nan was not going to be charmed. She had already given herself a stern talking-to about this very thing. 'I'm surprised you don't get around with the damn thing in your pocket.'

He made a face, mildly appalled. 'Nan! It's a historic document. My father's finest legal invention.'

'And how's the rest of your burgeoning practice, Donald?'

He looked hurt. 'Much like your hotel business, I imagine. I'm thirty-one years older than the next most senior partner. They don't invite me to the partnership meetings anymore. I don't get the memos, or even the financials, unless I ask. They've got computers on their desks these days and they didn't even offer me one. Which is fine, I suppose – what am I going to do with it? But it's … I feel mocked, sometimes.'

There was a discreet knock at the door, and a young woman who must have been Felicity came in. She placed a folder on the table between them and silently withdrew. Enmore flipped it open, poked his glasses back up his nose. 'Your mother entered into this deed with the Ardeleans in 1920, Nan.'

'So?'

'In 1920. And here we are in 1994, having the same old discussion.' He waved a dismissive hand at the parchment, with its sweeping strokes of ink. 'How old does the boy say he is, by the way?'

'Mid-twenties.'

'Goodness me. Very well.' He adopted the tone of a bored lecturer. 'I mean, you know this stuff. Lucy was granted a highly unusual form of legal tenure, a grant of title *ad structuram solum*, whereby the structure is owned but the land is rented, giving the landowner right of demolition and salvage upon default of rent. In effect, the building is security for the rent. Your mother was cleaned out financially by the time she paid the bills after your father … your father's untimely passing. She had the hotel built this way to save money.'

'So, we own our hotel. So, it's ours to take wherever we want.'

'Now, in a strict sense, that's true. But just as you retain ownership of the building and therefore the ability to have it stand wherever you please, so too my clients have the right to find it and exercise their right of recovery against it. The rent continues accruing even when the hotel is occupying other land. The timber has gained value, exponentially, as land uses have changed. No-one can grow cherry to such an age anymore. And the corner blocks are disappearing. Scarcity means value, and value means unbridled pursuit. The Cherrywood's debt has been sold and on-sold multiple times. Everyone clips the ticket, adds interest. So, it becomes larger as it keeps changing hands. You can't keep hiding in obscure corners of Fitzroy, Nan. As you well know, there aren't any these days. Avoidance simply doesn't cut it.'

'Disgusting,' Nan spat. 'Your father deceived my mother. She would never have agreed to this' – Nan waved her fingers at the parchment – 'this scam.'

'It's not a scam. My father built this whole firm on his flair for innovation.' He looked around himself as though to take in the entirety of Caspian Lawyers, although the view only extended as far as the frosted glass of the internal office windows. 'You've done a good job over the years of evading the debt collectors.' He paused, searching for the words. 'But the building seems to have become a little sedentary of late.'

She scowled at him. 'You know why.'

'We both do. Martha.'

She jabbed a finger into the surface of the table and her scowl deepened. 'You people have no ethics. You sent her to us so she'd fall for young Joseph and now the Cherrywood's stuck fast again. Another bloody sandbank in my life.'

Enmore had his hands up in surrender. 'Now, wait on, please, Nan. The partnership still values her, or they did until the other day. She's a very promising junior litigator. Insurance group.'

'Insurance! Nest of bloody thieves … I ought to kick her out on her bony arse.'

'Well, I should qualify that. One of the few things I do know about the goings-on around here is that she's been applying at every review to shift to the Human Rights group, and the Human Rights people have been begging to have her. Begging. But the partners figure she's worth more to them in Insurance. So they've blocked the transfer. Three times so far.'

'Hmph.' Somewhere inside, Nan was impressed by this.

'Trust me, the fact she found the Cherrywood is pure chance. Pure chance. And how could we have known the boy would fall for her, anyway?'

'Balderdash! It'll be another one of these *innovations* you people concoct round here. And you know it's killing me, too. Did you think of that?'

Enmore's eyes softened. A glimmer of something in there startled Nan: recognition, empathy. Fear. 'What do you mean?'

'Got a lot older in recent weeks. Since the girl moved into the attic. Don't try telling me you haven't noticed.' She flicked her hair, a relic of a past armoury of allure. She'd felt the time in her hips and back as a tightening, and in her ankles and knees as swelling and grinding. She was sleeping less and less, and her vision was fading to a fogged approximation of the world. Every day brought a new, small problem that stayed. 'Call off these Sandbank Demolitions people.'

'You know I can't.'

'Who came up with that name, anyway? Is it supposed to be funny, mocking my father?'

'They are given to rather dark amusements, these people. But the signs are everywhere, my friend.' A flash of pity on his handsome face. 'You might see them if you got out more. Someone will always appear when there's money to be made from someone else's pain.'

Enmore closed the folder and sighed, and Nan knew what it was now, the thing that had rattled him. The same process was speeding up inside him. 'Nan, I really do enjoy our tussles. And I don't want to see our entanglement come to an end. I don't know what would become of me if I didn't have a roaming boozer to kick around. Can't you do *something*? Sell the building to us. You could house yourself and Joseph and even the girl, if it's your wish, get to wake up in the same place every morning. Invest the balance and pay yourselves a stipend. Why must we be locked in this—'

'It's not for sale. Wasn't for sale in 1920. Wasn't for sale in 1960. Isn't for sale this year. I don't know how you communicate with these clients of yours – probly send a load-bearing curlew to Central Europe or something – but you can tell them this from me. I will never hand over the timber. I don't care what this grudge is about or how far back it goes. My family have been through untold grief over it. Capitulation has long ceased to be an option.'

'That saddens me, Nan. It's upset me every time you've said it down the years. And seeing you cornered like this, I am sadder still. I will convey your response. It's a fax, not a bird, by the way. And Nan ...'

'What?'

'It was never about the Wrenfethers, you know.'

'What on earth are you talking about?'

Enmore suddenly looked tired. 'It's not about the Enmores, and it's not about the Wrenfethers, either. It's not about the Ximenons, even though they go generations back from the man who persuaded your father to bring the timber here and build the paddlesteamer. People have traced the feud everywhere. The relevant part for my family concerns a place called Mardakan, on the coast of Azerbaijan. A Caspian port where they were doing business—'

'Caspian? As in Caspian Lawyers? How have I never been told this?'

'They financed my father into launching his legal practice. *This* legal practice. Dark amusements, as I said. But the old Europe stuff ... it's buried under layers of corporate indifference now, don't you see? The people in this building don't have the slightest interest in an intergenerational grudge. Sentient timbers, moving buildings ... The senses in them that might have registered such things are deadened, cauterised. Somewhere, one of this lot has a beach house weekend with an old school chum, only he's a banker, and they laugh about the problem file, bet a bottle of Grange on it. You can't imagine the contempt. Testosterone knows no tradition.'

Nan tapped the surface of the table, a drumbeat over the muffled sounds of people talking in corridors and cubicles. Enmore was right. He and she were stubborn old wretches taking up valuable space in a temple to youth and aggression. The things that had motivated them had passed into history and none of it mattered beyond the small inconvenience of them occupying a meeting room that was needed for more urgent business.

'So, the girl is a chance encounter ...'

'Yes. I've had her looked into. Only child, a short-lived early marriage. No connections anywhere.'

'Someone could've conspired to drag her into it.'

Enmore considered this, fingers steepled under his chin. 'It won't be anyone here, I can tell you that. And I've never had such instructions from the client.'

'Joseph is an innocent,' she said with newfound urgency. 'I hate it that you think he can be used in this way.'

'He's been there since the start. He knows the score.'

'He's barely left the building!'

Again, Enmore lifted his hands in a gesture of hopelessness. 'They don't listen to me here, Annabelle. They don't talk to

me. Doddering old fool trying to work the coffee machine or
the printer. But I maintain' – he leaned forward – 'it is they
who have lost relevance, not me. It is they who have forgotten
why we exist, which is to serve our clients and not ourselves.
I couldn't be sorrier, but you're up against the only person in the
building who holds to the old ways.'

Nan saw in him the tired obstinacy she herself felt, the habit
of intransigence. 'We're both at the far end of life, Donald.'

'The Cherrywood is in its last days now. And you are. And
yes, I am. You can't control this anymore.'

Nan hated the room. She hated the plastic smell, its medical
austerity and its punishing silence.

'Don't bet on it.'

THIRTY-FIVE

Nan returned from the city, tired from the walking and the trams and the lifts and the rest of it. She stood on the footpath assessing the hotel's encirclement of wire, peeled back the cut section by the front door and let herself in.

The lights were off, the bar lit by streams of daylight cutting around the edges of the blinds. The smells of her lifetime persisted: beer, timber, cigarettes. Something else under them, something sour. She would need to think about that.

The stools had gathered under the western windows. There were sounds in the boards, the timbers of the walls and floor more talkative than usual. This gave her pause to think a little. She tapped the barometer that hung by the door. The needle swung urgently to 'CHANGE'. The smell, the glass. Something was afoot, and she didn't think it was a move.

It was then she noticed the figure on the floor.

The girl, Martha. Whatever now? In jeans and a t-shirt. No shoes. Breathing, and although she knew her to be a bit scratched up by the shower thing, there was no sign of a major injury on her.

'What's going on?' Nan asked loudly, figuring it was a reasonable place to start.

Martha spun and sat up, crossing her legs. 'I was ... What do you want?' There was hostility in the girl's voice.

'My pub. I can want what I want.'

309

'I've never seen you leave here. Where have you been?'

Nan arched an eyebrow. 'Coles Cafeteria, dear.' She took a stool and sat down facing the girl on the floor. 'You were looking at the ceiling.'

'That woodwork. The big … knot thing up there. What is it?' The girl pointed, and Nan followed her gaze, surprised by her own lack of hostility. If this Martha had been sent as a saboteur, then they had chosen an agent with remarkable powers of observation.

'Jupiter joint. It's the giveaway, but the drinkers never look up. Maybe some of them'd figure it out if they did.'

'Jupiter joint?'

'The heart of the thing, I always thought. Shipwrights had their signature ways of joining timbers. You don't just bolt them together, especially if you've got any sense of history. You cut them in so they lock. An expert could say, ah, that work's from Liverpool, or Hong Kong … some local tradition to solve a design problem given the tolerances of the local timber, the demands of the local seas, and so on. Ever notice the treads on the staircase, how they slope towards the back?'

Martha nodded.

'They're the blades of the paddlewheels. Each one's got a steel rod through it where it was mounted in the wheel. Perfect for stairs. Used to put the wind up poor Joseph when he was young, what with his father and all.'

She watched Martha's face as she spoke, and saw the little flickers of understanding, guesses confirmed, hypotheses proven. The girl was every bit as clever as Enmore had suggested.

'Almost everything around you is made from cherry timber. The keel's an exception, but almost every other bit. The whole thing was a floating forest. Cherry trees are beautiful things, but they're not so tall, see? The shipwright has to get a forty-foot beam out of a twelve-foot tree, so what's he do? Ordinary ones use metal plates, steel bands. But not the real artisans.

'This stuff, the Rosstrevors did it, Port Melbourne. Which is *int-er-esting.*' She slowed on the word, giving it emphasis. 'He was a Scot, I think, way back – I'll have to ask him – but he made that Jupiter joint up there, which is a thing handed down from the Romans. So, how'd this old Scot learn it?'

They gazed upwards together for a moment in silence.

'Incredibly complicated. No power tools, of course. Apparently the inside of the join has two pegs that lock it, facing in different directions so it's got three-dimensional strength. See the – if you lean this way' – she tipped at an angle on her stool – 'looks a bit like a lightning bolt from side on. The French called it *le trait de Jupiter*, because Jupiter had a lightning bolt. Funny how things get passed down.'

'Why did a shipwright build a pub?'

'Rosstrevor? He didn't build a pub. That joint up there was originally part of the keel. You know, given the size of the thing, there would have been maybe five or six of these joints along the length of it, though I've never found the other ones in the hotel. And besides, the keel broke, so …'

She knew she had the girl now, had her riveted. She had sat up straight, alert, like she'd been hit in the arse with birdshot.

'You're sitting on deck timbers. They correspond exactly to the dimensions of the original steamer. Nobody wanted to trim them. See the bits of caulking in the corner?'

Martha's eyes, full of wonder, followed her pointing finger. Ah yes, Nan had her. And realisation would dawn in three, two—

'This building was a ship?'

'Aha. Well, a paddlesteamer, also called the *Cherrywood*.' Nan stepped behind the bar to the shelves of spirit bottles and the decorations dotted here and there between them. She stood below the picture of the paddlesteamer, reached up and unhooked it, then passed it to Martha. 'Ever so briefly, I sailed on it.'

'So, this is the paddlesteamer?'

'Yes. Read the back.'

A newspaper clipping, glued onto the back of the frame and varnished over so it was golden with age. Above the text, a photograph and a headline: '"Saunterings" by Myles Wintergreen.' The launch of the PS *Cherrywood*. Terrible events, the death of Rosstrevor, the shipwright. Such a bland opening, such casual handling of the violence. Nan watched Martha's pupils darting across the lines, watched the growing horror, racing down from the grainy photograph.

When it was clear she'd finished, Martha looked up. 'I read this at the State Library. Ages ago. But I didn't ... Jesus.'

It was the photograph that tied it together. The times Nan had read the piece as a small girl, racked with grief, she always went back to the photograph. The tall man, ancient-looking, long limbs bundled into a chore coat. Grim-faced, his hand resting on the shoulder of an adolescent boy. The boy in his own version of the coat, in oversize trousers, oversize shoes. The curved timbers of a ship's bow stretching away behind them. The caption:

> Prior to the tragedy, shipwright Coramand Rosstrevor poses by the bow of the incomplete vessel with his son, Joseph.

Nan studied Martha, who studied the image. 'Joseph,' Martha was saying. 'Adds up, I guess. April 1919. He'd be Joey's grandfather.' She was smiling as she said it, but, watching her closely, Nan knew the smile concealed a terrible disorientation. 'He's the son, then he's an orphan, and ... lines up with the evidence ...'

Nan waited for the girl's fine mind to work its way to the answer, but the shock had silenced her.

'He's your Joey,' Nan said quietly, and for the first time she felt sorry for Martha, sitting there holding the frame like a weapon that had discharged without warning. Dark-eyed, dark-haired, the boy had barely changed.

'He …' Martha was choking on the words, struck mute by the idea. 'He told me, but I wanted to misunderstand him.'

So, Martha had dug deeper than Nan had initially thought. 'He told you?'

'He said he was here at the very start.'

* * *

Nan suggested they walk, and Martha dumbly complied, edging her way through the cut wire and standing in the street with tears on her cheeks.

The sky was half-clouded, the trees feeling their way into the season, cloaked in new leaves. Nan had watched the girl walking the streets on such a Saturday, a year before. Searching, it was clear. And she had felt supremely confident it would come to nothing, that the girl, like so many other drinkers, would give up in confusion, never to be seen again. But this one had persisted. This one had made a case to be taken seriously, had become a danger and had weathered the backlash from the hotel. This one had to be reckoned with.

They found a café, dark and half-filled, ordered lunch and sat. Over the years, Nan had wondered if it would ever become necessary to explain it to an outsider. How she would do it, how it would *feel* to do it. And now it had become necessary. They waited for the food and she felt Martha's eyes on her, expectant. There was a new power in the girl, an unshakeable conviction. Maybe it had to do with staying through a move: her world indelibly marked by it.

'I was a child,' Nan said. 'I was a little girl. Impressionable. And these big things were happening around me. My father committed suicide when I was seven. I loved him like all the stars in the sky.'

Martha gasped at this. Nan saw her sympathy was genuine and it inched the girl closer to Nan's esteem.

'I'm so sorry,' Martha said. 'That's awful.'

'Seven is a particular age to lose an idolised parent. You have to reframe everything.' The coffee arrived. Nan touched the side of her coffee-glass to test the temperature, but did not drink. 'It drew me towards my mother. Resourceful woman. She had some money – not a lot by then, bit of old family money – and she had the timbers from my father's paddlesteamer.

'Even then, there were people who were after the timbers. Mum once said they were from an extinct strain of cherry that was gone from Europe. The stuff was priceless. Would've been worth – I don't know – a hundred thousand pianos in Melbourne at the time, the Wertheim factory in Richmond … You take a huge paddlesteamer's worth of timbers, extinct timbers that … sing. The potential value of it boggles the mind.

'And we needed money. Coming from Scots aristocracy to St Kilda, and then to Fitzroy, was a massive social fall. St Kilda and Fitzroy now, they're not so different. Back then, though, St Kilda was sea and sun and fresh white paint, and Fitzroy was the slums, the world after my father left us. Brick and mud and clouds. As a kid, it felt like they'd built a whole suburb to be his headstone.

'Mum was grieving, of course, and the timber came to represent a connection to the love she'd lost. I didn't fully understand it at the time, but like some families might preserve a room, or a wardrobe of clothes, there was this timber, and the timber was central to everything he'd been striving for. And it was a valuable asset, but Mum would never have parted with it. She saw it as her job to use it well, to finish whatever it was he hadn't finished. I never agreed with her, by the way. Things would've been very different if we'd offloaded it and sailed back to Scotland. But then, I was … angry.'

She faltered and stopped. A closed door. For a moment, there was nothing but the hiss and burble of the Gaggia, the clatter of glassware.

'The pub opened early in 1921. I think my mother had this aversion to the publicity my father had attracted for his boat – so there was none of that. It just opened for trade one day and people started coming in. She hired women as her staff, always. I can't remember her ever taking on a man. She said women were less corruptible, and the drunks might be happy to take a swing at a bloke – this was her logic – but even the worst ones would think twice about hitting a woman. In front of others, at least.

'So, we ran the pub, and when I say "we", I was there in the mornings for the sweeping and mopping and in the evenings for the meal service, and on the weekdays, I was at school in between. Alfred Crescent to Grade Six, then Falconer Street until Leaving, and I left. I was fourteen by then and Mum needed the help.'

'It all sounds so … normal.'

'It was.'

Martha frowned. 'But it couldn't have been.'

'Why not?'

'Well, there's the … When did the pub start moving?'

'I suppose from quite early on. There was nobody who could have noticed it was happening. Joseph just stopped going to school one day. I don't even remember how it happened. Neither of us was allowed to have friends over. Mum was sociable enough – it wasn't that we were recluses. We could go to other kids' houses. She must have known word would get out and there'd be trouble. So, I used to tell the other kids we'd moved house – which we had, in effect, but we were still in the hotel.

'Within our family – the three of us, I mean – it was a part of life, something that happened from time to time. And then, when I was about sixteen, I took a fancy to this man, Norm Casamento. Silly thing, just bloody immaturity. This older man who seemed very worldly. The other drinkers laughed at his jokes. In retrospect, I think he was a fence. Always had something to sell. Rat with a gold tooth, he was. He paid me attention and I was flattered. Mum was completely unimpressed. She knew Norm well, and I think he'd probably tried his charms on her – ha! That was never going to work. But for me, it was a way of rebelling.

'The hotel didn't react, at first. I think it sensed the infatuation, and Norm's pretty obvious lust. None of it was love. Not' – and here she stopped, looked down – 'not a *replacement*, you know?'

'No – what do you mean?'

Nan's tone became more careful. 'Not a replacement for the idea of love we grow up with as children. The one that falls apart on you as the price of becoming an adult. Anyway, I dug my heels in, and Norm knew he was on a good wicket, winking and groping with the publican's daughter, so things developed. He'd get beaten up now and then, dragged off by the cops, and we wouldn't see him for a few weeks. Then he'd be back in a new suit, full of piss and wind, selling radios or boxes of sherry. He proposed, and Mum and I fought about it, and, in the end, she gave in because she had no choice. The hotel stopped moving for a while around the time of the engagement. That's really the only time – until recently – I can remember it staying put for an extended period. It was the love that was going on – some approximation of love – and the fact that the pub was doing so well then. Mum was raking in the money, so the building was safe from the bank and the lawyers. So, there you go. At the tender age of eighteen, I became Mrs Casamento.'

'This might sound rude, but it seems so unlike you.'

Nan laughed. 'It was. What on earth was I doing? But youth's like that, isn't it? Things that seem ridiculous in retrospect were justifiable at the time. Wasn't much like Mum to allow it, either. I'm sure we both knew that this man wasn't going to deliver me from the slog of hotel life. I mean, he spent his days in there –

how was it going to be an escape? And before you ask, no, I wasn't knocked up. Norm wasn't ... I never fell pregnant to him. He wasn't exactly dynamite in the sack.'

Martha gasped and giggled, and Nan chortled with delight. Then her face fell. 'Would have been nice, I always thought. Having children.'

Their food arrived, greasy things. Nan tipped pepper over hers. She watched the girl take a paper napkin and place it carefully over her lap. She watched her wait until Nan picked up her own cutlery. Observations you learned to make over a lifetime in hospitality.

'We lived in the double suite, two doors down the hall from where I live now. Norm couldn't believe his luck. Everything a thirsty shagger might need, in easy reach. Course it wasn't enough. He was gone in eighteen months. Took off with a girl named Sal who'd been doing weekend shifts. Can't believe I didn't see that coming, either.'

'Oh God, that's bloody awful.'

'All for the best. The hotel hated him – he was hurting himself constantly. Cut his lip on a chipped glass once and sat there bleeding into his beer. And he had the same experience you had in the toilets – he got locked in. No-one came for him till I was cleaning up in the morning, and he was blue with cold. So, he might've had a thing with Sal but, really, he was scared off, and that was fine with us.

'Around this time, I did a lot of thinking about my parents. My father was this mythical figure who had died so bloody dramatically. And I'd got so angry with him – oh, I worshipped him, and he rejected me in his final days when he was very depressed. I took it on myself and it made me hate him. I was confused and ... and I've carried it around with me down the years. When you came along, a lot of it came up again, and – I'm sorry – I've not been much fun to be around.'

'It's fine, really.'

'It's not fine, Martha. I've been fucking poisonous.'

A smile passed between them and the matter was buried.

'Anyway, you got me thinking about him and me again. Something I haven't done in a while, so thank you. And I've come to an understanding. He was just a bloody dreamer, you know? A lovely dreamer and then he was gone. And my mother had to stick it out, had to be there and raise me and find money and do the hard things. She didn't have time to agonise over who she really was and what her destiny was. "Rubbish," she'd say.

'I had to grow up to understand her sacrifice. Who knows who she might've been, if she'd gone back to Scotland and remarried? When I was little, I tailed her around while she barged her way through all these condescending men – I thought that was what you did, you know? As normal as a hotel moving in the night. It was only later I came to see how tough it must have been.'

'What happened to her?'

'She did it all with, you know, with grace. Strength. "Out of the strong came forth sweetness," she liked to say. Wasn't the only woman in Fitzroy running a hotel – there were women's names on liquor licences for lots of reasons. Their husbands were involved in other businesses, or they'd been widowed by the war, or the husbands were drunks and layabouts. Mum was one of a kind. Never lost her Scottish accent, and she ran the place with this air of authority. Very sharp wit, very practical.'

'The thing with time … She's no longer with us?'

'Never altered things for her. She died of lung cancer, ages ago. Never smoked, but you may as well have in those days – at least you had a filter stuck in your mouth. The place was hazy with smoke most nights. Clothes stank of it, your hair … She died in her room, forty feet from where she worked. There was no handover of the hotel. She started coughing, I took over running the bar while she was sick, and she was dead in six weeks. Again, no fuss. Never wanted to be an inconvenience.

'You know, the thing that's stuck in my memory: the GP came over at the very end – this was the war years, um, 1941 – and he pronounced her deceased, and when he did, on the death certificate, he wrote "widow", and I was so furious. I would've been – how old? – twenty-eight, and you didn't answer back to a doctor, but I said to him she was a bloody publican, and he gave me this smile and asked me if I needed something to sleep. Fifty years, and all I've wanted to say to him was *Fuck you*. I spose it's never the thing you say at the time, is it?'

'Well, fuck him.'

'Thank you, dear.'

* * *

They sat with their smeared plates while the café emptied. Nan didn't want to get up and move back to the hotel. How much more of the story did the girl need in order to understand the looming predicament?

She didn't need to know about those unbearable first months after her father's death, the months her mother spent stalking round the timberyard. Counting and measuring, calculating. Taking her to every meeting, while she argued a better rate for the storage, demanded security when she found out there were thieves looking to pilfer the glorious timber.

Ormiston was the man who owned the yard. A gruff man who liked to drink beer in the afternoon, working his way through wooden crates of tall bottles. The brewery would deliver a pallet of them every few months, drop it in the yard near his shed, and he'd attack the tower of beer with a bottle opener and a tin mug.

Was Ormiston the first time, Nan wondered, that her mother had got a whiff of the old beer smell, the collection of ideas it carried, from ease and conversation to boorishness and violence? Was the smell of beer the smell of men? Was his shickered presence the first inkling her mother had had, the crucible of the transition from vessel to public house? A pub. A cocoon in which to wrap up those men like Ormiston with their unending thirsts. Cage them in the glorious timber, a boxed-up pump that answered their thirst and took from them money and urine.

Lucy withdrew to a room in the Elwood house, and there, at a window overlooking the bay that had taken her husband, she drew her plans. At first, it was painstaking, cumbersome, and it felt like work to her. Annabelle would read in an armchair in the corner, or she would draw, anything to offer quiet company. Even at seven years of age, she understood Lucy was trying to transform her agony into something useful, trying to force them both towards a light she could not yet comprehend.

* * *

By the first Christmas after Thomas's death, more or less a year since they had arrived in Melbourne, Lucy had completed the drawings. By an act of obsessive calculation, she had factored in every lineal yard of the timber, and many of the brass fittings, the minor signage, the glazing and the heavy steel. Boxes of rivets were assigned new roles, light fittings and ceramics and copper ware, and even the soft furnishings that had been saved from the wreck and stored properly – all of it applied to new uses.

Yet when she took it to the most reputable builder in the northern suburbs, Messrs Dawson, Deane and Gummow, she was met with scorn. They pored over her plans and pronounced them unworkable. Why, there was not a straight line in the structure, they observed. Dawson pointed his cigar-cutter at the grease drainage system, an ingenious recycling of the steamer's boiler, and declared the floor could never be built to the weight-bearing capacity necessary to hold the thing in place. 'The entire edifice will move in the wind,' added

Gummow, scratching at his moustache. 'These *attics*!' scoffed Deane. 'Totally impractical.'

Lucy held back the tears that were threatening, rolled up the plans and took her daughter by the hand. 'You're wrong!' she told them. 'And I will prove it to be so.'

At Walker and Moss, later the same afternoon, the plans were unrolled again, this time on the tray of a small truck parked in the yard of the business. Walker was tall and thin with a fine head of hair, and he listened in gloomy silence, poring over the paper. A long, careful finger traced its way along Lucy's lines.

'Why this way?' he asked politely at one stage, and Lucy explained the flow of rainwater from the roof. He wanted to know about the ceiling span across the downstairs bar, and whether a beam could hold it, or if it might require a pillar there. Lucy recognised this as a reasonable query and not an attack, and she wrote it in her notebook.

'You truly have these materials at your disposal?' he asked, and Lucy confirmed she did.

'But I will have very little money beyond that,' she confessed. 'Nobody will finance a widow, you see. We will need to come to some sort of payment arrangement.'

The tall man seemed unconcerned.

He began to make notes of his own on a separate piece of paper, muttering, counting on his fingers, unrolling the stubbornly curled plans to recheck details. The third time the plans rolled up, he took a handful of small rocks from the corners of the truck tray and placed them so the paper would lie flat.

'I would need six months,' he said, finally. 'The price would be in this range.' He showed her his workings and she smiled and shook his hand. There would be enough money to build the hotel.

The problem was, there was almost no money left to buy the land.

* * *

There was, at that time, only one solicitor practising near Elwood: a man named Enmore, who had an office he'd grandly titled Caspian Chambers, on the verge of Washington Lagoon. The position, looking west down the natural slump in the land that formed the lagoon, afforded him an uninterrupted view of the sandbank on which the *Cherrywood*, and Thomas, had come to grief.

Lucy took little Annabelle with her to meet Enmore. Annabelle was tired: she had been hauled across town, on and off trams and carriages, reciting a litany of 'yes, Mama' and 'perhaps, Mama'.

Wallace Enmore was a small man, bursting with energy; a relic of another era in a black serge suit filled with belly and thighs, a waistcoat with a watch on a chain, his moustaches bristling like the face of a walrus. As is often the case with such a man, the more Annabelle watched him, the more she thought he was younger than the get-up was intended to convey. His glasses were fine and did not distort the planes of his face. She suspected they were there for show.

Lucy had explained her circumstances to enough people that Annabelle could hear the phrases coming. The situation spoke for itself. Enmore's pen swooped and scoured over successive pages. He refilled it, blotted, resumed the scrawling. And when Lucy was done telling the story, he reclined in his wing-backed chair.

'The timber,' he said slowly. 'Cherry timber, you said.'

'Yes. It was why my husband named the vessel the *Cherrywood*.'

'And your understanding was, he came upon this timber through an acquaintance in the shipping trade?'

'Yes. A Sardinian, a Mr Ximenon.'

'Z-Y-M ...?'

'No. I have seen the name in correspondence.' She spelt it correctly for him.

'Aha, yes.' He wrote the name out and held up the piece of paper to examine the word. Then he put it down again, and his tone changed. 'Mrs Wrenfether, I do not know why we are resorting to such complexity. The answer is obvious, is it not? You have possession of a large amount of high-quality timber. It is milled, cut to lengths. You need only sell it to reverse your fortunes.'

'That is not what I'm asking you to do.'

'With the greatest of respect to you, madam, this hotel of yours is a waste of the resource.' There was a strange edge, something ardent, in the solicitor's voice. 'The potential for fine joinery, for craftsmanship ... Do you have any idea of the demand for pianos—'

'I am aware. You needn't trouble yourself. I will not consider a sale.'

'But madam—'

'No, Mr Enmore. The task for you is to implement my plan to build the hotel. With that timber.'

The solicitor's features compressed into a thoughtful frown, then an eye glinted from under the brows. 'Can I confirm, there is no doubt the source was this Mr' – he held up the sheet of paper again, pretended to squint at it – 'Mr Ximenon?'

'We have been through it, sir. As far as I know, he obtained the timber from Central Europe. There is no doubt about the chain of title, if that's what you are asking me.'

'Oh!' He smiled. 'Oh no, no, no!' And he adopted a pose that suggested deep contemplation. Annabelle looked to her mother, proud that this unlikeable man had failed to intimidate her.

'Difficult, yes,' Enmore began, drumming his fingers on the desk. It was unclear whether the thoughts he was articulating were for Lucy's benefit or his own. 'Asset position ... having regard to *income*. Not so easy, no. And in the drafting, the usual approaches are not – *no*! Inadequate and unsuited to these circumstances. A novel approach ... something dextrous ...' And directed more clearly at Lucy now: 'I will need approximately three weeks to devise a strategy.'

* * *

In fact, it took Wallace Enmore five months to deliver his promised strategy. Five months of living in limbo in the Elwood house, as Annabelle's mother made ever-smaller adjustments to her hotel plans. Five months of polite reminder letters, met with curt dismissals – 'Mr Enmore is a very busy man' – the only variation from which was a request for a copy of the hotel plans, and which Lucy laboriously made and sent. Five months of living off the diminishing rump of the Deal and Wrenfether fortunes. With each passing day since his death, Annabelle's idea of her father had changed, so she worried at times that her anger and her grieving might be altering him beyond recognition. If she thought about him too hard, he might vanish under the pressure of her summoning. He had made a shadow of himself in his final days and it was hard to see out from beneath it. But somewhere further back, he was this bright and unlikely creature, capable of anything in the world. At times, she dared to ask her furious self if he had been the one in need, and if it was she who had failed. But mostly she was baffled, and the bafflement fed the anger all over again.

When Lucy was finally called to meet with Mr Enmore, she and Annabelle once again took the tram and walked the streets to the pompous Victorian terrace by the saltwater lagoon. The sun was warm with the new spring and there were wading birds in the water, blossoms in the tea-trees around its margins, and the sunlight fell invitingly on the white facades of the beachfront buildings. Annabelle watched her mother staring westward at the inshore shallows of Port Phillip Bay, knowing what it was she was seeing. She gripped her hand more tightly and her mother allowed herself a perplexed smile, then hurried them on.

* * *

At his desk again, having been made to wait while Enmore went through the self-important rituals of his office, Annabelle felt her mother's impatience.

A letter, pushed across the desk. A copy of the same letter in front of Enmore, which he was reading from, betraying an assumption that Lucy would find the reading difficult.

An exquisite invention, if he did say so himself. Much rummaging in precedent, old treatises. A form of tenure, little used, which would harness the value of the timber asset, and avoid the need for a costly investment in fee simple. '*Ad structuram solum,*' he pronounced, with such theatrical gravity that Annabelle thought the words might summon a genie from his closet in the corner. But there was no pop of gunpowder smoke. There was something duller, something Annabelle didn't fully understand, at first. Lucy would have her hotel, but it would never rest on owned ground.

Many years later, when she made the acquaintance of Donald Enmore, the son of this narcissist, Nan learned the reason for the five-month delay. Wallace was deeply in debt to the Ardelean family, who were longstanding patrons of the Enmores and had provided the funds for him to launch his law office. The man could hardly believe his luck when the subject of an ancient Ardelean grudge had come to him unbidden.

He had written to them in Azerbaijan, recommending an investment, one that would secure them a line of income – and a right of repossession – from a nascent hotel venture in the hardest-drinking quarter of the city. The letter enclosed a copy of the plans, to which Wallace Enmore had pinned a note:

> *You may recognise that the intended building material incorporates*
> *your Ximenon timber. Anticipating your interest, I have pressed*
> *the woman for a sale, but she will not be moved. Thus, my*
> *slightly indirect approach to securing the timber.*

The reply was instantaneous, though it took ten weeks to arrive
in a letter smuggled out of Red Army–occupied Baku.
'Proceed with greatest urgency.'

THIRTY-SIX

Someone had booked the Cherrywood's dining room for lunch, somehow, for the following Thursday. So soon after a move, this kind of availability ought to have been impossible. If nothing else, the wrapping of cyclone wire ought to have put them off. Another alarming sign, Nan decided.

They were a family of seven, sundry cousins and grandparents, celebrating the birthday of a large and milky-looking adolescent boy. They had to be brought in through the wire, made to feel welcome inside the ramparts of the siege. The whole thing seemed so ridiculous, so awkward. But Joey and Martha had discussed it and they felt sure they could cater the event by themselves.

They bought ingredients using Martha's savings, bodgied up a menu. Whatever the family didn't order, they would eat themselves later. They spent the morning loading ingredients into the cool room, which Joey had switched on the previous night. They lit the burners on the hob, cleaned the lines and sipped off pony glasses of draught, hooked up a fresh container of post-mix lemon squash, made salad dressing and baked bread rolls. As Nan sat at the bar pretending to be furious at this intrusion, she glanced at the two of them bustling around each other and she felt their love as keenly as they did.

They offered her first choice off the menu they'd created. 'I'm eating eggs,' she declared sourly, and it felt better to be difficult. Sitting on this same stool in 1976, she had handed the business over to Joey. It was the same place she'd sat, alone, when the phone rang and she'd learned of her husband's death, on the floor of another pub only a suburb away, back in 1954. The same place she was when her mother, a woman sapped by grief and hardship, succumbed in the summer of 1941.

The Cherrywood had moved often that summer, on unbearably hot nights, under smoky northerlies from the faraway plains that bowed to thundering sou'westers deep in the night. Nights when the boards banged and the windowpanes rattled and the occupants of the building spoke of disorientation, dizziness, disturbing dreams. And in the mornings, they would be streets away, serving new customers as though it had never happened.

This was change again now. These sounds from the kitchen, despite their gentle intimacy, were the birds rising from the first tremors. Change, coming again, and she was not ready for it.

As Joey and Martha prepared the dining room for lunch, Nan realised another gathering was afoot upstairs. Thuds through the ceiling, the squeak of a beam. The tiniest puffs of dust coming down. She went to the kitchen, where Joey and Martha moved in harmony, and she saw the key to the Committee Room was missing from the pegs behind the door.

They never notified her of the meetings. There was no signal of any kind. They would simply begin to assemble, and they would expect her presence. Gibbering aunts downstairs, this lot upstairs. The timing couldn't have been worse.

When she went up to the first floor and heard the stirrings behind the door, she did not immediately enter the room. She went instead to her own room and chose the most outrageous gown in her collection: a wild jade-green Gina Fratini with flowing taffeta sleeves that she'd found in an op shop and for which she had pulled an Elizabeth Taylor glare as she'd handed over four dollars. She put on her rhinestones, did her makeup, added heels and a cloud of perfume. Then she stormed down the hall and swung open the heavy door of the Committee Room.

It was a long, wide space, crossing the full width of the building, its far corners gloomy enough that, even squinting, Nan was unable to find detail in them. The heavy drapes were pulled across so the only light was the dim glow of the chandelier above the table and a series of vertical spears around the edges of the drapes.

Nan's gaze was drawn, anyway, to the middle of the room, where the devils had gathered in groups, on the armchairs, in factions at the table, standing in clusters in the corners of their Pandaemonium. They stared when she entered, eyes like Goya's goblins in shades of impatience, mischief and sly appreciation of the outfit. She could smell the tide, see the old wounds and stories on them. Unseen birds shrieked and bickered.

Nearest to her was Hanif the bladewright, diminutive and smiling, a heavy leather glove on his left hand. He was the greeter at Rosstrevor's gate, who had come to her mother and offered to guard the stack of timber seven decades ago, his face crevassed by a million wrinkles then and now. Down the table, another group, among them Silas Whittle the stoker and his son, both in overalls, sooted and worn. Silas had on his yellow beanie; the boy had settled for a Greek fisherman's cap.

There were others, mostly from the shipyard but also from the complement of the paddlesteamer and from the years before and afterwards. An orchardist and his family. Ormiston, the salvager. Mack, Van and Will, Joey's three friends from the bar, who'd died in a flipped car near Kew in the early eighties. The charred man who took care of the electricity – Nan had never known where he wandered in from, but he had been one of them for as long as anyone could remember. The twins, bearded and filthy and clad in appalling scraps of canvas and hessian, whose job it was to crawl inside walls and under floors and over the roof, repairing and restoring, who had always been part of the structure, as deeply entwined with the frames and the bearers as the rats were. And the rats, scuttling about the floor in gleeful celebration of this lot.

There were children, urchins, perched on the pelmet above the drapes. They grinned mischievously down on the gathering. Women gossiped below them in languages lost from Central Europe, some dressed in bunched skirts and bustles, some in rags. One of them, elegantly dressed, was remonstrating with a small boy who clung to a light fitting on the wall. Unable to get him down, she swung a blow at him with a closed parasol and it connected with a fleshy *thwack*.

Their chatter was an entanglement of invasions, occupations, insurgencies and appeasements, exiled monarchs and hermit deities. The Caucasus, there in Ingush, Karbadian and Avar, English that had been bent to fit the Scots, the Londoners, the Americans and the locals. Wathaurong, Taungurung, Woiworung. The sounds intersected, knitted and clashed, and under them lay a static of inarticulate yips and barks and the whoops of children. There was no sign of Casamento, she noted with relief. Maybe he'd attached himself to Sal's descendants by now.

All up, there were three, four dozen of them, exuberantly at home in this room, the room that the hotel allowed them, where it took them into its embrace. She caught a whiff of smoke, foreign and thickly narcotic. Mad, jaunty music playing somewhere, full of pipes and discordant strings that whipped and screeched. As soon as Nan registered the sound of it behind the voices in the room, it stopped. The voices were beginning to recede too, as they came to attention.

At the far end of the table stood two figures. One was Rosstrevor, improbably tall and thin. He was curled forward over his own chest, hunched, but also tilted at his hips, the shape of his body made vague by an overcoat that hung like a sack down his torso and concealed his legs. He moved very little, and the movements were stiff and awkward.

To his left, the massive bulk of Oremu. Nan recognised him immediately, although it had been years since they had spoken. He must have come directly from a taxi shift: he was in pale-grey formal shorts, a light blue work shirt with pockets that buttoned down over the expanse of his chest, and a dark bomber jacket, left open. His dark face, the slight fuzz over his skull, the look of gentle abstraction. He was why they were here, she felt quite sure, but his face betrayed no nervousness about it.

Rosstrevor and Oremu. *Poor bastards*, she thought. Fixed in place, revisiting this forever.

The room had fallen silent now, but for the squeaking of furniture as people took their places at the table. One large timber chair remained vacant at the near end, intended for her. As nobody made any move to open the meeting, Nan spoke her mind. 'Be wonderful if someone'd actually invite me to one of these things.'

It was Rosstrevor who replied, in his bitten-off way. 'You found us easily enough, Annabelle.'

'Things seem to have got quite out of hand, Mr Rosstrevor.'

'Aye, they have. See if we can fix it, eh?' The shipwright looked at Oremu, who nodded solemnly. 'Might bring us to order, then.' On the wall behind Rosstrevor, almost lost in the gloom, hung the large clock that bore his name across its face. It had stopped at 12.15 on the terrible day of the paddlesteamer's beaching and been recovered during the salvage, then hung in the bar for years, so the useless Norm could fondly note it was right twice a day. 'Better'n your strike rate,' Nan would retort. At some point after Norm's departure, after her mother's death, Nan had moved it here to the Committee Room, where it kept vigil, but never time, in the empty chamber.

Rosstrevor cleared his throat and began. 'We have managed to stay ahead of the Ardeleans for years now,' he said. 'Decades, moving when we had to. Annabelle, you have been very accommodating in that regard.'

'Has to,' came a hectoring voice from among the women. 'Her bloody family wot set it up like this.'

Rosstrevor ignored the interruption. 'The building's our responsibility.' He indicated the assembled crowd with a sweep of the hand. 'Business has always been yours. Suited us very well up till now. So, we moved and we moved. Ardeleans did their snooping, chasing, and we stayed ahead.' He stopped and his voice changed. 'But it's clear that we're running out of places to go.'

There was more hubbub and consternation at these words, voices shouting over each other until Rosstrevor silenced them with a raised hand.

'We know what love does. Let's speak plainly.' *You mean you haven't been?* thought Nan. 'Love stops the hotel from moving. Right now, exactly when we need to be on the move, young Joseph has gone and fallen in love. *In the hotel.* You've all seen her. Nice lass, I'm told, only the building doesn't like her and it's trying to expel her. Splinter in its skin, trying to push her out. But the boy is stubborn, and so's she – stubborn and smart. Other times, we've seen things develop and the girls have been driven off, but neither one's shifting this time. So, it's an impasse. She won't leave, and she's lived through a move now, which means she's gradually joining us.' He looked around at them. 'The hotel is in danger.'

He paused again, and Nan admired his command of the room.

'Oremu here comes to answer to us. Might be said – *might* be said, don't want to prejudice anything – it was he who brought the girl into our midst. So. Over to you, sir.' He looked mildly at Oremu, who stirred now, shifted in his seat and looked up, reluctant.

'Go on,' said Ormiston.

'Someone had to do something,' the carpenter began. 'I've asked you all, many times. *Do something, do something.* I saw this coming. Mr Rosstrevor here says there's a handful of places left in Fitzroy. I take passengers, I listen. Sit in the rank outside Caspians. Turn the light off for the wrong people, on for the right people. The partners, you know – I was after the big bosses. Get a partner in the cab and I listen. Developers were buying up the corner blocks. The Ardeleans' debt collectors were trying to pin us down. I've told you these things.'

A wave of grumbling swept the room and, to Nan's ear, it had a tone of concession to it. In any event, no-one heckled him. She decided he was right.

'So, I came up with the idea. The best lawyer in the enemy's law firm. Waited and waited, and I got her one day, heading out. Brought her here. The idea was, she'd see the hotel, she'd be drawn into this world a little. She has a conscience – I knew from listening to others talk about her. So maybe we could have someone on the inside, working against the Ardeleans, and who knows whe—'

'You tried this years ago with Bird!' one of the twins spoke up. 'Nice chap, lovely chap. Where'd it get us? He's *still* on the inside, and it hasn't changed a bloody thing!'

'And look what happened,' said the same woman who had interrupted earlier. 'You stopped the hotel moving, and—'

Someone else, a man in a boilersuit, yelled over the top of her and pointed at Nan. 'And it means you're killing the old lady!'

Nan was not prepared for the sudden attention.

'Are things changing for you?' Rosstrevor asked her.

'Changing,' she repeated. 'Do you mean by that, am I ageing? Sure. Don't know if it's his fault.' She indicated Oremu. 'I'm old anyway. In the normal course of events ...'

'We don't *do* the normal course of events,' one of the gossipers interjected.

'Have you spoken to Joey?' It was young Will who'd asked, poking his long hair aside with a finger out of habit. The question hung there, addressed to Nan, but the collective gaze fell upon Rosstrevor, who in life had loved his son and had no means to reach him now. His agony coloured the room.

'Of course,' Nan replied. 'It hasn't got me anywhere. He loves her. This could wind up with him leaving the hotel, but—'

'Good!' snapped the gossiper.

'But he wouldn't last out there in the world. He's simply not made for it. So his fate is my fate. Is that what you want?' She glared fiercely at the gossiper, who melted back into the shadows.

'What would become of the timber if all of this ended?' It was Oremu, whom everybody seemed to have forgotten. 'We talk about it ending like that's a disaster, but perhaps it's the natural conclusion.'

Rosstrevor made an impatient gesture. 'It would fall into the Ardeleans' hands.'

'And why is that so wrong?' asked Oremu. 'Far's we know, it was theirs in the first place.'

'I've heard a dozen stories about the damn timber.' It was Ormiston. 'And none of em are true. It's trouble, is all.'

But Rosstrevor's gaze never left Oremu.

'You talk like that, you bring the girl into our hotel – makes me wonder whose side you're on.' It was another of the old women, a long-ago violinist. 'Maybe it's *you* who's gotta go.'

From down the table, another voice. A man of average size, dressed in a royal-blue naval jacket and placed conspicuously alone: Carville. He stood now, sorrow in his eyes and grog blossom on his nose, but his face retained the bright hope of affection it always did, like a golden retriever's or a politician's. There were sneers and some hectoring along the lines of '*Him?*' He waited for the room to settle. 'If you'll permit me.' More jeering. 'Being well versed in catastrophic error … um, this meeting needs to decide. Is it Oremu who needs to do something to fix what he's done? Or Annabelle? Or you, Mr Rosstrevor? Seems, if I may, the three of you have horsies in this race.'

'Bit rich coming from *you*.' Rosstrevor's rudeness was striking for its rarity, and his comment elicited a chorus of hissing. He indicated with an angry nod that Carville should sit. 'Very well. I will put it to the meeting like this. Who votes young Joseph should leave?'

His boy, Nan cried inside. *He is offering his boy!*

Three hands, belonging to the kids who had been on the drapes earlier. No-one took them seriously.

'He's too important to the place,' said Nan. Rosstrevor's relief was clear.

'Alright then, who votes we drive the girl out?'

'If we leave it alone, the hotel's gonna do it for us,' said Silas Whittle, who seemed as surprised as the rest of the room that he had spoken.

'She might be hurt,' said Nan. 'And I have become fond of her, I have to say.'

The room voted. There were substantial numbers in favour.

'What about just allowing it to take its course?' It was Carville again. 'The hotel stops, the Ardeleans will get their hands on it. Nan here will age and die, which is – no offence – the natural course of things, and so will Joseph and the gir—'

'Her name's Martha,' said Nan irritably. 'Can we stop calling her "the girl", please?'

'Through the chair, please,' someone muttered. Rosstrevor nodded his thanks.

Nan ignored the exchange. 'And apparently it's not even the Ardeleans anymore. It's just greedy people.'

The violinist was focused on Nan. 'Pretty strange that's your concern when ol mate here's sentenced you to die.'

'He hasn't. He's asked for a vote on it, and besides, I'm not worried.' A stir passed through the room. Whatever could she mean? Nan let the murmuring take its course. She had been thinking a lot lately. They voted. Five hands only, but it was enough.

'So,' sighed Rosstrevor. 'The only real motion we seem to have passed is that the girl has to go, and we have to expel her.'

'You're wrong about her!' Oremu shouted. Over all the years, Nan had never heard Oremu raise his voice. 'Give her time, damn you. She'll produce an answer.' His conviction drummed the timber. The room was cowed into silence, and it was left to Rosstrevor to break it.

'Oremu, you brought her to us. I'm afraid you will have to get rid of her.'

'I'm telling you, she's a good person,' he insisted. 'I have spent a lot of time with her. Not talking, just with her. You are not putting enough faith in her.'

Rosstrevor shrugged. 'We've voted. It's the only way these things can be resolved. You'll have to redirect her somewhere else.'

'She doesn't have another home anymore!' Oremu lowered his head, defeated. He stared at his hands, resting on his lap. In the silence this created, there was a single *pop* on the roof above the room. No-one noticed the first one, but there followed a volley of sounds, loud and clear. Necks craned towards the ceiling.

Pop. Dunk. Poonk. The sounds became louder and closer together and before long there was an insistent hammering on the roof, coming on with petrichor and speeding up to a drumming sound so intense that individual notes were lost.

Nan sensed the tension this new development had instilled in the room. Whatever else had been expected of the meeting, this had not. The gathering had got itself tangled in a moment in which nobody quite knew how to give voice to the unease.

It was Carville, laconic once again, who put words to it. 'Anyone expecting rain?'

THIRTY-SEVEN

When the devils had gone back to wherever it was they went, Nan surveyed the empty room.

It was filmy where the light cut through it, deep in shadow elsewhere. This was a space she had played in as a child, hidden in from visitors, where she'd gone to think or to cry when the need arose. Like every other room in the building, she believed her connection to it was more profound than the connection the wraiths had, despite the air they contrived that it was their anointed headquarters.

If they were always there, she had thought many times, it was reasonable that her parents should be too. If her father had fallen victim to the timber and its capricious loves and hates, if her mother had poured her effort and her ingenuity into preserving and venerating the same timber, then why were they not afforded a place in the mad pantheon of shipwrights and knife-men that appeared to her? Why could she not see them one more time, if she wished hard enough to summon them into being? They had as much entitlement – more entitlement – to be here before Nan as the boiler attendant and his son did, or the captain whose incompetence had set the disaster in motion. It was a terrible thing, she reflected, to miss your parents every day, deep into the years when one's own life is in decline. She had no way of knowing – had never had the conversation to know – whether this was everyone's fate or only hers.

She got up slowly, felt the creaking again, coming through the chair and continuing into her body. Down the hall, she found Martha in the spare room, seated at the small, plain Victorian writing table that had washed up in the pub sometime in the forties. She had her back to the door and was staring out the window at the rain. Her elbows rested on the desk. Between them, there was a document, folded over at one corner. Her fists rested against her temples, and the end of a pencil poked from the right one. She seemed lost in concentration.

Nan suddenly felt a pang of sorrow for her, uprooted and pulled into the hotel's ineluctable grasp, a victim of old grudges she could never have foreseen. As everyone connected to it was.

'Martha?'

The girl jumped, spun around, and Nan saw she'd been crying. She sat on the bed behind her.

'How'd the birthday party go?'

'They gave him a blazer.' Martha sniffed. 'What's wrong with people?'

Nan laughed. 'So, we were talking. You want me to explain the rest?' When Martha nodded sadly, she wondered if she had some insight into what was going on. 'Good,' she said, then: 'Shit. I don't know where we'd got to. Bloody mind's going on me now. Alright.'

She sighed. 'Anyway. So, you understand my mother had this place built. From the scavenged hull of my father's paddlesteamer. Ribs, spars, decks, fittings. Every bit of it's in here, everywhere, if you know where to look. And then she got on with life. She had responsibility for me, which maybe helped. They kept saying to her, "Go back to Scotland, start again." But the way she saw it, that would've been another betrayal of my father. An abandonment of his vision, even though he'd never thought of opening a pub.'

'And Joey?'

'Joseph. He was an orphan. His mother died when he was very young – no-one I knew had any memory of her. He was fourteen years old when his father, the shipwright, died, and he came to live with us.'

'Oh, so that explains it,' Martha murmured.

'It was just after the disaster,' Nan continued. The word they always used, a euphemism, a conversation killer. It was 'the disaster', and any more descriptive term was unwelcome. 'He already worked for his father in the shipyard, which was a pity. He was very academic. When the disaster happened, Rosstrevor had only recently renamed his yard "& Son", believing Joseph would soon begin an apprenticeship and become a shipwright. But, of course, everything changed.'

Nan saw the changing thought in Martha's eyes. 'Didn't he ever fall in love with someone?' The look on Martha's face was somewhere between curiosity and distress, a reading of the history that said he had never been a part of the world. A trace of jealous interest, a working of the Cherrywood's puzzle.

'No. He was just a boy for a long time and then he aged a little, became more or less the person you see now. Impossible even to tell whether he was ever interested.' She was hedging, and she saw the expectation in Martha's face. 'There's been girls. But you're the only one who's ever got this far and not been frightened off. Or driven away ...' A grim smile.

'Nan!'

'Aren't you glad I did that?'

Nan watched it washing over Martha. How could she understand that Joseph, at twenty-six, had been loved by them – by her mother and then her – for nearly seventy-five years? That their love was so fierce, so protective, they believed it would shield him against time itself? Searching for the words to explain it took her back there, back to a day when the pall that covered everything had lifted slightly to reveal the perfection of his open, trusting face, the thatch of his dark hair.

'Once he'd settled in, doing his grieving, same as I was, he came to belong to the hotel. Knew its crannies and corners, the patterns in the runners, which boards were squeaky, same as I did. Fourteen-year-old boys were everywhere on the streets of Fitzroy back then. They moved in pushes and they were ruthless – they'd roll drunks for their coins. A fatherless boy sleeping in a hotel could easily have resorted to that life.

'But from the start, Joseph was *separate*, you know? Apart from the world. We should have recognised something odd was going on, but we took a while to twig. It was the building that protected him. In uncanny ways. It'd hurt people it didn't like, or people who threatened it, but it never harmed Joseph, and it made sure he never came to harm. There was this cloak over him, somehow. He could stand toe to toe with a foreman or a footballer because he had that, and besides, he was forthright. Calm, very much like my mother. There were some ugly nights in the public bar, of course – that stuff's unavoidable – but Mum and Joseph, they could take the oxygen out of it simply by being there.

'And the thing was, he never left the bar. Mum would go out from time to time, not much, but enough that she knew the world. She'd take me. Both of us felt this pull, tidal, you know, to be back here as soon as we could. But not Joey. He refused to come with us. It wasn't a thing anyone else noticed – except me and Mum. People would recall seeing him in the dining room, or serving behind the bar, fixing a broken window. But if they were talking about a game of footy at Brunswick Oval, or a fight in another pub, or a town hall meeting over in Moor Street, they would never mention Joseph being there. He never was.

'Now, if I told you this like a folk tale, the next bit would go "the boy grew tall and strong". Well, he didn't. I wonder if that's to do with hardly ever leaving the building. He was always so slight, had that preference for dark clothes. The pale skin. Wore his hair long, years before this was a fashionable thing to do.' The years went on and on, thought Nan. So many things happened. But somehow not all of them happened to Joey.

'Joseph and I grew up together' – she waved an airy hand around her – 'but the hotel was working on us differently. I got older than Joey when I was around fifteen, and our relationship started to change. It was hard for us to keep up with it. The years started to move us further apart, imperceptibly at first and then faster over time. There wasn't a drinker who stayed long enough in here to detect it. Mum knew, of course, but then Mum had lived through a lot.'

'Didn't it feel strange to the two of you?'

'Why would it? For one thing, every child is experiencing life as something brand new. It took years to understand this wasn't normal. Same thing for understanding that the hotel is sentient.'

Martha gasped to hear it said so plainly, and the reaction was secretly pleasing to Nan.

'It spoke to us and understood us, and sometimes it defied us. It could be scary at times. But again, we assumed this was the way of the world. And I look back at it now – a building designed by my mother in her grief, built from timbers that cost my father his life, probably cost others their lives way back – why wouldn't such a building carry some spirits in its boards?

'The thing that did feel strange was the differences between us. Right from the start, I could see the crew that attended to the building. Wreckers and builders, procurers of things, coming and going around the time of the moves. I still see them. Joseph could see them too – like the boys from the car crash—'

'Will.' There was a faraway look in Martha's eyes. 'Will and Mack and Van. *I* saw them. They were ... dead?'

'Oh, dead, alive. Let's not get bogged down in specifics. Anyway, for whatever strange reason, Joey could never see his father. On the other hand, I never see my parents, but Joey does. He saw my father from the day he arrived, and over time Joseph was the emissary between them and me. It broke my heart at first, but after a while I found it comforting. Anyway. Feels as if we were both spared the visions that were too much for us.'

A movement across Martha's face as though she was about to ask a question. A hesitation, a change of mind. Then: 'I wanted to understand this thing for myself, but sometimes I think it's beyond me.'

'Go on.'

'Why does love stop the pub, and stop time within it?'

Nan took a long time to choose her words. 'See, nothing else matters. Everything's capable of reduction to nothing. We're nothing much, you and me. Every beautiful thought. Every deed, Martha. We're just flesh, soil. We're stardust.'

Her voice cracked. She pressed a fingertip into the table as a new adamance took over. 'But love persists and it won't conform to any rule, and most especially it evades time. Our loved ones die, but we insist we'll be reunited by our love, as though it's a means of transport through barriers like distance and even death. Somewhere deep down, we know love's the infinitely greater force. So why wouldn't it stop the hotel in its tracks now and then? The more you consider it, the more obvious it is.'

Martha stared at Nan in wonder. How wrong she'd been about her.

'When I look into Joey's eyes,' she continued, 'I see my beloved brother. I'm standing at the mast of my own life. I'm sure our bond is stronger than whatever handful of days I might have left in this cranky old body. Consciousness subsides. Our ideas, our grudges and preferences and desires, briefly outlive our weary flesh, then they go too. But love remains, dear. Or to put it the other way round, love's perfection can only be expressed as its defeat of time.'

Martha sat trying to capture what she'd heard, as though it might fly away. Then her instincts caught up. 'So why does it only happen within the pub?'

'How do you know it's the only place where it happens?' Nan watched now, to see whether more explanation was needed. It wasn't.

'I love him, you know.' Martha's face was resolute.

'I know.'

'I tried to tear us apart. I thought it'd save the situation. But I'm not prepared to do it anymore. And now things are in crisis, aren't they?'

'Yes. Yes, they are. The hotel has almost nowhere left to go. The demolition crew will start to take it apart as quickly as they can, and I imagine they will try to disperse the timbers so this isn't repeated in the future.' She hesitated.

'And you and Joey?'

Nan waited, thought. 'There's two ways of looking at it. If we're thrown out in the world, time will take its natural course. Joey has the bulk of his life ahead of him. But I'm surplus to requirements.'

'And the other way?'

'Neither of us is equipped to live in the world. It'd devour us.'

They sat in silence, imagining a world in which the hotel no longer existed. Like any form of extinction, it was hard to visualise while the life under threat went on. The ordinary domestic sounds of the building were obscured by the drumming of the rain outside. Still the seals held firm, Nan thought. Still the Cherrywood was watertight.

It was Martha who eventually broke the silence between them. 'There must be some reason you wanted to tell me this.'

Nan felt the dread rise up again. Why couldn't they keep talking and let the rain suspend time?

'There was a meeting just now. I'm a – what am I? – I'm a separate arm of government in here. I run the business. But the crew, devils I call em, they run the building. There's a separation of powers. They've been furious ever since my mother signed the lease – it means they're on the run all the time.'

'A meeting?'

'A meeting about what to do.' Nan looked directly into Martha's eyes and watched as the realisation dawned.

'They want me to go,' Martha said.

'Yes. Joey stays. I stay. The hotel will move on without you.'

'I've been in here through a move! Inside the place! You can't expel me now. I'd have to go back to, to …'

'It's not me doing it, Martha. I tried to warn you off, back when things were reversible, if you recall.'

'Oremu can bring me back.'

'Oremu's under strict instructions. You can no longer rely on him.'

'I can find the pub now,' Martha said defiantly. 'I've figured out the possibilities.'

'I am going to ask you not to,' Nan replied stiffly, and then, as the sorrow found its way into her voice, she added, 'Please.'

Another current inside Martha, another line of thought, evident in the sad beauty of her eyes. The conversation was tearing into Nan like the realities had teeth and claws.

'What will happen to you?' Martha asked. So typical, Nan thought, to consider someone else in her moment of exile.

'I'll figure it out.' Even as she said it, Nan knew her own complicity in this unfortunate business was breaking down. Martha's sincerity was taking the ground from under her feet. She didn't want to burden the girl with more than she needed to hear. Martha did not need to know it was possible to become tired of living, of outliving loved ones. Tired of being angry. 'I've outlasted everything that could've killed me,' she said. 'Do I have to fall down the stairs?'

Nan looked at the rain beading on the window.

Martha seemed lost in thought. 'So the *Cherrywood* wasn't just a ship,' she suddenly announced.

She was right, Nan thought. It was a vessel, an amphora for a desiccated heart. 'My mother loved reading Dickens,' she

said. 'Her favourite was *David Copperfield*. She used to read it
to me when I was little, and the thing that stuck with me was
Peggotty's boathouse – do you know about this?'

Martha shook her head.

'It was a boat, on the shore, with people living in it. In the
story, Dickens has the boat upright, but his illustrator drew it
inverted and Dickens never corrected him. Nobody knows
why – it's a mystery. Anyway, my mother read me this story
during the nights when my father was dismantling the wreck of
his paddlesteamer. We were … losing him then. I went to the
beach once, don't know who with, and I watched him working
with these labourers. They started taking it apart at the top, the
beautiful decorative detail. So those timbers were stored away
first, became the bottom of the stack in the yard. By the time
he'd finished, the timbers from the waterline and below became
the top of the stack. So, at that point, the boat was inverted. And
I must have got it confused in my head – I was only little – and I
couldn't separate the Dickens thing and the illustrator from what
my father was doing with the paddlesteamer. And of course,
when they built this hotel, they started with the top of the stack,
which was the bottom of the boat. So, the bottom of the hotel is
the bottom of the boat again, with a little modification to make
it flat.'

The sadness etched on Martha's face had not diminished. If
the story had given Nan comfort back then, it was having no
such effect on Martha.

'The point is, the Cherrywood is standing the correct way
up, keel at the bottom. Had it been otherwise, it would have
been' – she rolled the words in her lips – '*quilles en l'air.*'

An inquiring eyebrow from Martha.

'Keels-in-the-air. Buggered. The way my mother had it
built, she held out some hope of a return to love.'

Faintly, faintly, above the din of the rainfall, Nan heard
the sound of the cyclone wire outside. Then the corner door

of the public bar. Someone was breaching the imprisoned pub. Martha must have heard it too, as she got up first. They headed downstairs. Nan flicked a light switch on along the way, but nothing happened. So, they'd done the power, too. Or the building crew had withdrawn labour in support of the committee's daft scheme to remove the girl.

Joey stood in the bar, silhouetted against the windows. His hair was wet: the noise she'd heard had been him returning from outside. The engine note of an exhausted Ford Falcon sounded from the street, followed by the *chuck* of a car door. When she looked out there, Nan found Oremu standing like an obelisk under the narrow eave of the Cherrywood. Raindrops swung in the wind from the upper storey, most landing wide but the occasional one splashing on Oremu's forehead. He did not blink.

Joey appeared next to Nan in the shelter of the doorway. When he spoke, his voice was heavy with foreboding. 'What's going on?'

Oremu's dark eyes were filled with concern. 'It's time,' he said.

THIRTY-EIGHT

Nan had a sense that things were speeding up, that everything should be done in a hurry. She didn't know whether that would mean visitations from the loved and the lost, but the voices inside her head were shifting now. Sometimes they were inaudible, mere static. Sometimes she heard her own voice, rattling off to-do lists: *Talk to the girl. Set fire to the law firm.* But sometimes the voice sounded alarmingly like her mother's.

Let this business go.

Listen to your father. I've long since forgiven him.

She was overwhelmed by a need to be alone. She glanced at Martha. 'This'll have to wait,' she told her. She left the bar and headed up the staircase. Along the passageway, a skirting-board rat in flight to concealment; evening light soaking in through the window in the bathroom door.

It hit her at eye level when she reached her room. The small rectangular area where the drawing had been taped, for – how long? Seventy years? Gone. The paint where it had been was brighter, so it left an estimation of itself.

This was something. She placed her fingertips on the door, listening with them. Nothing, of course. What did she expect? The same thing she had always expected, year after year. She opened the door slowly, preparing herself, and there he was, sitting on her bed. He did not look up at her entrance, so she was looking at the side of his face, the line of his jaw that was once a prickled surface she had probed with childish fingers before he would mock-roar and pretend to bite them. His eternal self, at thirty-nine.

'Is this a good time to talk?' he asked.

She walked around the bed to face him, hands on hips. 'Nineteen-thirty would have been a good time to talk.'

He inclined his head slightly, allowing the barb. He was in his good suit, the one with the waistcoat, and the hat rested beside him. His hands were on his lap, holding the drawing, tilted up as though he had been studying it.

'Where's Mum?'

'She's fine, she's at peace. She lived a good life, didn't she?'

He was still looking down, perhaps staring into the mandala. 'So much, so much …' He looked up into her eyes and she saw the full weight of all his sorrows there. 'So much *time*.'

'Why?'

'Which why do you want?'

'Why did you leave me?' The question hung in the air. 'I was seven years old, for God's sake. How could you do something so destructive?'

'How could I leave you? How could I leave your mother? I had lost perspective, lost hope, dear girl—'

'I'm not your *dear girl* anymore. I'm an angry old bag. You killed so much more than yourself that day.'

He squeezed his eyes shut at this. 'You are my dear girl and you will be forever. I beg you to find a way to forgive me and let go.' Tears had sprung in the creases of his closed eyes.

'I was sad, and I was ashamed.'

She watched him weep, moved between pity and fury and a desire to be safe in his arms again. 'I was wrong, Annabelle.'

She felt a terrible doubt that he was there at all. She couldn't move for fear he would vanish, she would awaken, the spell would be dissolved. 'Why have I spent my life dealing with a bunch of shit-can collectors and scorched goblins when you could have been here?'

He smiled. 'I don't know the ways of these things any better than you do.'

'So.'

'So. When you walk out of this room, I won't be here anymore.' He smoothed his hands over his thighs, a habit of his, signalling the approaching end of a conversation. 'Can you forgive me?'

She was clenched, immovable, stricken.

'You don't have to say anything. Just let go of this' – he looked around – 'and the Ardeleans, and the lawyers and the rest. Let Joey walk out and get old. And you – stop fighting yourself and let nature take its course.'

'And then what?'

'And then I'll know about you and me.'

She was silent, broken.

'I never stopped loving you, dear girl.'

Now she was weeping and she wanted to clutch at him, to prevent everything being the way it was: ephemeral and unfair. He was holding up the drawing of the mandala now.

'Can I keep this?'

* * *

Downstairs, the beginnings of a plan. Rats and mice, scurrying in Martha's heart.

Joey and Oremu had waited together outside, indifferent to the rain, while Nan was gone. Alone in the bar, Martha had finished reading. The document had given up its secrets. She pressed it in half lengthways and stuffed it in the inside pocket of her coat.

She went outside, took Joey by the hand and drew him back into the darkened bar, kissed him slowly. The cold rain on his cheeks transferred itself to her face, and there was a trembling in his body that she could feel through her own. She felt a terrible sense of responsibility now, that whatever happened to him, for better or worse, would be her doing. And deep beneath that feeling, harder to place: that his fate was also hers.

'Would you come with me if I left?' she asked him.

His hands were resting on the nape of her neck. 'All this is over, isn't it?'

'Changing. Over.' She looked around the shadowed space where so much life had been transacted. 'It's never going to be what it was. I feel like I stumbled in one day and caused all this.'

'It couldn't go on,' he said. His face brightened. 'Tell me about your big idea.'

'I can take us somewhere safe,' she answered. 'You and me. And I don't know what it'd be like, or what would happen to you ...'

'Nor do I.'

'But we could do it together.'

He frowned.

'What?'

'I ... I mean ... who am I if I'm not here? And who are you if you aren't your other self? Maybe we're only *us* because of this building. It's the way we came together. If we started again, we might be two different people with nothing in common.'

'You don't want to let go of the Cherrywood, and that's why you're saying that. I know you're scared, and fair enough. But I didn't find this building. I mean' – she laughed – 'I did find this building, thanks to ol mate outside, but I didn't just find this building. I found you. And I'm not going to leave you on your own. I would never do that.'

Footfalls on the stairs, a hollow *clock* on the floor of the bar as one of Nan's vintage pumps made landfall. Martha thought she looked distracted. At first, Nan seemed trapped by the spell of the bluish streetlight falling through a leadlight window to her left, then she went to the barometer by the door and tapped it. The needle responded, passing through 'SQUALL' and, with a quiver, resting on 'DELUGE'.

'We need to move quickly,' she said.

As if in response, Oremu came inside. The darkness deepened as his body blocked the light from the doorway.

'Oremu, thank you for bringing me into … this.' Martha realised her words could also be taken as a rebuke, and she smiled awkwardly. The carpenter seemed at a loss for an instant, then lifted his arms and she embraced him, marvelling at his impossible bulk. She sensed a wonderful tenderness in him: she would never know what it was he had hoped to achieve in bringing her here, but his good intentions were beyond doubt.

He stood back and offered her his hand. When she accepted it, he placed his other hand over both, and hers disappeared in the grip. She looked down at the massive hands and saw that the letters on the interlaced fingers now presented as a bunch that looked like 'LEAVE'. He said nothing, only looked at her, and in his eyes she saw his steady, calm integrity, which gave her all the fortitude she needed. Then he left.

'Right,' Martha said to Nan once the taxi was gone from the street. 'The Sisters, around the corner. You've been here this long, you must know of them, right?'

'The community centre? Since before you were born, young lady.'

'I was thinking it might be a good place. For now.' Nan and Joey looked at each other but did not respond. Martha stepped through the door and started walking into the rain and out of the protective lee of the Cherrywood. After a few steps, she checked to see if they had followed. She saw Joey's panic, his frightened eyes darting from the hotel to Nan, to her, and back again. Every loyalty in his life was laid bare on his face – to the Cherrywood, to her and to this woman who had been a sister all his life. And alongside them, the terror of doing this thing, of stepping into the world.

Neither of them moved, nobody spoke. Martha stood in the rain, waiting, until at last the two of them passed through the door. Nan stepped down onto the corner threshold and did not look back, but Joey paused in the doorway, his body half in the light of the outside world. He placed both hands flat on the doorframe, rested his forehead on them and closed his eyes, and there he remained, perfectly still, until Martha went and put her arm over his shoulders.

Nan was the only one with an umbrella, and they walked the glittering streets in a tilted formation underneath it, with her at its centre. The quiet houses reminded Martha that the most distinctive thing about the hotel was its failure to conform among all this plain masonry.

The community centre was only five minutes' walk, but it was enough for the rain to find its way into their clothes and hair by the time they arrived. It was Thursday, a night Martha hadn't visited before. She pushed the door open and food smells flowed down the narrow hallway to meet them, along with the sounds of the clientele: voices, cutlery, chair-leg screeches and banging pots.

When they reached the end of the hall, Martha's instinct was to turn into the kitchen. Instead, she forced herself to stop and took Nan by the hands. 'I'm going to take a seat in there,' she said, looking over her shoulder into the dining room. 'With Joey. Could you—'

'Bring you some food?' Nan offered, and Martha knew then that she understood. 'Go on then.'

Artifice had no place under the fluorescent tubes of the dining room. Everything was exposed, every naked marker of survival. The light fell on Martha and Joey, along with the eyes of the regulars. They had crossed a Rubicon where the hallway carpet ended and they were clients now, lost souls like everyone else in the room. Joey looked so disoriented that the fear rose in Martha's throat as she sat with him: *You have betrayed him.* But she hadn't. She hadn't.

It was Hunza pie night, a regular favourite Martha had experienced before. Those who'd been rostered as waiters were carrying out huge trays of it: frozen spinach, cheese and rice, cheap enough to feed forty. The Pakistani clients had introduced it a few years back, and, to dispel any suspicion among the Anglo crowd, the Smoking Nun dubbed it 'green and white pie'. It could be eaten with tomato sauce, and so it was.

Looking back through the servery window from this unfamiliar perspective, Martha saw the Smoking Nun at her usual station, bent over a hot sink with a Winfield on the burn. It was Nan who surprised her. She was at the nun's side, had taken a tea towel from a folded pile and was rubbing her wet hair with it.

* * *

The Smoking Nun looked up at her old friend, assessing her.

'You right there?'

'What?'

'It's a food service area. That's a food service thing.'

'Oh.' She looked guiltily at the tea towel. It smelled of cooking. 'Sorry, love. Wet as a speckled trout.'

The nun indicated the dining room with a flick of the carving knife. 'What am I gonna do with these two? Feels odd having the girl on the client side.'

Nan peered out the servery window at the crowd: vacant, argumentative, loud, quiet, needing and despairing. She could see Joey's nervous eyes scanning the room, his fingers tapping on the cutlery. Martha sat close beside him, her shoulder touching his. She had that sheaf of papers, reading it again, focused.

'Don't know,' Nan said, eventually. 'I've got some of this figured out, but I reckon young Martha's got her own ideas about what happens next.'

'Well' – a long drag flared the burning end of the Winfield – 'they can stay if they want. She already knows the ropes, and he'll pick it up.' She ashed, exhaled at the ceiling. 'Your mother always said he was wasted behind a bar.' She rested the cigarette and went to the cool room, returning with a bucket of ice cream. A grunt as she lifted it onto the steel bench. 'What about the pub?'

'Haven't worked out the details yet. Just got to keep the Ardeleans away from it. And their grubby lawyers.'

The Smoking Nun cackled wickedly. 'You always had a thing for that – whatsisname?'

'Who?' Nan reddened.

'Enmore! You *know* you did!'

'He's older than you are. And uglier.' She flicked the tea towel and it snapped loudly against the nun's hip, eliciting a shriek.

'So, you reckon it's cursed?' The nun took down a stack of bowls from an overhead cupboard and began scooping ice cream into them.

'Pfft. It's not cursed. Goodness me, how long have I known you? Just good timber in bad hands.'

'Ha! Ask me, you oughta burn it.'

'Remarkable no-one's done it yet, the trouble it's caused. You told Bird about this?'

'Yeah. He's over that side. Look – already heading her way.'

Nan leant on the counter and watched as Bird's long frame weaved between the tables and chairs, heading for Martha. She picked up two bowls of ice cream and worked her way between the tables to Martha and Joey. Behind her, she heard the Smoking Nun's barked 'Oi!', but she didn't look back. She plonked the bowls on the table as Bird reached them.

'Bird!' She feigned surprise and so did he.

'Nan!'

'It's been an eternity.'

Bird seemed a little flustered by the interception, and Martha even more so.

'What are you doing here?' she asked him. 'I mean, hello. And what are you doing here?'

'Can I sit?' he asked, and when Martha nodded at the chair beside her, he shook Joey's hand, then turned to her. Nan had given up the pretence of delivering the food and sat across from them.

'You must be wondering why I wasn't at work the last few days,' Martha said.

There was a long silence between them. Bird finally broke it. 'Martha, it hasn't been a few days.'

She looked at him blankly.

'It's been six months.'

Nan watched the shock of it slam into Martha. 'What … *how?*'

'I've never lived in the hotel, Martha. It's not for me to say. But I'm so relieved to find you here.'

'W-what did you think had happened to me?'

'Well, I'm only a contractor, of course. I don't work at the firm. So, you hadn't contacted me, they hadn't contacted me, and it was only a diary reminder I'd done to check in on you at the six-month mark. They said you were long gone, they'd assumed it was your mental health, after Heidi—'

'I know about Heidi,' Martha said quietly. 'I told her to do it.'

'Ah. Good. Anyway, they cleaned out your office and hired someone new. Never made the least inquiry. I thought about things, thought about your taxi to Fitzroy all those months ago, and on a hunch I rang Shirley.'

'Shirley?'

Bird nodded towards the service window, where a plume of smoke billowed under the fluorescent light and a beady eye watched the four of them.

'She's *Shirley*?'

'Doesn't suit her, does it? She'd helped me before, that time I told you about with the … the episode. I spent some time here, client-side, sorting myself out. And I had a few interesting rides with Oremu. So, it was a hunch she'd know something, and she did. See, I still come back Tuesdays and Thursdays. Sit with the men, guide the speaking group. And what do you know, you were doing Wednesdays. I found out you'd moved into the hotel, and you were' – he smiled in Joey's direction – 'happy. Once I knew you were alright, I left it alone.'

'The time,' Martha said, frowning. 'I should have known about the time.'

'That's my fault as much as yours. I know some of what goes on with the hotel, from knowing Nan, but I didn't understand the true nature of the problem.'

'Back when we spoke, you told me it didn't matter whether all *this*' – she couldn't help herself; she looked at Joey – 'exists. Objectively. That what mattered was what I was experiencing.'

'Um, I'm right here, people.' Joey seemed amused, but Bird had taken the question seriously.

'And you want to know why I didn't say it was real when I knew it was.'

'Yes. You could have saved me a lot of pain.'

Bird smiled kindly. 'No, I couldn't. You're too analytical. You had to figure it out. If I'd told you straight up that what you were experiencing was real, you would have doubted me, and doubted yourself. It had to be you.'

'So that's done? It's over?'

'You tell me, Martha. Doesn't matter what I think.'

Nan looked at the poor girl who had, knowingly or otherwise, chosen this fate. The words weren't hers to say, but she wanted to tell her, finally, that she wasn't mad: the world was.

'That's it, then,' Martha said, eventually. 'I'm never going back.'

In the kitchen, the Smoking Nun was leaning on her elbows on the service bench, fingers pushed into her steel-wool hair. Nan watched her lift herself and return to work. Nothing Shirley did was ever done for display. Everything was work, humble and well directed.

'Well, gotta go,' Nan said to the three of them.

Martha looked at the rain beating on the windows across the room. 'Go where?'

'Things to do.'

'What are we ...?' Martha looked at Joey. She had been so decisive at the Cherrywood. Now, the full weight of her responsibility for him weighed down on her.

Joey looked to Nan, and the look did not seek consent or even advice. He had no need to reach for words. The long arc of their history together was enough to make his intention clear. Nan looked back, with sorrow and love, with complete acceptance.

'We're staying here,' Joey said to Martha, finally.

'What does that mean? What does it mean for you?'

'Let's find out.'

THIRTY-NINE

The stench made itself known on the third day of rain.

This was the Saturday, a day of loneliness. The power was still out. Nan began smashing the barstools – wheezing with the effort – and feeding them into the public bar fireplace, which had been unused for fear of an inferno since Joseph took over the bar. Or fear of a drunk falling into it, which had indeed happened in the forties.

The blaze gave off light and warmth, and Nan patrolled the deserted bar, listening to the drumming on the windows and the furtive trickles and drips the building created as it shed the water.

She sniffed the air thoughtfully. Pungent, rancid, sharper than mere damp. The most obvious culprit was a dead animal lodged somewhere – under the temp-rites or behind a fridge. A rodent that had overextended in its quest for a morsel too far back in a tight space, wedged and decomposing. Or the food in the cool room, perhaps. She swung the door open and sniffed. The motors were silent, but the room had retained its chill, and the smell was no worse there.

Nan wished she had Joseph and Martha to test these theories against. She grimaced, gripped the edge of the bar and breathed, mouth open, to dispel the nausea. The pub was deathly still under the sound of the rain. She'd been lonely before, she told herself, and it hadn't been fatal. She let her nose lead her. 'Be rotting myself, soon enough,' she muttered into the gloom near the stairs. 'Might as well get used to it.'

Now she was closing in. She walked the length of the staff side of the bar, then stopped halfway along. With a grunt, she lowered herself to a squatting position and peered into the gloom under the bar. She felt dizzy down here, and the cracking noises from her hips were alarming her. She sat on her backside with her legs extended in front of her and thought about the problem. The temp-rites and the fridges offered no clues. The rain drummed away at the outside of the Cherrywood, and she thought some more.

An idea occurred to her.

She shifted sideways a little, exposing the old trapdoor in the floor, two heavy brass hinges at one end and a brass loop next to her thigh at the other. She tugged at the loop, a memory in her hands. The hatch came free, and as she swung it upwards, the supporting arms underneath it locked in position so it stayed upright. The solution to the lack of a cellar was an ingenious design feature drawn up by her mother – a false floor under the bar.

The waft of stale air from beneath was so foul she battled to withstand it. She reached an arm over her head and slid open a drawer under the bar, fumbled around blindly until her hand closed around a torch, which she poked into the darkness. Two steps led into the shallow void, and as she swept the beam from side to side, it picked up quivering curtains of cobweb. She reached a little further, felt the blood rush to her head and steadied herself with a firm hand on the lip of the cavity. It would be alright to lie down, she thought, here, just for a moment. The others would find her, eventually, and take her to bed.

She recovered, swept the beam again, and it found a curved surface. The side of a large cylinder, rusty and stippled with rows of rivet heads. The grease-trap, originally the paddlesteamer's boiler, rigged into the pub's plumbing to rot down the cooking refuse that flowed from the kitchen. Its upper surfaces were unremarkable. A little rat shit, more cobwebs. But its underside was another story. It had burst along a seam, and thick, putrid globs of grease were oozing from it in sickly yellows and greens and browns, streaked here and there with the black of some foreign substance.

She lowered the torch beam to where the bare earth was visible, a metre or so down. Where the earth *would've* been visible: now the ground was submerged under a layer of molten fat, glistening in the light, making little suppurating pops and slurps as it flowed. She circled the beam, and the extent of the spill went further than she could see, forming a lake under the whole building. Hard to conceive that the tank could hold so much, but then, the birthday party had all wanted parmigiana.

What a time for the grease trap to fail, she thought.

To fail.

Perhaps not to fail, but to purge itself. It had taken nearly a century for the welds to give way, and they did it the day after the Ardeleans took possession.

The old girl was responding now, answering the taunts with a prank of her own. She was starting to fight back.

* * *

Martha appeared at the door in the mid-afternoon.

Nan was surprised after the finality of their conversation at the community centre two nights before. Just when she was beginning to quite like her, Martha had left the hotel, forever, and was now part of that other building, the lives of those other people. And she had taken Joey out into the world. She felt at peace about their decision, so Martha's arrival at the door was a shock, and she stared for long enough that the girl cocked her head to one side.

'Nan?'

She made a fussing noise and stood aside to let her in.

'Why are you covered in cobwebs?' As Martha stepped into the room, her nose scrunched in disgust. 'Jesus, what's that smell?'

'Grease trap,' said Nan. 'She's burst. I think the pub's passing comment on the repossession.'

Martha was taking a satchel from her shoulder.

'Someone's come on business.'

'I've worked it out,' Martha said.

Lawyers. Nan felt a flare of the old suspicion. 'Humour me. What have you worked out?'

Martha reached into the bag and took out a bundle of papers. Nan recognised it firstly as the document Martha had been working on for days, and then, looking more closely, she recognised it for what it was: a copy of the Ardelean deed. It was covered in Martha's pencil markings, arrows joining one paragraph to another, underlinings and annotations, stretches of highlighter, sticky notes. The corners were curled.

'Mr Enmore would be very cross.'

'Mr Enmore will never know,' said Martha. She smoothed her hands over the document, looked up and smiled. 'It took me a while,' she began. 'Understanding the *ad structuram solum* idea, the rules that have built up around the pub over the years. What will happen to you, what will happen to' – her voice betrayed her faintly – 'to us.'

She flipped three pages, folded the document over itself and rotated it to face Nan.

'There. Under "Right of Recovery". Read it.'

Nan fished her glasses from the pocket of the mohair cardigan she'd chosen to combat the chill of the un-powered hotel. The document's typeface was unfamiliar: over the years of tormenting Enmore about the deed, it was always her demanding he recite it. Now, here were the words, arranged in their martial rows.

'Right of rec— Ah. Here we are. "The Grantor shall" – who's the Grantor, for Pete's sake?'

'You.'

'Well, why don't they just say so? "The Grantor shall grant to the Grantee"' – she glanced over her glasses – 'that's going to be the Ardeleans – "the right to recovery of any sums remaining unpaid at any time, against the premises known as the Cherrywood Hotel ..."'

She stopped. 'Do I have to keep going?'

'Yes!' Martha was hopping slightly in her seat. 'This is the good bit.'

'Lord,' grumbled Nan. 'You reckon there's a good bit? Er, where ... right. "The Cherrywood Hotel, whether such building be known from time to time by any other name or trade in any other style, and wheresoever located within Fitzroy or elsewhere."' Nan dropped the document contemptuously, looked up again. 'So, they've got us cold. The pub's theirs, by any other name, and wherever it lands.'

Martha could barely contain herself. 'Remember what you told me about Peggotty's boat? The pub is built the same way up as the boat, and everything in it is a piece of the boat.'

Nan sat perfectly still, letting the logic settle in her mind. Then a sly smile appeared. 'Building, building, building ...'

'Exactly,' Martha said, and she lowered her voice to a whisper. 'The Cherrywood is also the *Cherrywood*.'

'Oh,' Nan breathed. 'And the *Cherrywood* isn't a building.' She clapped her hands in delight, and the colourful resin rings on her fingers made clacking sounds in the silent bar. 'It's time we summoned the devils.'

FORTY

The stirrings began after dark, faintly audible above the rain's steady rhythm.

Nan first heard them by the short yelps and whistles they used to communicate outside the building, footfalls here and there. The quiet tap of a ladder touching the exterior wall. They were discreet. More than that, they were uncanny. The years of furtiveness had taught them a language that punctuated, but never punctured, the night.

Gulls gathered on the pitches of the roof: Pacific gulls, big and ungainly. Not the regular scrappers but heavy black and snow-white birds that approached petrels in size. This lot were garrulous, with orange rubbery feet and huge beaks; they settled in for the show and were not at all put off by the rain. They mobbed the slate, rising and resettling to the rhythms of their own squabbles.

The devils had come and gone all through Nan's life, in exactly the numbers needed to perform a specific set of tasks: to connect the wiring, change the street signs or phony up a takeaway shop next door. But they were no longer out there in ones and twos. This was an even bigger complement than had attended the meeting. Every one of them, every shadow she had seen in passing since she was seven years old, was gathered at the foot of the building, every gargoyle alive. They hopped in impatience, hyenas on a carcass.

This was the reckoning, then. The rain had not paused over the days and nights, had not even backed off to a drizzle. On Victoria Parade, in its little triangular block of grass, the weather station would be recording numbers unheard of since the gauges and dials were screwed to their posts. Outside the Cherrywood, in the street, drains had backed up into pools filled with swirling leaves. Every slump in the road had become a pond, every gradient a rapid. The new rain built in intensity until it had a weight to it: pedestrians bent at the shoulders under it; trees shivered and lay over with the force of it.

Around ten pm, Nan poked her feet into a pair of Hunter wellies, took an umbrella and went to stand in the street. None of them paid her any heed, busy as they were with their work. They had torn the cyclone wire from the facade and it lay in a coiled heap on the nature strip. The Ash Man, charred and wild, eyes burning brightly under the clumps of his singed hair, was releasing the power cables that had been feeding the Cherrywood its electricity. They were live, and Nan felt foolish at the realisation that Sandbank Demolitions had done nothing more than trip the fuse box. Even as she watched him, the Ash Man held a naked wire in his fist and it spat sparks as the raindrops struck it.

They moved their ladders around the front wall now, extended them to reach high on the facade. They would place a ladder, and then a small boy in a peaked cap, to whom this one job seemed allotted, would give it a shake to ensure its solidity before stepping back. Then one of the others would climb up with his jemmy bar to attack the cladding.

It made her heart cry out to see the violence of it, but she knew their work was precise, and their hearts carried an even stronger loyalty to the timber than hers did. When they prised off a board, they would carry it back down the ladder as though they had rescued a living thing, and place it softly on the ground, rather than toss it from where they were. The reason for doing it the slow way was clear: they did not want to damage a single piece.

There was an unsettling quality about the work, something that rendered it not quite real. The devils moved over the building, but the building was still there, even while it became something else. Nan watched it, squinted her eyes, un-squinted them as the shadowy figures hovered over the surface of the precious timbers, levering them out of their places to reveal hollows that weren't quite hollows.

At first, she thought the devils were transparent. She watched one prising nails with a claw-hammer, apparently suspended by a belt from a rope. No, that wasn't it. Something was happening to her perception of the structure behind the man, but the wall was not visible through him.

Next, she thought the light was playing tricks. Like watching the thinnest layer of incoming water rushing over sand: the sand remained in place, immutable, while the water threw patterns of bubbles and shadows and foam, so that a fixed reference point, such as a shell, might disappear briefly then reappear seemingly in a different place but without having moved, and – that wasn't it either.

She knew what it was now. It seemed as though the devils and their work were being projected onto the hotel, creating a convincing illusion of change, while the essential structure underneath had not changed. Change only moved over its surface. So strong was this sense of layered reality that Nan looked around behind herself to ensure there wasn't a projector somewhere.

Another devil worked in the piles of planking at the feet of the ladders, water running off his hat as he stooped to his work. He was using the claw of a hammer to gently ease the nails out where the planks had come down with them still embedded, pocketing the nails as he went. When he had finished a batch of the planks, he went to the corner door facing the intersection, carrying with him a short stepladder. He placed it across the large timber step at the threshold and stood on it so his head was level with the top of the door. Here, he reached up and prised away two broad planks that lay across the lintel below the beautiful lunette window. He lifted them down, exposing a long signboard beneath them.

Nan felt the rush in her heart, and she came forward to stand at the foot of the stepladder and gaze up. The devil ignored her, busy with his work, but enough of the street lighting fell upon the corner of the pub that she could see the swirling cursive across the hidden board. The years fell away and she was a small girl again, watching her father at work on the wreck of his dreams, lifting down the very same piece of timber: the *Cherrywood*'s nameplate. She was standing on the beach when he did it. He was on the sandbank, separated from her by a narrow channel of water. She saw in his face – and recognised it clearly, despite her age – the loss of all hope.

And she had stood in another street somewhere else in Fitzroy, as her mother supervised a carpenter nailing the board in place above the door of her new hotel. On her face, the stubborn determination, the refusal to submit. And now, standing below it as it was taken down once again, Nan didn't know what she should feel. She bit down on the tears.

The board came free, and, despite the deluge, it released a little swirl of dried bird's nest and dust. The worker leaned it carefully against the wall and poked his pinch-bar back into the cavity in the cladding. Another sign below it, one she remembered differently. It had been a legal requirement at the time she'd had it made, but it was also a point of pride: 'Annabelle Wrenfether, Publican'. The prestige of it, the assurance of hospitality. The point at which she took her maiden name back, when Casamento had gone for good, and it was her and Joey and the hotel and her mother's unspoken pride.

The devil was prising carefully now, lifting each corner of the tin sign from its nails. It had been a Saturday morning, the anticipation of football in the afternoon. The signwriter brought it around in his car, exchanging it for a crate of claret, for he was a drinker. He stood it with a metallic scrape on the footpath, then took the nails from a pocket, the winter sun shining on them both. She had seen the concern in his eyes and asked what the matter was, and he had replied, 'Doesn't say missus, missus,' and she understood he worried for her reputation now her dumb-as-dogshit husband had done a runner.

The devil had the sign off the framing and was lifting it carefully to the ground.

'What are you going to do with it?' she asked, more sharply than she intended. But he didn't speak. He tucked the long nameplate and her tin sign under each arm and took off around the back of the pub. And immediately she understood. Her signs would be re-affixed as stern plates.

* * *

The building was no less graceful as it was stripped back. Rather, it appeared to be changing shape before Nan's eyes. Now it appeared curved: not in ways she could readily identify, but in ways that eluded her. A *sense* of curvature rather than any measurable thing, an inchoate notion that a female form had long been hidden under the squared planes of masculinity.

The hotel wasn't changing from one thing into another. It was unburdening itself, emerging from under the unwanted carapace of planking to reveal another shape, another purpose – another skin of timbers that had not had to weather the decades but looked new and fresh and perfect.

Other devils came forward in mariners' boots, pushing wheelbarrows, and they loaded the discarded planks onto them. The longest ones they left in place on the ground, and Nan soon saw why: out of the rain there came a massive Clydesdale, a grey mare with a white blaze down its nose. It was a beautiful thing, a gentle thing, and it stood patiently by the front of the Cherrywood. It was drawing a long wooden cart that oddly combined the old world and the new, made from timber but with the wheels and suspension of a car. They slid the long planks onto this cart and the horse waited while they did it, its coat and mane and the feathering over its hooves plastered down by the rain. The hooves themselves, big as dinnerplates, stood in puddles that nearly obscured them. The street gutters had filled and were overflowing up onto the narrow nature strips bordering the footpaths. Every movement splashed, although Nan did not feel cold. She could sense her clothes sticking to her back and her legs, but it did not concern her. Once they had removed the planks from the upper half of the walls, an area that roughly corresponded to the upper floor and attics, the devils took the ladders down and laid them on the cart so that they covered the top of the pile of planks. Then they produced ropes, which they lashed firmly over the load.

She walked around to the front of the patient mare, and found Rosstrevor standing there. Again, he looked misshapen in his heavy, wet cloak. The rain ran off the wide brim of his hat. He held the reins in a broken hand.

'You know where you're headed?' she asked.

'Yes, missus,' he replied, and she smiled at the formality of it.

'See you there, then.'

FORTY-ONE

The door to the community centre was propped open by a wedge of scrap timber. There was plastic sheeting on the floor of the hallway, a touchingly worthless effort to preserve the trashed carpet. There was no food smell, no singing or ping pong clatter. The sounds from the doorway were ones entirely unfamiliar to this place.

Nan entered, struck as always by the sense of the building opening from this wombat-burrow hallway into a spacious cavern. The kitchen to the left was empty and in darkness. The blue pilot flames under the hob were the only sign of life.

The dining room, however, was lit and filled with noise and activity. The cartload of timber had arrived ahead of her, and had been brought through and piled on the floor, again on a protective layer of tarpaulins. A saw bench had been set up beside the pile, and a crowd had formed around it. They were not regulars, but rather the Cherrywood's familiars: one on a drop-saw, another gluing and clamping thicknessed timbers into laminated sheets, others sanding and planing. Some worked at the ping pong tables, ripping away with the same pinch-bars they'd used to de-clad the hotel, now taking the tops from the tables.

They smashed away at the asbestos sheeting in gleeful indifference to the fibrous cloud they were creating. Hanif, grinning happily at no-one in particular, was heading out the

369

side door with a shovel and a collection of large shards under one arm. The Ash Man steered a path between the tables wearing a backpack vacuum cleaner, the scream of it adding to the cacophony in the room. He ran the suction head up someone's leg and ducked the flurry of angry punches that resulted. The table frames, liberated from their tops, were being sanded and lacquered, then wheeled to another station where the brand new cherry-timber tops were being attached.

The planers howled in the echo-chamber of the dining room, headlining a layered racket that combined the vacuum, sanders, a saw and the background roar of the rain. The devils yipped through it all, some directing others, some arguing, provoking, or celebrating the completion of a task.

The finished tables stood in neat rows on the far side of the room, in front of the red velvet curtain that marked the speakers' stage. Here, Nan could see the carpenters had already finished a beautiful ceremonial lectern, made from sanded and polished sweeps of the glowing cherry.

Gluers and clampers were at work on benches, presumably intended for the speakers' audiences. Others prowled the open stretches of the dining room floor, looking for defects in the boards, then taking their measurements to the cutting benches.

Nan moved into the long side room that adjoined the dining room, where the singers gathered on Wednesdays. Here, too, was a cluster of activity. The upright piano, which had always borne the mark of a fist in its front panel, along with cigarette burns and scratches, had been stripped back to its soundboard and strings, and it grinned a full set of felt hammers as it was rebuilt in cherry. The ugly tin pedals had been replaced with what Nan recognised as the brass bellows pedals from the paddlesteamer's furnace. The air in the singing room was rich with sawdust and linseed oil, as well as the mysterious odours of the devils themselves: smells neither pleasant nor noxious but compelling, and otherwise beyond recognition.

Nan returned to the dining room. Against the far wall, she could see three figures, and at first she mistook them for devils, but it was Martha and Joey, almost leaning into each other's bodies, and beside them a shorter figure. The three of them wore dust suits and respirators. The shorter, third person raised a gloved hand to the rubber skirt of their respirator and lifted it up, slipping a lit cigarette underneath. A deep draw, then a plume of blue smoke. The nun, trading one pulmonary death's head for another.

When they saw Nan, Martha took Joey by the arm and began to lead him over. The nun, apparently content to leave this moment alone, screwed her finished dart into the lid of a paint tin and wandered off. As Martha and Joey approached Nan, Martha's eyes indicated the air around them and its likely payload of lethal fibres. Nan followed them outside, and they stood together under a small portico that rattled in the downpour.

Martha and Joey took off their masks – Martha shook free a lock of hair that had become trapped under hers – and they were smiling, almost shy.

'This alright?' Nan asked.

'It's perfect,' Martha answered. She hitched herself up onto the handrail of the portico and sat there, the dust suit making a crumpling noise as she rearranged herself. 'You know, I was thinking about how badly I wanted to be doing something that meant something.'

'What on earth do you mean, girl?'

'The work I was doing. It was just money going around in circles. Everyone takes their cut, sends it off around the circle again, and it shrinks and spirals until it disappears. I was so desperate to get into the Human Rights group, like it was the land of fucking Oz. But it's pretty easy to practise remedial philanthropy when you've already taken the money out of someone else's pocket, isn't it?'

'Good thing you've had your epiphany,' Nan said. 'You won't be welcome around those people anymore.'

Jock Serong

But Martha's smile hadn't dimmed. Clearly, the prospect of banishment held no terror for her. 'Yeah,' she said. 'Think I'll do this for a while.'

'This?'

'Help run the place. Figure out the money problems, get some funding.'

They both looked at the nun, who was heaving a plastic rubbish bin across the room.

'She's got no succession plan,' said Nan. 'And she's the last of her kind. You might be taking on more than you realise.'

'Bah. It'll be fine. But what about you?' The girl, worrying for her again.

'I'll be right. I'll come back and check on the finished product when these freaks have nicked off.' She hugged the girl, held on to her slightly too long. 'You're a good soul, young Martha,' she whispered.

They drew apart and she took Joey in her arms. He was used to her embraces. She had been doing this to him for seventy-five years: reaching up when he was her towering older brother; taking hold of him with a measure of reserve when he was her equal; drawing him in for consolation, for company, as she became his older sister and his guardian, his pilot in the overwhelming world. And less so in recent years, seeking the comfort of his arms as the elderly co-tenant in their dying, sentient domicile.

He held her at arm's-length, his head tilted in affection. 'You still worrying about me?'

She nodded, momentarily lost for words.

'I'm fine,' he said. 'Really fine. The sky hasn't fallen in, Nan.'

'Look at her,' she said softly in his ear, her eyes turned to Martha. 'You have done so well.'

She never saw either of them again.

FORTY-TWO

The walk back to the Cherrywood had become significantly more hazardous. Rivulets had formed on the footpaths. Holes had filled with water to unknown depths, and concrete pavers had begun to lift and move as hidden torrents raced under them. The trees shook down showers of water that felt like denser patches in the rain.

Nan hurried through the darkness, well after midnight, with her umbrella speared into the night ahead of her. The Cherrywood loomed over the trees, undiminished despite its recent flaying. The windows were in darkness, with the exception of the middle one on the first floor: her room. A small hurricane lamp, installed by the devils. Its buttery light filled the window now, making a lighthouse of the building.

They were still in the street, hours after she had left them, but the nature of their work was different now. They stood in water, knee-deep in places, that flowed eastward under the Cherrywood and off towards the distant Yarra. On the far side of the pub, it carried rainbow slicks from the escaping grease. The street was empty. The residents had shut themselves in, and the only evidence of their presence was the occasional glimpse of light behind the blinds of a front window, or a wisp of smoke caught by the streetlight as it escaped a chimney.

It had been a long day, and Nan ached everywhere. But the rain offered comfort, a promise of renewal. Her toes had gone numb, but her hands, buried deep in the pockets of the raincoat she'd worn, were tingling with warmth. Her breath was visible in the chilled air, billowing in a way that reassured her. The raindrops were heavy enough that they streaked through the little cloud of her breath and broke it into smaller wisps before expending themselves in the lake at Nan's feet. She sensed the work was almost done. A thick hawser snaked across the street to where Oremu's taxi waited on the far side. It remained slack for now. She still didn't understand how this was going to work.

Silas Whittle watched from across the street, arms folded and face obscured behind his saturated mop of thick white hair. Now he approached the Cherrywood, lowered himself to his hands and knees in the water so only his yellow beanie remained visible there like a mooring buoy, before he disappeared under the front of the building. She worried for him: what if it got dammed up under there and he drowned? But what would *drowned* mean to Silas Whittle, a man fifty years dead? He emerged a short time later and exchanged yips and hand signals with the others. He must have found the thing he'd wished to inspect, and the nature of the gestures indicated everything met his approval.

While the discussion proceeded among the workers, the momentum of the flowing water increased. Nan stood on the small island made by the base of a street tree. From here, she could see the flow was beginning to back up against the west wall of the hotel. She would have to wade to the door to get in.

And there were other ropes, she saw, not just the one that had been laid out in the direction of the taxi. Ringbolts at the three visible corners of the building, each securing a cable, and crews forming at the end of each rope. Mooring lines, the source of all the damned trouble.

A whistle pierced the dark. It was followed by a bang, and the pub shuddered. Suddenly, it was adrift, and the cable crews were straining, hollering, as the building surrendered to the pressure of the water. The brakelights of the taxi split the darkness, there was a short squeal of tyres and the hawser pulled taut. The crews took up their choruses of yips and whistles and the pub spun anti-clockwise, crashing through a tree. Over the roaring of the rain and the water and the din of the crews, the taxi revved and the tyres squealed again, and the air filled with the unmistakable stink of burning clutch.

A streetlight came down in a shower of sparks, its timber pole felled by a cable under tension. The crunch of a rubbish bin, flattened under the wall of the bistro. A tearing, popping sound that might have been tree roots or snapping pipes. More shudders, the sound of breaking glass from deep within the Cherrywood.

Slowly but unerringly, the pub headed out onto the street, where the torrent was rolling east. The taxi revved again and, with a jolt, the building made another quarter-turn, so its corner door pointed downstream like a bow, and Nan saw with perfect clarity the vessel within it, the one it had ached to be. She saw how its true shape had eluded her, as a long series of groans marked its final separation from the terrestrial world.

A figure emerged from the dark: Carville, sodden but alive with excitement.

'Miss Wrenfether, please,' he said, reaching out both arms, and Nan understood she was to be carried. She edged herself down the small slope of the tree's base and leaned tentatively into his arms. He took her weight with surprising ease, and began to wade across the street to the corner door.

Oremu stood at the door of his taxi, vast and immovable in the swirling kinetics of the night. The water was at the blocks of his bare knees and it raced under the mudguards of the taxi, but he was unconcerned. His head inclined slightly and he half-raised a hand in farewell. Nan returned the wave, and she felt the movement of Carville's head next to hers as he watched the exchange. The Cherrywood strained at the taxi-anchor. A breaking wave was forming against its back wall.

'We must hurry,' Carville said, slightly out of breath now. As they were passing along the side wall, he tripped, but then recovered. There was a commotion in the water where a patch of light fell beneath the streetlight opposite them. Nan squinted to see slippery backs surfacing and disappearing.

'Eels,' Carville puffed. 'Coming out of the drains.' Ordinarily, this would have horrified Nan, but it seemed to belong to this night. 'Rays under our feet, too,' he added. 'Don't know where they've come from.'

They reached the front door and Carville set her down carefully on the top step. 'You okay?' he asked, and she nodded. Something was bothering him, and he looked up at her with eyes that appeared, to Nan, unexpectedly clear and truthful.

'I'm sorry,' he said. 'I've always wanted to say it. I ...'

She took his face in both hands and kissed his forehead. He smiled, and was gone.

The Cherrywood lurched queasily under its restraint. The water wanted its way with this persistent obstacle. Nan braced herself in the doorway with the darkened public bar behind her, and in front the sparkling night with its random pools of illumination.

Oremu climbed back into the cab, slammed the door with a splash, and the headlights laid their beams over the street that was a river now. The strain on the hawser was so great, the vehicle seemed to be creeping backwards. The engine roared into life once again and Oremu reversed the cab back towards the hawser; for an instant, it slackened, and he threw open the door, dived out and swiftly unhooked it from the towbar.

The Cherrywood was released. It swung from side to side, keeping the corner door as its leading edge as it voyaged down the street. At the doorway-bow, Nan rummaged in her pocket and found the yellow plastic lighter she had picked up off the bench at the community centre, bearing the message:

Fitzroy Community Centre
Ping Pong · Choir · Speaking
Meals Every Night

She rolled the thumbwheel: it sparked and lit. The open door was moving slightly with the motion of the building, and she caught it and closed it behind her, felt the ancient familiarity of the latch in her fingers. Despite the swelling of the water, the mechanism clicked home exactly as it always had.

She was immensely tired now. Her joints ached in unspecified ways and a headache had formed behind her eyes. She let the tiny flame guide her through the public bar, her hands out seeking balance. She stopped at the banister of the staircase, laid a hand on the brass cap of the newel post and waited for her breathing to slow. The pub bumped against something, shook a little. One foot, then heave. Another foot, another heave. She stopped again, gripped the rail. Recommenced. And in this way, she slowly ascended to the first floor, expending the last of her energy and the last of the gas in Shirley's promotional lighter. It died just as she opened the door to her room and the warm light of the hurricane lamp took over.

Everything was as she liked it: the beads and the marmoset, the Kentia palm in the shell casing, the flight of weedy sea dragons pinned to the wall, the pictures, the ottoman, the screens. Her shoes lined up in low racks, her gowns hung in the open-fronted wardrobe. She fussed a little over the hurricane lamp. She couldn't drape her favourite veil over it, she realised, so she hung the fabric over the window instead, then raised it a little and looked out.

The street, the trees and houses, the neighbouring shops with their awnings and signs, the streetlights glittering in the sliding mass of the water – all was receding from view. And there in the strange open space left by the Cherrywood gathered the devils, the children splashing about, the women standing in conversational clusters, Hanif with sledgehammer lowered by his side, the Ash Man, the Night-Can Man. And fronting them, a small group comprising sodden Silas, Oremu and Carville, and, at their centre, the lopsided and broken figure of Rosstrevor, who appeared to perceive her presence at the window, and raised an arm in farewell.

Then, as one, they all walked out into the rain, headed in the direction of the community centre, diminishing in the darkness until they were an uncertain collection of shadows.

The rain was loud overhead, punctuated by the thuds of the birds' feet on the roof, and the noises made the room all the more a place of solace. She kicked off her shoes, undressed, and, in the lamp's glow, she dried her hair with the bath towel that hung behind the door, then chose the warmest flannel nightdress she could find in the chaos of her chest of drawers.

She stood by the bed, anticipated the relief of lifting her sore feet off the floor. The covers were tossed about, but she found an edge and climbed under, pulled the blanket to her chin and felt the hotel moving beneath her.

There was nothing left to do.

FORTY-THREE

The Cherrywood burst out of the side streets into Alexandra Parade, close by the newly redundant public pool – the lighting of which had been left on overnight and now cast an eerie blue glow across the muddy water surrounding it.

There was no traffic on the roads, no pedestrians. The streets had been abandoned. The hotel teetered as it bumped over a kerb, riding the remnants of its slick of grease out into the centre of the roadway. Had Nan been looking out the window from her elevated vantage point, she would have seen the lane markings, the elongated turn arrows and the ghostly reflectors under the shallower parts of the great sheet of water that lay over everything.

The land tilted slightly from left to right, west to east, at the mouth of the wide thoroughfare. It was in this direction the water pulled, and so the hotel followed. The road was broad enough that it was divided in the middle by a median strip, visible only by the trees that had been planted along it. The Cherrywood veered towards them, crashing heavily into one, before resuming its course downstream. A tall industrial chimney loomed above the north side of the road, old bricks shiny with rain, and as the hotel neared it, the pace of the flow increased sharply and the pub was sucked under an overpass, missing the underside of the concrete span by inches.

On the far side of the bridge, the pub emerged back into
the open void of the night. In her room, Nan had sensed the
brief silence overhead before the rain resumed its hammering
on the roof. The stream swung south and the pub left the road,
passing through a low fence, which it collected like a finishing-
line streamer that then trailed behind it. It touched briefly on the
grass of an open hillside, then plunged down an embankment.
The barbed-wire whiskers of the fence collected grass and clods
of earth, and the birds on the Cherrywood's roof rose and
resettled irritably – all this mayhem had upset their roost. But
worse was to come: the pub now slid at alarming speed into the
boiling torrent of the Yarra River.

There was a tremendous splash, and the waterbirds – the
various grebes and crakes that inhabited the reedy bank – took
to the wing in fright. The ground floor was briefly submerged
as the building nosed into the river, but the windows and the
caulking of the inner timbers held tight. The Cherrywood found
its equilibrium again, along the waterline that was formed by
the bearers of the ground floor, and it settled and bobbed in the
deeper water as if deciding which way to go. But it could only
go one way. Upstream of it, cascades of muddy water poured
over the basalt shelf of Dights Falls, the intersection of the river's
freshwater and saltwater lives, and downstream a small peninsula
of land had been completely engulfed, so the hotel floated in a
wide and turbulent pool as the splash it had made radiated away
to the banks.

The Cherrywood had found saltwater again, for the first
time in seventy-five years. And if it were possible to see from
beneath, in the hurrying past of a water rat, the pub would have
appeared as a dark mass suspended over the basalt bed, a shadow
in the sodium vapour half-light and the glow of other indistinct
sources: houses, offices, factories by the river. The storm flow
conspired with something in the hotel that willed it onward,
and it rolled southeast with the river, hemmed into the narrow

channel between the rag trade factories of Collingwood and the eucalypts of Yarra Boulevard. Dawn was still an hour away, a dark and secretive time for such happenings.

The framing and the delicate latticework of the Cherrywood's upper storey passed between the draped branches of the eucalypts. The weathervane, untouched by the night's remodelling but surrounded by the Pacific gulls, sailed serenely at the height of the topmost branches, and the canopies of the trees were the green sea that the bronze ship rode upon. The timber picked up the gleam of the streetlights as the building passed them, and it glistened in response.

Near the end of Johnston Street, as the river's velocity began to build again and bright plastic milk crates and street litter spun past, the hotel struck the base of an ancient redgum and became entangled. The tree had grown there before the city knew itself, had seen another era of smoke and song and afterbirth, and had survived the making of the streets and the buildings and the hunger for timber and firewood and the city founders' hatred of random nature. And now it stood in opposition to an untethered thing that people had made, which was swinging erratically east.

The water built up against the back wall of the hotel, and it forced its weight against the ground floor windows. An observer, had there been one in that drowned world, would have worried that the pressure would burst the delicate panes and that, having access to the space inside, the rampant water would crush the timber shell like a discarded carapace and send its fragments flying.

But that didn't happen.

A mid-blue Datsun station wagon, lifted off its tyres by the torrent and tennis-balling its way down Johnston Street, clipped the lounge bar end of the hotel and dislodged the Cherrywood from the grip of the tree. The pub emitted a groan as it came free, and the station wagon took its own route through the eddies as both pub and car reached deeper water over what had been a road bridge. The Cherrywood slipped over the leafy tops of council shrubs and again found its way out into the muddy mainstream of the Yarra. The light from Nan's upstairs room fell warm on the angry river, the lighthouse cut adrift and borne upon the very seas it was lit to indicate.

Under the Catholic scowl of the Abbotsford Convent, the river swerved west, then looped around to flow east again in a reversed 'S'. Despite the retention of its corner-door bow and its mighty keel, the Cherrywood lacked a rudder, and had long since parted ways with its paddlewheels, the combination of which meant it had no means of steering. As the bends in the river screwed tighter in the hilly landscape, the building slammed helplessly into the banks, over and over again, picking up signage and more fencing materials, and waiting each time for the current to catch a corner and continue the voyage. Each of these impacts sent a percussion through Nan's upstairs bedroom and, correspondingly, through her bed. She woke each time from fitful slumber feeling slightly older, fainter and more confused.

The meandering ended at Victoria Bridge, where the river's channel ran true enough to pull the pub straight through the middle arch, and the span was high enough to allow passage. Again, at the Hawthorn Bridge and its sibling rail span there was clearance, but each time the gap was slightly smaller, as though the Cherrywood was being squeezed into a funnel between water and overhead structures.

Around the bend at Leonda and under the Swan Street Bridge, and Nan felt the drama of the massive beams passing at lethal speed just over her head. She felt it through the building, through the bed and in her body, and she wondered how nothing inside her or in the bones of this wilful edifice had anticipated the danger earlier. Moments later, the river reached its easternmost point and began to swing southwest, head first into the breeze that carried the rains.

Nan sensed the change of direction in her body, and the nearby concrete mass of the South Eastern Arterial overhead. She felt the threat of it, but also the knowledge that this was preordained. The Cherrywood was not destined to wind up a pile of scrap timber at the feet of the Scotch College rowing sheds. The river would have its way, but this, she felt sure, was a prelude to a fate and not the fate itself.

The freeway bridge was lit horizontally by the headlights of stranded cars on both sides. Unseen drivers behind rain-speckled glass would blink and wonder if they really saw a whole building, slate roof and attics capped by a spinning bronze weathervane, steaming past on the swollen Yarra and disappearing into the night. The downpour obscured it, made the vision partial enough to dismiss as a figment, swept away in seconds by the wipers. Anyone on the road at that hour had been recently or was soon to be sleeping, and figments were everywhere.

A night-lit train, the first of the new day, ploughed overhead on a rail bridge. Dawn had broken, but its light was no more than a rumour, diffused and directionless. The rain was entering its fourth day, apparently inexhaustible.

The westward momentum of the river increased, and with it the Cherrywood's speed. Ahead, the MacRobertson Bridge cut the river from north to south, a metre lower than the peaks of the hotel's roof. Again, the threat manifested in the body of the reclining woman. Again, she was resigned to the outcome. This, or another thing. It would happen, she knew, as it was meant to happen.

The beautiful wooden fretwork of the Cherrywood's upper storey raced towards the flat concrete face of the bridge. The pub did not veer; it made no contact with the banks or the riverbed. The gulls, sensing the danger, lifted off the roof and flew over the bridge, anticipating new roosts on the other side, on rafts of splintered timber.

It was the humblest of interventions that saved the Cherrywood, and Nan, from obliteration. Having no forewarning of the coming rain, only a week before, a works crew from the river authority had strung a rubbish-collecting boom across the river, metres upstream of the MacRobertson Bridge. Long experience had taught them that the westerly run of the river picked up the trash that accumulated in the corners and the bends, and it could be easily scooped here where the straight run ended. Now, the Cherrywood hooked the plastic floats of the boom and lurched to a halt as the anchors on the banks began to strain. The attics swayed over so the weathervane pointed an accusing finger at the face of the bridge. The water pushed mightily against the rear of the pub and began to wash up the wall. Slowly, inexorably, the Cherrywood began to capsize.

In the upstairs room, Nan was tipped out of bed and bundled onto the floor. Her landing was soft, on a pile of clothes she had been dumping there for weeks, waiting for the right day to do a good wash. The Kentia palm in its shell casing pot tipped over with a crash, and the marmoset wound up among its fronds.

The hotel listed further. The river increased its pressure.

On the north bank, the boom was anchored to an iron ring in a concrete block, and it held. But on the south bank, the heavy steel peg the workers had driven into the earth began to work loose, churning up clumps of grass and shards of clay plumbing.

The Cherrywood lay at forty-five degrees, with the upstairs windows of its downriver wall half-submerged. Upriver, a large and embarrassing expanse of its underside was exposed to the world. The hotel, thus inclined, stood at less than half its full height. And so it was in this position, when the peg eventually gave way, that the Cherrywood was shot free, able to pass under the MacRobertson Bridge before it righted itself, trailing sixty metres of barbed wire fence and the festive bunting of a forty-five-metre plastic rubbish boom.

On the downstream side, as the hotel righted itself, Nan rolled gently back towards her bed. But the shock had stripped away the dreaming, and she stood up with her hands outstretched, uncertain what to do next. The bends continued, following the snaking course of the freeway, though in truth the freeway had followed the course of the river.

The hotel passed Herring Island, a kink in the river's course that had been straightened by blasting, back in the years when the Cherrywood was new. The blasters had drunk at the bar, and it was Nan who took the coins from their dynamitey hands. The hotel slewed north here and would have run into a disused quarry if not for a Parks barge that had been left on a punt cable. The keel snagged the cable and the building spun clockwise, knocking itself back into the stream.

The bridges now were low-slung from bank to bank, flooded under, and, crossing over them, the hotel shuddered as the pedestrian railings made contact with its foot-beams. The river pressed westward, heavy with the stormwater of the eastern suburbs. In Nan's room, the ride had become easier, and her body – experiencing none of the violence that had characterised the first part of the journey – was lulled by the faintest swaying. The hotel had become her gondola. She climbed back onto the bed and the undulations separated her from her weary body and summoned her dreams.

Her eyes strained in the soft light to study the ceiling of her room, searching for traces of leaks. She rolled over with some considerable effort and examined the floor. Everything was dry. The saturated world outside had swollen the timbers so their joins were tighter than ever.

By now there was an emerging logic to the journey, an inevitability about the fact that the river was taking the hotel, would not abandon or maroon it, had intentions for it. Or perhaps the hotel had plans for the river. Had there been another soul inside the hotel, and had that soul thought to ask Nan what was going on, she would have replied that this was exactly as expected.

Onward, downstream, the banks flattened out on the inner-eastern floodplains, and the true riverbed was hidden by the clay-stained water spilling out into the suburbs, where the residents would labour for days, sweeping mud from their homes.

The gulls had resettled on the roof, confident that the last of the guillotine bridges had been negotiated. The flying foxes of the Botanic Gardens hung inverted in the bare trees like gourds, and at the sound of the Cherrywood's approach, this pile of timber hurtling through the gauzy night, they rose and circled. And then the river's sudden climb northward was ended by the granite and bluestone piers of Princes Bridge, the city's aorta, and the Cherrywood aligned itself to sail under the central arch span.

Nan, restless again and plagued by visions of the saturated night, climbed from the bed once more and stood at her window, watching the bridge pass above, a shadow-line of demarcation where the suburbs crossed into docks, gardens to wharves. This was the river's prime meridian, its noon or its midnight, giving way to the industrial past, to the river's delta. The rivets in the iron girders of the bridge flashed by, close again, close enough to panic the maddened birds. They drew themselves into a vortex and spun high around the white lacework of the Arts Centre spire on the southern bank. Up-lit by the powerful search-beams illuminating the spire, the gulls were reduced to points of light that swirled and rose and fell against the brutal bulk of the city skyline.

Birrarung had woken. The water was up in streets that hadn't felt it for sixty years, when last the river invoked its ancient rhythms: to flood, to purge. Water in the streets, in the drains, trickling and gushing into the veins of the city and leaching down, down through the basalt and into the aquifers that flowed underneath, water flowing under rock: rivers below and below and below.

The minor bridges of the city were inundated. The Cherrywood sailed effortlessly over them, and inside Nan felt her fate drawing nearer. She ran her fingers over the pictures: her mother and father, the paddlesteamer, the day they opened the hotel. Joseph, at fourteen, at twenty, and forever at twenty-six. She lit a cigarette, savoured every morsel of smoke, let her body sway gently in response to the water's coaxing. The yellow light flickered and steadied.

She thought of her father, not as he was in his final disillusionment but as he had failed to see himself: a visionary who had tried mightily to bring his dream to realisation. If only he had felt the comfort of knowing he shone so brightly for her. So much heartache might have been averted. He had been hard on her at the end. She in return had been bitter for most of her life. But peace was at hand.

The Yarra was wide now, wide enough to swing a vessel, as her father had hoped it would do. The light retained its muddy quality, refusing to define itself: the rain had settled into a soaking drizzle.

Her mother now, wise and steady. The thing she had sacrificed, her talent for drafting, had reappeared in Nan, passed in the blood bond between mother and daughter. Neither of them had found the space in their lives to explore that talent, and it would end with her, here. Cause for regret, perhaps, or resignation. No life could attend to its every possibility.

Shipping containers forested the foreshore here, behind the steel ships that had carried them. Oil tanks, gasworks, pipes and gantries and smokestacks. The scale of the river became unrecognisable, the hotel as unimportant as any other floating thing. Backswept cuttings led to the chemical plants, the shipping terminals, the bulk loaders.

And Nan was tired, so very tired. She saw the mandala again, expanding and multiplying in perfect symmetry, filling with colours that glittered in faraway light.

The Westgate soared overhead, so far above that the gulls, which had returned, were content to stay put; south of the bridge, the underside of the hotel was bathed in a stream of hot water from the cooling jackets of Newport Power Station, while the cold drizzle washed the timbers that were exposed.

The hotel was leaving the river now, carrying its payload of gulls and the woman who aged beneath their feet. The empty Committee Room, the rooms for hire that had hosted the lonely, the lustful, the ambitious and the hopeless, and Lucy and Nan, briefly Norm, and Martha and Joseph. The bistro in darkness, the public bar that had seen so much. The kitchen, wiped down and gleaming in isolation, the stairs curling to darkness.

The water under the Cherrywood had been salt for miles now. As it cleared the rocky fingers of the breakwalls, it slowed and began to release the particles it had collected: lead, copper, zinc, cadmium and mercury, hydrocarbons, pesticides, herbicides, paper and plastics and carcasses, soil and clay and grass, all flocculated so that the turbid mass was reborn as seawater, mournful green in the soft light. And along with the rest of its burdens, the river unhanded the Cherrywood. The bay widened and spread before the hotel, which still drifted south under its own momentum.

It spun once, a full and graceful circle around its own axis, then straightened. Beneath it, the silt had given way to a clean bed of sand, flat and shallow. Life gathered to receive the nutrients borne on the overspilling river. A massed march of spider crabs in numberless abundance, stepping over each other and over flounder and flathead and blind sharks and scallops and grasses, over a dumped safe, a lost pendant, the milk teeth of children and the bones of drowned men, the fossils of evolution's spurned anabranches, the settled heavy metals of industry and the other detritus of a century and a half's abuses. The secrets and riddles and tragedies a river collects and keeps and transports to its outfall: the Cherrywood was one among these now, deposited at the end of the line and serenely adrift.

It lay two miles from the sandbank that had once claimed it, reborn and concealed by the weather.

In a nondescript mid-century building, back in Fitzroy, the boy who was Nan's brother and her son – and neither of those things – would be starting again. He had love. He was freed from pursuit now, and the vaporous world he had inhabited was made solid. The generations that had missed their mark, over and over, had aimed truly.

The gulls alighted and flew to a channel marker, where they settled on the lantern, and on the roof of the lightkeeper's quarters, at home and cawing happily on a crust of weathered guano. The Cherrywood's sole passenger now was Nan. She had returned to bed, to the position she had adopted at the beginning of the voyage, with the covers pulled to her chin, her head cradled softly in the pillow. The world outside was grey and indistinct. The fishing boats were harboured, the yachts and the leisure craft penned and trailered and moored. The shipping had ceased and the silence of the busy channel evoked the rarity of a stopped press.

In all the monochrome realm of the bay, in the clouded air, the sharp light of the channel piles was smothered from view. Only close by – where there was no-one – might a warmer glow have been detected: the yellow lantern light of the Cherrywood's upstairs window. Nan lay quietly behind that window, listening as the rainfall whispered over the calm surface of the sea.

ACKNOWLEDGEMENTS

This story came from dreams and memories of mine, but it became *Cherrywood* through the generosity of others.

To my early readers and listeners Dom Serong, Kerryn Underwood, Robert Gott, Damien Newton-Brown, Ed Prendergast, Nick Batzias, Jo Canham and John Sutherland, thank you for offering sensible comment on what were then wild speculations.

For their ideas and research suggestions, thank you to Ashley Kalagian Blunt, Damien Wright and Andrew 'Gigs' Gigacz. My thanks also to John Mitchell for sharpening Bird, and to Alecia Bellgrove and Tim Covey for the river science. Some of my Enid Blyton ideas began with an essay by Steve Wasserman, 'The Magic Faraway Tree', which included Adam Phillips's conception of dislikes as the fuel of desires.

I owe a lifelong debt to Howie McCorkell, who taught me a way of seeing Melbourne that was more like Silas Whittle's.

Books — of course there were books. These included Clare Wright's *Beyond the Ladies Lounge: Australia's Female Publicans*, the Fitzroy History Society's *Fitzroy: Melbourne's First Suburb*, Bernard Cox's *Paddle Steamers* and Martin Amis's *Koba the Dread*.

A nod to Raphy for the wine-glass harmonic, to Justin Kurzel, and to Waanyi woman Judy Watson for her *watershadow* installation at Shadow Spirit, Melbourne 2023, which intersected in some deep way with Darran Anderson's ideas about Calvino's *Invisible Cities*, published on Literary Hub in 2023. Then there's Calvino himself, who revelled in strangeness as our natural state.

A note on the Smoking Nun: while I won't dwell on the origins of other characters in this story, I need to make an exception here. Some readers may recognise her from a profile I wrote for *The Monthly*: she is drawn from the life of Sister Brigid Arthur, a great woman and good friend who works tirelessly for Melbourne's asylum-seeker community. She hates fuss and has never been a smoker, so she may be cross with me. You can support her work at www.basp.org.au

The twin pillars of this novel, which stood strong throughout and did not wander around Fitzroy, were my publisher at HarperCollins, Catherine Milne, and my agent, Melanie Ostell. Both have been indefatigable, enthusiastic, clever and patient, and I cannot thank them enough. I am also grateful to editors Kim Swivel, Scott Forbes and Elizabeth Cowell, and to designer Darren Holt for his wonderful cover.

Lastly to my brilliant family – Lilly, Raph, Leetie, Hum and Dee … yes, Ondine – thank you for putting up with all my hullabaloo, and for filling my life with yours. I love you all.